The Iowa Award

The IOWA AWARD

The Best Stories from Twenty Years

SELECTED BY FRANK CONROY

University of Iowa Press Iowa City

University of Iowa Press, Iowa City 52242

Printed in the United States of America

Design by Richard Hendel

Printed on acid-free paper

Library of Congress Cataloging-in-Publication Data

The Iowa award: the best stories from twenty years/selected by Frank Conroy.—1st ed.

p.   cm.

ISBN 0-87745-313-6, ISBN 0-87745-333-0 (pbk.)

1. Short stories, American.   I. Conroy, Frank, 1936– .

PS648.S5I58 1991   90-5220

813'.0108—dc20   CIP

96 95 94 93 92 P 5 4 3 2 1

Contents

Introduction

Once upon a time—and in truth it was not so long ago—American writers working in the short story form could make a living doing exactly that. The magazines—*Collier's, Saturday Evening Post*, and the like—paid handsomely. It was not just F. S. Fitzgerald getting the equivalent of thirty thousand dollars per; any number of people made big bucks. And below them were hundreds of writers getting by fairly well. It was no golden age, however, since most of the stories were junk, or close to junk, just as today most of television (which killed the magazines) is junk, or close to junk.

When the money went away fewer people worked in the form, but the general quality began to rise. The literary standards of the few general magazines continuing to print fiction—the *New Yorker, Atlantic, Esquire*, for example—were significantly higher than those of the mass-market magazines that folded. The quarterlies had always had high standards, and they became a major venue. So too, bit by bit, the university presses. The University of Iowa Press has kept the faith for twenty years and has contributed significantly to the forces responsible for the current resurgence of interest by the big houses in serious short fiction. So a celebration of sorts, like the publication of this book, seems both earned and appropriate.

It should be noted that the short story as a form is famous among writers—infamous, maybe—for its excruciating difficulty. All good writing is hard to do, but the short story especially so, perhaps because it lies somewhere between poetry and the novel and contains elements of both. There is, generally speaking, narrative, with something that resembles plot but is unlike plot in a novel. There is, generally speaking, a high degree of compression, but not the hypercompression of language and thought we associate with poetry. Few novelists make good poets, and vice versa. The short story writer draws from both genres to create the unique interior dynamics of this younger form.

The stories in this book cover twenty years, but they are all modern short stories, by which I mean things have moved past the kind of story executed so well by de Maupassant and others. The hair sold to buy the watch fob, the watch sold to buy the combs. A life of penury wasted to buy real diamonds to make up for the lost ones, which were only paste. A linear, logical kind of development, often cunning and crafty as in, for instance, Saki or Maugham. Chekhov, Joyce, and the modernists went after a more organic form, shapes determined in part by the nature of the material discovered in the act of writing. The modernists rely on different kinds of surprises than those of de Maupassant or of, say, Shirley Jackson in her famous old-fashioned tale *The Lottery*. They have opened up surprise far beyond plot twists, they surprise us in different ways, and more deeply.

It may be that part of the crisis of postmodernism is because in our advanced materialism and spiritual confusion we are no longer so sure what it is we want to say about the world in which we live. If the novel leans toward the past, as I suspect it usually does, then the short story may be an especially valuable form in the current atmosphere. Very close examinations of significant events. The search for the large suggested within the small. Short stories often dare to talk of the *now*, about what is going on in the right now of the time in which they are written. The novel may increasingly be answering questions, but the short story increasingly seems to be posing them. Who are we? Where are we? What is happening?

Read on.

The Iowa Award

Elba

Marly Swick's short stories have appeared in the Atlantic, Redbook, North American Review, Iowa Review, Indiana Review, *and* McCall's, *among other places. She has been the recipient of a National Endowment for the Arts grant, a James Michener Award, and the Wisconsin Institute of Creative Writing fellowship. She teaches fiction at the University of Nebraska.*

"Marly Swick's accomplished stories are wholly contemporary in their grasp of the American situation and wholly traditional in their establishment of rounded, complex characters who live beyond the pages that define them here. Swick has a finely focused, kaleidoscopic awareness as a writer; she takes another look, and another, and gives us certain, varied renditions of mobile, restless people coping with broken, constantly realigning families, fashioning new selves that incorporate reunion, abandonment, and an always hard-won forgiveness. Marly Swick's A Hole in the Language *is a lovely, funny, deathly sorrowful, essentially hopeful, wonderful collection of stories. She is a writer with wisdom and new information, and we can only hope she'll be widely read."*

JAYNE ANNE PHILLIPS, 1990

Mother, who wanted to keep her, always thought of her as some wild little bird—a sparrow, let loose in the wide world, lost forever—but I knew she was a homing pigeon. I knew that at some point in her flight path, sooner or later, she would make a U-turn. A sort of human boomerang. So even though I had long since stopped expecting it, I was not surprised when I walked down the gravel drive to the mailbox, which I'd painted papaya yellow to attract good news, and found the flimsy envelope with the Dallas postmark. I didn't know a soul in Dallas, or Texas for that matter, but the handwriting reminded me of someone's. My own.

I walked back inside the house and hung my poncho on the peg by the door.

"Still raining?" Mother asked. She was sitting in her new electric wheelchair in front of the TV, painting her fingernails a neon violet. Mother's sense of color was pure aggression. This was one of her good days. On the bad days, her hands trembled so that she could barely hold a spoon, let alone that tiny paintbrush.

"Just let up," I said. "Sun's poking through." I handed her the new *People* magazine, which she insisted upon subscribing to. "You know anyone in Dallas, Mother?"

"Not so as I recall." She dabbed at her pinky with a cottonball. Mother was vain about her hands. I was used to how she looked now, but I noticed people staring in the doctor's waiting room. She had lost some weight and most of her hair to chemotherapy, and I guess people were startled to see these dragon-lady nails on a woman who looked as if she should be lying in satin with some flowers on her chest.

"Why do you ask?" she said.

I opened the envelope and a picture fluttered into my lap. It was a Polaroid of a sweet-faced blond holding a newborn baby in a blue blanket. Their names and ages were printed neatly on the back. Before I even read the letter I knew. I knew how those Nazis feel when suddenly, after twenty or thirty uneventful years, they are arrested walking down some sunny street in Buenos Aires. It's the shock of being found after waiting so long.

"What's that?" Mother said.

I wheeled her around to face me and handed her the Polaroid. She studied it for a minute and then looked up, speechless for once, waiting for me to set the tone.

"That's her," I said. "Her name's Linda Rose Caswell."

"Lin-da Rose." She pronounced it phonetically, as if it were some foreign gibberish.

I nodded. We looked at the picture again. The blond woman was seated on a flowered couch, her wavy hair just grazing the edge of a dime-a-dozen seascape in a cheap gilt frame. I hoped it was someone else's living room, some place she was just visiting.

Mother pointed to the envelope. "What's she say?"

I unfolded the letter, a single page neatly written.

"She says she's had my name and address for some time but wanted to wait to contact me until after the birth. The baby's name is Blake and he weighs eight pounds, eight ounces, and was born by cesarean. She says they are waiting and hoping to hear back from me soon."

"That's it?"

I nodded and handed her the letter. It was short and business-like, but I could see the ghosts of all the long letters she must have written and crumpled into the wastebasket.

"I guess that makes you a great-grandmother," I said.

"What about you?" she snorted, pointing a Jungle Orchid finger-nail at me. "You're a grandmother."

We shook our heads in disbelief. I sat silently, listening to my brain catch up with my history. Forty years old and I felt as if I had just shaken hands with Death. I suppose it's difficult for any woman to accept that she's a grandmother, but in the normal order of things, you have ample time to adjust to the idea. You don't get a snapshot in the mail one day from a baby girl you gave up twenty-four years ago saying, "Congratulations, you're a grandma!"

"It's not fair," I said. "I don't even feel like a *mother*."

"Well, here's the living proof." Mother tapped her nail against the glossy picture. "She looks just like you. Only her nose is more aristocratic."

"I'm going to work." My knees cracked when I stood up. "You be all right here?"

Mother nodded, scrutinizing the picture in her lap. "Actually, truth to tell, I think she looks like me." She held the Polaroid up next to her face. "She's got my profile."

I felt the pleasant warmth of the sun on my shoulder blades as I walked along the path paved with sodden bougainvillea blossoms to the garage I'd had converted into a studio a few years back. I'd moved my painting paraphernalia out of the house and repapered the spare bedroom. Mother sewed some bright curtains and matching pillows for the daybed. Then we were ready for guests, and I guess we enjoyed this illusion of sociability, even though the only person who ever visited us—my mother's sister—was already dead by the time we readied the guest room.

I spent hours in the studio every day, painting still lifes, and they were hours of perfect contentment. From my studio, I could hear the ocean across the highway, but couldn't see it. Sometimes when I was absorbed in my painting, in this trance of light and color, it seemed as if my brushstrokes and the rustle of the waves were one and the same.

After Mother and I moved to Florida, I developed a passion for citrus fruits. I liked to look at them, and I was always fondling them. When I was pregnant, the only food I could tolerate was oranges. I lived on oranges. One afternoon while I was wandering around Woolworth's, wasting time before returning to the motel, I bought a tin of watercolors just on impulse. That afternoon I sat down at the Formica table in our kitchenette at the motel and painted a picture of a red china dish with one lemon in it. As soon as the paint was dry, Mother said, "My, I never knew you had such an artistic bent," and taped it to the dwarf refrigerator. Even with my big belly, I felt like a proud first-grader. From then on, hardly a day's gone by that I haven't painted something.

My father back home in Baltimore made it clear he wasn't awaiting our return. Seduced by sunshine, we decided to stay in Florida after the baby was born. We moved out of the motel into a rented house on Siesta Key, and Mother enrolled me in an adult art class. The teacher, an excitable Cuban, nudged me to enter some local art shows. Now galleries as nearby as Miami and as far away as Atlanta sell my work on a regular basis. A local newspaper reporter interviewed me a few years back and quoted me as saying, "Painting is meditation on the moment, no past and no future." Mother sent my father a copy of the article, which he never acknowledged, although he continued to send us monthly checks, like clockwork, until the divorce settlement. I thought maybe the quote offended him.

The evening of the day we received the Polaroid, after the supper
dishes were cleared, I spent a good long time in front of the medicine chest mirror. I felt as if I were saying good-bye to someone.
Then I climbed up on the toilet seat and from there onto the rim of
the sink. Using a washcloth as a pot holder, I unscrewed the light
bulb. It was one of those guaranteed-to-outlast-you 100-watters.

I carried the offending bulb into the living room. Mother was
hunched underneath the pole lamp browsing through some old
black-and-white snapshots, the kind with the wavy edges.

"Just hold on a sec," I said, as I unplugged the lamp and fumbled
to exchange light bulbs.

"What're you doing?" Mother said. "It was just fine the way
it was."

Mother always got nervous when I tried to change anything
around the place. She would have appreciated living at the scene of
a murder, sealed off by the police, with no one allowed to touch
a thing.

"I'm putting in a brighter bulb," I said. "You're going to ruin
your eyes."

"That's too glary." She squinted up at me as soon as I plugged
the lamp back in.

"It's much better." I slipped the 60-watt bulb into my pocket.

In the bright light I recognized the pictures she was looking at,
and even after all that time, my stomach muscles clutched. They
were snapshots we had taken on the drive down here to Florida
from Maryland almost twenty-five years ago. I had a new insta-
matic camera my father had given me for my birthday, before he
found out, and I couldn't resist using it, even though I knew that I
would never want to look at those pictures.

"Look at that." I picked up a picture of Mother holding a basket
of nuts at a pecan stand in Georgia. She was wearing a patterned
sundress with spaghetti straps, and she had a bird's nest of blond
hair. "Imagine," I said. "You were younger there than I am now."

I handed the picture back to her and squeezed her bony shoulder. She reached up and patted my hand. It was hard to guess who
felt worse.

I picked up another snapshot—Mother in her bathing cap with the rubber petals that resembled an artichoke, posed like Esther Williams in the shallow end of a swimming pool.

"I'd forgotten that bathing cap," I laughed.

"I'd forgotten that body," she sighed.

Some of the motels had small pools. Looking at the picture, I could smell the chlorine. At night, under the artificial lights, the water turned a sickly jade green. It was summer, and after a hot, sticky day in the car, nothing looked more inviting than those little concrete pools surrounded by barbed wire, but I was embarrassed to be seen in my bathing suit with my swollen breasts and swelling belly. I would post Mother in a lawn chair. Sweating, chain-smoking, she would dutifully keep watch in the steamy night. If anyone headed toward the pool, she would whisper, "Pssst! Someone's coming!" and I would scramble up the chrome ladder into my terry-cloth beach robe. But more often than not, we would have the pool area to ourselves. Sometimes after I was through in the water, she would breaststroke a couple of slow, tired-looking laps before following me back into our room with its twin, chenille-covered beds.

Mother leafed through the little packet of snapshots as if she were looking for some particular picture. There were more shots of her—smiling beside the Welcome to Florida sign, clapping her sandals together in the surf, lugging a suitcase up the steps of an unprepossessing motel called the Last Resort. I was struck by how tired and young and lost she looked in those pictures. In my memory of those days she was strong and old and bossy. You could see in the pictures just how much it cost a woman like her to up and leave her husband, even if he was an inflexible, unforgiving, steel-reinforced ramrod of a man. The irony was that right up until he stopped speaking to me, and for a long time after, I loved him more than I loved her. I had always been a daddy's girl. I still dream of him occasionally, and in my dreams he always treats me tenderly.

"There!" Mother suddenly held a snapshot up to the light—triumphant. "There you are!"

There I was. Sitting behind the wheel of our '57 Buick (which we just sold ten years ago, all rusted from the salt air but still running), my telltale belly discreetly concealed by the dashboard. Trick pho- tography. I seemed to be scowling at the gas pump. I was moody and sullen during the entire drive south. She did what she could to cheer me up—bought me fashion magazines and let me play the radio full blast. I had turned sixteen but didn't have my license yet. At night, even though all she wanted was a hot shower and a soft bed, she would give me driving lessons in the parking lots of the motels we stopped at. She would smile encouragingly while I stripped the gears and lurched in circles, barely missing the few parked cars with roof racks and out-of-state plates. She rarely mentioned my father, who had promised to teach me how to drive before he disowned me, but once I sauntered out of the ladies' room and caught her crying in a pay-phone booth at a gas station just across the Florida state line. Her tears relaxed something in me, just long enough for me to put an arm around her and say, "I'm sorry. I know it's all my fault."

"No," she hugged me and petted my hair. "It's his fault. He loved you too much. He thought you were perfect."

I jerked away. "I don't want to talk about him," I said. "Ever."

The whole time Mother and I were packing up the Buick, my father was in the backyard pruning the azalea bushes. I heard the angry little snips, like a dog snapping at my heels, as I trudged up and down the stairs with armloads of books and clothes. When the car was all packed, Mother and I sat in the driveway, warming the engine. We sat there waiting for him to stop us. Finally, Mother cleared her throat. "Well," she forced a brave smile. "I guess we're off."

I opened the car door and ran to the backyard. I threw my arms around my father's bent waist as he stooped over an unruly azalea. "I don't want to go!" I cried. "Don't make me go."

He shook me off and went on snipping.

"Don't you even love me?" I wailed and stomped the ground like a five-year-old.

"Look at you." He pointed the pruning shears. "Who could love that?" Then he grabbed a handful of the oversized man's shirt I was wearing and sheared a big, ragged hole that exposed my pale balloon belly.

I turned and ran back to the car.

Mother shuffled the pictures into a neat stack, like a deck of playing cards, to put away. She used to be a dedicated bridge player. After we moved, she tried to teach me a couple of times, but I have no head for card games, and anyway, you need more than two players.

"Wait a minute," I said. "What's that one there?" I pointed to an oversized picture on the bottom of the stack.

"I don't know if I ever showed you this," she said, "come to think of it." As if this had just now occurred to her.

The picture had its own private envelope. I slipped it out and turned it right side up. It was the kind of picture that hospitals used to give you, of a nurse wearing a surgical mask holding a sleeping, wrinkled infant.

"Where'd you get this?" I sat down on the edge of the sofa.

"I make friends," Mother said. "I talk to people."

I stared at the sleeping infant, wishing it would open its eyes.

They never showed me the baby in the hospital. Back then, they thought it would be harder on you. I suppose maybe today it's different. Most things are. They told me she was a girl, that she weighed six pounds something, and that she was perfectly normal, but that was all. I never asked to know anything more. I was just a kid myself, a schoolgirl. Since then, I have read novels and seen movies where these unwed mothers—cheerleaders and prom queens—suddenly develop superhuman maternal instincts and fight like she-cats to keep their babies. All I can say is I never felt any of that. I felt like this thing had leeched into me and I couldn't pry it loose.

Your body recovers quickly when you're that young. Sixteen. I remember walking along the beach a few days after being released from the hospital, just bouncing around in the waves and screaming. The pure relief and joy of it. Suddenly I didn't even care that my whole life had been ruined, that my parents were disgraced and now separated as a result of my wantonness, that I didn't have a high school diploma, and that I'd only received one postcard from Tommy Boyd.

I wasn't even in love with Tommy Boyd. It happened the first and only time we ever went out. My boyfriend of two years had just thrown me over because I refused to do anything below the waist. I went to a friend's party with Tommy, hoping to make my boyfriend jealous, but when we arrived, the first thing I saw was him making out with Julie Mullins on the Mullins' riding lawn mower. (It was summer and the party was in the backyard.) I was so upset, I started drinking and flirting, and somehow I ended up in the back seat of Tommy's brother's car, doing everything. I was crying before he ever touched me. It started out as comfort.

The postcard was of the Painted Desert. He and his older brother were driving cross-country that summer, disciples of Kerouac, before college started in the fall. In an exuberant scrawl he listed all the places they'd been. Then at the bottom, when he'd run out of room, he printed in letters nearly invisible to the naked human eye that he was thinking about me and hoped I was doing okay. He even called me from a pay phone once in California and held the receiver out of the booth so that I could hear the Pacific Ocean. I listened to the surf and sobbed for three minutes before the operator said our time was up. I try not to think back, but when I do, I don't blame Tommy Boyd. Never did. And I didn't blame my boyfriend because I loved him. Who I blamed was Julie Mullins. That is the way girls thought back then, before the women's movement raised their consciousness. It came too late for me. I feel closer to Tess of the D'Urbervilles than to Germaine Greer.

I handed the hospital picture back to Mother. We sat there for a minute listening to the geckos and the rain and the palm fronds scratching against the sliding glass doors. Mother picked up the remote control device and hit the "on" button. As the picture bloomed into view, I said, "Did I ever thank you for what you did? Taking me away and all?"

She just nodded and mumbled something, flipping through the channels. She settled on Masterpiece Theater. We had watched that episode together earlier in the week, but I didn't say anything. I picked the new *People* up off the coffee table and said I was going to read in bed. She nodded obliviously and then, just as I reached the hallway, she said, without taking her eyes off the screen, "You going to write to her?"

"Of course I am," I bristled. "I may be some things, but I am not rude."

"You going to invite them here? Her and the baby?" She swiveled her eyes sideways at me.

"I haven't thought that far," I said.

"Well, don't put it off." She slid her eyes back to the television. "She's been waiting twenty-five years."

I went to my room and changed into my nightgown. It was a hot, close night despite the rain, and I turned on the overhead fan. Mother and I dislike air-conditioning. A palmetto bug dropped off one of the blades onto the bed. I brushed him off, whacked him with my slipper, picked him up with a tissue, and carried him at arm's length to the toilet. I'd forgotten it was dark in the bathroom. I had to go back for the light bulb, climb up on the sink again, and screw in the 60-watt bulb. Crouched on the sink's rim, I caught sight of my face in the mirror and instinctively, like a baby, I reached out and touched my reflection. Then I brushed my hair and creamed my face, satisfied in the soft light that no one would ever suspect I was a grandmother.

The next morning by the time I had showered and dressed, Mother was already in the kitchen, eating her cereal. In the stark sunlight, she looked bad, worse than bad. The spoon doddered its way between her bowl and her mouth. The trembling spoon unnerved me. I feared it would not be long before I'd have to tuck a napkin under her chin and feed her like a baby. I felt my eyes swimming and stuck my head inside the refrigerator.

"You sleep?" I asked her. Mother and I are both thin sleepers.

I grabbed some oranges off the back porch and started to squeeze myself some fresh juice.

"I dreamed she came here with the baby. We were all sitting out on the lanai playing cards, even the baby. We had a special deck

made up just for him. Only she . . . ," Mother hesitated to invoke
her name, ". . . Linda Rose looked exactly like that dark-haired re-
ceptionist in Dr. Rayburn's office with the big dimples. Isn't that
weird?"

"I've heard weirder." I tossed some cheese and crackers into a
Baggie. "I'll be in the studio," I said. "You want anything before
I go?"

Mother shook her head, dabbing at some dribbled milk on her
robe. "I thought I'd just write some letters," she said. "You got anything for the postman when he comes?"

"No, I don't." I plunked her cereal bowl in the sink and sponged
off the counter.

"You worried she's going to be trouble or ask for money? For all
we know, she's married to a brain surgeon with his and her Cadil-
lacs. Dallas is full of rich people."

"She didn't mention any husband at all," I said, getting drawn
into it despite myself.

"Maybe you're worried 'like mother, like daughter.'" She was
leafing through a rosebush catalog now, pretending nonchalance.
"It's no disgrace these days, you know. Nowadays you'd be hard-
pressed to think what you could do to disgrace yourself."

I lit a cigarette. Since Mother had to quit smoking, I tried to
limit my smoking to the studio, but every once in a while she got
on my nerves.

"Give me one," she said.

"You know you can't." I exhaled a smoke ring, followed by another one. They floated in the air like a pair of handcuffs.

"Just a puff," she pleaded.

Mother had smoked two packs of Camels a day for over thirty
years. She liked to say that nothing could be harder than quitting
smoking, not even dying. I put the cigarette to her lips and held it
steady while she took a couple of drags. She closed her eyes and a
look of pure pleasure stole over her features. Then I felt guilty.
"That's enough," I doused the cigarette under the faucet.

"Maybe you're worried she'll be disappointed in you," she said.

"You know, that she's had this big fantasy for all these years that maybe you were Grace Kelly or Margaret Mead and who could live up to that? No one. But you don't have to, Fran, that's the thing. You're her flesh-and-blood mother and that's enough. That's all it'll take."

"Could we just drop this?" I wished I hadn't doused the cigarette. When she got onto some topic, it didn't make the least bit of difference to her if you preferred not to discuss it.

"You call me if you need me," I said.

She nodded and waved me away. When I looked back at her through the screen door, she was sitting there, frail and dejected, with those watery blue eyes magnified behind her bifocals, massaging her heart.

The studio was mercifully cool and quiet. I stared back and forth between the blue bowl of oranges on the table and the blue bowl of oranges I had painted on the paper clipped to my easel. I dipped my brush in water and mixed up some brown and yellow on my palette until I got the citrusy color I was after. I wondered if she, Linda Rose—there *was* something in Mother and me that resisted naming her after all these years—had inherited my eye. Maybe she had it and didn't even know it. Maybe she had been raised all wrong. Which was entirely possible, starting out with a tacky name like Linda Rose. She probably grew up twirling a baton and never even picked up a paintbrush. I would have named her something cool and elegant like Claire, not something that sounds like what you would call a motorboat.

As I focused on my oranges, the rest of my life blurred and faded away. I didn't give Linda Rose another thought that afternoon. Then I did what I always do when I finish a painting, my ritual. I lit a cigarette and sat in a canvas director's chair against the wall, facing the easel. As I stared at the painting, I gradually became more and more attuned to my other senses: the clatter of birds in the banyan tree, the salty breeze, the ache in my lower back, the taste of smoke. When I was satisfied that I was satisfied with the painting, I reached for the blue bowl, selected the most fragrant orange, peeled it, and ate it with slow deliberation, section by section, like some animal eating its afterbirth. Then I washed my hands and headed

up the path toward the house to fix mother her lunch.

Mother was crying in front of the television set when I walked in.

"What happened?" I peered at the set expecting to see some melodrama, but it was just a quiz show. The contestants looked hyper-cheerful.

"I can't get this open." She handed me her painkillers, which were in a plastic vial. "You forgot to tell them no safety caps." Her quivering lips and trembling voice were a study in reproach.

"What if I did? It's certainly nothing to cry about." I pried the cap off and handed her the pills. "Here."

"I need some water."

I brought her a glass of water with a slice of lemon, the way she liked it.

"It seems like a little thing," she said, "but it's just one little thing after another. Like an old car. This goes, that goes. Pretty soon you're just waiting for the next part to give out."

"That's no way to talk," I said. "Come on now."

A couple of times she lifted the water glass up off the table and then set it down again as if it were too heavy.

"Here." I picked the glass up and tilted it to her lips. She took a few sips and then waved it away. Water cascaded down her chin.

"I don't believe in my body anymore," she said. "It won't be long now." She closed her eyes, as if she were trying out being dead. It scared me.

"I sure as hell don't know what's got into you," I shouted. I was rummaging through the kitchen cupboard. "You want Gazpacho or Golden Mushroom?"

"Don't shout," she shouted, motoring herself into the kitchen. "I'm not hungry."

I sighed and opened a can of soup. Even in summer, Mother and I lived on soup.

"We're having Gazpacho," I said. "Chilled."

I poured the soup, threw an ice cube into each bowl, and stirred it around with my finger.

"I was thinking about what you'll do once I'm gone," she said.

I pushed her up close to the table, like a baby in a high chair. She ignored the bowl of soup in front of her.

"You've never been alone before. I don't like to think of you here all by yourself," she said.

"Maybe I'll like it."

"Maybe." She picked her spoon up and pushed it around in her soup. "But I doubt it. Just close your eyes for a minute and imagine this place is empty except for you. . . . Come on now. Close them."

"Jesus Christ." I sighed and slammed my eyes shut.

"How's it feel?"

"Peaceful." I glared at her. "Very peaceful." But, in truth, this shiver of loneliness rippled along my spine.

"You write to your daughter," she said.

Then, as if she'd exhausted that subject, she nodded off to sleep, wheezing lightly. When I turned my back to wash the dishes, her spoon clattered to the floor. I wanted to stuff her nylon night-gowns into an overnight bag and drive her to the hospital where experts would monitor her vital signs and, at the first hint of fail-ure, hook her up to some mysterious life-support system until I was ready to let her go, but I simply picked her spoon up off the floor and rinsed it under the tap.

While Mother slept, I sat out on the lanai staring at a blank sheet of stationery until sunset. I had never been a letter writer. Even thank-you notes and get-well cards seemed to call for more than I had to say. Once or twice I'd tried to write a letter to my father—in the spirit of reconciliation or revenge, depending on my mood—but the words seemed to stick in my mind. In the old days, when Mother still kept in touch with her friends up north, I used to mar-vel at how she could fill up page after page, her ballpoint flitting across the calm surface of the scented page like a motorboat skim-ming through water, her sentence trailing along in its wake like a water-skier holding on for dear life. Chatting on paper, she called it. I preferred postcards. When Mother and I took a twelve-day tour of Europe for my thirtieth birthday, I sent back El Grecos from the Prado, Turners from the Tate, Cézannes from the Jeu de Paume. I don't have many friends, and those I have wouldn't expect more than a couple of hasty lines on the back of a picture postcard.

Mother didn't even bother with postcards. Over the years, her letters had shrunk to notes and then to nothing. At Gatwick Airport, going home, I bought a biography of the Duke and Duchess of Windsor to read on the plane. I have since read everything I can find about them. I understand them, but I don't pity them. Their fate was a simple equation. When someone gives up the world for you, you become their world.

I sat on the lanai for hours in the wicker rocker—the smell of oranges from a bushel basket at my feet mingling with the lilac-scented stationery—pen poised, trying to think what I could say, what she would want to hear:

Dear Linda Rose,

Last night I slept with your picture under my pillow. Every year on your birthday mother and I would try to guess what you looked like and what you were doing . . .

Dear Linda Rose,

What is it you want from me? Our connection was a purely physical one. I have never shed a tear on Mother's Day.

From behind me I heard the faint whir of Mother's electric wheelchair crescendoing as she steered herself down the hall and across the living room to the lanai. The blank white stationery looked gray in the dusk.

"Did you write her?" She was wheezing again.

"Yes." I shut the lid of the stationery box. "You take your medicine? You don't sound good."

"Never mind me. What'd you say? Did you ask her to come here?"

"Not exactly." It was cool on the lanai, a damp breeze from the ocean. I buttoned my cardigan. "Are you warm enough?"

Mother dogged me into the kitchen. I took a package of lamb chops from the refrigerator.

"Where's the letter?" She was sorting through some stamped envelopes, mostly bills, in a basket on the sideboard.

"I already mailed it." I stuck the chops in the toaster oven. "You want instant mashed or Minute Rice?"

"Don't lie to me." She jabbed me in the rear with her fingernail. "I'm your mother."

"Just leave me be." I turned the faucet on full blast to drown her out, muttering curses, but I knew she would wait. I shut the water off and set the pan on the burner to boil.

"Even half-dead I'm more alive than you are," she said.

In the bright overhead light she looked more than half-dead. She looked maybe 60 or 70 percent dead.

"You need a swift kick in the butt!" She wheeled her chair up behind me and tried to give me a swift one, but her toe only grazed my shin.

"Goddammit, I tried to write it," I said. "I kept getting stuck."

"I'll help you!" She stopped wheezing and something inside her rallied. Her spine snapped to attention. "I always could write a good letter."

I imagined I could hear her brain heating up, words hopping around in there like kernels in a popcorn popper.

"Get some paper and pencil!" she commanded. She was chipping nail polish off her thumbs, something she did when she got worked up.

The chops were spattering away in the broiler. The water was boiling on the stove. "After dinner," I said.

The phone rang. I hurried out of the kitchen and answered it in the hallway. "Hello?" I said. There was silence, then a click, then a buzz. I hung up.

"Who was it?" Mother asked, as I set a plate of food down in front of her.

"No one. They hung up."

"I'm not hungry," she said.

"Eat it anyway." I dissected the meat on her plate into bite-sized pieces. "There."

After dinner, to make amends, I offered to paint mother's nails for her. Mother graciously accepted. One thing about her, she can recognize an olive branch. Her chipped purple nails looked unsightly in the 100-watt glare. She closed her eyes and swayed her

head in time to the music on the radio. I shook the little bottle of
Peach Melba and painted away with the furious effort of a child
trying to stay inside the lines of a coloring book. My breathing
slowed. My hands steadied themselves. My concentration was perfect, dead on. Nothing existed except the tiny brush, the shimmer
of color, and the Gothic arch of each nail.

"What's that?" Mother said. She opened her eyes.

"Schumann, I think." I started on the second coat.

"Not that. I thought I heard a car door slam."

"I didn't hear anything."

A second later there was a loud pounding on the front door. It
startled me and my hand skittered across Mother's, leaving a trail of
Peach Melba.

"Told you."

"Whoever it is, we don't want any." I set the brush back in the
bottle. "Religion, encyclopedias, hairbrushes . . ." I stood up and
patted mother's hand. "Be right back."

"Don't unlock the screen door." She peeked through the drapes,
careful not to disturb the wet nail polish. "Well, he's got himself a
flashy car for a Fuller Brush man."

I put the chain on the door and opened it a crack. "Yes?" I said,
peering into the darkness.

"Who is it?" Mother yelled from the living room.

"It's George Jeffries," a man's voice said.

I flicked on the porch light to get a good look at him.

"Who is it?" Mother yelled again.

I didn't answer her. A second later I heard the whir coming up
behind me. She came to a stop right beside me.

"Hello, Lillian. I didn't mean to scare you," he said. "I would've
called. I guess I was afraid you'd hang up on me."

"You're right. We would have." She was wringing her hands,
smearing the nail polish all over.

"You could still slam the door in my face," he said.

"Good idea," Mother said, but I was already unlocking the screen
door and motioning him inside.

The disturbing part was we didn't shout or cry or bare our souls to one another. We drank iced tea, then brandy, and conversed like three old friends who had lost touch with each other and were trying unsuccessfully to recapture something. Mother made a few barbed comments, tossed off a few poison darts, but my father just bowed his head and said, "You're right," or "I'm ashamed of myself," or "I deserve worse," and pretty soon she gave up. I could sense his shock every time he glanced at her. He didn't look that well preserved himself, but she could have been his mother.

I was mostly quiet. I couldn't believe that this thin-haired, mild-mannered old gent was my father. The main thing I felt was gypped. He told us how he'd been married again, lasted about eight years, then she left him. He wouldn't say who it was, but once he slipped and said Genevieve, and Mother and I exchanged glances. We knew it was one of her old bridge club members, a divorcée with three kids I used to babysit for. My father went on about those kids—the drugs, the shoplifting, the wild parties, the car wrecks—and implied it was what did the marriage in. I figured it was his backhanded way of telling me he realized that I hadn't been so bad after all.

"Why now?" I said when he finished. "Why'd you come here after all these years?"

"I don't know," he said. "Awhile back someone named Linda Rose Caswell contacted me, said she was your . . . said you were her . . . that some agency had given her your name and wanted to know how to reach you. After that, I started thinking."

I nodded. The three of us were silent, not a comfortable silence.

"Then a couple of days ago"—he fumbled in his breast pocket— "she sent me this." He offered it hesitantly. It was another Polaroid, almost identical, except in this one the baby was crying.

I nodded and passed it back to him.

"We got one, too," Mother said, not one to be outshone.

"Then, I don't know," he shrugged. "I just packed my suitcase and started driving." He tucked the picture back inside his pocket and cleared his throat. "What about you? You haven't told me much about what you've been up to. I'm here to listen."

"We lead a quiet life," I said. "There's not really much to tell."

"It's a nice place you've got here," he said. We'd bought it with his money, mother's divorce settlement, but, to his credit, he didn't seem to be thinking about that.

"You should see Fran's paintings," Mother said. "She's famous around here."

"That so?" my father said, smiling.

"You know how she exaggerates," I said.

"Well, I'd like to see them. In the morning." He looked at his watch. "I'm beat. You gals know a reasonable motel nearby?"

I looked at mother. She shrugged.

"We can put you in the spare room," I said.

"If you're sure it's no bother . . ." He looked at my mother, but she was busy chipping away at her thumbnails.

"It's no bother," I said. "The guest bed's all made."

That night, after they were both asleep, I sat down again with Mother's stationery and a shot of whiskey and wrote to Linda Rose. It was a short note, but this time the words just came. I told her it would mean a lot to Mother and me if they could come visit us—Mother was too sick to travel—and I offered to pay their plane fare. It wasn't much of a note really, under the circumstances, and once I sealed the envelope, I found myself adding lines to it in my mind.

It was after midnight and stone silent on the island except for the waves. My mouth felt dry, as if I'd been talking out loud for hours and hours. I chose an orange from the bushel basket sitting on the floor next to the rocker, bit into it, and spat the peel out onto the porch floor. They were runty, greenish juice oranges from the small grove out back. The trees were so old they'd sprouted dark, spiny thorns. But their fruit was sweeter than those picture-perfect oranges you see in the supermarkets. From California. Imports.

As I sucked the juice out, I closed my eyes and imagined Linda Rose sitting across from me on the wicker sofa, telling me all about herself while the baby slept contentedly in my lap. I breathed in his baby smell of powder and sour milk. I felt his soft warmth, a pleasant weight against my belly, radiating inward. I began to rock, crooning in harmony with the squeaky floorboards, and as I rocked, I began to pile oranges on my lap, one after another, hugging them to me, until my lap was full of oranges, heavy with oranges. And then, for the first time all night, I felt something. It could have been the avalanche of oranges, shifting in my lap, but it felt more like it was on the inside, more like something under the skin, something moving there inside me.

The Ice Fisher

Starkey Flythe, a graduate of the University of the South in Sewanee,
Tennessee, was managing editor of the Saturday Evening Post *for ten years.*
His stories have appeared in the Best American *and* O. Henry *volumes,*
and he has also published poetry. He lives in South Carolina.

"Magnanimous, intelligent, and fully imagined stories, in an astonishing
range of voices, about modern folk, young and old, male and female,
black and white, deeply engaged in their life pilgrimages."
GAIL GODWIN, 1989

Denny Harrell presses against the school wall trying to keep his underwear pants from falling down. He grips the elastic waistband,
which has failed after service to five older brothers, in his fist hard
enough to choke off the circulation in the bottom half of his body.
Except for his being alone while the other children are playing, the
pose appears fairly natural. His face is red, though. His eyes sting
from not crying.

When the bell rings ending recess, while pretending to scratch
his back Denny creeps to the rear of the line filing into the cafe-
torium. He thinks of it as a crematorium. He will be burned alive
on the low stage when he sings, "I Dream of Jeanie with the Light
Brown Hair." The underwear, made of hateful wool of a quality to
last forever, will fall below his short pants. He will have to let the
waistband loose when he gestures, as Mrs. Hutson, his fifth-grade
teacher and the music mistress of the school, has instructed. He
imagines he can drown the titters and snickers of the other students
with his singing. Actually his voice is clear and strong, without a
waver. He likes to sing. He looks straight at his audience and opens 21

his mouth wide. He sneaks his breaths skillfully, has huge lungs for nine. His torso looks like a barrel with toothpicks for legs.

The teacher in charge of getting the children to their seats suddenly stares at him. Denny puts his hands up to his mouth in the pre-vomit sign, eyes wide, cheeks puffed out, hand to mouth. She calls, "Harrell! Denny Harrell! Where are you going? Get back in this line!"

But Denny is in the boys' basement, pulling down his short pants. He takes off his shirt. The underwear is in one piece, an arrangement, he thinks, of almost historical significance. He tears open the buttons of the underwear, heavy as a wet blanket, protection and elasticity dead after six hating owners. He is surprised at his violence, but wads the underwear suit into a sodden ball and throws it over the booth hoping for a direct hit. He is not good at sports. There is a satisfying ploop. His father, whose favorite sport is ice fishing, will come back with him and make him retrieve the garment. The thought of fishing through the toilet for the vile underwear curdles his stomach. Only then the bathroom will be full. The boys in his class who never choose him for teams will point and whistle and laugh and his father will be on their side. When his father takes him ice fishing on weekends and he endures the misery of sitting on a bucket in a tiny shack filled with cigar smoke, his father always asks Denny, "Did they pick you this time?"

Denny sees himself in the broken mirror over the sink, his tiny penis like a nib on some machine, on a sink disposal, to stop it running or get it started after it has chewed up a spoon.

He puts on his clothes; he looks five pounds thinner as he rushes to his place by the stage. Mrs. Hutson beams at him, relieved.

After a nursery-rhyme act in which a first-grader jumps over a lighted candle, nimbly, while the fire marshal looks on, Denny comes onstage; Mrs. Hutson strikes the piano. The notes reek of meals past, giving the tune a pizza flatness. Denny's voice is full of force, out of all proportion to his undernourished appearance; the audience, squirmy on the uncomfortable benches, is silent. The music pours over them with a calm that defeats the planned derision of the older boys.

Denny's confidence is free of malice or competition, joyfully

technical. When he sings, "I dream," the listeners think of the
power of dreams to make wishes come true, to prophesy, to rest
them, to create an escape, and they are quiet.

The older boys never choose him, but each is aware he can sing
and anyone who can do something is important: fart in class so the
teacher can't see; play catcher close enough to the plate to make
overhead-pops outs.

The clapping is spontaneous. It roars from the back, runs down
the side aisles, surprises Denny. He stands, face open to the crowd,
happy, unconsciously milking the applause until boys in the back
are whistling and banging on the benches. Mrs. Hutson holds up
her finger for silence but she is drowned. Finally she says, "Please,
please. Perhaps Denny will oblige us with another number? Would
you like that?" Denny senses the response is to a game, an answer
to the folly of Mrs. Hutson's putting a question to the pit, the
knowledge classes will be delayed. There is pleasure, though, in his
being the cause of pleasure.

Mrs. Hutson whispers him off the stage to the piano. They agree
on "Tenting Tonight." She has not had time to instruct him in the
elocution, in the inane gestures of grade-school performance. She
has to make up for it by explaining the words.

"Brother has been fighting brother in this terrible war," she says.
"Both sides are losing. They are hungry and tired. Many are
wounded and sick, far from loved ones. Before the soldiers lie
down on the cold ground, they sing this song."

Someone moans "Boohoo," but the mockery is short-lived.
Denny stands very straight, his voice pours out, pure and full. Without Mrs. Hutson's gestures, the effect of the song is simple and sad.
He draws the words through the tune a little behind the tempo (she
must speak to him about that) until it is almost a lullaby and the
students, tired from recess, stare, wide-eyed, frozen in the moment
before sleep. When he finishes, the words die into a long fall of
quiet. The children are more asleep than awake, metamorphosed
somehow into the gray and blue soldiers around the campfire.

Mrs. Hutson lets herself cry behind her glasses, thinking of the

South, her background the only superiority, romantic superiority, she has over the other teachers. She imagines the salted and burned fields, the disenfranchised men, Jeff Davis in chains. Her grand- father was from New Jersey, though. The moment is long. Some students are thinking of tests next period, hoping they will be put off. Another teacher has a different picture of Denny, always against the school yard wall, his hands behind him. A visitor, Dr. Sydenstricker, in the audience, an annual visitor at the request of the school district music teachers' association, thinks what a beau- tiful voice.

Billy Sydenstricker is the choir master at the Cathedral of St. Mary the Virgin. The choir operates a school next to the cathedral, a day school. The choir is heavily endowed. Billy goes to every school in the district looking for boy sopranos. Usually, if they have the voice, he can't purify their diction, *Cheeses* for *Jeezus*. Or they are shy and hide behind the choir screen. There are four places be- hind the choir screen at the foot of each row. They are all taken and there is a waiting list. Or they bring discipline problems.

"It's a great opportunity for him," Denny's mother, Rayanne, tells her husband, Hugo.

"I don't want my son growing up to be no mackerel snapper!" he says.

"You don't have to convert, the brochure says," Rayanne tells him, not quite convinced herself. "It would cost us six thousand dollars a year to send him there."

"It would cost us ten thousand dollars to send him to the moon, but we ain't going to."

"He'd learn a lot about music. They take these nice trips in sum- mer. Go to Rome, Italy, and France. Europe."

"I want him to stay here with me. I want to take him ice fishing. I want the boys to choose him!"

"Who's better to choose? Some kids who don't like him anyway, or a school where he'll have teachers interested in him? You never get that, do you, that some people just don't like you and they're never going to choose you? He might get into rock and roll. They make a good living. They get rich!"

"No, not going, that's that!"

The following Monday, Rayanne takes Denny, dressed in another pair of hand-me-down wool underwear, a talisman to protect him against her disobedience, to the cathedral school.

The brothers smile condescendingly at her and Denny as if they comprise the whole of Protestant literature and art, its temporariness in the face of Giotto and Dante and Michelangelo. The nuns, out of the mystery of their veils and long dresses now, try to out-ordinary the ordinariness of Protestantism.

But Dr. Sydenstricker takes them into the cathedral. From the concrete block of the church she and Hugo sometimes go to, this soaring miracle is a solace of myth and sorrow and triumph.

In the church—ribbed like the inside of the whale that spit out Jonah, she hears from the very back pew Denny's voice, white and high like a beam of light caught in the vault, a voice to make her unafraid of Hugo, or guiltless of her own wrongdoing. He sings hymns—she can't think they are Catholic songs, maybe the choir master has a book from their church to make Denny feel at home—and she feels for moments like the Virgin Mary herself, brimming with observations she must keep in her heart. Would Joseph have struck Mary, though?

"You took him where?" Hugo demands at supper. He already knows—his bus went right by the cathedral and, luck being luck, there they were emerging.

"If I told you not to and that was that and you still went on and did it, you must have a very good reason, probably better than my reason for not letting him go, that I don't want him to be a sissy and I don't want fried fish stinking up the house on Fridays, right? I forgive you. And just in case," and he comes across her mouth with the side of his right hand, hard, clean—she thinks of it as Denny's voice, on key, perfect pitch—how can Hugo be so deadly accurate?—an inch one way or the other would've saved her. A random inch.

Her jaw is so sore she cannot open her mouth to eat. She needs to lose weight, she tells herself. Hugo apologizes. "How could I?" he demands. His eyes menace. She thinks he will hit her again if she doesn't answer.

Five sons, plus Denny. The youngest lying about his age like his brothers to get into the Marines. Sending an allotment home. Hugo supported the armed services—"the happiest days of my life," he said whenever Rayanne thought he should say he was happy with her. "I want all my brats in it. Denny included. He don't show no signs of wanting to join. It's time he should be asking about it." Like his remark they could send Denny to the moon or China. She risked being hit to say, "Well, neither do I," and he hit her.

She was raised in a family where to be male was to be violent. Her mother never reprimanded her father for letting go about things, chided him for not. She felt more secure knowing his fist could protect her, anywhere she walked in the neighborhood, than she would have knowing his paycheck never deviated as it always did, between factory and home.

But Hugo's not being able to see any difference in people—perhaps it is like acceptance of his hand across her face, a male prerogative—makes her nervous and, after making her nervous, makes her determined. Denny is going to that school and will open his mouth in the procession.

The first Sunday he is to be in the choir, scrubbed white as a piece of tallow, Hugo is called in to work overtime. Rayanne thanks God and tries to cross herself, imagining she is hitting all the wrong places.

She puts on a hat she hasn't worn in years, forces her too-fat fingers into short gloves, and lopes for the bus. Denny has been picked up hours earlier by a van from the church. She sits in the back, astonished at the casual dress of people coming and going, paying very little attention to the priest at the altar. And then the children march in. The organ notes pound the stone floor. The descant rises above the general tune and the singing of the congregation the way an eagle would soar over sparrows. Even above that she hears Denny. He comes close to her pew in the procession.

A motet at the offering throws the voice back to her, to every ear in the congregation with the intensity of sun magnified by glass. He is hidden, so she cannot see him. But she knows his voice and she can imagine perfection.

Leaving the cathedral she wants to tell someone. But no one seems friendly. Stinging sleet drives her back into the vestibule to wait for Denny. They have a half-hour practice before he can leave. Rayanne is embarrassed by her hat, the shortie white gloves. People talk, but not to her. Nervous, she thinks words mean nothing. The priests could have cocked their fingers and everybody would have flocked to the altar; the man preaching the sermon might have shaken his head. No! Hugo hit her; she knows what that means. When the children open their mouths, music is more important than words. Music goes through the body, pulls strings, makes chords with what is already there. Only words go through the mind. The music hangs in her ears like water lilies in a pool, sweetening and filling the air. She feels Denny's voice is somehow the sex she has never understood or felt pleasure in with Hugo, satisfying and long, an act perfect if never repeated or if repeated a thousand times.

When he comes to her, his face is that of another child, holy, dazzling, beautiful. He cannot stop talking to her, telling her everything that happened, what they said to him. The priests complimented him. Singled him out. Dr. Sydenstricker wanted him to sing a solo at the end of the month. He marched in the procession with some boys who lived near. He could ride with them.

Hugo is waiting for them when they get home.

"What's for the old man's dinner?" he asks, furious. She has forgotten, or, having remembered, thought she would be home in time. She tears into the kitchen. Denny's bright face ravishes the sullenness of Hugo's overtime, his disappointment at not being able to go out to the lake and bore a hole.

Hugo has heard something. Over the unsatisfying lunch he tries to remember who told him, or if he told someone at the plant about Denny's boys' choir, or how the choir director found him. It is something about organists. Or choir masters. He drinks another beer to clear his memory.

During the week he sulks over Rayanne's getting Denny into the school, over Denny's enthusiasm, his new friends, the face that seems less and less like his own, and happier and happier to be so.

Sunday morning, Denny gone, he tells Rayanne he is going out to see if he can find somebody to go ice fishing with him. He looks funny, she thinks, his clothes vaguely like her hat and white gloves, but she lets it go, is determined to make up for last Sunday's dinner.

Hugo goes to the cathedral, walks up the center aisle to the front pew. He glances from side to side, tries to ape the genuflections and crossings of the people sitting around him, saying out loud as he touches his forehead and his chest, "Head, gut, tit, tit." No one pays any attention to him. He crosses and recrosses his legs: his dress boots with very high heels have sharp inner points, which cut into his thighs and bang his ankles when he stands or kneels. He cranes his neck to see Denny, tells an old woman in black sitting next to him, "My son!" She stares blankly. He says, "Sounds just like a girl!" She moves to another seat. Her hearing aid catches the gleam from the bank of candles with a money-box in the middle. He gets up in the middle of the creed, goes over and drops a coin in, blows out a candle, all the while trying to remember who told him.

When the priests hold the host up, he leaps from the pew and gallops to the altar. He looks right, left, to see what to do, holds the wine a long time to his lips, his heavy, hairy hands forcing the delicate white fingers of the priest tight on the foot of the chalice. He stands five minutes in the middle of the choir searching for Denny, finds him, and winks.

In his seat he stretches his arms over his head and yawns loudly, uncomfortable in being uncomfortable, miserable for having come. He wishes, kneeling, his legs too long, his frame too big for the narrow pews, that he had the same habit of faith as these people around him. During the endless prayers, said rapidly and to no one

in particular, his eyes dart back and forth between Denny and Dr. Sydenstricker's arms, with slits in his surplice, waving the air when the children sing. His lips mouth the words, his eyebrows move up his forehead as if they were leaving his face altogether. At an amen, he touches a boy's head. Hugo stares at his hand on the shiny gold hair, the large ring on Sydenstricker's finger, the way the hand lingers. It begins to come back to him. Hugo turns red.

After the mass, he waits and waits for Denny. What has happened to him? Finally, Hugo strides back into the church and finds a door into the parish hall. The mood of the acolytes and priests, the women taking the flowers from the altar and locking up the silver, disturbs him. They are cheerful, as if they were cleaning up after a party.

"Where's the choir?" he demands of the crucifer who is polishing the brass cross.

The boy points to a flight of stairs. Hugo hears a piano, like the sound in a bar. He imagines Denny leaning in the bend of the instrument the way he saw a woman at a concert on television. He takes the steps three at a time.

There are two gothic doors at the top. He throws open the door on the right. The choir, still robed, is going over and over a phrase. Dr. Sydenstricker stops, looks at him with irritation. Denny is in front, standing, a sheet of music in his hands. Hugo plunges into the middle of the room, feels the humiliation of Sydenstricker's cold inquisitive stare.

"Touch him! I'll find out!" he shouts, realizes with each word he is saying that something is wrong. The silence puzzles him. He expects Sydenstricker to answer in kind, craves the simplicity of a fight. The boys, till now only mildly interested, used to interruptions on Sunday, mothers who have to take sons early, priests making suggestions about the music in the service, now turn their attention to Dr. Sydenstricker. Hugo feels in the false exuberance of their glance that they are allies. He swells bigger and bigger; his words seem to kill the music lingering in the room. The more he

threatens, the more aware he is of some mistake, some cat of innocence let out of the bag. The boys now stare at him. Denny's face
and mouth twist in pain. Hugo is reminded of Rayanne's face after
he hit her; a dead silence blocks out his presence. The more he
talks, the more the silence punishes him. He is moving back against
the wall, out of the center. Denny is praying to his new god that
Hugo will not identify himself as his father. Hugo grabs the door
handle. "You come downstairs, Denny!" He slams the door.

Denny wishes that Hugo was wilder. They could have understood a madman. But there was a vile reasonableness in what he
said. The other boys look at Dr. Sydenstricker, who feels curiously
sunk, unable to defend or explain himself. Idiot! He has never
touched one of them.

He stands up by the piano, looks at Denny, and blows into his
pitch pipe. They finish two glorias, neither prompted nor corrected
by Sydenstricker. "That's all," he says and turns his back to them,
standing at the keyboard, stacking music. He sees Denny, whose
eyes are wet. He hates the tears, despises himself for bringing
Denny into the fold. What has Denny told his father? What do the
other children tell theirs?

Hugo is waiting for Denny. Denny lowers his head. Hugo puts
his great hairy hand under his face and lifts it up. It is so different
from his own face. Rayanne is always saying, "Why won't you leave
him alone? He's different. He doesn't want to go ice fishing." Hugo
looks at her in Denny's face and thinks of her, or himself thirty
years from now when they will look so much alike strangers will
think they are brother and sister. Isn't that what love is, his face
demands of hers? Making somebody *like* you? He looks at Denny's
face again. It is so different. Denny has put his hand up to take his
father's fist away. He takes the hand dutifully and they cross the
street. He wants to ask him what he is mad at Dr. Sydenstricker
about, supposes it is the same thing he is mad at Rayanne and himself about. Denny has the feeling he is leading Hugo. He hopes
they are not going ice fishing. If he catches a cold, he won't be able
to sing. He thinks of the space between the water and the ice, of the

trapped air, the fish with no way to escape but Hugo's bread-baited
hook. He tries to pull his hand free from his father. His underwear
pants, the one condition Rayanne exacts of him for going to the
choir school, sag. She is waiting dinner on them but Hugo decides
to go straight to the lake.

Wyoming

Miles Wilson has worked for the U.S. Forest Service in Oregon and California and has been a partner in a small logging company. Director of the Southwest-focus M.F.A. program at Southwest Texas State University, he has published widely in such journals as the Georgia Review, Iowa Review, Sewanee Review, *and* Southwest Review.

"Frontier stories in the best sense: fresh, sharp, and rambunctious."
GAIL GODWIN, 1989

McGrath had been driving three days, I-80 all the way from Indiana into the breadbasket of an ugly blizzard that gave him something to think about. One day to Council Bluffs, one more to Cheyenne, and now sluicing in the wake of a Redball Express rig somewhere west of Laramie. He had caught the truck on a sweeping climb east of Elk Mountain and decided to tuck in behind. Now, even with chains, he wouldn't be able to get around; the north lane had drifted in to wall him off.

McGrath checked the gauges. It seemed prudent, but he knew that probing invited bad luck, his attention wiring the Volvo into the socket of his uneasiness. Skip, a philosopher-mechanic in Bloomington who worked only on Peugeots and Saabs, had debugged the electrical system as a favor to a friend. More precisely, Skip had promised only to induce the bugs to migrate into redundant circuitry where, left undisturbed, they might remain. Skip was of the opinion that Volvo built a good marine diesel and that their electrical systems had been designed by a German engineer who subscribed to Gurdjieffian electrokinetics and had never forgiven the Swedes their neutrality in World War II. Skip had spent three days drinking akvavit and reading Schopenhauer in preparation for the job.

The Volvo belonged to McGrath's wife, who now belonged to someone else. They had bought it from a colleague in the English Department at Bowling Green to which McGrath also no longer belonged. He was driving to San Francisco, to the MLA Convention, for an interview with Jenijoy LaBelle—Vonnegut, Fielding, Margaret Mitchell?—about a one-year replacement position at Long Beach State.

The Redball's logo was right in his face, and McGrath dropped into second as they squared off with another hill. McGrath had figured wrong. A Brown Ph.D., six years of carving up his dissertation into articles, servicing the department, tight with a couple of senior professors and cordially suppressing his gag reflex with most of the rest. Even that last year when suddenly, inexplicably, it all hung in the balance, sending off to that outfit in Boston that filled in, at five dollars a whack, blank student evaluations in a variety of inks and handwriting and with whatever comments you sent along. And it had come to this: adrift in academe, out of it now for a semester, willing to take even a migrant labor job, stooping over rows of freshman essays: "In our modern world of today everyone has their own opinions about life." Jenijoy LaBelle—Poe, Tom Robbins, Ringling Brothers?

A cornice of ice broke off the back of the truck and McGrath swerved sluggishly, missing the chunk with his tire but taking a thick whump somewhere around the oil pan. The oil light remained blank and oracular. Had it worked when he started the car after gassing up in Laramie? McGrath took a slow drink of rum to shore up where the blow had caved part of his stomach in.

By one o'clock in the afternoon McGrath had made Rawlins, driving with his knuckles the last twenty miles, dervished by a ground blizzard. Snow-dazed and ringing from the slap of chains, he followed the Redball into a truck stop. Inside, he spread out the map. A hundred miles in three hours. He'd given himself two days' slack, and that was gone. He'd have to put in, say, thirty-six hours in the next forty-eight to make the interview. Already, the ache of the road had gotten beneath the husk McGrath folded into whenever he needed to make good time over long distances.

The waitress set down a cup of coffee without asking, and McGrath ordered a hamburger. He poured cream into the cup and loaded it with sugar. When the burger arrived, he layered it top and bottom with catsup and covered his mound of fries with the rest of the bottle.

Road-stunned, McGrath's eyes wandered the map. West of Rawlins, a state highway went north and stopped. No town, just stopped. A cartographer's error, bad planning, a metaphor? In Wyoming? McGrath combed his memory. No writer he knew of had ever come from the state. Pound? No, that was Idaho, or maybe Washington. Wyoming, a wind-sucked vacuum in the literary map of America. What if he took that road?

He saw the dress before he really saw the girl. An electric floral print: orchids, hibiscus—McGrath's grandmother had raised them—and half a dozen other improbable tropical exotics he couldn't name. The girl's hair was long and straight and almost the color of parchments he had seen once in the British Museum. The rest was ordinary: plain face, serviceable figure, maybe twenty-five, a springiness in her walk as she approached the register, her center of gravity not yet migrated to her hips. She paid her bill and passed across the room near his table. She saw him watching her, but he was too weary to look away. Her eyes were ash-gray and yes, she flickered a smile and went on through the doors into the alcove that buffered the room from the weather.

McGrath finished his sodden fries and left a rueful tip. In the lee of the building, the Volvo's windshield had filled with snow. McGrath unlocked the car and ducked in. In the stunted light, the girl bloomed in the passenger seat.

McGrath woke up entirely. The girl was attentive but perfectly at ease. Before McGrath could imagine what to say, while card after card skittered face down from the deck—what kind of sucker was he being played for; was this unguessed good luck; hadn't he locked the passenger side and what about his manuscript, his Leica, his

Slazenger (who would play in Wyoming, how could anyone fence

it?), in fact, the whole affectionate debris of his adult life piled on
the seat behind him?—before he could arrange any of this into a
hand he could play, the girl raised a cautionary finger and leaned
forward to blow on the windshield. In a sure and elegant hand, she
wrote across the pearly film:

mute

Abby

from: Abora Wells

to: west

And on the evidence of the colons and the lowercase *w*, and because he could not think of what else to do, when the girl turned
from her writing and smiled again and nodded at the ignition,
McGrath turned the Volvo over and they set out.

The first ten miles or so he had to settle into the weather again
and the little detonations of adrenaline as the Volvo yawed, even
with chains and tethered in ruts, in a wind that had shifted and now
surged broadside against the car. When he had fallen into the erratic rhythm of it, he reached under his seat and took another pull
from the rum. He offered the bottle and the girl tipped it up, deftly
blocking the top with her fingertips. She touched her tongue to
them and made an exaggerated face.

McGrath laughed. "Old Paint Stripper, specialty of the house."

The girl breathed, spun the words out of her index finger.

Find another house

The blizzard seemed to have let up some, but the wind came
like a blind, enormous drunk, and the running snow had begun to
drift into the open lane. It was colder now too; the Volvo's heater
couldn't keep up with it. McGrath turned on the radio. KBOY gave
him the price of feeder hogs in Chicago, how many head of cattle
had been shipped to Omaha last week. He walked the dial across
the band, then switched to FM. Poised among the static was a
strong station, playing an arrangement for flute, drums, and some
stringed instrument he couldn't identify. It sounded like the score
for a Kurosawa film. When it was over, the DJ, his voice like a
stoned dream of speaking (McGrath could be convinced that all

FM stations in the country were plugged in to one announcer, operating from a Vaseline-coated sauna in Boulder, Colorado), produced the call letters KHAN, and the radio went dead. McGrath spun the dial, hoping for static. The generator light hadn't come on, and he was about to pop the cover over the fuses when the girl pointed. McGrath had to lean above the wheel to follow her finger past the crescent of compacted snow that surrounded the wipers. The antenna had snapped off, leaving an ice-crusted stub.

McGrath shrugged and worked on the bottle again. They were not making good time; at thirty-four, McGrath was not making good time.

How did you get here?

McGrath turned to look at her. He had been wrong about her eyes. They were more green than gray, the iris flecked with amber. It must have been the fluorescent lights in the truck stop.

"I-80 mostly from Bloomington. Bloomington, Indiana. I was staying with friends."

No. How did you get here?

McGrath guessed. "I used to teach. I used to be married. She took off with a graduate student, some goofy leftover from the sixties. I'm going to see about another job in California."

The same thing?

"More or less."

The girl frowned at this and settled back. McGrath's thoughts idled ahead. He wondered if they would be sleeping together that night. He tried to erect the possibilities, but his imagination was chaste as a ghost. They topped a rise and McGrath looked north. Rail lines ran along the freeway. An empty gondola car lay tilted against a bank on what must have been a siding. The snow had drifted over the lower lip of the car and was filling the cargo space. Before today, McGrath could not have believed in such a wind. The Volvo seemed suddenly like a model of itself, set down by accident in a world where the scale was terribly wrong. Where only the distance of Wyoming was proportionate to the wind and the veteran cold. The thought of it made McGrath's teeth ache.

The girl was at the windshield again, but not writing. Breathing
and working, first with her finger, then her nails, and finishing the
foreground with her hair spread between her fingers like a brush,
she unscrolled a panorama of plains and beyond them a forest folding back into domed mountains, all of it bisected by a great river
that flowed improbably from the plains away through a rift in the
mountain line. McGrath scanned the detail, then took the scene in
whole again. It was stylized, a pure act of imagination, yet it seemed
absolutely right, more credible than a *National Geographic* diorama.
It felt a little like he thought Kenya might. McGrath realized he had
been holding his breath.

"Are you an artist?"

The girl leaned close to the windshield, puffed her cheeks, and
blew over a spot at the river's edge. She drew a stick figure, then
added an outsized head, a caricature of McGrath. The head was set
on backwards, and an amplified toe of the stick man was dipped
gingerly in the water. The girl put her whole face into a smile that
had no referent in his inventory of expressions.

He watched the scene as little rivulets of condensation began to
run and the cold ate it all away. The whole thing remained clear to
him long after it was gone.

They gassed up in Wamsutter and McGrath asked the girl if she
was hungry. She shook her head and they went on, into the deep
afternoon, scuds of thinner gray breaking through now and then
above the ground blizzard. Later, the light failing steadily, McGrath
caught sight of something off to his left and no telling how many
hundreds of feet up. Broadside to him, it was flat and rectangular,
metallic, about the size of a house trailer. Tumbling, it disappeared
until the wide surface came round again. It veered extravagantly
and, before McGrath could point the girl to it, was lost in the driving snow.

The light had been gone for some time when the girl began to
play. The instrument sounded like a harmonica, but with greater
range and resonance. Call it a mouth organ, thought McGrath. She
built the piece layer by layer, and McGrath sifted the memory of his

wife's scuffed collection of classical music. Nothing stuck. When the girl was finished, he asked her.

Me

"No, I mean the composer."

Me again

"What do you call it?"

Anything you like

"But you must have a name for it, something to call it when you want to remember."

I just made it up. You give it a name for me to remember

"Wyoming."

The girl tooted her instrument like a circus calliope.

Sometime around midnight they broke over a summit after an imperceptible climb. Ahead, a rinse of lights made McGrath squint. He couldn't remember the last light he had seen. The snow was banked so that even whatever eastbound traffic there might have been was shielded from view. Closer, a gargantuan American flag stood out straight in the floodlit wind; closer still, a sign above the drifts: "Little America." McGrath played a flashlight across the map. Such a thing did exist, confirmed by Texaco.

He pulled in to gas up again. The place looked like an outpost on the moon, snow-chromed and antiseptic as an operating room. The boy who took his money told him to shuck his chains. The road west was spotty with bare pavement; he'd chew up his tires in no time. As McGrath unraveled the chains, he wondered how the place got any help. A two-story, multi-wing motel that must have had hundreds of rooms, a coffee shop the size of a school cafeteria, rank upon rank of pumps. There wasn't a town, nothing for at least fifty miles. Did Wyoming have gulags? McGrath seemed to remember that it had been a Republican state for a long time. And James Watt. Maybe Little America was staffed with bureaucrats who had fallen from his grace and been posted there—the extremity of the interior.

McGrath had to take off his gloves to manipulate the chains. When he got back in, he could barely curve his fingers around the wheel. The girl took his hands in her own, guided them under her dress. She didn't flinch when she took her hands away and closed

her thighs on McGrath's glacial fingers; she didn't stiffen when he
began to move them as the feeling came back. There had been
something so attentive in her doing this that it drained the act of all
erotic content. Bowed toward her, both palms facing away from
him like a mendicant, McGrath thought he was going to weep.

When his fingers tingled, he withdrew them and felt around
under the seat for the rum. And because he couldn't trust what else
he might have said, he left it at "thanks."

Unchained, the Volvo skittered less than McGrath had expected.
The wind settled in at a steady 20 mph or so, and the blowing snow
sheeted across the road. The moon had broken out behind them,
and McGrath could see patches of pavement, like a dark arctic sea,
that appeared wherever the plows had gouged through the snowpack. McGrath relaxed a little. Unclenched, he felt the weariness in
his thighs and back, tasted the peculiar tarnish, the transcontinental
casing in his mouth. On wobbly legs, his prospects teetered west:
Jenijoy LaBelle—Barth, Pynchon, Borges?

You could throw it away—let it all go

McGrath muffled the flashlight against the seat but did not turn
it off.

"What?" He was afraid that he knew.

You must decide. Now, I think

"Yeah, well, I don't know." McGrath tried to pick his way. "Sure,
I suppose. Why the hell not." What was a promise to her?

The cold clamped him like an imperative from the end of the
earth. The girl had rolled her window down. She leaned around
the bucket seat and brought up his overnight bag, setting it on the
hump behind the gearshift.

Jesus, that's what she meant. She was calling him on it. McGrath
swerved wildly, then leveled at once into a lunar calm.

"Why," he said steadily, "the hell not."

The girl did not respond, and McGrath drained the last of the
rum.

"Well, go ahead."

You must do it

"I can't throw and steer; you drive?"

Yes

McGrath didn't need the flashlight anymore. The moon had broken through altogether and he could read by its light. He stopped the car and they squirmed around each other. McGrath looked back, checking for traffic. Only Wyoming, thirty-four years of it. And the moon, hanging like a wild ace for those whose luck had run out.

The girl went through the gears a little mechanically but without hesitation. He was, McGrath saw, in capable hands.

The whole thing went quickly. He had no urge to linger, did not look back, even as his manuscript flapped away behind them, giddy at the thought of some cowpoke turning up a weather-beaten page: "As J. Hillis Miller suggests, the self-referential nature of all structures—indeed, their deconstructive plasticity—has called into question the *logos* of 'beginning, continuity and end, of causality, of dialectical process, of organic unity, and of ground.'" The air was at him like a bibliography of pain, burning his nostrils, blurring his sight, the ache coming back to his fingers. And it was all so light in his hands as he lifted it up and turned it loose in the slipstream. He was rolling up the window when he felt her hand on him.

Everything

McGrath checked the back. "That's it."

Not quite

It came to him that he was all that was left.

The girl twisted in the seat and in a quick sweep had her dress off over her head. Under it, there was nothing else. She handed the dress to McGrath and he caught the scent of cinnamon as he let the wind take it away. Turning, he watched it blossom above the snow.

He came out of his own clothes reflectively, handling each piece as though he had been a manikin dressed for a costume ball.

Done, McGrath leaned back in the seat and let his weariness have him. He warmed up quickly, and soon even the little spasms in his legs went away. Beside him, the girl's torso was lit like a crescent, curving into her thighs and away in the dark.

"What do you do?"

The girl arched forward.

This

McGrath rode the answer to sleep.

He woke once. The moon had shifted and was pouring over her shoulder into her lap. Sleep-sluiced, McGrath registered the amber thicket that arose there, spreading down her thighs as far as the moon lit them. He went back to sleep.

He woke again at dawn, the perimeter of light widening at his back. When she saw that he was awake, the girl eased the Volvo to the side of the road and stopped. She was wearing woolly stockings and a sheepskin coat that she must have hidden under the seat. She smiled at McGrath and was gone. He scrambled into the driver's seat and was half out the door calling "Abby, Abby," when she turned from the median and stopped him with an imperial motion of absolute command. She turned again, at the top of the driftline, made another gesture of, what—permission, benediction, regret?— and disappeared down into the eastbound lanes.

Pure forsakenness sucked at McGrath, and when it was done he feels like uncirculated silver, untarnished by handling. As he drives away, accelerating west—the Volvo skating, freelancing it over the patches of snowpack—the instrument panel lights up like a slot machine and McGrath cups his hands for the payoff. The lights go out and then McGrath is across the border—welcomed to Utah by the governor himself—and he fogs the windshield to write his name across it, his vapors retrieving part of the scene of mountain and plain, and with more of his breath brings the whole thing back with the stick man, yes, now out in the current astride a raft. And singing "Jenijoy LaBelle," McGrath cups his hands again for riches, claps for the luck of Salt Lake City as he passes through, naked and shining, a vision out of the east, and then the lake itself, the salt flats, the high desert and the Sierras and on down, all the way to the edge of America.

The Venus Tree

Michael Pritchett currently lives in Shawnee Mission, Kansas, where he works as a freelance writer. He received his bachelor's degree in journalism from the University of Missouri in 1983 and is presently working on his M.F.A. through the low-residency program at Warren Wilson College in Swannanoa, North Carolina. He is also at work on a novel and a new collection of short stories.

"Michael Pritchett's haunting and austere stories linger a long time in the mind. His characters seem to be exploring their way through a world of clues and secrets and his writing has such persuasive force that the reader shares in their explorations, coming to understanding as they do. His style is strong and unpretentious, often capable of real unforced poetry. His images seem compounded naturally out of the weather of his people's lives."

ROBERT STONE, 1988

A long time ago, at a place where two rivers came together to form one broad river that ran to the nearby sea, there grew a tree. It grew in a rain forest that was as full and deep as night.

The tree rose three hundred feet above the forest floor and its thick canopy stretched out as though it were the sky. The branches of this tree stretched down until they brushed the face of the blue river and the rolling waters carried away the yellowed leaves that fell from the rich canopy. The bottom of the river's deep channel was carpeted thickly in these same yellow leaves.

Water birds of all colors came to the shade of the tree in the afternoon when the sky was clear and the morning rains were past. Hidden in the shade, they stood still in the clear water, spearing the minnows that came near, seeking cover amid their silent orange legs.

The birds would stay on until the sun passed away and slid down into the jungle to sleep for the night. At dusk, the birds moved out into the

*river's deep water and, packed tightly together, would wait out the night
and watch for the alligators that sometimes ventured out beyond the
muddy shallows and cattail beds.*

*When night began settling around the tree, and the canopy had
changed from brilliant green to black, the canoes came from the village
upriver. Lovers, moving through the water without torches or other light,
making almost no sound with the sandalwood oars as they dipped them
into the river, came down to the tree.*

*The young men came in the lead canoes. Their black hair was combed
back with water and their skin shone under the growing moonlight.
Bare-chested, they were first to pull their dugouts onto the shore beneath
the tree; as they did so, they beat the shallows around them with the flats
of the paddles to frighten alligators that might be lurking.*

*With the canoes ashore, they waited in the shallows for the women to
glide in so that they might pull the boats in for them and help them onto
dry ground. The women came in their bridal dresses, made from cotton
that had been dyed in the purple berry of the very tree to which they had
come. They wore bright flowers in chains around their waists, and their
bare breasts between the long streams of their black hair were moistened
with banana oil.*

*Alone now, beneath the canopy, surrounded by the night calls of giant
toucans and banana parrots, the young men separated from the women
and allowed them to go about the gathering of the purple berries of the
tree. The women plucked the hard berries from the tree in clusters and
held them in the aprons of their bridal dresses. When there were enough,
they came back together and arranged the clusters in rows on palm leaves
that the men had spread out on the soft grass.*

*When all was ready, the lovers paired off so that each was kneeling
on the opposite side of the berry clusters from her true love. The women
lit tightly wrapped bundles of flower petals and slow-burning roots and
placed them on the palm leaves where they might smolder and fill the
air with sweet smoke.*

*When the hour was right, and the moon had risen until the light was
falling between the leaves of the gently blowing branches, each of the
young men took up a cluster of the tree's purple berries and held it in the
palm of his right hand.*

If the spirits favored him that night, then the young man either was visited with the knowledge of love for the young maiden kneeling before him or was visited with the knowledge of the desires of the flesh. This knowledge was said to emanate from the tree itself and might infuse itself into every heart of every young lover to kneel beneath its branches.

If the young man was visited with the knowledge of love, then by putting the cluster of berries back on the palm leaves where he picked it up, he made a promise to wed his true love one year from that moment and to make no efforts to taste her love until their wedding night.

But, if the young man was visited only by the knowledge of the desires of the flesh, then he was forced to eat the cluster of berries he had picked up from the palm leaves. If he was able to do this, then he was allowed to take his lover deep into the jungle, away from the tree, and make love to her until morning.

In the morning, she would return to the village alone and send men back into the jungle to find his body and bring it back up the river, where, after the burning of a raft of his belongings and a pile of flowers gathered by the girls of the village, he would be wrapped in vines and palm leaves and set adrift in the river so that the spirits of the other world would find him and care for him.

"What if he couldn't eat the berries?"

"Well, then he had to leave the village and the girl and he couldn't ever come back."

"What if she had a baby? Then there wouldn't be any dad around."

"If she had a baby, the baby was cared for and loved just the same as the babies of the other women in the village. Children were sacred and nobody cared where they came from."

"Okay. Good story."

"Thank you. Now sleep. I mean it."

After every night's story, Abby stands naked beside the sink on the bathroom scale. She steps off, face serious, and puts her feet into slippers with the faces of rabbits. Robe half-on, she scuffs over to me and sits.

"I'm very fat and very beautiful," she says.

She's not fat. She's a good hundred and fifty, but not fat. When she stretches out in bed, any fat fades into strong lines. I have less muscle. A lot less when you throw out the physical aspect.

That time is almost the only time we touch. She tips her head back and I start at her throat, working my fingers along the gentle sag of her jaw, rubbing deep along the hairline, seeing without seeing.

I put what I can into the touches, moving down to the hollows of her breastbone, then down again to the light scratch of her underarms. She drops to her elbows toward the end, making of her torso a flat, solid surface as firm as earth. Her belly has the wrinkled memory of Linden in its lines but her pelvis points down to her plump vulva as surely as a stream channel.

She works on the next night's story while we're still wide awake, talks through it out loud, with the lights out and the window letting in the muffled night.

"Here's something I was thinking about," she says. "I'm wondering if they shouldn't change that line in the Bible that says, 'And the lion shall lie down with the lamb.' I say they add a line that says, 'And two years later, the lamb shall develop a reduction in weight and a chronic and persistent superficial gland inflammation and shall die of a gross failure of his immune system.'"

"You think there's a story in that?"

"Oh, there is. Believe me. If you only look there are good stories all over."

When she has something she can work over in her mind, without me, I go to sleep. I hear her get up three or four times in the night and write in her spiral notebook, then I feel her weight on the bed again.

Linden gets her bath in the morning. Abby sits wide-legged in the soapy water, her big breasts tan on the small billows of suds. Linden sits between Abby's thighs with her own knees up, a scale model of Abby, closing her eyes tightly, waiting for the rinse.

Abby gets the plastic pitcher ready and Linden stands up, steadying herself on Abby's round pink knees. Abby pours. It's a cold rinse. Linden shrieks and does a war dance in the steaming tub.

I come in after Linden has gone to school and Abby is crying. She holds the end of the toilet paper to her face with the other end still attached.

"That buckle mark is still on her bottom," she tells me. "I wonder sometimes if it's ever going to go away."

"It will."

"I'd like to call that fucker up and invite him over for a romp in the hay."

"Go ahead. I'm looking for a job today."

"Huh. And get the clap for my trouble. No, thank you very much."

I wet my face to shave. There's no reason to stop for Abby's emotions. They come and go like nesting birds. She's already dried up when she wraps her arms under mine and works her way between me and the sink.

"What's this about a job, Nelly?" she says. "No jobs. People are for their presence."

I have shirts I cannot wear. I have shirts that were never sewn for mortals to wear. Buttons and buttonholes have no real relationship to Abby. Sleeves go on and on without limit, or stop short at the elbow. She makes shirts until we all go weak from the exertion and fall into bed, and at dawn she is up again, sacrificing the lives of curtains, tablecloths, to the vigilant black Singer.

I try to stand clear. She is dizzy with giving and she talks in her delirium to the sewing machine and the dusty windows, to me, sort of, and to June wafting along the sidewalks outside.

"My mom called me 'Poor Heart,' when I was little," Abby says. "I made doll clothes for everybody so they would like me and when they didn't and I came home bawling, she called me Poor Heart. You know why? Not because she was sorry, no. Because my heart was empty. She meant I was giving all my heart stuff away and keeping nothing for myself."

She sighs a little, then, a long time later, she sits back and says,

"My, how I've changed." And laughs.

Giving is what put her here. She gave for a dishwasher that drifted into the restaurant where she works and then in a few weeks drifted out again.

"He was small," she says. "And clean. At my age you go for the possible, not the beautiful."

I've asked her his name.

"None of them," she says. "I don't remember any names. The faces, though." She taps her temple. "Keep those right here."

"So really," I say, "it could have been any of them."

"You've heard that old joke, haven't you? Two ladies are sitting in a veterinarian's office with their little dogs on their laps, and one says to the other, 'Well, that's a nice-looking dog, what's it doing in here?' The other woman looks embarrassed and says quietly, 'It's sort of embarrassing, but he's got syphilis.' 'Syphilis!' the woman says. 'How in the world did he get syphilis?' 'Well,' the other woman says. 'He claims he got it from a tree!'"

June ends with Abby waking me at two in the morning to talk about stories.

"Nelly," she says, her round, shiny face very close to mine. "You've got to work on your stories. You've got to give them a beginning, a middle, and an end and you've got to make them mean something. There has to be a point."

The warmer our summer gets, the more she has to say about points, about purposes. We watch TV with Linden between us on the deep couch. Linden leans on Abby's shoulder but throws one of her small legs over one of mine. Abby talks in a fever, explaining and explaining the plots and motivations of the characters to all of us, even herself. I don't stop her. I doubt she could stop. Linden sleeps and I try, but Abby is tireless and the rooms fill up with the blue light and a haze of her words.

Later, Linden moans on my shoulder when I take her up the stairs and the sound is like "Dodo." When I tell Abby, she gets wet eyes and stops unbuttoning her blouse.

"That's yours now," she says and she takes a hard, sudden hold on me that pulls me down. The ring where her fingers held burns for a moment. "Understand?" she says.

"No."

"That's what she called him when she was just little."

"She was sleepy," I say. "She just thought I was him."

"I'm telling you," she says, serious. "It's yours. Be wise and take it."

She weighs and then comes out to where I'm stretched on the bed and eases onto me like I am a rubber raft on deep water. Her hair carries the smell of cold grease from the restaurant and another, deeper smell. The blood of meat.

After a breath, she rolls over, pulling me on top. My thin legs slip between the soft fold of her thighs and I can't stop my hips from pushing just once against that joining.

She wedges an elbow between us then, and shakes her head.

"You ought to go to the bank and talk to my friend," she says. "You'd like each other. You could share these things."

I'm speechless when she says that. Not because of what she said—she tells me about the girl at the bank all the time. It's how she says it, how easily she gives. She gives away herself. Now she gives away me.

July fifth, we celebrate my birthday at the hospital. Abby is sitting on the metal table, swinging her tan feet, a box of Puffs on her knee. On Tuesday, it was sniffles and a lot of quiet. Thursday, I was up for an hour before I realized Abby was still in bed. Light was falling on her fingers and she was turning them in it, the rest of her perfectly still, her eyes wide and dark around the edges.

I dropped Linden with the neighbors and we drove along in sunshine with rain falling in thick spats on the windshield of my truck.

"Well," she says, when we pull into the hospital lot. "I wanted to wait to give it to you later, but here's your birthday present."

She looks up to the sky and, following her gaze, I see it, too.

"I don't know where I'll keep it," I say.

"Don't. Give it to somebody else."

In the room, they give her a surgical green gown. We're adrift in white and only the lights seem to be affixed to the ceiling. It's the first time I really see, with the pale green, with the painful white, that Abby's color is not so good. Her face seems gray like the stone of statues, like a goddess of legend.

In minutes, we're in Ben Franklin's, buying the new bottle of ampicillin. I hold it in my pocket, sure and brown, a mojo against all the things I imagine but can never see.

There's a story I heard about a Chinese prince who wanted to find the most perfect pair of goldfish for his garden pond. He was willing to pay any price for them and he sent out a messenger to tell the kingdom of his wishes. It just so happened that one of the young court attendants, a boy of fourteen, was in love with the prince and he wanted to be the one to find the beautiful goldfish. So he sent a message to his grandfather, an old gardener in a nearby kingdom, to find these goldfish and to send them to him.

The old gardener, having age and wisdom on his side, went to his own prince, knowing that the prince possessed a most excellent pair, each of the fish fully ten inches in length with papery fins and a color like polished gold, and easily the most beautiful in the entire Mainland.

He humbly suggested to his prince that he might improve his negotiating position with the neighboring kingdom if he would satisfy the other prince's wish and supply him with the remarkable goldfish.

So, the following day, a royal entourage made the long foot journey to the other kingdom with the goldfish. The two princes met in the palace court and the gift of the most beautiful pair of goldfish was made.

The boy was very pleased because, by way of explanation, his prince came to understand that it was he who had arranged not only the gift of the goldfish, but also the meeting of the two kingdoms on a very favorable occasion.

At the end of the meeting, as the visiting entourage was preparing to depart, the prince took the boy aside and said, "You have served me well and been so clever that you are probably the finest thing I possess. Therefore, I must now make a gift of you to the prince of our neighboring kingdom to show my good faith and my desire to promote health and welfare between our kingdoms."

And so he gave the boy who was in love with him to the neighboring prince and the boy never set eyes on his prince again in his lifetime.

Abby listens to the story, buoyed by pillows without pillowcases in the middle of our wrecked bed. She has slept fifteen hours. While I talk, quickly because her tiredness is so heavy in the room, she looks at the alarm clock on the table. I know she is counting up the hours she has slept.

"That's it?" she asks me.

"It's just one I heard," I say.

"Keep working on it," she says. "And don't tell that one to Linden. Not until she's old and fat like us anyway."

It's two in the afternoon on a Sunday, and Abby is asleep. I'm trying to be in other places, trying to push myself into other rooms, but I never get far. Linden roller-skates on the runner in the hallway and bumps the wall every now and then for balance. The bumping sounds are big and muffled, like something is trying to get down the hallway and into Abby's room.

But Linden's skates are fierce on the floor above my head. I feel better knowing it won't get past her.

Downstairs, I'm sitting in the kitchen on a chair, looking down both hallways. One leads to the living room and the other leads to a small laundry room, a bathroom, and a short hall that ends at the stairway that goes upstairs.

I'm just looking at the designs, the way Abby's pans are hung with nails on the wall, the number of towels stacked on top of the washing machine, the kind of bleach bottle on the shelf above the white metal sink.

I'm trying to see her plan in all of this.

By four, I've worked my way to the third step from the top and

Linden is sitting on the top step. She's breathing hard and the sweat stands out on her pink face like a fine oil.

The skates are still on. She wears a top Abby made from kitchen curtains. Grape clusters, purple, red, and green, are dyed into the fabric. With tan arms and her one black braid, Linden looks like a Latino princess. I tell her so and she just bites her upper lip and fumbles with the lacing of the plastic skates.

"I wish we had a tree," she says. "A big one with big branches."

"You'd climb it?"

"I'd sit under it."

"And the boys would swarm like bees."

She fumbles more and more with the lace.

"Who knows," she says.

When Abby wakes in the evening, she is as pink as the roses in the bedsheets. I don't know why I don't have a shirt just like it. She rubs under each side of her jaw. Her damp hair clings to her cheeks. She makes me rub, too, and I feel what she means—no more swelling.

While I'm still holding her moist throat, she says she wants to go to the Fun House.

"We have to celebrate every time," she says seriously. "That way, we'll also celebrate the time it doesn't go away and we'll have a reason to be happy that we won't be able to get out of."

I nod, agreeing, but I can't seem to say anything. I'm trying to turn my face some direction so she won't know she's holding up better than I am. When she wriggles the nightgown up over her head, I wipe my face and make it out of the door into the hallway.

In the truck, Linden clicks her skates together, toes and heels, toes and heels. Abby let her keep the skates on. "For luck," Linden had asked. I wish I had a pair, too.

We come off the dark highway into the strip malls of Raytown and coast into the lot behind Fun House Pizza. Linden struggles for a few yards across white gravel, then hits the smooth downhill walk and glides, legs stiff, arms straight out to the door. Because of the skates, she's not really on the earth with the rest of us. I admire her for finding a way to do that.

Inside, we each take a hand and tug her along. Passing video games on both sides, Linden suddenly stops and points.

"That's us," she says.

When we look, there's a carnival mirror. It is us. But we're pushed down to two feet tall and stretched three feet wide. There's more to us than there ever was before.

Abby's smile opens like wings on her face and flutters there before slipping away. She bends down and covers Linden as if to make of herself a cocoon around both of them. While she cries, I look into the mirror and try not to see how frightened I am.

At bedtime, Linden lies down beside Abby in a nightgown with a pale blue bow at the throat. I tell them both the tree story. Linden snores lightly through the ending.

"What if he couldn't eat the berries?" Abby asks.

"Well, then he had to leave the village and the girl and he couldn't ever come back."

"What if she had a baby? Then there wouldn't be any dad around."

"If she had a baby, the baby was cared for and loved just the same as the babies of the other women in the village. Children were sacred and nobody cared where they came from."

"Okay," Abby said. "Good story."

"Thank you. Now sleep. I mean it."

The Seeney Stretch

Sharon Dilworth, originally from Detroit, now lives in Pittsburgh, where she teaches English at Carnegie Mellon University. She is currently working on a second collection of short stories, Women Drinking Benedictine.

"Sharon Dilworth's writing is animated and sympathetic, wry and aware. Her characters are vivid and unpredictable. She is able to convey a sense of life lived in time and place with great immediacy. The reader senses a complete world in the control of the author's sensibility; it is this, I think, that establishes the excellence of her work."

ROBERT STONE, 1988

He says the gray skies confused him. Surrounded by the trees losing their fall colors, the leaves almost all gone, my husband shot Colin.

"I was a hundred feet away," Patrick says. He stands in front of the fireplace, one foot on the brick hearth and his long arm stretched along the mantel. "Why didn't he say something? How come he didn't see me?"

Two policemen sit side by side on the couch. Their pressed blue pants have identical creases running down their legs. They hold matching coffee cups and only the one's blond mustache reminds me that I am not looking at a mirrored image. He asks Patrick to tell them again what happened just before he fired the gun. There is nothing cold about their questioning. They are hunters too. Duck, not deer, and they understand the silence of the woods, the sharp rustle of a sudden noise.

"I should have seen him," Patrick says. "His face at least. Why didn't I see his face?" Patrick puts his head in the crook of his arm and talks to the floor. He is still wearing his long underwear shirt,

53

and the collar is dirty from sweat. He has been answering questions for almost twenty-four hours. First up in Marquette County and now down here, but I don't see any sign that he is tiring. His energy scares me because no matter how many times he tells it, I don't believe the story of the gray skies.

The policeman without the mustache leans forward and takes a white powdered doughnut from the tray. "It doesn't make any sense," he says. "Third day of deer hunting and the kid's wearing his vest in his jean pocket. What was he doing? Asking for it?" He bites into the doughnut and the crumbs fall onto his chest.

Patrick took Colin deer hunting up north near the Seeney Stretch. The land is dense with birch and poplar trees and the hunters wear orange vests so they can be spotted miles away.

The policeman turns to me, the crumbs balanced on his shirt. "We're not sure if Colin got lost or what. He could have ended up back at camp by mistake," he says.

I nod. My legs are crossed and I push against the floor with my heel, letting all the weight go back in the chair. The thick carpet muffles the noise.

"Was Colin having any problems?" the other policeman asks. "You know, like the runs, diarrhea? Did he get drunk the night before?"

"We had some beers the night before," Patrick says. "But not that many. Everyone just kind of fell asleep after an hour or two."

"Is there any reason you can think of why he didn't stay with John or that group?" The policeman coughs and sits forward.

"I don't know," Patrick says. He moves away from the fireplace and paces in front of the bay window. "He seemed okay. Maybe bored with the whole idea of hunting. I thought he'd like it, but it was really cold. It rained the whole time we were up there."

"The other group can't remember when Colin disappeared," the policeman says. "All of a sudden they realized he wasn't with them."

Without asking if anyone wants more, I go into the kitchen to start another pot of coffee. I pull the filter tray out slowly, listening to their conversation. I want the policemen to feel comfortable. No awkward empty cups. Outside, the rain catches in the wind and beats rhythmically on the storm windows. The coffee drips into the pot. A dirty brown color, it becomes rich only after the pot fills past halfway. I take the washcloth hanging on the faucet and wipe up the spilled granules on the countertop.

I thought the affair would end once I started teaching again in September, but the second week of school he was sitting on the back steps with a black and orange cat in his arms. He sat quietly, petting the cat's head, making a small clicking noise with his tongue.

"I have to get rid of her," he said without looking up at me. "She's been hanging around our house for a month and my mom wants her gone before it gets too cold. I thought you might want her."

"Patrick's allergic to animal hair," I said. "We can't have any pets in the house." I was always mentioning Patrick to Colin, but he ignored or seemed to ignore the fact that I was married. "Can you take her to the humane society?"

"They won't take stray cats," he said. "Not without money."

"What are you going to do with her?" I asked.

The cat jumped out of his lap and began to explore a small pile of leaves under the steps. Colin unzipped his leather jacket. It was too warm a day to be wearing such a heavy coat, but I stopped myself from saying anything. Colin had told me he bought the coat because he thought it made his shoulders look bigger.

The cat knocked her head on the steel bar under the lawn chair and it collapsed. The sudden noise frightened her and she ran under the table. Colin went over and picked her up.

"You're getting heavy," he said. "I wonder if you're pregnant." He held her up in the air and then tucked her inside his jacket, turning her around so her head stuck out at his chest.

"You're going to take her on your motorcycle?" I asked. I moved closer to him, touched by his display of tenderness. "I don't think that's a good idea." I could hear the teacher in my voice.

"Why not?" he asked. He balled his fist and swatted it in front of the cat's face. She tried to grab at him, knocking her paw in the air—she hit at nothing. "Won't you, girl? You'll be okay. I'll take her down the highway a mile or so. There's a new subdivision where I can drop her off."

"She's got claws," I said. "You take her like that all trapped inside and she'll attack your chest."

"Do you think she'll be scared?" The urgency in his voice surprised me.

"Yes," I said. "Let me take you in the car."

It was the first time we had ever gone anywhere together. I thought it would be all right because of the cat. I could always tell Patrick I was just helping Colin get rid of the cat.

Colin kept her on his lap until we got to the highway and then let her into the back seat. He bent forward and turned on the radio. He flipped back and forth, along the stations, listening to a song for a minute before switching.

We drove to the construction site where the new roads were caked with wet mud. The afternoon had started to cool down and I rolled up my window.

"This is good," Colin said. We had pulled into a circular court, where the basements of the new homes had been sunk and sections of plywood were strewn on the cleared land. "We can drop her off here." He turned around to the back seat and started making the clicking sound with his tongue again.

"No one's living around here," I said. "They haven't moved in yet."

"She'll be okay. She's not afraid of squirrels or rabbits or anything."

"But there's nothing to eat here," I said. "She'll starve to death."

"Let me drive," he said. "I'll show you a good place. It's further down the road, toward the parkway, where they haven't started building."

"You don't want me to drive?"

He shook his head. I stopped the car and moved over to the passenger side. Colin didn't get out of the car. He brought his hand up to my neck and made a circular pattern on my cheek with his finger.

I could smell the fresh leather of his jacket. The top button of my
blouse was loose and he played with the thread until it fell off into
his hand. He stuck the button in his mouth and showed it to me
between his teeth.

"You can take your shirt off here," he said. "No one will ever see
us out this far."

Usually when we made love I kept something on. It had nothing
to do with getting caught, although I had implied this to Colin. I
didn't want him to see me naked. I already knew his legs were
shorter than mine, that his hipbones fit inside mine.

I put my finger up to his lips and he drew his breath in, sucking
my finger with the button. His teeth were sharp and it hurt. I
pulled my finger out and let him undo the rest of the buttons on my
shirt. The cat crawled along the top of the seat near our heads.
Colin picked her up and tossed her in the back seat. He took off his
jacket and folded it on the dashboard. The car stayed warm in the
afternoon sun. He pushed at my shoulders until we both slid down
the seat, our legs caught under the steering wheel. He closed his
eyes, the skin around them creasing with concentration. When the
car horn blew, we both tried to sit up right away. He was on top of
me and I only caught a glimpse of the car—a funny orange color—
before his weight crushed me back down into the seat. I grabbed
my shirt off the car floor and put it between us. My heart was
racing.

"I know that car," Colin said. He kept his head up, staring out
the window. "But I can't tell who's driving."

"Is it Patrick?" I asked.

"No," he said. "Who drives that car?"

"Are you sure it's not Patrick?" I pushed him off me and pulled
my shirt on. I started doing the buttons, my fingers too nervous to
pull them through.

"Positive," Colin said. He sat all the way up, turning around to
look out the back window. I heard the car pull away.

"Are they gone?"

"I think it was this kid from school," he said. "I'm pretty sure
that's his dad's car."

"Did he see you?"

"Yeah," Colin said. He reached for his jacket and pulled it on without his shirt. The cat jumped in the front seat and began pulling at the plastic strings wrapped around the steering wheel.

"Colin," I said. "You don't tell people about us, do you?"

He shrugged.

"Do you, Colin?"

"No one that would care," he said. He looked down at himself. The dark leather against his pale skin. "This is how Jack Nicholson wears his jacket. I wouldn't mind looking like him."

I sat up and finished buttoning my shirt. I was ashamed, imagining how I would ever explain that he was nineteen. Colin sat beside me, talking about wanting to act like Jack Nicholson. I made a promise that I would stop it. I would just stop it. I told him to put his shirt on and I dropped him and the cat off around the block from his house. But the affair was still going on when Patrick surprised me and told me he had invited Colin to go deer hunting.

The coffee makes a finishing noise and I carry it straight into the living room. The steam travels quickly and hits my chin. I put my hand on the top of the pot, holding it there, until it burns.

"Just another mystery," the policeman says. "Seems like with hunting accidents, there's always something no one can explain."

I walk around and fill their cups. Three doughnuts are left on the tray and I pass it around too, but no one takes one. Patrick is sitting in the rocker. With his head back on the green pillow, he stares across the room at the policeman.

"Last year we had a real hunting mystery around here," the policeman continues.

"That's right," his partner agrees. "Right in this area. There was a father and son team who headed out first Thursday of the season. They were supposed to be up near Gaylord by midnight. They packed the car and drove down the driveway and that's the last anyone saw of them."

He pauses and both policemen shake their heads.

"What happened?" I ask.

"Disappeared," the policeman says.

"Did they find them in the woods?" I sit down on the carpet beside Patrick. He rubs his stocking feet together. I put my hand over the arch of his foot to make him stop moving. His nervous energy reminds me of a kid.

"Never found either of them. Ever," the policeman says. "No explanation. Nothing. Not even a real clue."

His partner finishes the story. "The case has been open for a year. A year and four days and we don't know any more now than we did when we first started investigating."

"But was it a hunting accident?" Patrick asks. He gets up from the rocker and moves back to his place in front of the fireplace. He knocks the painting crooked when he leans closer to the mantel. "How do you know it had anything to do with deer hunting?"

"Maybe not," the policeman says. "But it sure started out that way." He looks over at his partner and nods. The two of them get up, just when I thought they would stay all afternoon.

Patrick walks them to the door.

"Accidents happen every year," the tall one says to Patrick. "You'll go crazy if you start blaming yourself. It just happened. It's no one's fault."

He calls Patrick "buddy" and I hear Patrick laugh. I think they are playing games with each other, each telling the other that everything will be all right.

I crawl across the room and rub the doughnut powdered sugar into the carpet. The front door is open and the sound of the rain on the cement disguises the rest of their conversation. I breathe in slowly, refusing to let the panic take over. I am afraid Patrick wants to tell me that he shot Colin on purpose and I don't want to hear it, even if it's true. The door slams; with nothing to do with my hands, I kneel and reach for a doughnut. Patrick comes back into the room. When he touches the end table for his coffee cup, I can hear the static shock.

"Do you think you could sleep?" I suggest to him in the silence of the room. "You look exhausted." It's not true but I want to be alone. It makes me nervous to be around him.

"I'm not tired," he says. He finishes the coffee and then plays with the cup, balancing it on the back of his hand.

"You must be," I tell him. "There are some sleeping pills in the bathroom. Your mother left them last time she was here. I'm sure it would be safe to take those."

"No," he says. "I don't want to be out of it."

"But you should try to sleep," I say. "It'll be quiet. I can unplug the bedroom phone."

I collect the coffee cups and pile them on the doughnut tray. I carry them into the kitchen and a second later Patrick follows. He won't look at me, but talks to the wall, right above my head. I sense his fear of being alone, but also the unease he feels at being with me.

"I want to talk to John," he says. "I want to know what the police are telling him."

"Why?" I ask. "Why should it be any different than what they're telling you?"

"Because I'm the one who fired the shot," Patrick says. He stretches his arms over his head and rests them on top of the door frame.

"Do you think there's something they're not telling you?" I ask.

"Not you too, Jessie," he begs. "I've got everyone asking me questions. I don't need you too."

"I'm sorry," I say. "I didn't mean anything by it." I dump the rest of the coffee into the sink and put the cups in the dishwasher. It is nearly full. I get out the soap from under the sink. It's a new box and I can't open the silver triangle on the side of the package. I take a dirty knife from the basket and try to pry it open. Patrick holds out his hand for the box and I give it to him.

"I just don't understand." I stop myself from saying anything more.

"What?" Patrick asks slowly. "What don't you understand?"

"Why did you have to take him hunting at all?" I say. "I don't understand why you had to bring him up there in the first place."

"Jessie," he yells. "Jessie. Colin was a kid. I took him hunting because I thought it would be good for him."

The word "kid" stings in my ear. Patrick's face is white and I am

afraid to look at him because I can hear him crying now. I stare at a
stain on the floor in front of his feet.

"I thought he'd like to go hunting," Patrick yells. He throws the
unopened box of detergent on the counter and walks to the back of
the house. The bedroom door slams. A minute later I hear the radio. He never falls asleep when he listens to music.

I go out to the garage without my coat. It smells of bleach from
when I tried to get rid of the oil spots in the middle of the floor.
Protected from the rain and cold, I wander around looking for a
T-shirt of Colin's. He left it in the house one afternoon, walking
home in his cutoffs. When I found it two days later stuffed under
the couch, I threw it in the garage. As I walk around, I start throwing things away in the open trash can: a month-old newspaper, a
paintbrush without a handle. His T-shirt is hidden behind the lawn
rake, dirty with fall leaves. I pick it up and whisper his name. It's
soft against my cheek. I kiss the cotton, trying to bring him close to
me once more.

It was the first week in June. The heat had come without warning, following two months of cold spring.

"I need a rag or something," he said. He had knocked on the
back screen door and then called out when I didn't hear him. "I cut
my foot."

"How bad is it?" I asked. The back door was usually kept closed
and it took me a few seconds to find the latch. The lock was tight.
The silver knob pressed into the soft skin under my thumbnail
when I released it. "Is it bleeding?"

"I think so," he said. He ran his tongue back and forth over his
front teeth. The heat was dry.

I didn't know his name, but I told him to come into the kitchen
where I could look at his foot. He sat down on the chair in the corner
instead of at the table. It's a kid's stool left over from the woman who
sold us the house. I use it to reach the cupboards above the stove.

"Take it off," I said. "Let me look at it. Maybe whatever it is is
still in your foot."

I turned on the faucet and let the water run warm before wetting the washcloth. Blades of grass clung to his bare ankles and he brushed them off onto the linoleum. I held the damp cloth against his foot for a minute and then looked at the cut.

"Do you think it needs stitches?" he asked.

I knelt in front of him and pushed the skin around the cut, soaking the cloth with blood.

"Can you feel anything in there?" I asked. "Does it hurt?"

"Not really," he said.

The skin pulled away from his foot. "Is it glass?" I asked.

"I don't know," he said. "It shot into my foot. At first I thought it was a stick, but then I felt the blood."

He pulled his T-shirt over his head, grabbing it up from the back. He brought it up to his face and dried the sweat on his forehead and then ran the T-shirt down his stomach, following the dirty lines of sweat on his skin.

"It's my brother who usually does your lawn," he said. "He's the one that should be here, but he's still at hockey camp."

I remember looking at his chest. It was pink from the heat. There was one drip of sweat around his nipple and I moved my hand to wipe it off. He grabbed my wrist when I touched his skin.

"What's your name?" I asked.

"Colin," he said.

He was still holding my wrist when he took his T-shirt and brushed it back and forth across his chest. He shivered and his nipples hardened.

"Are you older?" I asked. I couldn't remember what his brother looked like.

"My brother's only fifteen."

"That's right," I said.

"I just turned nineteen," he said. "I'm legal now if you ever want to go out for a beer."

"Really?" I said. "Go out for a beer?"

"Sure." He shrugged and I knew he was embarrassed.

I had to do it. I pulled my wrist from his grasp and touched his skin above his breastbone. He pulled away in surprise. He was so young, so surprised at my touch that when I saw him blush, his

cheeks flamed with uncertainty, I kept my hand on his chest. I let
my fingers move slowly back and forth over his nipple. The fine hair
dampened with sweat. If he hadn't closed his eyes I would have
stopped, but he relaxed in the stool and I let my hand move up to
his neck and he dropped the T-shirt and when he touched me, I
pulled his head down to mine.

Patrick came home two hours later. I was out on the deck, just
standing there. The wood slats were warm beneath my feet. He
asked me what I was doing and I told him I was looking for a spar-
kler or a nail. I told him Colin cut his foot mowing the lawn.

"His name is David," Patrick told me.

"No," I corrected him. "That's his brother." The sun was hot and
I put my hand on the patio table for support.

The affair had been going on for more than a year when Patrick
walked into the living room one night with one of the bathroom
towels. My hair was still wet from the shower I had taken after
Colin left.

"This smells like sex," he told me.

"It's our towel," I told him. "Why should that surprise you?"

"Smell it." He put the towel to my face and I could smell Colin in
the damp terrycloth.

"So what?" I pushed it away and went back to reading the
magazine.

"Are you sleeping with someone?" he asked. His face was drawn,
and I found it painful to look at him.

"Is it David?" he asked. He brought the towel up to his face
again as if he could discover who it was.

"David?" I had been thinking of Colin and when he said David I
thought of Colin's brother. It took me a minute to realize he was
talking about one of our neighbors, a good friend of Patrick's who
had recently been laid off from his job. He was home during the
day and his wife worked. "David Enderby?" I said. "Of course not."

He didn't mention it again, but one time I found him looking through the pockets of my raincoat and, when I asked him what he was doing, he shook his head. "Protecting myself," he said. "Just protecting myself."

"Protecting yourself from what?" I asked.

"Against surprise," he said.

I knew what he was talking about, but I dropped the subject. I'm not sure how Patrick found out about Colin. But I was positive he knew. It was something in the way Patrick continually brought up Colin's name. It was the way he treated Colin like a child—the way he kept reminding me that Colin was young, someone who was harmless, someone who had no effect on our lives, but someone who was just there, like a toy.

The house is getting dark, but I refuse to put on any lights. I want to stall the night. In the living room, I flip the cushions on the couch over and the crumbs fly to the floor. I sit down and face the window. Outside, the street lights are not lit; the day hangs on. There is a film of dust which always comes with the winter. I wipe it off and brush it down the side of my jeans. My hands are dry. I suck on my finger until the nail softens. I bring my teeth down on the nail and feel it give. It hurts when I rip it off. I spit it on the rug. My hand looks uneven as I hold it in front of my face. The skin is raw and I bite the rest of my nails, tearing them off until all my fingers hurt.

The shadows in the room shift, and Patrick is standing in the doorway watching me.

"Couldn't you sleep?" I ask.

"No," Patrick says. He comes over to the couch. I can't see his face until he kneels in front of me. "What am I going to do, Jessie? What should I do?"

Colin's T-shirt is in my lap and I tuck it under my leg. "Don't," I say. "Don't think about it."

He puts his head in my lap and I can feel the dampness of his tears through my jeans. He rubs his face in my legs. I reach up to turn on the lamp and he lifts his head. The dark circles under his eyes show for the first time.

"It's all right," I tell him. "It's going to be okay." I take his hand

and we stand up together. He follows me down the back hallway to
the bedroom. The blanket is pushed to the end of the bed. I sit and
turn the radio down. Patrick takes his clothes off before lying beside me. I hear the change from his pocket as it falls on the wood
floor. Patrick is very strong and his weight crushes my chest, but I
do not move. His face rests at my neck and I still feel his tears. My
muscles tense. I hold him tight and come right away. I keep my
hands on the back of his neck and we stay together until he shivers
and moves off me.

Patrick turns to the wall. His breathing quiets after a moment. In
the silence, I try to imagine the woods, the spidery trees against the
sky, the dull color in the air from seventeen days of rain. It reminds
me of when Patrick and I went camping in the Upper Peninsula
and first discovered the land around the Seeney Stretch. The man at
the Mackinac tollbooth warned us about the fires.

"They're right at the Seeney Stretch," the man said. "Always has
been a problem spot."

We told him we didn't know where it was.

"Two hours north of here," he said. "Just when you think you
can't stay awake any longer you'll hit the Seeney Stretch. It's a
thirty-eight-mile straightaway. Drives the truckers crazy. They're always driving off the road. Think they see something. A light or
something shining on the road."

The day was bright with sunshine. Patrick and I thanked the man
for the warning. As we got closer to the park entrance, the sky
clouded over. Patrick predicted rain. We lost sight of the horizon,
driving deeper into something we couldn't see. A state trooper on
the side of the road flagged us down and told us about the fires.
They had been burning underground for months, he said. The dry
summer was bringing them above ground and the grass and trees
were burning faster than the fire fighters could control them. The
police were afraid for the deer, who were too scared to run from
the flames. The heavy smoke made the land look like the end of the
world. We drove down the straightaway, counting off the miles on
the odometer. Patrick had to drive under the speed limit to keep

the car on the road. The entrance to the park was clouded over from smoke, like a fog that wouldn't lift. We stopped for only a minute, deciding to drive north into an area Patrick knew from hunting. I wanted to get away from that stretch of land as quickly as we could. By Munising, the sky had cleared and we camped at Picture Rocks on Lake Superior, the clear blue water letting us forget what was behind.

The Anniversary

Abby Frucht's first novel, Snap, *was published in 1988. Her new novel,*
Licorice, *recently published by Graywolf Press, examines abandonment, loss,
and desire in a disappearing town. Frucht lives with her husband
and sons in Oberlin, Ohio.*

*"In Abby Frucht's perceptive short stories, the details of everyday domestic life
expand into half-suggested depths of meaning that can transform ordinary
situations and relationships into something more serious and universal."*
ALISON LURIE, 1987

It is a Friday evening, far too hot for early September. The humidity has been building since noon, and everyone seems pleased with
the rainy forecast for the weekend. They talk of rain as if it were a
loved one coming home after an absence. Of course the air condi-
tioning is out; Martha dreads the moment when the conductor
calls her stop and she'll have to stand up, yanking the backs of her
thighs from the vinyl seat like two Band-Aids torn from a wound.
She is wearing her tennis dress, not what she usually wears on the
LIRR but she had planned a game with Gloria after work. Gloria
hadn't shown up. Martha dropped her dime in the club phone, calling. Her hands were trembling. She phoned Gloria's office, but nobody answered. Then she phoned Gloria's home, but her daughter
picked up the phone, so Martha kept silent, not wanting to worry
her. Maybe something has happened to Gloria. Maybe Gloria is
lying on a subway platform. More likely Gloria stopped for a drink
and forgot their date, which is just as well because it's too hot for
tennis. Martha is glad for an excuse to wear her tennis dress home
on the train, instead of her suit and stockings and high-heeled   67

shoes. She is comfortable in her tennis shoes, her bare ankles, her bare arms. The tennis dress is appliquéd with daisies.

When the conductor calls out Hicksville she shuts her eyes. An ancient habit. Six years ago Tom divorced her and moved to Hicksville with a girl who played the piano. The girl was twenty-two, and Martha has never been given the satisfaction of seeing her. Still, when she imagines her, she sees her from behind, seated upright on a piano bench, her hair swept up and fastened with a wicker clip, the pale floral folds of her skirt falling nearly to the floor, her long fingers dancing on the ivory keys. She must have long fingers if she plays the piano. She is still twenty-two, still playing Elton John. The two of them live in a tiny house, one of those identical houses you see from the tracks in Hicksville. The houses are gracious and have parlors in them. Tom drinks scotch; a decanter is filled with the amber liquid. Martha doesn't know which house is theirs, but she is certain it is one of those houses that line the tracks. They are all alike. It doesn't matter which is theirs. Frequently, above the screech and whine of the train, she hears the faint sweet cadence of notes being struck on a piano.

"Must be a hundred degrees on this train," says a young woman sitting next to her. She is sweating and reading a newspaper and she smells of deodorant. Martha is always glad when a woman sits near her instead of a man. Once on this same train, years ago as a newlywed, she dropped her handkerchief in the lap of a man who was sleeping. It was a hot evening, like this one, but in June when she knew she was pregnant, and she wiped the sweat from her face and somehow let go of the handkerchief so it floated to the man's crotch. She couldn't bring herself to pick it up. She remembers staring at it nervously from the corner of her eye. When he wakes up, she told herself, I'll say, "Excuse me but I seem to have dropped my handkerchief." She rehearsed the phrase a million times. "Excuse me but I seem to have dropped my handkerchief," with a discreet tilt of her head toward his lap. But then he grunted in his sleep and tucked in his shirttails. He tucked the handkerchief right into his pants so only a lacy corner remained visible over the belt.

She felt guilty about that for years. She had a vision of the man going home to his wife, chatting with her in the bedroom while he

undressed, first his sweaty shirt, then his pants, then the handkerchief falling to the floor at his feet. How could he explain? Martha imagines them going through life, their marriage irreparably al-
tered, a bitter air of puzzlement between them. She wonders what
became of her handkerchief. Lately, thinking about it, she finds herself laughing. The laughter is deep in her belly but genuine. She
wonders how something that once seemed so cruel has turned
funny. She imagines she has grown full of spite.

Shifting in her seat, Martha edges toward the window and crosses
her legs so the open newspaper no longer brushes against them.
She wishes it were winter. In winter, at dusk, the view from the
train is not nearly so dim. There is snow and the light hits it, and
maybe there are snowflakes whirling and falling, fine dry flakes so
the air is filmy and white. She would get home, start a fire, sit with
a book and a glass of wine until she felt hungry or sleepy. She is
proud of the fireplace. They both were proud of the fireplace when
they bought the house; set into the wall between the living and dining rooms, it opens onto both. It is the saving grace of the house,
which is split-level and ordinary, part of a development in which
the houses are mirror images of one another. When they purchased
the lot, they requested a house in which the kitchen and garage
faced south, the bedrooms north. The builder mixed up. He built
the house backward, so the kitchen faces north; when you walk in,
the stove and sink are on the left. She felt turned around, misplaced, as if she were cooking in somebody else's kitchen. The open
fireplace made everything better. When Tom moved out, she made
a point of building herself a fire every night when it was cool, and
eating dinner on the couch while her son sat close by on the floor,
his salad plate clinking on the slate of the hearth. She looked past
him through the flames at the shadows moving on the pine-paneled
walls of the dining room, and asked about his day. She likes to think
of herself as a good mother, a friend. Her son is named Tom. He
looks like Tom. She loves her son but has never been able to like him.

Now, because it is dark, and summer, she sees only the reflection
of her own face in the window of the train. It is a plain, calm face,

lined around the mouth, with ice-blue eyes that she avoids looking into directly. Today is her anniversary. She and Tom were married eighteen years ago today, in the chapel of a country club with velveteen paintings hung on its walls, and then they went to Portugal. Tom wanted to see a bullfight, but Martha couldn't stomach the idea of watching as an animal was killed, so they compromised. In Portugal the fighters only tease the bull and stick him with darts but don't murder him. They saw four fights in a week. There was much fuss made in the arena; the matadors and picadors marching around in fancy brocades, waving cloaks and weapons, and then the furious bull snorting and heaving and bowing toward the crowd. The crowd seemed subdued. Children cried and were slapped. By the end of each show, when the frustrated bull was led from the ring, he was decorated with his own blood, scarlet threads that swung from his slippery back. Tom smiled and went on stomping his feet. Leaving Portugal, in a cab on the way to the airport, Martha put a question to the driver, who spoke some English. "Why do the people of your country seem so sad?" she asked. Then she wished she hadn't, because he turned toward her and stopped watching the road. "They're not sad," he said. "They're just unhappy."

"I am not sad," she tells herself now, her face mouthing the words back at her from the window. "I am just unhappy." She thinks of her son. Tom Junior was born sad. Sadness is in his genes and he cannot shake it off; it's like a rotten name you have to live with. He is on his way home for the weekend, this minute, on the Throg's Neck Bridge in that broken-down car he played with all summer, both hands on the wheel, trembling. Traffic scares him. A lot of things frighten him. When he was very small she took him to the beach and put her bathing cap on and he screamed and ran away from her. Things like that. People pick on him. He phoned her last night from the state college in Oneonta where he has just started his first year. "Mom," he said, "I'm coming home for a little while." He explained that he and his roommates, three other boys with whom he shared a suite in the dormitory, weren't getting along. Martha wondered, what does he mean they're not getting along? Are they all not getting along with each other, or are the

three of them simply not getting along with him? "But they were
matched with you on a computer," she found herself saying. "You
had to fill out that form and they matched you up with those boys
on a computer."

"It's a piece of trash," Tom said. He had pulled himself together. "Their computer's worthless. Everyone's switching roommates. Anyway I'm coming home. I'll go back Monday but I have to come home."

He hadn't mentioned the anniversary so she supposed he had forgotten about it. Previously they celebrated it together, just the two of them, just to have something to celebrate. They sat at the table in the dining room and ate a nice dinner and bad-mouthed Tom Senior and laughed. She liked to hear him poke fun at his father's tightfistedness. No money had been forthcoming to pay for his schooling. Or for his harmonicas. Tom Junior has six harmonicas, each tuned to a different key, and they cost fifteen dollars apiece and Tom Senior has not paid for a single one of them. That always gets a good laugh. But her son makes a habit, during these dinners, of trying to convince her to go out with other men. Some men have tried to get close to her over the years but she's turned them down. The idea of getting stuck with any one of them seemed ludicrous. Sometimes she has difficulty thinking of these men as men and of herself as a woman.

Turning from the window, Martha sees that the young woman reading the paper has left. The newspaper, rolled up on the seat, has been secured with a red rubber band. She wonders what kind of a woman would put the rubber band back on her newspaper when she has finished reading it, and she plucks at the rubber band with her fingernail until noticing that there is nobody else on the train with her. A heavy silence clings to the heat. The train has reached the last stop, her stop. She gathers her things, her tennis bag with the racket zipped to the outside, stuffed so tightly with her suit and blouse and high-heeled shoes that she couldn't quite close it, and her shopping bag with the Entenmann's cakes she bought at a bakery close to the office. She hunts for her purse. For a minute she thinks she has misplaced it but then she finds it in the shopping bag along with the cakes. She opens it and takes out her hairbrush. Her hair has recently been cut and shaped, so when she brushes it has a pleasant bounce. She brushes for a long time, keeping an eye on the sliding door to the compartment. Any minute, someone will come through and kick her out. She thinks if she still smoked cigarettes she would smoke one now. Then she stands up, and her thighs make that harsh sound as they are peeled from the vinyl seat.

The station platform is bare, bathed in a yellow light from the tall naked lamps that line the tracks. Because the train pulled in from the west, she is on the wrong side and has to climb the tinny steps to the footbridge that crosses over. But the air is damp and smoky and on the bridge it seems fresher; there is a breeze up there that smells of leaves.

Her car is parked in the long-term lot beyond the rows of cabs and the circular drive, in the dark. She is glad about the dark because suddenly she feels silly in the tennis dress. Her shoes make no sound as she crosses the pavement. At the car she stops, puts her things on the ground, bends over and rummages in the Entenmann's bag for her purse and keys. When she stands up there's a man with a hand on her shoulder. "Tom!" she says, because his face is in darkness and she thinks maybe her son has surprised her at the station, but it is not Tom because the man has a knife and has raised it to her throat.

"Lady," he says. "You got your car keys, lady?"

What's happening? she thinks, and throws the keys at his feet and ducks but he grabs her and makes her pick them up.

"I don't want your damn car keys," he says. "I want you to get in the car."

"You want me to unlock the car," she is saying. "You want me to get in the car," because she has heard that if you talk to a mugger like a human being then maybe he won't hurt you.

"Don't hurt me," she says.

"Very smart," he says, because she is working the keys in the lock, shoving each key in and yanking it out and fumbling.

"I don't have my car keys," she says. Her teeth are chattering. "I must have . . . they must be," but he slashes her skirt with his knife.

"Lady," he says. "Do what I say."

She opens the door and for a second they stand there and look into the dimly lit interior of the car and at a pack of cough drops lying on the seat.

"Get in," he says.

She is thinking of the knife. She can think of nothing but the knife and the extraordinary noise it made when it cut into her skirt. Surely someone must have heard it, surely the cab drivers chatting in their smoky circle near the cabs heard it.

He has struck her arm, hard, with his fist, and she finds that she is seated in the car although she can't think how she got there.

"Move over," says the man.

He pushes her onto her back on the seat so her knee hits the steering wheel. The horn. The horn hasn't worked for ages but she pushes against it anyway with her knee, hoping to get a sound out of it.

"Don't kill me," she says. "Don't."

He has climbed into the car. He is leaning over her with the knife poised between their two bodies and he is grinning. She sees that he is terribly young.

"Now," he is saying.

"What?" she pleads. "Now what?" because she doesn't know what he is talking about. He slashes at the skirt again.

"Please," she says. "What? What do you want? Take the keys. The car. Take it."

"You know what I want."

"I don't. I don't know." Because she doesn't. The cakes? The tennis racket? Why won't he take it then and get away from her?

"Take it," she says. "Don't hurt me. Take what you want. I won't stop you."

But then there is the high wail of a police siren and the flashing red light as it pulls into the station drive.

After what seems like a long while she pulls herself up, gripping the steering wheel and pulling herself forward until her feet touch the pavement and she is sitting on the edge of the driver's seat looking out into the parking lot. It was not a police car after all but an ambulance that is parked at the station entrance with the light still turning and the back doors open. She sits there dully and watches the commotion. Only after someone has been carried out on a stretcher and the back doors have been slammed shut and the ambulance has driven off with its siren screaming does she realize what it was he must have wanted from her.

"Oh god," she says.

There is a bruise on her arm where he struck her and a spreading pain. Not much pain but she imagines it will get worse after a while as the shock wears off. She wonders if she is in shock. She doesn't know. She doesn't think so. She might call the police. There are phones in a row between the benches to the right of the station entrance. But she would have to walk through the parking lot to get to them. She thinks of screaming. If she screams, someone will come running and she can ask them to escort her to the telephones.

But what would she say to the police? There was this boy, and he pushed me into my car.

And she has nothing to show for it. Nothing but a slash here and there in the ridiculous pleated skirt of her tennis dress.

She pulls the Entenmann's bag and her tennis bag into the car. She puts them on the passenger seat and searches for her keys. They are dangling from the door. Then she starts for home, forgetting to turn on the lights until she is halfway across the parking lot and realizes that it's dark and she can't see anything.

Connor's Lake

*Born in Des Moines, Iowa, in 1945, Lucia Nevai lives and writes in New York
City. Her stories have appeared in the* New Yorker, New England Review/
Breadloaf Quarterly, Fiction, Literary Review, Iowa Review, Prairie
Schooner, Mademoiselle, *and others. She is the mother of two
sons and stepmother of two daughters.*

"The stories in Star Game *are full of energy, invention, humor, and feeling.
Whether they deal with a steamy sexual encounter, an alcoholic spinster
organist, or a folk-art commune, the range of sympathy and generosity toward
all the characters is remarkable. Lucia Nevai is a new writer
to watch and to celebrate."*

ALISON LURIE, 1987

Connor rides the bulldozer like a motorcycle, hatless in the March
cold, his eyes wild above his neat brown mustache. Cursing and
reprimanding the earth, he charges up the retaining wall on the
dozer and backs down to the right, packing the dirt down, packing
it down. Digging his own lake is making a madman out of him. No
one in town will ask him how it's going anymore. They're sick of
hearing about it. The word is out not to give him excavating jobs—
he'll get aggressive and start talking you out of what you want to do.

Meanwhile for him it's no picnic, freezing his butt off every day
from dawn to dark, digging a mudhole nine feet deep and an acre
wide where his beautiful field used to be. A lot rides on this lake,
the least of it being a hundred dollar bet with the agronomist from
Albany who told him he'd never get water to stick in that field.
"Kroydek or Kroychek, whatever the fuck your name is," Connor
shouts into the wind, "there's clay, goddamn it!" He sincerely
hopes there is.

Connor works until the dirt and the sky are the same color of purple, then he climbs down off the D-6 and walks up the hill to his cabin. It's hard for him to take any pleasure in his shower. The hot water comes in one stingy, erratic stream—he has to hold himself beneath it ingeniously so that most of the water breaks into a thin wall which warms his broad young back. A shift in weight diverts a trickle to the front to catch his chest. The mud runs off him and down the drain, but there's never really enough hot water to let him forget the two things he's afraid of most: digging a lake that won't hold water and Kaitlin with the long pointed breasts in the health food store who keeps giving him two pounds of dried pineapple rings for the price of one. He feels wary. Connor has never lived through such a prolonged period of being absolutely uncertain that he is doing the right thing. When he steps out of the shower, the towel he grabs is musty and soiled. He pities himself.

Connor sits in his green DeSoto in the Newmans' driveway for ten minutes before getting out, looking at the glass wall Richard put in the north side of the barn. It was a year in the making, the glass wall. Now the Newmans have the best barn in the woods. The design is impressive, trapezoids of glass angled artfully in the diagonal cedar siding. Richard designed it, but the installation was too much for him. He had to hire people to finish it last November so he and Lilly wouldn't freeze to death. It cost a fortune.

Connor is jealous of Richard's trust fund. Everyone is. Everyone who's left, that is. Of the ten couples who bought properties in the Minnisink woods in the early seventies, only four and a half are left. Connor counts himself the half. He and Gita were the first to discover that farmhouses and barns on several acres could be had cheap in Minnisink. But now he's alone. He's been alone since January. He thought it would be much easier than it is. The truth is, he doesn't know what to do with himself. He couldn't get through the week without Richard and Lilly.

The Tiffany lamp over the round oak pedestal table is turned on. Connor watches Lilly's long beautiful hair fall forward, soft as corn silk, as she leans across the table to line up a knife and fork in front

of one of the chairs. He watches as she moves patiently back and
forth from the counter to the table with wine and glasses, two big
pottery plates, bowls of salad, and a basket of something. Of course,
Richard doesn't deserve her. His car isn't even in the driveway. If
Connor had a wife like that, he'd be home for dinner every night.

Connor wipes his mouth with a napkin which he takes a good
look at for the first time. To his consternation it is made of stiff,
batiked cotton. "Jesus Christ," he sneers playfully, tossing the napkin onto the table, "does everything in this house have to be a
craft?"

"*I* made those, Connor." Lilly takes him seriously.

He looks at her. She seems a little distracted, but her high white
brow is clear of the telltale Richard-trouble furrows. "Where's
Richard?" he asks.

"In the city. Realizations."

"I thought he finished that seminar."

"He started the second level of classes. Tuesdays and Thursdays.
He leaves at four and he's back at two."

"I hate that shit," Connor scoffs. "Fortunately, he doesn't try to
talk me into it anymore."

"It's good for him," Lilly insists. "It keeps him from being depressed, keeps him working."

"That's all fine and good," Connor says, pushing back his chair.
"But he acts like a person is betraying him unless they do everything *he* does. I mean, I have realizations of my own. And one of
my realizations is that his realizations are horseshit."

Lilly smiles and Connor basks in the approval of her twinkling
blue eyes. "It's about time." He grins, referring to her smile. She
yawns a large comfortable yawn and stretches her arms up over her
head, arching her back. Connor is tempted to ogle the outline of
her pretty breasts in the blue turtleneck, but instead he stands up
and pulls his jeans out of his crotch. He reaches across the table for
Lilly's plate and stacks it on his own so all her gravy slides up under
his rim. He takes her buttery knife and neatly licked spoon and lays
them side by side with his own sloppy utensils. He sets her wine-

glass and his on top of the plates with the silver between the stems of both glasses and carries the whole tidy mess to the sink.

He washes everything off methodically with hot running water and some new Swedish natural bristle brush Lilly has come up with. She sits at the table, inert, pressing the tip of her middle finger into the stray salt crystals which catch the light on the unwiped table. He sees her vitamins by the faucet and remembers she's pregnant. He decides he'll take her out to dinner tomorrow so she won't have to cook. Richard too, if he's home. "Why don't you go lie down?" he says proprietarily.

"That's what I'll do," she says, rising and pulling the chain on the Tiffany lamp. Scowling in the dark of the kitchen, Connor scrubs every last bit of Beef Bourguignonne off the black dutch oven and wipes it carefully round and round inside with Lilly's soft white towel.

She's sleeping on the sofa when he comes in to talk. Connor unfolds the afghan and tries to arrange it over her, but it won't reach—her ankles stick out. He positions a fragrant quarter log on the grate and builds the wood around it so the fire will last a long time. Then he lies back on the Oriental rug with a hard little needlepoint pillow under his head. He wonders if Kaitlin flirts with all the health food customers or just him. She's young and almost pretty. She's not intense or high-strung. He's read all her T-shirts. He's measured those long legs against his. He's never had a young, long-legged girlfriend who could give him all the pineapple he wanted.

Round and round, someone is rubbing Connor's shoulder. He climbs slowly out of his dream of being in the post office, screaming at someone who is fucking up his mail. He opens his eyes. Lilly is leaning over him.

"Connor," she whispers, "time to go home."

"What happened?" he asks.

"Nothing. It's late."

"Did we make love?" he jokes. She looks tense and impatient.

"Time to go," she insists. The furrows are there, loud and clear on her white forehead.

"What time is it?" Connor says soberly.

She hesitates and then answers, "Four-thirty."

"Oh, shit. Poor angel," Connor whispers. Richard is seeing the girl from Realizations again. Connor rises slowly to his elbows and then pulls himself into a seated position, gathering Lilly into his arms. She lets him hold her. "Sure you want me to go?" he asks. "I could stay and give you a nice back rub or we could go back to sleep and then go out to breakfast together."

Lilly stiffens slightly and pulls away just enough so that the polite thing for Connor to do is release her. He lets his arms fall to the Oriental rug. He is disappointed. Lilly is too goddamn proud. She wants Connor's car out of the driveway before Richard or anybody else sees it. Appearances first—even though they're all best friends.

All the way back to his house in the dark, Connor can't help wanting Lilly's little game to be tricked up. He can't help wanting Richard to come home early one of these nights and find Connor and Lilly singing "Wake up Little Susie" in perfect Everleys harmony by the fire. Or eating a whole strawberry-rhubarb pie right after they baked it. Or standing outside by the spruce tree listening to the mockingbird.

He wishes Richard would come sailing over the hill at sixty miles an hour right now. He'd like to see the expression change on his dissipated, selfish face as Connor's DeSoto passes him coming from the glass-walled barn. Let Richard be jealous for a change. It would be good for him. Connor thinks this all the way back along Route 38, but Richard's blue Volvo does not come into view at any point.

He parks by the road and sits in the car. He needs to be held. He needs to be hard. Instead of walking into the house and falling asleep in his stale gray-sheeted bed, he wanders down the hill. In the violent, bloody mess of the spring dawn, he kneels in the mud at the edge of the gaping acre-wide hole. It lies there in terrible judgment of him. He remembers what it looked like as a field, its golden silk knee-high with red sumac and white milkweed. He remembers the way the grass would part when anyone walked through it.

Panic rises in Connor's blood and he feels overwhelmed with loss. He sees Gita wading through the field, so skinny and so intense in her long cotton skirts and baggy sweaters. He used to ridicule her for going into the woods with her homeopathic pamphlet listing the Bach Flower Remedies. He wonders why once they were married, he began to despise everything that made her happy. He hopes this is not the closest thing to love that he will ever feel. He's baffled as he remembers the day in January when he found the torn-out page with the list of infusions for despondency. *For despondency through lack of confidence: larch. Despondency through self-reproach: pine. Despondency through anguish: sweet chestnut. Despondency due to embitterment: willow.*

The red slowly drains from the sky. All that's left by six is a pink cast on the stubbly bleached winter grass of the hill. The lake bed is mottled with saturated-looking stretches of gray. "Clay," Connor announces. He leaps to his feet and punches the air with his right fist. "Kroychek, you bastard!" he howls. "Get out your checkbook! There's fucking clay!" He jumps up and down in the mud, hugging himself. By fall, the lake will be filled. By spring, the mud will have settled and the water will be clear. By summer, the lake will be alive with salamanders, leeches, fish eggs, and cattails. Forget-me-nots will bloom on the banks. Turtles will sun themselves on the rocks. All that life will have come from the water.

Connor runs up the hill to shower and shave. He won't work on the lake today. The clay is there—he can relax, finish the hole on weekends. He wants to get back into the swing of things, go into town, hustle up some basements, get a landscaping contract. But first he'll celebrate. He'll buy himself a big breakfast at the Sunrise Diner, read the paper, smoke a cigar, and then, at ten to ten, when Kaitlin pulls into the parking lot of the health food store in her Jeep, sleepy and sexy, fumbling for the key, Connor will be at the door, ready and waiting with a great big order for dried pineapple.

Charis

Russell Working is a reporter and fiction writer living in Oregon. His stories have been printed in the Paris Review, TriQuarterly, *and other publications.*

"This collection introduces a writer of unusual promise. Refusing the easy ironies and glassy surface of most contemporary fiction, Russell Working's stories enact our uncertain and restless longing for freedom and transcendence— resurrection—against backgrounds and circumstances startling in their vivid actuality. Raw, abrasive, urgent, these stories jangle the nerves and haunt the memory."
TOBIAS WOLFF, 1986

To the best of Len's recollection, he met Charis on New Year's morning, just after two o'clock. There had been a party. He remembered talking to her. The crowd had finished the last of the champagne, and Len had an image now of a corpulent drunk (someone he knew from work, maybe) sprawled unconscious on the couch, mouth open, a red party hat crushed beneath his head with its string cinched under his jowls. Len knew that as he went for his coat he bumped into her, a tall, striking blonde in a black dress, whom—he was now becoming increasingly convinced—he had spotted through the crowd but had not had the opportunity to meet. Did he introduce himself? Did she toss back her hair and smile beautifully and perhaps say, "Pleased to meet you, Len. I'm Charis"? He remembered her mentioning she had noticed him earlier, "But you were so deep in conversation I left you alone." She said, "You remind me of someone I used to know." "Who is he?" Len asked. "Nobody, really," she said. "He died in an explosion at an aluminum plant down in Longview." "I often do that to people," Len said, "remind them of someone."

Later, as he tried to piece together what had happened, he found to his vague interest that his memory not only of the previous night but of significant portions of the preceding year was blank.

Len asked, "Did we eat dinner together?"

"No."

"But there was a New Year's party. Somebody kept blowing a whistle in my ear."

"Yes. At Sean and Julie's. Do you remember who they are?"

"Of course."

Charis twisted the watch around her wrist. "I don't mean to be rude."

He shrugged. "I know I spent the night at your house."

"A couple hours of it."

Len set aside the steel rack so the plastic tube would not bisect her face.

Charis said, "You shouldn't lift that."

"Why not? What do you want me to do, ring for a nurse?"

"I'd be glad to do it."

"Thanks, I'm not paralyzed." The man in the next bed looked at Len, and Charis smiled at the bed rail. Len considered his reflection in the television screen on the wall against the ceiling (his hospital-issue pajamas open on his wiry chest; arms at his side, one palm upturned and the other down; his hand inserted with a three-inch-long, pliable needle connected to the intravenous tube), and he decided that even unshaven and messy-haired, lying in a cagelike bed, he was not an unattractive man.

He ventured, "And we made love?"

"Don't you remember?"

"Yes, of course. I'm just stating the things I recall."

"I thought it was a question."

"No, it wasn't." Actually, the only thing he could remember was an electric blanket that had been turned too high, but he did not wish to be undiplomatic.

Charis asked, "Do you remember the paramedics?"

"No."

"You were sitting on the edge of the bed talking to them. You were quite lucid—funny, in fact. They asked you what drugs you had been taking, and you said, 'Cocaine.' You pointed to the table in the kitchenette and said, 'There's a whole bowl of it in there.' The one paramedic got up and looked at it with his eyes bugging out and said, 'Good heavenly days! What's the street value of this? $20K?'"

"I took cocaine?"

"Um, no. You were kidding him. It was the sugar bowl."

"Oh."

"I guess he was pretty naive. His partner, the woman, was laughing. She said he came from this Missouri Synod Lutheran family who owned an apple orchard near Wenatchee."

"Huh."

Charis said, "Do you remember anything else?"

"Not much."

"Do you remember my name?"

"Of course. Charis."

They laughed. Charis stood up and patted his arm. "I've got to go," she said, and then, digging in her purse as she walked to the door, "I'll drop by this evening." Len called, "You don't have to," but she was gone, clicking down the hall in her high heels—a dry, aberrant sound amid the padding of the nurses' white sneakers, as if her heels were made of bone.

Len groaned and began adjusting the angle of his bed with the electric controls—bending the knees, a little higher, then back down a bit, raising the back—until he was positioned like an astronaut awaiting launch. There was a sensation he wished to alter in his back, legs, arms, buttocks, and neck. He considered the sensation and its name. He ached. He felt as if he had spent a day pitching bales of hay onto a flatbed truck. Then his eyes were closed and he knew he had slept, but he wished to keep them closed and think. Periodically he awoke and lay like this, or the nurse woke him and he opened his eyes and put capsules in his mouth and drank a glass of water. He attempted to recall what he could of the party and what had happened, and by the time the nurse brought his dinner tray he had recovered several fragments, shards of memory to dust off with a camel's hair brush and tag and classify. The older memories of the past year, he saw with relief, were returning of their own accord.

Charis had awakened him in the middle of the night and asked, "How are you now?"

"What?" Len groaned.

She was leaning over him and pressing his cheeks between her hands, her breasts hanging in her diaphanous nightgown. Traces of mascara ringed her eyes, and her blonde hair was tangled. "How are you doing?" she whispered. "Are you all right?"

"I suppose so, considering I've had maybe an hour's sleep."

"You just had a seizure."

"What?"

Charis' chin quivered. "You stiffened, and you thrashed around kicking and woke me up. You drooled all over the place. I can't believe how strong you are. Your fingers were fanned out, and I couldn't even squeeze them together."

"A seizure?"

"Yes."

"Oh, my head hurts. Maybe that's it. I thought it was the champagne. Hey, how come I'm all wet?"

"I tried to bring you out of it by dashing a cup of cold water in your face."

"Did it work?"

"No. You nearly drowned until I rolled you onto your side."

"Oh."

"Do you want to get back in bed?"

Len looked around. He lay on a hardwood floor, wrapped in a twisted rope of sheets, beside a heating vent. A tuft of dust dithered in the warm draft. He climbed into bed. Charis collapsed on the mattress beside him and brushed his hair from his eyes.

"Do you have epilepsy?"

"No."

She touched his belly. "Maybe I should call a doctor."

"No, don't," he yawned and fell asleep.

Sensing the motion of a vehicle, Len lifted his head long enough to survey his torso, lying flat on a raised bed, draped with a blanket (a red cross on the blanket: an inverse Swiss flag), and foreshortened like a painting in a Spanish cathedral of an interment, only reversed, viewed from the head. The pink-and-emerald lights of a marquee (TONIGHT ONLY: Two for one after Midnight HAPPY NEW YEAR!!!) swept his body and disappeared in the silent cruising of the van. He asked, "Did I tell her about it?" "Shhh," said the woman in the blue jacket. Len asked, "Wasn't there someone else who could do that?" "Yes," she said, "I'll tell you who later." Relief overwhelmed him, and he lay back.

Light suffused an entire field of vision and intensified into a sun moving here and there, burning green zigzags on his retina, yet a voice like that of a man said, "Don't look at the light. Watch this. Wherever it goes, I want you to follow it with your eyes."

Len looked and in an act of will caught sight of a fleshy blur a few inches from his eyeballs.

"That's right. Just watch my finger. Good." And then distantly the man said, "I guess it's all right to let him go now." The pinpoint of light and the finger went away, and several young women in white unstrapped the canvas bands binding his ankles, knees, wrists, elbows, and chest. Len was dressed only in a canary yellow pair of briefs whose fly was printed with a caricature of Satan and the words "I'm a little devil." He blushed and looked around for his clothing.

"Don't struggle or we'll tie you back down," said an Oriental in a white coat who tugged on a wispy vandyke. He asked, "Do you have epilepsy?"

"No."

"What drugs were you taking last night?"

"None."

"You sure?"

"Yes."

"What's your name?"

"Len Demarest."

"Good." The doctor helped Len sit up and asked, "Do you remember your address?" Len repeated a sequence of numbers and letters that seemed familiar, while the nurses watched, the broad-faced one, a black woman, chewing on a pen. The doctor nodded at his clipboard. "Do you know what happened to you this morning?"

"I had—" What was the word? Somewhere a synonym rattled a cup against its cage, but Len silenced it: "I had a seizure."

"You had three of them. Grand mal seizures. Two at your girlfriend's place and one in the ambulance."

Then the doctor asked a dozen other questions, kneaded Len's neck, prodded his scalp, knocked on his knees with a rubber hammer, did everything but shake a talisman and attempt to suck the demon from his patient's head, and finally said, "Well, I think this should do," and, scribbling on his clipboard, "Mr. Demarest, we'd like to keep you here several days for tests. We need to get to the bottom of whatever's causing this. I've got you on Dilantin now, and that should keep you from any more convulsions for the time being." Convulsion, thought Len: explosion, implosion. The doctor sniffed and left the room, followed by the nurses.

Len's clothes had been wadded up and tossed on a chair against the wall, and he glanced at the door, then hopped from his stretcher, snatched up his pants, and struggled to pull them on. The room reeled and he balanced himself by holding the rail of the stretcher while his pants dropped to his ankles. A black nurse entered and said in surprise, "Oh."

Len pulled up his trousers and climbed back on the stretcher with them still unbuttoned. He lay down. The nurse introduced herself. She had an unusual accent and said she was from Montreal. "Pleased to meet you," said Len.

The nurse said, "For a moment I thought you were dressing so you could sneak out on us."

Len inched toward the head of the plastic surface, which clung to his back, and said, "No. I wouldn't make it to the front door, let alone back to my apartment. Not without help, anyway."

She laughed and pushed his stretcher out of the room.

Len's parents arrived just after Charis departed. His mother

rushed in and kissed him, laying a bouquet of roses wrapped in green plastic on his chest, and his father opened one eye wide and comically arched his eyebrow and shook Len's hand. "They treating you all right?" he inquired. Mrs. Demarest's face was puffy and red from crying, but she began arranging the flowers in a vase on Len's dresser and asked, "Now, who is this Charis you were with? Somebody I ought to know about? She sounded very nice when she spoke to me on the phone this morning." Len said, "I don't know." She winked and said, "Oh, come on." "No," Len said, "I really don't remember." Mrs. Demarest plucked a dead leaf and opened her mouth to protest, but when she saw his expression, she took the vase over to the sink and filled it with water and said nothing.

"Mom."

"Yes," she said, her back still to him.

"Do you remember the story about the mining camp that Aunt Carla told us when she got back from her vacation to South Dakota?"

"Honey, Aunt Carla hasn't been back to South Dakota since she came to Seattle in 1941 to work at Boeing."

Mr. Demarest said, "Yes, she has. What about that trip?"

"Hal, she only got as far as Missoula before she had her first heart attack and they had to fly her back. You remember."

"Mom, wait. On that trip, didn't she say something about people mining for gold in a graveyard?" Len's father was pacing the room, nodding once at the patient in the next bed. Len said, "It was in a town in the Black Hills."

Mrs. Demarest set the vase on his dresser. "I don't remember that story."

"Yes," Len said, then cut himself off.

Mr. Demarest paced the room and squinted with his glass eye at the posters on the wall (the only one Len could see advertised a production of *Tannhäuser*) until Len realized what was the matter and turned on the Rose Bowl game. The Huskies were playing Michigan. Len's father sat and gripped the armrest of the chair and said with relief, "First quarter."

Charis did not come that evening—not while Len was awake, at any rate. He dozed but fought to rouse himself; he dreamed he was shaking his head, slapping his face, rolling out of bed onto the floor, and still his eyes would not open. He dreamed about the whiteness of his room. The nurse woke him for dinner. "Your parents said they'd be back tomorrow," she said. Afterward Len chatted with the man in the next bed, Cal, a middle-aged patient whose gray hair was matted in locks and draped across his balding head. Cal said he was an accordionist.

Len said, "Professional?"

"Sure."

"Where do you play?"

"Lots of places: dances, parties, clubs. I even played at a wake once. Don't laugh; they paid well. It followed an open-coffin funeral for this beautiful sixteen-year-old girl with a figure that would knock you dead, and everyone was so sentimental they kept requesting her favorite pop songs and stuffing bills in my tux pockets." Cal grew distracted and stared out the window beside his bed.

"What are you in here for?" Len asked.

"I'm paralyzed from the neck down. I got a little movement in my right hand that I think is getting better. See me twitch my fingers? Pretty exciting, huh? The doctors can't figure out what the hell is causing my problem. Probably a tumor or something in my brain, just like you, I guess. That's why we're in neurology. I told them to crack my skull open and have a look round, but the sons of bitches won't do it. They say it's too risky."

As Cal spoke, Len recalled a joke he had made to Charis, and he winced and clutched the sheet with his toes. Then he asked, "Is there much of a view over there? I can't see very well from here."

"Nah. Just the other wing of the hospital and some damn sculpture."

Len tried to think of something to say, but Cal muttered, "Would you mind if I closed the curtain between our beds? I'd like to get a little shut-eye."

"No," said Len.

Cal bit like a snapping turtle on a piece of plastic tube that bent around from behind his bed, and the curtain buzzed on its track

and encircled his bed.

The next morning there was no sign of Charis. Len was slightly nauseated when the orderly brought his breakfast, and he ate only half an apple that was browning on his plastic tray. His mother dropped by for half an hour, then departed, saying she would be back that evening, after his father got home from work.

At twelve-thirty Charis arrived, carrying a canvas bag and a thermos.

"Want to sneak out of this place?"

"Sneak out? What for?"

"I don't know. I thought we might take a ride on a ferry, have a picnic somewhere, something like that."

"I don't think I could get past the nurses' station."

"Sure you can. I asked them if you could join me for a cup of coffee in the cafeteria now that you're off of the intravenous fluids, and they said okay."

Len laughed and glanced at Cal, who shut his eyes. "All right. Can you slip my clothes out for me? They're hanging in the closet."

"Sure. These?"

"Yeah."

"They look familiar."

"Right. Similar to what I wore the other night."

As they walked past the desk, Charis slipped on her sunglasses and grinned at the black nurse with the broad, familiar smile. She looked at the thermos. "Enjoy your coffee," the nurse said. "Thanks," Len called.

They drove to the terminal below the Pike Street Market on the waterfront and caught a ferry to a small island in Puget Sound. The sky was pale blue over the dark sound, and cirrus clouds streaked the southern horizon. To the west the Olympic Mountains were stark and icy above the hills and evergreens. Later Len remembered drinking tea while they stood on the balcony at the bow; he was unsure where they had gotten it. He pinched his tea bag and scalded his fingers. Charis mentioned the cold port wind, and he turned his collar up. A gull hovered low over the wake alongside the ferry; it seemed to be slipstreaming. Len flung his tea bag in the sound. The gull lunged at it as it fell steaming to the water but missed, fell away, and circled back to look for it. Charis bit her lip. Len watched her and tried to remember something (a dream, maybe, about the open front of a ferry, with cars parked on the pavement that slipped over the green scudding sea), but when she glanced at him the sensation vanished.

"Beautiful," Charis said.

"Pretty nice weather for January."

"It is. Can you believe it snowed last week?"

"Oh."

"You remember? It might have been the week before that."

"Did we do something that day?"

"No. Well, I'm sure we did, but not together."

"Of course not. Silly me. We didn't even know each other then."

Charis gave him an odd look. Her nose was turning red in the cold, and he suggested they go inside.

After landing at the island's dock, they walked along a road that curved southward, past scattered wooden houses with moss growing in fistlike clumps on the shingled roofs, until they came to a grassy park that sloped to a boat dock and a clear, pebble-strewn marina. They sat at the sunny end of a picnic table beside a tilting Douglas fir that was oozing sap. They were on the leeward side of the island, and the air was still and brisk and smelled like salt and turpentine. They removed their coats—Charis was wearing a sweater and skirt, Len his tuxedo jacket and ruffled shirt and slacks (one leg of which was crusted with cheese dip, which he had elbowed from the table while impersonating Richard Nixon at the Kitchen Debate). Charis opened her bag and spread out a tablecloth, on which she set a loaf of rye bread, sausage, cheese, fruit, and a bottle of wine.

She handed him a napkin and said, "Dig in," and then Len saw he had missed something and she was repeating, "Have they figured out what's causing those seizures?"

"Not yet. They'll be testing me tomorrow: EEG, CAT scan, the works. They ought to figure it out. And they say they have medication that completely controls these things, so no matter how it turns out I'll be as good as new. I'm on something now. Dilantin and something else."

"Good. Have some wine."

A mallard waddled about a few yards away in the shallows, watching them. As they finished eating, Charis tossed a scrap of bread to the bird. The mallard gobbled it and stared at them with its thumbtack eyes. Mallard drakes always reminded Len of the simple toys that children build from sets: a bill inserted in the green-black head, a ring like a washer separating the head from the neck, a squat body that made you want to punt it like a football, and flat feet. A group of ducks out on the water began quacking and paddled closer. "They're hungry," said Charis.

Len dipped a piece of bread in his wineglass and tossed it out to the water's edge. The pink scrap crumbled in two, and the ducks squawked and fought over the pieces. The drake got one fragment, and a hen snatched up the other. They turned up their bills and shook their heads and tried to swallow the bread, and the flock parted and chased the two until they managed to choke their bread down.

Len and Charis laughed. He put his arm around her. "They love it," she said, "here, give me that loaf." She tore off a piece of crust, dipped it in wine, and flung it underhand to the birds. They flapped and fought each other. A drake emerged from the melee and gulped the scrap on the run.

Len and Charis roared with laughter. They crumbled hunks of bread, soaked them in wine, and threw them to the ducks. The birds wobbled about nipping each other and flapping their wings. Two drakes pursued another out over the water, tipping the surface with their feet until they got airborne; they swooped crazily and chased the other bird back to another part of the bank, where they pounced on it and nipped at its feathers. Two mottled hens fought over a pink rock until each had bit it; then they wandered in opposite directions. Charis giggled and swigged her burgundy. Sometimes a duck would stumble to the shallows and stoop to fill its bill;

it would raise its head and bob its throat and gulp down the salt water. Down drifted along the shore.

Charis said, "That's enough. Look at them, the poor things!"

"Just one more for the big guy."

"Don't, he's drunker than the rest—he ate half the bread. Stop it." She tried to grab Len's wrist.

"One more," said Len, tossing the scrap to the mallard. The bird gobbled down the bread, then weaved its way up the beach before collapsing. It thrashed about and beat its wings on the pebbles, then opened its mouth and heaved, jerking its head forward.

"Jesus!" said Len.

"The poor thing," said Charis.

Len tiptoed toward the bird, but before he reached it, it fled flapping across the water. A green feather stirred on the bank. The mallard paddled to the dock. The rest of the ducks shook themselves and quacked at Charis as she packed the leftovers in her bag and dumped the remnants of their wine on the trunk of the fir. They never got to the coffee. Instead they returned to the terminal and caught the next ferry back to Seattle.

As the ferry approached the Seattle terminal, they again stood at the bow on the second level. The sun was setting behind them, and the wind was bitterly cold, but they leaned on the rail and watched the drivers returning to their cars below and revving their engines. The dark green water boiled against the oil-stained pilings, and a group of men on the dock unhooked a chain and prepared to lower a ramp to the car level. Len and Charis reentered the overheated interior and stood among the crowd of people rustling about buttoning their sweaters and coats.

Len said, "I feel strange."

Charis took his arm. "What do you mean?"

Out of an infinite number of inquiries and arrangements of words, she chose to toss out the one that was tied like a millstone around his neck—and although Len, Leonard, Leonardo, I immediately forgot the question, what horrified him was the sea into which her words sank him (couldn't she have chosen other means?) or, rather than a sea (outside, though skin is porous), an implosion of white dread: Len, do you need to sit down? Wasn't there a crowd that pressed us at that level too, backs puffy in their winter coats? Listen, come over here and sit down, Len. Didn't the window fog as we looked out on the churning green-white froth? Are you going to be sick? Whispering, do you want me to help you to the bathroom? Len! Didn't this attract the interest of a crowd with stale chewing gum breath while our muscles tingled and cramped? As if a fluorescent tube exploded (the particles of glass sting and prickle the skin), something flashed.

Pressed back against the windows and chairs along the walls as Len reached down, the people laughed. A man with a scruffy beard lifted his backpack from the floor (unaware that the bellyband still hung, bright orange, to the ground) and said, "Well, that's one way to clear a crowd away from the exit." They laughed again. Our tormentors required that we hang up that instrument: the one with the keyboard and collapsible structure: saying—"Len," she said. "Please. Can you understand me?"

"Can you understand me?" asked the redheaded man with a crust of acne around his nose, his face pockmarked. He wore an embarrassingly bright yellow shirt (perhaps there had been a tie like that, painted with a nude woman, which someone found around his neck when he woke up in the presence of ladies). He was finished with the light.

"Yes, doctor. Len Demarest."

"Almost. It's Glen Demarest."

"What?"

A nurse whispered and pointed at the clipboard.

"Oh, I'm sorry, you're right. It's Len. Can't read the handwriting here. Now, I'm going to mention three things, and I want you to remember them and repeat them when I ask. Think you can do that? Great. Listen carefully: lightbulbs, the color red, and Park Place. Now, where do you live?"

Len recited an address.

"You got the address right, but this is Seattle."

"What did I say?"

"You said Geneva."

"I went there on vacation last summer."

"Good. I'm glad you remember that. Okay, can you tell me those three things I asked you to remember?"

"No."

"Come on, now. Try."

"I am. I can't remember."

"Very well." The doctor made a note on his clipboard.

Len said, "Where is—where is she?"

"You mean your friend?" The doctor scowled. "I haven't the slightest. She evidently told the paramedics she would follow them here in her car, but she must have gotten lost in traffic." He whispered to the nurse, then added aloud, "I ought to just leave you tied down there," smiling. "Seriously, I hope you won't try to slip out of here again, Len. You know, you're in here of your own free will. If you want to check out and leave, nobody will strap you to your bed. But I trust this afternoon has convinced you of the importance of these tests we're going to run. We've got to find out what is the matter with you."

"Yes, I know."

"Good. It's about time you understood the seriousness of all this."

A black nurse entered Len's room and spoke in a melodious accent. Her laugh was deep, and she was short and busty and rather overweight.

"Where are you from?" asked Len, and she laughed.

"Do you want anything else?" she said.

"No, thanks. Nurse? I guess I had another seizure."

"Yes, you did."

"On the ferry."

"Yes."

"What happened?"

"We haven't talked to your girlfriend yet, but the paramedics said it hit you while you were getting off. I guess she knew a little better what to do this time. She said this one man yelled at her to stick her fingers in your mouth to keep you from swallowing your tongue, but she told him to shut up."

"Why was I naked when I woke up here?"

"Um, your clothes were wet. They undressed you in Emergency."

"Wet?"

"It seems that after your seizure you unbuttoned your pants and urinated on the floor, and you got it all over yourself."

"Ah. In front of everyone?"

"I don't know who all was there. I think probably no one saw it except your girlfriend."

"She's not my girlfriend. I doubt I'll ever see her again."

"Oh. I beg your pardon."

"That's all right."

"At least she won't try to sneak you out again. That was very bad of you—both of you."

"Nurse? Wait a second."

"Yes?"

"Uh, do you know her name?"

"Whose, the lady you were with?"

"Yes." Len looped the plastic tube over his elbow, out of the way, and sat up with a groan. His muscles ached. He saw his reflection in the television screen. "I forget her name."

"I'm not sure. It might be in your file."

She left the room. A few minutes later, as she was walking past carrying a bedpan, she stuck her head in the door. "Charis," she said.

"That's an unusual name," said Len.

"I know. I never heard it before."

"What's your name?"

She shook her finger at him. "You'll just have to remember; I'm not telling you."

As people entered his room, Len awoke from a dream, only a fragment of which he could remember: he was carrying a golden, bejeweled orb through an alley that stank of rotting meat, but the orb kept slipping through his fingers and rolling behind piles of waxy cardboard boxes or under dumpsters. A tall, lean doctor nodded at him, but the others walked straight toward the curtain without a glance at his bed. One man held the curtain open as the others entered Cal's part of the room, then himself entered, and the cloth draped back in place. Someone spoke, his voice muffled, low, and uneven, like a tuba heard through the walls of a practice room.

Len clicked through the channels of his television set with the remote-control button. Cal's voice sounded indignantly: "Permanent! What the hell do you mean, permanent? When I came here they were saying a couple months, maybe three, and I would be better. I thought you had surgery that could fix me up."

Two doctors spoke at once. A voice won out, but Cal shouted it down: "I don't give a damn if I can go home! Are you saying I'll never be able to play the accordion again? That I'll have to have a nurse to wipe my ass for the rest of my life? I'm fifty-eight, damn you; I can't live another twenty, twenty-five years like this."

A doctor spoke, and the nurse flung aside the curtain and trotted from the room. The voice was soothing, but Cal sobbed: "God, this is ridiculous. I can't believe it. I mean, isn't it hilarious when you think about it? If I'd a-been in a car wreck, at least it would've made sense. You'd better not charge a penny for your tests and everything. I don't care if insurance does cover it."

The nurse returned, spraying a jet of clear liquid from a needle. Cal said, "Don't jab me with that. I can still bite, damn you! What is that? I have the right to know what you're doping me with."

Len rolled onto his abdomen and clamped the pillow tight around his head. He groaned and pressed his face in his sheets. Inject something lethal in his veins, and put him out of his misery. Toss his cadaver in the Montlake Canal. Let the birds pick him clean.

When Len woke up, someone had turned off the television, and his side of the room was dark. "Cal?" he called. The curtain shifted in the draft. Maybe he had already checked out.

A noise came from the hall: someone was leaning on the closed door, and her voice resonated through the wood: "That's all right, as long as you understand that you only have fifteen minutes left. Just a second, let me see if he's awake." The door opened, and the nurse said, "You have a visitor."

Len clicked on his light. "Okay," he said. "May I have an aspirin?"

"Do you have a headache?"

"Yes."

"Would you rather not see anyone right now?"

"No, that's fine."

"All right. I'll go get you something for your head."

She swung open the door, and Charis entered. She was pale in the fluorescent glow of the hall lights. "Hi," she said. She left the door open.

"Hello there. Have a seat."

"Thank you. I can't stay long."

"Want some candy? Sean and Julie left me some."

"No, thanks." Charis coughed and put a fist to her mouth.

Len said, "To tell you the truth, I'm surprised you came by. I thought I wouldn't ever see you again." She shrugged. He said, "You must have been pretty embarrassed."

"It isn't every day your date pees all over your skirt."

"I suppose not." Len opened and closed the top drawer of his dresser. "Hey, Charis, didn't you say something about me dying someday in an explosion? Remember, when we first met?"

"When we met? Oh, you mean at the party. No, no, no, that was just someone you reminded me of."

"Who was he? A lover?"

"He was my brother."

"I'm sorry."

"Yeah."

A nurse said from the hall, "Miss, I don't want to rush you out, but Dr. Amers is on the floor now, and he wanted to ask you a question or two in private. I'm sorry about that. I know you just got in."

"That's all right," said Charis. "Look, I'll be back in a minute, Len. Or if they won't let me back in tonight, I'll drop by tomorrow, maybe."

"Great." Though annoyed, Len disciplined himself to say nothing. "Take it easy."

"God!" Cal cried, and Charis started.

"Cal?" Len asked.

Charis scratched at a spot on her purse while he listened. She said, "He must be a joy to room with."

"He's all right," said Len. He pressed the call button for the nurse. "He usually doesn't talk in his sleep. He's pretty quiet most of the time."

Charis kissed him. "See you," she said.

Len laughed. "Good-bye."

"What are you laughing about? Have your lips turned ticklish?"

"No. It was nothing."

Charis smiled over her shoulder as she left and bumped into the nurse, who was entering. The nurse approached Len's bed. "Here's your aspirin," she said. "I'm sorry I forgot."

"No problem." Len swallowed the tablets with water from a paper cup.

"Well," said the nurse, leaning her bust on the bed rail, "she came back."

"What?"

"Your friend Charis. You said you'd never see her again."

"Yeah, I guess I did."

"Did you want anything else?"

"Oh, Cal was crying out a minute ago, and I thought maybe he needed some help, but when I tried to talk to him I realized he was unconscious."

"I'll check on him."

She went behind the curtain, and her squat form billowed the cloth where her shadow moved. She seemed to be making Cal's bed, tucking in the corners of his sheets, drawing her hand across his brow. Cal's light clicked out, and she reemerged.

"Good night, Len," she said.

"Good night, nurse."

"You still can't remember my name?"

He tugged on his lip and said, "I remember it was a Puritan name, something like Chastity or Prudence. What's so funny?"

"Nothing. You're wrong, though."

"It'll come to me. Hey, would you mind bringing me a TV
schedule?"

"No, but I think you'd better get some sleep before those tests
tomorrow. Sitting there for hours staring at lights and having wires
hooked to your scalp can be exhausting. And that woman asks a lot
of questions to keep your mind racing."

Len said, "Maybe she can save herself the bother and just electrocute me on the spot."

The nurse said, "That would be one way to keep you from running out on us."

She started for the door.

Len said, "Grace!"

"What?"

"Your name is Grace."

The nurse flashed her white teeth and laughed deeply. "No, but
you're close," she said, stooping to pick up a get-well card that fluttered from his dresser. "Very close."

Eminent Domain

In addition to his 1986 Iowa Short Fiction Award winner, Eminent Domain,
Dan O'Brien is the author of a work of nonfiction, The Rites of Autumn,
and two novels, Spirit of the Hills *and* Center of the Nation.
O'Brien lives in the Black Hills of South Dakota.

*"In these quiet, powerful stories Dan O'Brien takes on some of the larger
themes of American fiction—the loss of the wilderness, nostalgia for the West,
the end of individualism. At the same time he never loses sight of more personal
struggles—a boy coping with his mother's abandonment, a man on a rescue
expedition trying to recover his own feelings for his wife and their failing
marriage, an aging black man's love for a great hunting dog. O'Brien writes
about memory and longing in a voice so strong you cannot help but listen,
so gentle you must lean close to hear."*
MARY MORRIS, 1986

You can say a lot of things to a woman, but don't ever tell her not to
let the door hit her in the ass on the way out, because she won't.
She'll be gone before that door has a chance to slam and she won't
be back until long after the sound of that slam has stopped ringing
in your ears.

Willy Herbeck can be the meanest, most insensitive son of a bitch
the world has ever seen. He's dirty, sloppy, unsociable, old-
fashioned, moody, bullheaded, and ugly. But he's got class. I guess
that's why I married him in the first place, and that's why I moved
out on him, too. He's got an independent orneriness and when he
takes a liking to something he doesn't care what other people think,
he sticks by what he's said come hell or goddamned high water.

That's why when I heard that the state highway department had been out to buy the place and Willy had told them to get out, I

knew we were in for trouble. Willy, I said, it's a fair price. You
haven't sold fifty dollars worth of parts off this place since spring
and here they're offering you ten thousand dollars. He just sat there
and read the newspaper. They'll get it, I said, the law says you have
to sell. Bullshit, he said.

He hadn't even read the letters we'd sent him. I figured he was
confused or maybe couldn't read so I went out and offered him top
dollar right off the bat. They said he was a funny, hard-to-deal-with
kind of guy, so I thought, hell, give him the ten grand, move those
junk cars out of the way, and save everyone a lot of problems. He
said that there were one hundred and thirteen of them and they
weren't for sale, and I tried to explain that he had to sell, that the
highway was coming through and that there really wasn't much
choice. Then he grabbed me by the arm and led me back to my car
and put me in and said good-bye.

So I was stuck. It's my job to get the land that the department
needs and I don't get much time. I went and looked up his wife.

They told me she was young and good-looking and worked in
a cafe at the intersection of Route 50 and Route 27. I asked for
Shirley and the girl smiles and says she'll send her over. She brings
me a cup of coffee and I wait. When Shirley comes I can't believe
it's true. She's about thirty-five, blonde, nice body, white teeth.
That slob of a junk man must have something going for him. The
guy had to be fifteen years older than she was, he was dirty, rotten
teeth. I looked her over real good, figured there had to be something wrong with her; but if there was, I didn't see it.

I told her what I wanted. Said that Willy had practically thrown
me off the place and she should have a talk with him. It's a good
price, I said, and let me give you a little inside scoop, the state
ain't going any higher. She said she didn't think Willy would sell
and I explained to her that he'd have to eventually. She nodded and
asked if I needed anything. I said I was all set and as she walked
away I wondered why a gal like her was with a guy like Willy
Herbeck.

I did like the state man said, because he was right. I tried to talk Willy into selling the place. He was lying under the '48 Dodge in the front yard and I was trying to talk to him. Willy, I said, you can't fight them. They'll come and take it and put you in jail, that's what will happen. He didn't say a word. Keep it up then, I said, be a pighead. He said nothing. I kicked the Dodge, and that brought him out. You listening to me, I asked. Not much, he said. Well you better start listening to me, you're messing with the state, I said and pointed my finger at him. He looked back at me and said, Shirley, don't kick this car. It's a driver. Driver my ass, I said. They were all drivers; just needs a fan belt, he'd say, or a new wheel. They were all drivers, all precious pieces of junk and the truth is none of them were ever drivers. They all just sat and the people would come with good money and try to buy parts and Willy would just say, no, he didn't have it, and the people can see the thing they came for hanging off one of those junk cars and Willy pretends like he's never seen what they're looking for and tells them to get off the place. Now the state was offering him ten thousand dollars for the whole place and he was acting like they were someone who came looking for a gas cap.

Threatening and puffing up your chest is a waste of time. Nobody ever proved a thing in a pushing match, and nobody ever held onto nothing by talking about it.

After dinner he started going in and out of the house, carrying little boxes of things and kind of keeping them hidden from me. I was watching television and trying to ignore him. Finally he quit coming and going and sat down in his chair to watch television. What was all that about, I asked. Nothing, he said. Come on, Willy, I said, I know you're up to something, what was in those boxes? A little of this, a little of that, he said. I could see that he wasn't going to tell me what he was doing so I just ignored him again. But the longer I sat there the madder I got. I'd been living with him for a long time and I'd been bringing in the money ever since the first and now that he had a chance at ten thousand dollars he wouldn't

even talk about it. And then he starts sneaking stuff out of the
house. I couldn't stand it.

I screamed. Willy, what are you going to do about the state, and
what was in those boxes? I yelled a while longer and finally he says,
I guess I'll have to fight. And the second he said that I knew he was
serious and I knew that those boxes were filled with supplies.
Where'd you take those boxes, I asked, and he answered exactly
what I knew he'd answer. I took them up to the '26 Packard,
he said.

I've been buying land for the state for a long time and I don't
think I ever had one like Willy Herbeck. He must be a mean bastard. He even threw that good-looking gal out of the house for trying to convince him that we were offering him a good deal. I talked
to her the day after she got thrown out and she said she didn't care
if she ever saw him again.

I went out again, hoping that maybe he'd thought it over and
changed his mind. I was kidding myself, he was too mean to give in
to anything. I knocked on the door and nobody came. I cleaned
the dust off the window and looked in. Didn't look like anyone
had ever lived there. I walked around to the back. There were car
parts everywhere. Cracked engine blocks, old batteries, differentials,
transmissions, fenders, hubcaps, junk scattered everywhere.

Behind the house the land rose to what must have been a little
hilltop. You couldn't see any ground, nothing but wrecked cars,
and nothing new, all old, rusting, smashed cars. I glanced over
them all, then hollered to see if anyone was around. There was no
answer. As I turned back toward the house I noticed a license plate
leaning up against the house. I could see it was an old one. I
reached out to inspect it and inches from my outstretched hand the
siding on the house shattered, pieces of wood splintered, and I
heard the rifle shot. I hit the ground behind an engine block. A
voice boomed out from above, GET OUT. I looked up, and this
time saw a person sitting behind the wheel of the Packard at the top
of the hill.

They say that stainless steel is the best material to put bodies in for burial. When I die, I want them to cremate me, and put the ashes into a Stanley thermos bottle (they're stainless steel), and put the bottle in the glove compartment of the '26 Packard and not tell anybody where I'm at.

They came to see me at work and I told the sheriff, husband or not, I was staying out of it. The sheriff looked over his shoulder at the state man. He took a shot at this man, Shirley, now that's against the law and you gotta do something, he said. No, sheriff, I don't have to do anything, I said. The sheriff turned and led the state man into the corner of the cafe, I went on cleaning the counter. They were back in a minute. This time the state man was doing the talking.

He started off with, Mrs. Herbeck, I know that you're upset about all this and I know that when the state is forced to take over property that there are often serious adjustments to be made. I folded my arms across my chest and listened to him. You and your husband have had a falling out, he said. That's understandable, it's a trying situation. But, he said, and smiled slyly, this is not the time to alienate your husband. This is when he needs you most. Then he winked, and the time that you need him most.

I thought for a second. Okay, I said, I'll talk to him. He touched me on the shoulder and said, now you're thinking straight. He motioned to the sheriff and the three of us drove out to the place to talk to Willy.

When the sheriff stepped out of the car three shots hit the ground in front of him. He leaped back and said he was going to call the Highway Patrol. I told him not to do anything and got out of the car. They both yelled at me to get back but I didn't pay any attention. I knew Willy wouldn't shoot, and I knew right where to find him.

He was sitting in the driver's side of the Packard, peering out of the side window over his rifle barrel. Hold it right there, he said. Hold it yourself, I said, and walked over to the Packard. I looked into the backseat and could see that it was full of food and ammunition. What the hell do you think you're doing, I asked. I thought

you weren't coming back, he said. So I'm back for a minute, I said,
what the hell are you doing? Nothing, he said.

I took a good look at him sitting there in that old Packard, the
backseat full of food and ammunition and the tires all flat. He was
dead serious. You think you're protecting this place, I asked. He
wiggled his mouth around under his nose and I knew that meant
that he figured he was. Well, you're nuts, I said, you aren't protecting anything. You're just making a fool out of yourself. He rubbed
the black stubble on his chin. That don't much matter, he said. I
could see that there was no sense in even trying to talk him down
from the hill. I kicked the Packard. You're a fool, I said, they'll
shoot you dead as hell. He'd been staring down the hill toward the
sheriff and the state man but raised his eyes to look at me. Don't
kick the '26, he said, she's a driver.

He didn't listen to his wife the first time but I still thought he
might. Something had to be done, the superintendent was starting
to breathe down my neck. The sheriff said he'd give him a week,
then go up and get him. Evey day the sheriff and I would spend
hours at the junkyard, every evening I'd stop at the cafe and talk to
Shirley.

Once or twice a day the sheriff would call up through his megaphone, WILLY, YOU'RE GOING TO HAVE TO COME DOWN
HERE AND TALK. THE STATE MAN IS HERE AND HE'S
WILLING TO NEGOTIATE. But Willy would not come down.
And every time that Willy didn't answer the sheriff's message the
sheriff would say, he left, he must have just deserted the whole
thing, and the sheriff would step out from behind his car and smile.
Then shots would ring out from the top of the hill of junk and the
sheriff would jump back behind his car, grab the megaphone and
say, WILLY, YOU SON OF A BITCH.

I kept telling Shirley that the ten thousand would be her ticket
out of the junkyard. She's a smart gal, she knew what I was saying
but played dumb. She kept talking about what was the best way to
handle Willy, but she was smelling her share of the money and what

she was thinking was what was the best way to get that in the bank. I told her that if she talked him into the ten thousand that she'd be doing herself a favor, that she'd earned it, and I was telling the truth.

If she could just get him to take the cash, she could get her share and get the hell out of there. I'd seen it work before. A guy like Willy could drink himself to death with five grand and a gal like Shirley could get a fresh start. It's a fact of life and Shirley knew her facts of life.

Somewhere there ought to be a law that says you don't have to sell what you got just because someone offers you a good price for it. There ought to be a law that everything isn't for sale, and people should realize that happy is happy and when you got it you got it. Everybody should think about that, especially women.

I kept thinking about Willy up there in the Packard, fighting his little war for no reason, and all the time I was figuring, ten thousand dollars divided by one hundred and thirteen cars in the lot is eighty-eight dollars and forty cents per car. And that's a lot more than they're worth. At first I just got mad when I thought of it. There he was, king of the mountain. But this wasn't a game, it was for real. The sheriff wasn't kidding and it wasn't right that Willy was playing with my life in his game. After all, there wouldn't be a mountain of junk to fight over if it weren't for me. Willy didn't have the ambition to support himself over the years it took to collect all that. In a way that mountain was half mine. I began to hope that the whole thing would just be over.

On the Wednesday after the Thursday when the sheriff had said he'd give Willy another week, the sheriff and the state man paid me another visit. He's still up there, the sheriff said, he shot at me twice today. Now tomorrow we're going up there and get him out, and we won't be pulling our punches. This is about your last chance to talk him down. He talked like he meant it, and I could see that the state man was serious, too. Will you give it another try, Shirley, the state man said, it's in your best interest. I untied my apron. Yeah, I said, I'll try again.

So five minutes later I was walking up that hill toward Willy and
the Packard and I was thinking again about all those years of sup-
porting Willy and I could remember them by the heaps of junk I
passed. The '57 Chevy with the mashed-in left side had come in on
Christmas Day four years ago. I remembered because Willy left the
turkey dinner I'd made to go out and get it. And the '58 Edsel that
had been driven off a bridge was there, and the wire-wheeled Hud-
son from fifteen years before and the blue '62 Ford with the green
racing stripe, they were all there. I could see them all and could remember all the screaming and fighting that they had caused, and
then I saw Willy sitting in the Packard, his very first car, and before
I said anything to him I turned and looked over the junkyard. I saw
the view that he had from the Packard. I saw every junker—drivers,
he'd call them—and I saw every oily piece of junk that I'd helped
him collect. And on the horizon, still miles away, I could see the
ink-black exhaust smoke from the bulldozers and earth movers.

When she came down off the hill we asked her what he'd said.
She said that he hadn't said anything. Then the sheriff asked her
what she'd said and she said, nothing. They hadn't said a word to
each other. The sheriff frowned, turned away and kicked at the dirt.
Shirley turned to me and asked for a ride back.

In the car, she spoke first. You know, she said, I worked for that
business, probably more than Willy. I nodded my head, I could see
what she was getting at. I figure, she said, that since Willy can't talk
to you, that I should. I nodded again. I'd been wondering when
she'd get around to dealing, she was a woman, she could get Willy
to do like she wanted, no matter what he wanted. I think, she went
on, that I can convince him to take your offer. This time I smiled, it
had paid off. She'd put the ultimatum to him and they'd take the
money and she'd be wearing new clothes in a week. Good, I said, I
knew you could convince him once you saw what was best. But
what, I said, would happen if he still says no, if the sheriff has to go
up. She turned to me and said simply, they'll have to shoot him.
Then she asked me to turn down a side street and told me to stop in
front of a wrecking service. Let me out here, she said.

When two people agree to spend their lives together it seems to me that they gotta be able to pick up the slack for each other. When you live with someone you gotta be able to know that her little hands will scrub the inside of the pickle jar when it's empty, if you'll unscrew the lid when it's brand new.

The sheriff was there before the state man and me. There were four squad cars and the deputies stood behind them, wearing helmets and checking their guns. Sheriff, I said, I want to talk to him, I think I can talk him out of a fight. You had your chance yesterday, he said, time for talk is done. But you have to let her try, the state man said, it could save some trouble, maybe even a life. The sheriff frowned. How long, he asked. Ten minutes, I said. Okay.

It was just getting light when I started up. I called out to Willy as I went, to be sure he wouldn't shoot in the half-light. Willy, I yelled, it's Shirley, and my voice bounced in all directions off the gray forms of the junkers. Don't shoot me, I said, and halfway up, beside the '41 Studebaker pickup, I called again. Willy, I said, don't be pointing that gun at me. And this time he called back, shut up, he said. When I came to the Packard I could see him sitting there, his rifle barrel pointing out the window and the bill of his baseball cap pulled down low over his eyes. Hold it, he said, what do you want? They're down there waiting, I said. Yeah, he said, I heard them drive in. They're coming up, I said. It was almost light and I saw him glance in the backseat. Well, he said, I'm almost out of food anyway.

I walked over to the Packard. I got a deal, I said. No, Shirley, he said, I've made up my mind, I'm staying with this junk for the rest of my life, and he smiled and rubbed his nose with a greasy hand. That's the deal, I said. His eyes narrowed and I knew he was listening even though he acted like he wasn't.

I talked to Ray over at Ace Wrecking Service, I said. Willy still wouldn't look toward me. He said he'd move them for us, I said. Willy glanced at me from the corners of his eyes. There are one hundred and thirteen of them, right, I asked. He nodded. At twenty

dollars apiece for the move, that's four thousand five hundred and
twenty dollars, I said. That leaves us over five thousand dollars to
buy another piece of land.

He turned his head and looked at me, then motioned toward the
seat beside him. Get in, he said. I climbed over the stack of rusted
wheels that lay in front of the Packard and Willy kicked at the passenger's door from the inside until it came open and I sat down. We
can pick a new piece of ground, he asked. Sure, I said. He'll move
all of them, Willy asked. All of them, I said. And I can supervise, he
asked. I don't see why not, I said.

Willy cleared his throat and let the rifle barrel slip onto the floor.
It went through a hole in the floorboards. He stretched his oily arm
over the back of the front seat and leaned back. A new yard, he said
to himself and dangled his left arm over the steering wheel. Maybe
somewhere out by the dump, he said, I'd like that. And we looked
straight ahead, through the shattered windshield, the sun was coming up bright and we could see the black smoke from the bulldozers
just beginning to rise.

Little Bear

Robert Boswell has published two novels, Crooked Hearts *and* The Geography of Desire, *and has held fellowships with the National Endowment for the Arts and the Guggenheim Foundation. He teaches in the Warren Wilson M.F.A. program and is an assistant professor of English at New Mexico State University in Las Cruces, where he lives with his wife, Antonya Nelson, and their daughter, Jade.*

"Dancing in the Movies *is a powerful book, taut and stark, intense with human passion. Bluntly, bravely, Robert Boswell explores that gray borderland where betrayal mixes with trust, violence with love, despair with hope. The final effect is overwhelming.*"

TIM O'BRIEN, 1985

Joey Malone found Pfc Owens under a transport truck.

"You getting overtime?" Joey said.

Owens scooted out on his back. He held a black radiator hose in his hand. "They said it needed a new radiator. Look here." He bent the rubber hose to expose a crack. "I been lying under there a half hour thinking how stupid the army is."

He stood, skinny and black, threw the hose in a metal barrel, blew into his cupped hands. "Colder than Bejesus," he said.

Joey nodded. He looked out over the support unit and beyond it to the gray Korean landscape. When Joey had first joined the unit, the pointy canvas tents and six-wheel trucks, the single-axle trailers and barking officers had reminded him of the circus that came to Michigan City in the spring, setting up in a field near the prison. Now, he could see only trucks, trailers, and temporary quarters.

Joey stuck his hands inside his jacket, under his arms. "Sergeant Anderson said I'm ready."

Owens stomped his feet to fight the cold. "I'm staying," he said.

Joey and Owens were the last of Master Sergeant Anderson's training detail, organized to make men who had performed badly in combat ready to return. Owens, they had discovered, was a good mechanic, so good he would stay with the support unit indefinitely. He had tried to teach Joey, telling him to picture the engine running, the pistons shooting in and out like the legs of chorus girls they'd seen in a camp movie. Joey couldn't see it. His head was too full of army regulations and meaningless numbers, images of Indiana and a great blank fear of dying. He would have to return to combat.

"I have to report to him in an hour," Joey said. "He wants to *talk* to me."

"That's lousy, Joey. I'd take combat over that." Owens pulled a cigarette from his pocket, lit it, and inhaled deeply. "Luckily, I don't have to do neither. You, on the other hand . . ." Owens chuckled.

Joey laughed with him. "I, on the other hand, get screwed coming and going."

Owens laughed, spitting out his cigarette. "That's the looks of it." He picked the white butt off the ground and blew on it. The end glowed orange. He twisted dirt off the lip end. "My last cigarette," he said, looked it over again, and tossed it back to the dirt. "This very earth is swarming with bacterias, I bet." He wiped the tips of his fingers against his chest. "Probably a thousand on your shirt alone." He pointed at Joey.

A circle of dirt marked Joey's chest like a target. He wiped and slapped at the dirt. Sergeant Anderson had had him shooting at burning barrels from a ditch as part of his training.

"It's like I slid into home," Joey said.

"Always slide feet first." Owens took two steps, slid into the rear tire of the transport truck. "Feet first." He kicked the tire. "I stole fourteen bases once. In one game."

Joey had been a second baseman in high school, then a shortstop in Okinawa. "There was something I wanted to talk about," Joey said. "Really, something I want to tell you about."

"Michigan City?" Owens said. He was from Brawley, California; Joey from Michigan City, Indiana. They took turns telling about home. "Let's get out of the cold."

They crawled into the cab of the truck. "I've been having dreams about this," Joey said. "It was when I was a kid." His words fogged the windshield.

"Yeah?" Owens said. He blew into his hands again, clapped against his shoulders, rubbed his arms.

"I was ten," Joey said. "My brother was six."

"My brother's six," Owens said, glad to have a connection to the story.

"Nineteen forty-three, I remember that," Joey said. Eight years ago, walking to his friend's house on a street without lights, a night without a moon, Joey had tried to avoid the puddles. His little brother sloshed through them. *What's the point of wearing rubbers if you don't have any fun?* his brother, Dave, said. *Galoshes,* Joey said, *call them galoshes.* His brother shrugged, said, *Not what Mom calls them.* Joey shook his head. *Trust me,* he said.

Shelling sounded in the distance. Not really like thunder, Joey thought, louder, more explicit. To Owens, he said, "We spent the night at my best friend's house. Mickey Lawanda. His parents were out of town."

"Your folks let you do that? Mine would never. Not when I was ten." Owens slipped his hands under his legs to warm them.

"They didn't know Mickey's parents were gone. He lived across from the penitentiary." Three boys had huddled around the coffee table, reading newspaper clippings aloud to Joey's little brother, who couldn't read. They arranged the clippings in chronological order, passed around the seven pictures the newspaper had run again and again—blood on the tiled floor, the floral wallpaper, the bedspread, the ceiling, and Tomás "Pato" Rodríguez staring into the camera, his hands cupped over his ears.

"This guy, Pato Rodríguez, had killed his girlfriend with scissors," Joey said.

"Crude," Owens said.

"At least, they said he did. He didn't look like a bad guy."

His body had been no larger than a boy's, thin arms thickening at the elbows like the joints of tree limbs. Even in the grainy newspaper photographs, his brown skin looked soft. He couldn't speak English, which had seemed like crime enough. The boys didn't know what Pato meant or why he was called that, but they imagined it meant Tiger or The Knife. Mickey gave each of them nicknames. He labeled Joey "Mongoose" Malone. He called Joey's brother "The Spot" because of the large birthmark that covered part of his jaw and neck. He called himself Mickey "The Wonder" Lawanda. Joey's little brother's name had stuck. Everyone but family called him Spot Malone. Because of that night, Joey thought, because of Pato Rodríguez.

"We read the newspaper stories about the killing. We were right across from the prison," Joey said and crossed his arms against the cold.

As midnight approached, they stared through the small squares of glass at the prison, a hulking concrete box, dark against the dark sky. Mickey had said it looked like a devil's food cake with barbed wire icing.

"We turned on every light in the house."

His brother had run upstairs, turning on the lights in the bedrooms, hall. Joey covered the downstairs, turning on the lights in the kitchen, closets, dining and living rooms. Mickey went to the cellar, switched on the remaining lights. Joey ran out the front door, a misting rain covering his face, to be sure they had not missed a room. The house had become an island of light.

"What for?" Owens said. "Why the lights?"

"I'm getting to it," Joey said. "We all looked at the pictures from the newspaper one last time." Blood on the tiled floor, blood on the floral wallpaper, blood on the bedspread, blood on the ceiling. "We sat in the front room." They sat separately, each with his back erect, hands palm down on the arms of a chair.

"When they executed Pato," Joey said, "the lights in Mickey's house went dim." Two minutes after midnight, the state of Indiana pumped light through the arteries of Pato Rodríguez. Three boys sat in straight-backed chairs with irretrievable smiles until the few dim moments passed and the lights surged on again.

"What'd it feel like?" Owens said.

The windshield was fogged over. *With my words,* Joey thought, imagining that the story could be read there if you knew how to do it. "It was thrilling," Joey said. *It was frightening. It was terrible, beautiful.*

Nearby, a jeep started up, idled. Owens pulled his knees to his chest, wrapped his arms around them. "Think our deaths here would entertain anybody?"

Joey shrugged.

"Idiots and dogs," Sergeant Anderson said, spitting into a pool of motor oil as they walked to the jeep. "Korea's full of them." Anderson jumped behind the wheel. Joey got in beside him, looked over his shoulder at Owens next to another jeep, oil pan in his hands.

"Every war is just like this." Sergeant Anderson maneuvered the jeep around a puddle of muddy water. "A shithouse mess." He began talking about World War II, how the units were segregated. Joey found he could let the noise of the jeep drown out the words. Owens' regiment had been segregated. They were the last all-Negro unit, broken up after they had bugged out. Owens said the unit joke was that they were the asphalt crew because the army wanted to pave the way to Korea with black asses.

The jeep bounced hard. Mud sprayed from both sides. "Mud'll be ice by midnight," Sergeant Anderson said. "Whole country'll be ice in a week." Joey nodded at the sergeant. "Look here." Anderson switched on the headlights, although the afternoon was still light. He pointed to the road in front of them. "A man's got direction, it's like he's got an extra arm. Army's built-in direction, like what bats got—your own personal radar. *You* can see that, Malone. *You* listen. Most the idiots here never listen to anything but mess call and the sound of money leaving their pockets. That Owens," he threw his thumb back over his shoulder, "wouldn't listen to his own black mother."

Joey followed Anderson's thumb back, half expecting Owens to
be there. Korean children sat on a thin gray mattress, stuffing hanging out of it like intestines. "Owens is all right," he said and felt a
rush of panic.

Anderson gripped the steering wheel with both hands, switched
off the lights, accelerated. The jeep gobbled up the road faster and
faster. Anderson's face, Joey realized, was light green, like the meat
of a cucumber. The jeep swerved away from a spotted, yapping
dog, but the rear wheel caught it. A crack, as if they'd run over a
tree limb, and a short whistle. "Shit," Anderson said. "We kill it?"

The dog's head rose and fell slowly, rose and fell, like a toy dog in
the rear window of a car. "Dying," Joey said.

"My brother hit a dog once in Italy," Anderson said.

Joey waited, but Anderson didn't add to the story. The dog's
head finally dropped and stayed down, a dark lump on the road.
The jeep continued. The sky, in a haze of dust from the jeep, turned
khaki.

Half an hour later, the jeep stopped at a windowless, bare plank
building just off the side of the road. Over the door hung a yellow
sign with red letters: SUZIES SALOON. "Place is a pigsty. But so
is all of Korea," Anderson said as he got out of the jeep. Squat, with
hunched shoulders, a thick neck, and arms too short for his body,
Sergeant Anderson reminded Joey of a giant amphibian.

Anderson shoved a drunken private who blocked the door. Although the ceiling was low, the building had the feeling of a barn.
Joey could have turned it into an Indiana barn if not for all the GI's
crowding around wooden tables. Sergeant Anderson comman-
deered a table next to the wall. He grabbed a Korean woman by the
thigh. "Get us two beers." He smiled at Joey as the woman walked
away. "One time I was a kid and wouldn't eat my string beans.
Hated them. My father stuck a revolver to my head and told me to
clean my plate. Your father still living?"

"Yes, sir."

"I was mad at him, but I thought, hell, he's my father. My
brother Paul come in saying, 'He's a son of a bitch.'" Anderson
folded his arms. "We both enlisted young." He leaned against the

table. "World War II, Paul and I spent a lot of time in Italy. Got more pussy there than we ever dreamed of in the States." He reached across the table, cupped his hand around Joey's neck, pulled him slightly closer, then let him go. "Got a girlfriend back home— where is it—Michigan?"

"Michigan City, Indiana."

"Got one?"

"No, sir."

"Good. Man don't need a skirt home fucking the plumber while he's gone."

Joey nodded, stared at the table. He felt uneasy, threatened, wondering if this was part of combat training, if he might have to fight a table of drunks or make a weapon out of bottle caps and spit.

The Korean woman returned. Sergeant Anderson paid for the beers. "Completed the training, Malone. Another day or two we're going to join a unit at the front. The both of us. You're a soldier." He reached across the table. Joey took his hand. Anderson gripped it firmly, looked it over. "Important to know a man's hands," he said. They shook, then drank to Joey's accomplishment, the army, Anderson's brother, who had died in North Africa.

"Best beer in the world is in PI. San Miguel. Ever get the chance, go to PI. Heaven for a man."

Joey drank the beer, pretended to be interested. He thought he should ask what PI stood for or whether San Miguel was a place or a beer. He said nothing. The whole evening seemed like a test.

"Basically, I don't like women," Anderson said. "They want you to think you can't live without them. There's a lot you can live without. Sex though." He ran his thumb and forefinger across the end of his nose. "The thing about sex is you can't remember it. You remember the woman, the night, maybe how everything worked up to it. But sex itself can't be remembered. Like a shock or one of those dreams that never come back."

After an hour of drinking and talking, Anderson bought each of them a whore. Joey didn't want one. The sergeant said it was an order. "Next hole you'll be in won't be as warm as this one," he said

and shoved a girl at Joey. "She's Suzie," he said, "all the whores are
Suzie."

Joey took her hand, followed her through the bar and out a back door. Behind the building, a row of stalls stood like booths at the county fair. A cloth curtain covered the doorway. Inside, a dirt floor, a canvas ceiling ripped open into a smile.

Joey's whore was young and thin and wore a tomato red dress with white buttons the size of quarters. She lit a kerosene lamp. "Cold," she said.

Joey nodded, blew into his hands, shoved them into his pockets.

She unbuttoned the top two buttons, pulled the dress over her head. Her breasts barely lipped away from her chest. She sat on a regulation army cot, smiled up at him with crooked teeth. She said her name was Suzie, then pulled his pants down to his knees. In the cold, his testicles and penis looked like nothing more than a shriveled apricot and stem.

Joey watched the crooked teeth surround his penis, looked above her at the wall, bare except for an ill-framed still life of cabbage and celery. He looked above that, through the tear in the canvas ceiling to the sky. He'd had sex only once before. He began thinking of that night so his penis would get hard.

He had made love with June Norris on the outfield grass in the school ball park one night just before graduation. He remembered the sensation of being inside someone else, and afterward, while he still lay on top of her, she lifted her right arm into the air, pointed to the sky, and said, "Ursa Minor, the Little Bear."

Joey rolled off her, looked up at the stars. She pointed out Little Bear, and squinting his eyes he thought he could picture a bear cub. They lay on the grass and she pointed out other animals in the sky—a bull, a ram. The only one Joey could picture was the bear. June giggled, pulled her checkered dress, which was already pushed up to her chest, over her head. Joey ran his hands over her headless body. She pulled the dress back, bunched it around her neck. Joey thought her head looked like a bean, her lips a hilum. When he told her, she laughed, said he should plant the bean so she could grow another body.

June took his penis, rolled it back and forth in her hands like a child playing with clay. He remembered thinking she was beautiful but never telling her. She said that she was leaving Michigan City to be free, that everyone in the city was in prison whether they knew it or not. She was going to college in the West where not one person in the entire state knew her name. She had promised to write, but Joey never got a single letter. He thought if he were to write her now he'd say, "Suzie was nothing like you."

Anderson talked the whole drive back about being stationed in Italy, how his brother had bought him his first whore. Joey tried to listen, but his mind was in Indiana with his own brother, his father, even his mother, who had been dead for years. Joey was thirteen when his mother was killed crossing Water Street. In his last letter, his father had said the state was going to build a bridge over Water Street. This seemed to make him very happy. His father taught science in high school: the way a cell divides, the position of the earth in the universe. He had majored in English at the University of Indiana, but never taught anything except science. Joey's brother was beginning high school even though he still couldn't read. They'd just kept passing him because his father was a teacher and because he was a good shortstop.

Joey had played shortstop in Okinawa. He had been a shipping clerk and played for the Green Foxes, one of the regiment's teams. Numbers had given him no trouble then. He'd even kept batting averages. During his first few days in Korea, his sense of numbers had suddenly become confused. Fatigue, someone had told him, he would get over it. Instead, it had gotten worse. His head was as much a jumble of meaningless numbers as the bingo cage at the Michigan City Methodist Church.

In the middle of the summer, his battalion had been told they were being shipped from Okinawa to mainland Japan for six weeks of combat training. In the ship, they were told they would go to Pusan, Korea, for three days of intensive training. When they arrived in Pusan, they were sent to Chinju and combat.

Joey and the Green Foxes' first baseman lugged a .50-caliber machine gun into position to provide cover for the other men. Neither had ever fired a machine gun. Joey was given quick instructions. He followed them, but the gun wouldn't fire. Grease coated his hands and forearms as he went through the steps over and over. The clatter of weapons became more regular, louder. They could not get the gun to fire. Nearby, a corporal shouted coordinates into a radio again and again, then slammed it with his fist. U.S. planes flew overhead, unaware. The radio man stood, screamed numbers at the planes until his face exploded from a round of fire. Joey and the first baseman ran. Joey ran faster. When the first baseman was hit, he called out, "Cinnamon."

Joey wrote to his father that he'd escaped with just some shrapnel in his arm. When the medic dug the fragments out, they were pieces of skull. Joey couldn't finish the letter. Later, he found out the grease was packing grease and the machine gun wouldn't have fired for anyone. By that time, his head was a bingo cage. Since then Joey had been shuffled around Korea like the extra ace in a marked deck, until finally he'd been assigned for special training.

Back from SUZIES SALOON, asleep in his cot, Joey dreamed of Pato Rodríguez in the electric chair, hands free from their straps, cupped over his ears. When the lights dimmed, Pato called out, "Cinnamon." Joey woke, stared into the dark. He was sure of two things, that he hated Korea and that *his* death was out there, patient, walking in regulation boots.

Owens told Joey to just sleep. Master Sergeant Anderson had left camp without leaving orders for him. "Sleep," Owens said. "Enjoy the scenery."

Joey couldn't sleep because he was sure Anderson would be coming to take him to combat. "I hate Korea," he said.

"Got to stop the communists here or they'll be at your doorstep." Owens smiled.

Joey tried to imagine communists taking Michigan City. "I still hate it," he said.

"I hate being here," Owens said, looking from side to side, pulling on his belt buckle with his right hand. "I hate the fucking food the most."

"I hate it all."

"All of it?" Owens asked.

"All of it."

"The clothes, you hate the clothes?" He looked at Joey disbelievingly.

"I hate this uniform."

"I like the clothes." Owens smiled, looked down at his khaki T-shirt, jacket, pants. "They let you keep the clothes. And the tags." He held his dog tags to his face, read his name, looked again at Joey. "I bet you a jimmy you can't guess my blood type."

Joey thought the clothes didn't look bad on Owens, even though his T-shirt was inside out. "Bet a what?"

"A jimmy, you know, a favor," Owens said. "You win, I owe you. I win, you owe me."

"Type A," Joey said.

"It's O. Now you owe me one, Malone." Still smiling, he began to walk off.

"Owens, your shirt is inside out."

Owens stopped, looked at his shirt. "How can you tell?"

"Look at the collar."

He stretched the neck of his T-shirt out to look at it. "I think you're right." He looked back at Joey. "We're even."

Joey thought of Indiana like an alcoholic thinks of liquor. When he closed his eyes, he saw pictures: his backyard in Michigan City, the pitcher of lemonade his mother sets on the round table in the corner of the back porch, his mother in a yellow cotton dress, arms folded, smiling. He's playing catch with his father while his brother, only six, sits in the grass, rocking and watching. His father is teaching him to throw a curve, saying he is old enough now, his arm can withstand the violent snap of the wrist at the point of release. It's a warm day. The sun shines directly on his arms and face.

In Korea, the afternoon turned to a cutting cold. Sergeant Anderson had told Joey that winter in Korea was brutal. "Ever seen a

man turn blue?" he'd said. Joey tried to block it out by thinking of
Indiana, the smile that crosses his father's face as a pitch breaks a
few inches. He couldn't make it last. Something always returned
him to Korea: the smell of a rifle recently oiled, phosphorous clouds
rising on the horizon. He wanted to stay back there with his mother
still alive, his brother too young to know he can't learn how to read,
his father squatting in freshly mowed grass, pointing two fingers
toward a dish they'd taken to use as home plate. He knew that the
dream wasn't real, that it never had been. But his mind went there,
and for a moment the khaki uniform became jeans and a white
T-shirt, the flapping of the flag became striped sheets on the clothes-
line, the birds lining the top of the tent became cardinals perched
on a telephone wire, and even the leaves, as they turned, turned toward home.

Late afternoon with no sign of Sergeant Anderson, Joey and
Owens played cards in the cab of a truck with a burnt-out transmis-
sion. They played poker, but Joey had too much trouble keeping
track of the cards, so they played Go Fish, talked about California, Indiana, food, women. Owens said the problem with Korean
whores was that, basically, they were white. "White women don't
fuck worth a shit," he said. "Good to look at but no good on their
backs." After another hand of Go Fish, he retracted the statement.
"Truth is, this guy in basic told me that about white women. I
never really had much luck with women, really." A jeep rattled by.
Owens watched as if it meant something. "Truth is, I never had *any*
luck with women." He turned back to Joey, put the deck of cards
on the dash. "Look at this." He pulled out his wallet, opened it,
removed a photograph, and held it up to Joey's face. The photograph was of a beautiful white girl with long dark hair parted down
the middle.

"Who is she?" Joey asked.

"Her name is Barbara. I met her in geography."

"You go out with her?"

"You kidding? She gave me her picture when she found out I was going in the army." He turned the photograph to look at her again. "I hardly know her really. I seen her at school and stuff, but I don't know her mother or nothing. You think I'm stupid carrying her picture?"

"You mean everyone goes to the same school out there?"

"Yeah. Ain't no girls in your school?"

"Plenty of girls. No Negroes."

"Yeah. So this guy in basic told me carrying pictures of white women would either get me crazy or get me killed." Owens put the picture in his wallet, shuffled the cards. "He said I got the sickness of screwing black girls and pretending they're white."

Joey thought of himself with the whore, thinking of June.

"He's crazy," Owens said. "I never even been to bed with a woman, and he's telling me what I'm thinking." He began dealing the cards.

"Forget it," Joey said.

"What I'm worried about is getting shot up or killed, and I never do sleep with a girl. We *could* get killed here. There should be a rule."

"For the army or for the enemy?"

Owens laughed. "You think the communists would cooperate?"

"You think the army would?"

Owens took the picture back out of his wallet. He looked it over again carefully, then began tearing it into pieces. "If they ever do pass that rule, I don't want any doubt about me being eligible." He threw the pieces of photograph into the space between them in the cab. The pieces fluttered to the seat and floorboard like disembodied wings.

"We really could get killed," Owens said. "Especially *you.*"

"You have a 7?" Joey said.

Owens shook his head. "Think that's why Anderson took you to Suzie's?"

"What do you mean?"

"You know, the rule."

Joey shrugged. "I slept with a girl just before I left Michigan City."

"Really? You got a queen?"

"Go fish," Joey said. He told Owens about June Norris, the night on the outfield grass. He told him about her pointing to the stars, pulling her dress over her head. They played another hand of Go Fish, and Owens asked Joey to tell it again. Afternoon faded into evening, night. They huddled in their jackets, kept the flashlight pointed toward the seat. Owens made Joey tell the story five times. He liked the idea of animals in the sky. At midnight, they stepped out of the truck to look for Little Bear. The sky was too full of clouds. They climbed back into the cab.

"You think I could meet her?" Owens said.

"I don't know where she is. You have a 5?"

"You just asked for a 5. You don't know what college she's gone to?"

"Somewhere in Arizona or New Mexico. You have a 6?"

"Fish," Owens said, shaking his head. "I been to Arizona once. Nothing special." He spread his cards, closed them. "She'll be coming home for summer, won't she? I don't want to hit on her. I just want to meet her."

"Okay."

"As soon as we get out of this shithole," Owens said.

"Yeah," Joey said, "as soon as we get out of here."

"You think your pop mind me staying with you?"

"You could fix his car," Joey said, laughing.

"What's he got?"

"A Pontiac. A big one."

"Probably a lot like a jeep."

"Doesn't look like a jeep. Looks more like a boat."

"I wouldn't tell your pop I want to meet June," Owens said. "He might get the wrong idea. Got a 9?"

"Go fish," Joey said.

Joey lay on his cot, unable to sleep, trying to figure out why his brother could not read. He thought it might be his fault. When Dave was really young, Joey used to sit with him and hold a picture book open, pretending to read, making up stories to go with the pictures. He wondered if his brother thought reading was some mystical thing having nothing to do with black letters on white sheets of paper. He remembered taking a head of lettuce, peeling off a leaf at a time, "reading" them to his brother. He'd promised to show Dave how to read stories on plankboard fences, cardboard boxes, photographs. The fogged window of a transport truck, Joey thought. He began crying silently.

He often cried in his cot. One night he'd cried because Pato Rodríguez stood with hands cupped over his ears as words he couldn't understand flew at him. One night he cried because they were building a bridge over Water Street years too late. One night he cried because he was worried about crying so much.

He was crying when Sergeant Anderson walked into the tent, squatted beside his cot. The gray stubble on Anderson's cheeks made him look ghostly. Joey tried to stop crying, couldn't. Sergeant Anderson said nothing, waited, finally spoke, "When I heard Paul, that's my brother. When I heard he was dead, I cried. Bawled like you wouldn't believe. North Africa's an awful place. Not as bad as here, but awful." He rubbed his nose with his thumb and forefinger. "MacArthur probably spends half his time crying. Ought to, anyway." Sergeant Anderson waited again, but Joey still couldn't stop crying. "Tomorrow'll be better. Going to join a combat unit. The both of us. No more lolling around here."

He stood, then squatted again close to Joey, whispered. "Once, for a while, I heard this voice. Didn't tell me to do things, that was the frustration of it. I could hear it but couldn't make it out. I'd think, it's the wind, or it's my lungs, or those noises that go on in the back of your skull. But it was a real voice and one night I finally made it out. It was asking questions."

Anderson whispered so close that his stubble brushed against Joey's cheek. Joey stopped crying.

"It asked, 'How is it?' and 'What of it?' and 'What are you waiting for?'" Anderson paused for a long time, then put his hand on Joey's shoulder. "We're soldiers. Tomorrow'll be like old times."

"What old times?" Joey said.

"I'll take care of you. Way my brother took care of me."

As soon as Anderson left, Joey cursed him, angry to have been caught crying over his brother. He wanted part of his life kept sepa- rate from Korea.

During the first day of the fight for Hill 409, Joey kept low in a bunker, shot his rifle at a large-leaved tree in the distance. The drive from the support unit to the front had taken less than an hour. In minutes he was in the bunker. The hill was a long, gradual incline, wooded near the top. Some strategy was being played out, Joey was sure, but all he could make of it was that the North Koreans controlled the hill, firing from behind the trees and foliage, and the army wanted it. Joey thought of several alternatives to fighting over the hill—a trade could be worked out, graders could level the thing, citizens of Michigan City could pitch in and buy it.

Joey was ankle-deep in icy mud. When the call came to withdraw, his feet were as heavy and awkward as bowling balls. He tried to run, slipped, fell, the icy ground hard as concrete. He flattened himself against it, crawled. Beside him a man yelled, "Jesus, my father," stood straight up, hands at his face as if he'd remembered something important. Mud covered his right shoulder and arm, his helmet tipped slightly to the left, his startled eyes the color of wet grass. Joey knew the standing man would draw attention. He rolled left, began running clumsily. He heard a burst of fire behind him and a sound like a baseball landing in a mitt. He didn't look.

That night, huddled around a small fire with a dozen other men, Joey tried to imagine pistons moving up and down like the legs of chorus girls. He thought about the Green Foxes' first baseman calling out "cinnamon" as he died, as if he were trying to tell Joey something, to let him know what to expect. Joey had no idea what to expect.

Sergeant Anderson squatted next to him, put his arm on Joey's shoulder. "We'll take that hill tomorrow," Anderson said.

Let them have it, Joey thought. There were thousands like it in Korea that had no North Koreans at the top.

Before the night was over, it had begun to snow.

During the second day of the fight for Hill 409, Joey muddled forward slowly across the snow-covered ground. He was frightened, crawling on his elbows and knees. Snow soaked through his clothing, and he lost some of his fear in the cold. The crawling forced water into his boots. His feet grew numb. From behind, the firing stepped up to provide more cover. Joey believed he would die that way, from friendly fire, although the yellow flashes kept coming from behind the trees at the top of the hill as well. Suddenly the ground in front of Joey erupted. He flattened, unmoving, terrified. His right foot felt warmer. It took him a few seconds to realize he had been wounded. The boot was filling with blood.

"Malone!" someone yelled. Joey had to resist the urge to stand. "Malone!" To his left. A man motioning. A ditch. Three other men. "Malone!" The air filled with sparks. "Malone!" Joey started crawling, keeping his head low. His feet didn't respond. "Malone!" He began rolling toward the ditch. The sound of mortar rose and fell like a scream heard through a revolving door. Suddenly he began flying toward the ditch. The impact of the explosion swallowed its initial sound, but the reverberations clanged in his skull. Hands pulled at his arms. Beneath the echo of the bell he heard a voice. "You ain't even hurt, bud." The blue of the sky rushed out east and west, leaving an enormous white.

A pair of feet, Joey saw them in the tangle of legs at the end of the ditch, thought they were his. He tried to move them, but the thick boots whiskered with frost would not budge. He brought his right hand to his mouth, covered his fist with a cloud of warmth. He believed he was ready to die. The night was silent, dark, lit only by a quarter moon. He hoped his death would be like Pato's, that the moon would dim momentarily, then, with a surge of light, become full. Joey felt his eyes draw closed. "Cinnamon," he said, laughing. The quarter moon became dim, distant. He closed his eyes, opened them. The urge to close them became more insistent. He opened them one last time, saw the full face of the moon near enough to touch. As his eyes closed, he heard a voice say, "I've found you."

The woman in the silent shoes with a dozen dog tags hanging

from her wrist passed through the space between the beds. The man in the next bed tapped the floor so Joey would look at him. "I had the best treeing dog in Ballard County," he said.

Joey nodded.

The man pointed to his head. "The doctors here keep their heads in their hats, putting them on in the morning, taking them off before bed. They don't know what it is to be human."

"I had a dream," Joey said, "where the nurse had fingers strung around her neck."

"It wouldn't be so bad," the man said, "but I hate to leave before catching my limit."

They lay still. Joey listened to their breathing, believed the words had some value. He turned again, but the man had fallen asleep. Joey wanted to ask about his feet. Although everyone could see he had lost his feet, Joey couldn't help telling people. He wondered where they were. He thought the doctors might keep them floating in a large jar.

The doctors told Joey he was disoriented.

Dr. Perkins loved Joey's stumps, said he couldn't have had better care, that he was a showcase of army surgical skill. When Joey asked what he'd done with his feet, the doctor's face turned gray and he wouldn't say. He assured Joey that they were not in a laboratory jar. "The army does not keep feet," he said.

Joey stared at the end of the bed where his feet should be. He tried to spread his toes and could feel the muscles in the balls of his feet tighten, relax, threaten to cramp. "Phantom feelings," the doctor had said. Joey didn't believe him. Somewhere, floating in formaldehyde, his feet were dancing, he was sure.

Sergeant Anderson sat next to the bed in dress uniform, his back erect, his jaw set. He and Joey stared not quite at each other, one waiting for the other to begin.

"Proud of you," Anderson said.

"I lost my feet," Joey said.

Sergeant Anderson grimaced, tensed his neck. Joey thought he was holding something back as if angry. "I know, Malone. I know that." He looked over Joey's head at the wall.

They sat for several moments in silence. Joey felt he should say something. It dawned on him that he was going home and Sergeant Anderson couldn't control him now. Joey said nothing. Anderson's face was rigid, red, the muscles around his cheekbones thick and tense. Joey believed Anderson was about to burst into anger, say he should be proud to give his feet for his country. Joey looked away. It didn't matter, he thought.

When Joey looked back, tears were running down Anderson's face. "I searched for you. After the firing died down. If I'd gone another hundred yards, I'd found you. Finally did, of course." Sergeant Anderson cleared his throat, removed his handkerchief, wiped his face.

Joey again felt that he should say something. He had nothing to offer. Finally he asked, "What do you think they've done with them?"

"With what?" Anderson removed his dress hat, held it in his lap.

"My feet."

Anderson stared at Joey several moments, then crossed his legs. "Had to identify my brother by his hands. Most the rest of him was gone, just gone. I kept thinking, *This is Paul, this is Paul*." Sergeant Anderson put his dress hat back on, uncrossed his legs, then took his hat off again. "My brother had big hands, like a boxer's." He made two fists, held them at his chest. "What they showed me were two little cauliflowers."

"I can feel my feet," Joey said. "I can wiggle my toes."

"Everybody gets things taken away from them." Anderson stood. "Got to make do with what's left." He shook hands with Joey for a long time, then left him.

Owens came late, had to wake Joey to talk. It was after visiting hours, but the nurse made an exception.

"You all right?" Owens said.

Joey opened his eyes, looked at Owens running his hands up and down his arms.

"You all right, man? It's colder than Bejesus out there."

"I lost my feet," Joey said.

"That's what I heard. I'm sorry, Joey." Owens took off his green wool pullover cap, dusted with frost. "I got a deck with me if you feel up to it." He sat on the edge of the bed.

Joey raised himself up on one elbow. "What do you think they did with them?"

Owens shuffled the cards once, then looked at Joey. "They probably got a whole warehouse full of them."

Joey nodded. They played Go Fish. "Anderson worked it out that I could come," Owens said. "He told me, 'You can remake a human soul just like you can rebuild an engine.' What do you think of that? I don't think he's running with all his cylinders."

"You have a 4?"

"You just asked for a 4. He told me they took that hill the next day."

"So the communists are that much farther from Michigan City?"

Owens smiled. "Something like that." They played Go Fish again and again. Owens asked about the Negro in the next bed. Joey told him he'd seen the man crying during the night, his left arm, just a stub, twitching around like a propeller.

Owens shook his head, dealt another hand. "Tell me again. About June and Little Bear."

"It was the end of the school year," Joey said and told about the baseball field, June pointing, how she pulled her dress over her head.

When he finished, Owens walked over to the window. "Damn, Joey, more stars than you can imagine tonight. I know Little Bear is out there, if I knew where to look."

"Let me see," Joey said.

"How am I going to do that?" Owens said. They stared at each other for a moment before Owens began crying. "This fucking shithole," he said. He walked to the bed, slipped his arms under Joey's back and knees. "Be quiet," he said. He lifted Joey out of the bed.

Joey heard the nurse calling after them in a hushed voice. Owens carried him to the door and out into the night. The cold air wrapped around Joey's throat like a hand. The stub ends of his legs ached. He could no longer feel his lost feet.

Joey looked over the sky, blurred his eyes until he could make out the round buttocks and chubby head of a bear cub. He lifted his right arm into the air, pointed to the sky. "Ursa Minor," he said.

"Little Bear," Owens said.

They stared into a sky blistered with stars.

Rue

Susan Dodd has published two novels, No Earthly Notion *and* Mamaw, *and a second collection of stories,* Hell-Bent Men and Their Cities. *She has just completed a third novel,* The Return of Light. *Dodd has taught creative writing at Vermont College and the Iowa Writers' Workshop. She is currently Briggs-Copeland Professor of Fiction at Harvard University.*

"This collection is superb. Its breadth of imagination is what impresses me— Dodd's ability to range among varieties of character and situation; she is one of the most inventive new writers I have come across in a very long time."
FREDERICK BUSCH, 1984

Miss Rainey Roth of Wyoming, Rhode Island, did not believe in luck. Sixty-one years old, a self-sufficient woman with a business of her own, she had no time for hazy notions. People who believed in sudden strokes of good fortune, she thought, were simply seeking an excuse for idleness. Nothing was apt to help a person who wouldn't help herself.

This sensible attitude was not the least bit undermined or shaken when, on the fifteenth of September, Miss Rainey discovered she had won ten thousand dollars in the State Lottery. She became a winner (the word seemed remarkably foolish, applied to herself) not through luck, but through carelessness: someone had dropped the ticket on the path to her small herb and spice shop. Miss Rainey had never bought a lottery ticket in her life, and she wasn't sure whether her practical nature or her whimsical streak prompted her to save the numbered stub, to check it against the winning numbers announced in the paper a few days later. Either way, she was sure of one thing: she wasn't about to let the benefits of a rather silly accident alter her realistic outlook. Luck, indeed. Luck was largely a matter of paying attention.

Miss Rainey was accustomed to making decisions. She rarely sought advice, made up her mind with an almost savage authority. On the day her winnings were confirmed, she remained in the potting shed behind her house, where she put up flavored vinegars and scented toilet waters, potpourris and pomander balls. The scents from the drying sheaves of lavender and comfrey and sweet basil cleared her head. By late afternoon, she knew precisely what she was going to do with the ten thousand dollars which had fallen so peculiarly into her lap:

She was going to keep her feet on the ground.

She was going to pay off the remainder of the business expansion loan she had taken out two years ago with the Wyoming branch of the Old Stone Bank of Providence (an outstanding balance of $3,764.25, according to her records).

And she was going to get herself a proper divorce. Legal. Official. Once and for all.

The following morning, Miss Rainey phoned the bank. Mr. Gencarella, the branch manager, sounded like a rejected suitor when she told him what she was about. He congratulated her, however, and agreed to make the necessary arrangements. Miss Rainey made one more phone call. Then, dressed in the gray tweed suit reserved for important business, she walked to the foot of her driveway. Her coarse, curly hair, still more black than gray, was tucked into a wool beret the color of wild chicory blossoms. A silk scarf of peacock feather print was loosely knotted at her throat. With a gray-gloved hand, she reversed a hand-painted wood sign. "Open for Business . . . kindly consider the well-being of resident cats and visiting children. Drive with Caution," was changed to "Closed." No excuses. No promises.

The private investigator's office was in a nondescript six-story building in downtown Providence, within sight of the State Capitol. After checking the directory in the dim, narrow lobby, Miss Rainey took the stairs to the third floor. There was an elevator, but she was

not of a mind to wait for it. She needed to stretch her legs after the
long drive. At the top of the stairs, she followed a sign shaped like
a pointing hand: "Franklin R. Alfino, Room 302." It relieved her
that the nature of Mr. Alfino's services was not specified on the
sign or his door. She thought this boded well for his discretion.
The floor of the short corridor, speckled marble, was wet, and ammonia fumes made her eyes water. She passed three unmarked
doors with pebbled glass windows before reaching Room 302.

Its door ajar, Room 302 was just that—a room. Perhaps fifteen
feet square, windowless, uncarpeted. It contained one desk (gray
metal), three file cabinets (one oak, two green metal), a small black
safe, and a man in shirtsleeves who looked nearly as old as she was.
Miss Rainey was taken aback.

"I beg your pardon, I should have knocked," she said.

The man looked up slowly from the newspaper spread across his
desk. "No problem. Mrs. Roth?"

"Miss."

The man smiled. "Miss Roth. Come on in." He waved casually
toward a rickety folding chair she had not noticed beside his desk.
"Have a seat." He did not rise or fold his newspaper. "What can I
do for you?"

Miss Rainey occupied the chair gingerly and with the utmost re-
luctance. She could already see she had made a mistake. The office
itself did not disturb her, though it was certainly shabby and less
than clean. Still, it was utilitarian, like her own workroom in the
former potting shed.

The man, however, was nothing like herself. More to the point,
he was nothing like what she had imagined. A private investigator
should, to her way of thinking, look alert, energetic . . . perhaps a
bit sly. Mr. Franklin Alfino looked innocent and slothful. His narrow shoulders seemed pulled down by a center of gravity located in
his soft, round belly. He had very little chin, no hair to speak of,
and his brown eyes, too close together, looked sleepy. He reminded
her of a Rhode Island Red laying hen. She was hardly surprised
when he cackled.

"Don't like my looks, huh?" He leaned back in his swivel chair and stretched, exposing a rumpled shirttail. "That's the chance you take with the Yellow Pages."

"I beg your pardon?"

"Isn't that how you found me—the Yellow Pages?"

"In fact it is," Miss Rainey said.

"Figures." Alfino nodded. "Started with the A's, right?"

Miss Rainey felt herself flushing, as if she were caught in some ill-considered fib.

"Don't tell me Paulie Abrams is all booked-up?"

The fact of the matter was that Miss Rainey had ruled out Paul C. Abrams because she found his ad distasteful. She could muster little confidence in professional services commended to her attention by a large India-ink eye with spiky lashes. Franklin R. Alfino had been the second name in the phone book, limited to a simple line-listing. She had thought, or hoped, this might indicate reliability, serious-ness of purpose. His appearance in the flesh, however, did much to counteract that favorable first impression.

"I think perhaps . . ."

"Looks aren't everything," Alfino said. "Mannix I ain't. But you could give me the benefit of the doubt."

"Mannix?" Miss Rainey fingered the soft leather strap of her handbag nervously.

"The T.V. glamour boys . . . weren't you expecting somebody like that?"

"I do *not* watch television, Mr. Alfino. Nor have I had occasion to require the services of a private investigator previously. I didn't know what to expect."

"Let me tell you something, then—free advice." Alfino was grin-ning, and the expression made him look a good deal less sleepy. "There's sixteen of us—private eyes—in Providence. Another five in Warwick. I know all these guys, and you can take my word for it—none of 'em look much better than I do. Fact is, you could do worse."

Miss Rainey said nothing for a moment, a doubtful and worried crease in her forehead. Finally, while Franklin Alfino continued to stare at her, she smiled. "Pretty is as pretty does," she said.

The detective cackled. "So what can I do for you, good lady?"

"I wish to locate my husband," Miss Rainey said.

"I thought you said it was 'miss.'"

"I prefer it. My husband and I have been . . . estranged for some time."

"Okay . . . miss. What happens then—when I find him, I mean?"

"I would like you to make whatever arrangements are necessary for him to divorce me."

"You want to get divorced?"

"I want," Miss Rainey said, calmly and distinctly, "for *him* to divorce *me*."

"But—."

"I am willing to pay."

Alfino shrugged. "How much?"

"We'll cross that bridge when we come to it. In the meantime, he must be located."

"Whatever you say. Name?"

"Lorraine Elizabeth Roth."

"His, I mean."

"John Amos Dudley."

Franklin Alfino scribbled in the margin of his newspaper with a ballpoint pen. Without looking up, he asked in a monotone, "When and where, to the best of your knowledge, was Mr. Amos last seen?"

"Dudley." Miss Rainey sighed. "Commander Dudley. Point Judith Pier. He sailed for Block Island. The bluefish were running. He never came back."

"So he may have drowned?"

"He did nothing of the kind."

"How do you know?"

"Because he wrote and told me so. A postcard. Of the Watch Hill carousel."

"Have you got this card?"

"Certainly not."

"Don't suppose it'd help much, anyway. He tell you where he was going?"

Miss Rainey sniffed. "'Where the spirit moved him,' he said." She saw Alfino trying to suppress a smile. "Even *I* had to be somewhat amused, Mr. Alfino."

Looking sheepish, the detective asked, "Why don't you call me Frank?"

"I'd rather not."

"I'm sorry?"

"Nothing to be sorry about," Miss Rainey said firmly. "I am simply not one for informality in business dealings."

Alfino studied her, and she saw she had been mistaken: his eyes were alert as a chicken hawk's.

"Back to business, then . . . Miss Roth. When did you receive this card?"

"I believe it was the first of July," Miss Rainey said.

"Postmarked—."

"The first of July, nineteen forty-three."

Franklin Alfino rubbed his eyes with his knuckles, as if he'd had cold water thrown in his face. "Ho, boy . . . ," he said.

"*You* can divorce *him*," her father's friend Judge Brimford had told her in nineteen forty-four, in his pleasant walnut-paneled study overlooking Narragansett Bay. "There is no earthly reason why you need ever set eyes on the scoundrel again, my dear." Rainey's father had recently died, and the Judge, retired, attempted to offer her *ad hoc* paternal advice and judicious affection.

Rainey had thanked the Judge and done nothing.

"*You* can divorce *him*," a Providence lawyer had pointed out in nineteen forty-six, when Rainey was buying the farm in Wyoming with the intention of beginning a new and independent life. "A legal notice is published. A brief wait. Then, if he doesn't appear— which we may assume he will not—the divorce is granted. *Pro forma.*"

"But *he* left *me*," Rainey said.

"Immaterial."

It was not immaterial to Rainey. She had thanked the lawyer
and left.

"*You* can divorce *him*," Franklin Alfino told her now. "Much
simpler."

"So I understand. That is not, however, what I want."

Alfino sighed. "Have it your way."

"I intend to," Miss Rainey replied. She did not leave until she
had answered all the detective's questions and written him a check
as a retainer.

Driving back to her farm, Miss Rainey Roth felt cautiously op-
timistic. Perhaps Franklin R. Alfino was unlikely to set the world
on fire, but he knew how to take direction. And he was evidently
not as befuddled as he looked. The hourly rate he proposed to
charge for his services seemed reasonable. Besides, Miss Rainey
didn't relish the prospect of another go at the Yellow Pages. The
private investigators of greater Providence were probably not, as
Alfino had suggested, a particularly congenial or impressive lot.
Now that she had selected one, she might as well give him a chance,
the benefit of the doubt.

Ten days later, Miss Rainey was arranging bittersweet and marsh
grasses in lacquered Chinese baskets when she heard a car coming
up the drive. Although her automotive knowledge was limited, she
recognized the sound of a car in desperate need of a new muffler.
She winced at the unwholesome racket upsetting the late morning
calm, but kept on with her work. Footsteps scattered gravel on the
path outside. She glanced through the small window and saw
Franklin Alfino approaching the shop. She went out.

"You've found him?"

"Nothing yet. Sorry."

Miss Rainey tried to keep impatience from her tone. "What is it,
then?"

"Had to come out this way, your neck of the woods. How about
some lunch?"

"You want me to give you lunch?" she asked faintly.

Alfino tossed back his head and cackled, scaring off a squirrel from some nearby shrubbery. "I want to *take* you to lunch. There's a little tavern, not far . . . on the road to Exeter. How about it?"

Miss Rainey's usual lunch was a cup of sassafras or chamomile tea with saltines or a slice of buttered bread, and she frequently forgot to have that until three o'clock. She looked completely astonished at the detective's suggestion.

"Best cheeseburgers in Rhode Island. Chowder's homemade."

"I look a fright."

"Take off that smock thing and I wouldn't mind being seen with you." Alfino's eyes hooded sleepily. "Besides, I want to talk to you. Business," he said.

He drove more like a tourist than a detective—slow, aimless, his concentration adequate, but sporadic. Miss Rainey leaned back and looked out the window, waiting for him to speak. He did not. When he pulled up in front of the roadhouse—a place she had never visited, but assumed disreputable—she regretted the ride was over. The leaves were beginning to turn, and she realized that she always worked so hard at this time of the year that she scarcely had time to notice the colors of the season. "Bittersweet," she thought.

The Hilltop Tavern was as dilapidated inside as its exterior promised. The air was stale, smelling of beer, tobacco, cooking fat. Several men in work clothes sat at the bar, drinking and staring at a television screen high in a corner, suspended from the ceiling. Miss Rainey could see that they were watching an old horse opera. She thought she spotted John Wayne, huge, gravel-voiced, and very young. Alfino led her to a booth in the opposite corner of the room, and she chose the side of the table which placed her back to the television.

"Place doesn't look like much, does it?" Alfino said. The remark was offhand, but she got the feeling he was trying to gauge her reaction. She paused, pursing her lips.

"Pretty is as pretty does," she said at last.

The detective grinned. "Wait till the chowder—that's *beautiful*."

A stout middle-aged woman in a white nylon dress and an orange calico apron, who had been standing behind the bar watching television when they came in, approached the booth. "What can I get you?" No menu was on the table and none was offered.

"Chowder and a cheeseburger?" Alfino asked Miss Rainey.

"I believe just the chowder will do nicely, thank you."

He turned to the waitress, whose bored gaze was drifting back to John Wayne. "And bring the lady some johnnycakes, too. I'll have the chowder, onion rings, a burger medium-well, and a Narragansett draft. You want a beer?"

For a moment, Miss Rainey thought he was still addressing the waitress. "Oh . . . no, thank you."

"What'll you have to drink?"

"Tea?"

"Don't have it," the waitress said.

"Then a glass of water, please."

"You got any hard cider in yet?"

"Yup."

"Bring her one of those."

Miss Rainey opened her mouth to protest, but Franklin Alfino startled her speechless by reaching across the table and chucking her under the chin. "Trust me."

"That it?" the waitress asked.

"For now," Alfino said.

Miss Rainey waited until she felt sure the woman was out of hearing before she spoke. "Mr. Alfino—."

"I wish you wouldn't call me that." He sounded aggrieved.

"Please—."

"I know, I know . . . you don't believe in mixing business with pleasure." He hunched his shoulders and seemed to duck his rather large bald head. "But you did come out for lunch with me. How come?"

"I had nothing to offer you at home," Miss Rainey said.

Alfino raised his mournful eyes and smiled. "You're honest, I'll say that for you."

"I'm afraid I never learned not to be. I'm a very solitary person, Mr. Alfino. I've not had much need for tact and pleasantries."

"You went to college."

Miss Rainey felt accused by the flat statement. "That has nothing to do with it."

"Don't get your back up. I just meant you talk like a person with education."

"A young ladies' seminary. In Boston."

"A seminary . . . you mean like a priest? What, were you going to be a missionary or something?"

"A seminary was like a finishing school, Mr. Alfino."

"Yeah? Are you finished?"

She smiled.

"What'd they teach you there, on the level?"

"To speak like an educated person. Tact and pleasantries, too, I suppose . . . but I lacked the aptitude. Or have forgotten, perhaps."

"You're all right," the detective said. "Pleasant enough for me."

"Thank you." She felt flustered, like a schoolgirl.

"I'm going to college myself. Community college. Nights. Getting an associate's degree in accounting."

Miss Rainey blinked. "Why, that's very . . . commendable."

"Incredible, you mean." He laughed. "I'm sixty-four . . . don't ask."

"You look a good deal younger."

"Lady, you say you got no tact?"

Miss Rainey squirmed uncomfortably and the vinyl seat-padding under her squeaked. "You said we had business to discuss?"

Alfino's face resumed its somnolent expression. "I haven't been able to turn up a thing."

"So I gathered. I didn't expect this to be uncomplicated."

"Did you expect it to be expensive? Because I gotta tell you, the hours are mounting up."

Miss Rainey raised her chin. "I'll decide when I can no longer afford your services."

"Hey, don't get me wrong—I can use the work. But this could take months, and even then, it might be a blind alley. I'm just trying to be honest with you."

"Of course . . ."

"I hate wasting your money, when it'd be so easy to get you a
divorce without finding your . . ."

"Husband," Miss Rainey said firmly. "I am still married to him."

"Sure. And you don't want to be—that I can understand. What I
don't understand is—."

"You don't need to understand," she snapped.

The detective's nostrils and lips pinched, drawing together as if a
swift and shocking blow had been dealt to him. The waitress returned, and Miss Rainey looked away. Plates, bowls, and glasses
were set on the black formica table with unnecessary clatter.

Miss Rainey felt sorely distressed by her unintentional sharpness.
"I'm sorry," she murmured.

"You're right, though, it's none of my business—that part of it."

The waitress sauntered off again.

"I suppose that I *do* want you to understand." The admission was
clearly difficult for her.

"Never mind. Try the cider."

"He left me, so he should divorce me . . . people must take responsibility for what they do."

"You loved him?"

Miss Rainey looked severely at Franklin Alfino and did not speak
for a full minute. He waited, watching her face with eyes that were
alert under half-lowered lids.

"I did," she said finally. "But what's important is that I promised
myself to him. And John Amos Dudley promised himself to me.
Whether I loved him is beside the point, Mr. Alfino. I would have
kept my promise regardless. I *have* kept it, for thirty-nine years."

Alfino shrugged. "No disrespect . . . but what's divorce gonna
get you now?"

"Very little, I suppose you might say. But I've reached an age
where I don't care to leave loose ends."

Franklin Alfino picked up a dented soup spoon and stirred thick
white chowder in a gray plastic bowl. Behind wisps of steam, his
face was troubled. Miss Rainey reached for the pepper. Neither of
them started eating.

"May I ask you a question . . . a personal question, Mr. Alfino?"

"Shoot."

"What makes you go to college? Do you intend to become an accountant?"

His cheeks seemed to sag when he smiled, and the dark pockets under his eyes deepened. "I'm a little old to start over." He picked up a greasy salt shaker and held it, right-side-up, over his soup. "But I'm not . . . 'finished.' There are certain things still interest me, things I'd like to understand . . . I never really had a chance to learn them until now."

"Precisely." Miss Rainey nodded. "I want John Amos Dudley to look me in the eye."

"You think if he does you'll understand something?"

"I rather doubt it."

"But you'd have a chance to try?"

"I believe we understand each other, Mr. Alfino."

The detective leaned across the table and gently tucked a paper napkin inside the high collar of Miss Rainey's blouse. The bristly back of his hand brushed her cheek. "Your johnnycakes are getting cold," he said. "Eat."

Several weeks passed with no word from Alfino. Miss Rainey was not surprised, but she was restless. She busied herself in the shop, preparing for the holiday trade. The second week in October, summer returned to New England. For four days, the sun beat down on the tin roof of the work shed, making it unbearably hot. Crickets chirped at night. The cats, Oleander and Hyssop, seemed stupefied.

Miss Rainey tried not to allow the extraordinary weather to disrupt her autumn routines. She packaged extra sage and thyme for Thanksgiving stuffing. She tied whole cloves and nutmeg, cinnamon stick and cardamom seed in tiny muslin sacks and designed a new label with instructions for "Wassail Bowl." When perspiration dripped into her eyes, she swiped impatiently at her brow with the back of her hand and thought how the heat would dry the herbs quickly, sealing in their flavors. She kept busy. She kept her feet on the ground. And she kept thinking of John Amos Dudley, who had courted her in a late Indian summer like this one, wed her the first

week of Advent. Rainey had worn a silk shantung suit the color of
champagne—it was wartime, Chantilly and satin were considered frivolous. Her bouquet of white tea roses was bordered with
lavender and rosemary. Lavender for luck. And rosemary for
remembrance.

John Amos Dudley was a local boy made good by war. A Lieutenant Commander in the Navy stationed at Quonset Point, he
fought the enemy on paper. He was tight-lipped and clear-eyed
when Rainey's father inquired about the specific nature of his duties.

Commander Dudley was a serious young man. Only Rainey
Roth, with her high spirits and her quick tongue, could make him
laugh in uniform. He was the son of a brakeman for the Providence
and Worcester, and his family lived in a modest house near the rail-
road station in Westerly, Rhode Island. His mother had died of a
stroke during the hurricane of '38, and his father's heart had failed
the following year in a freightyard outside of Boston. John Amos
was their only child.

Rainey met him at a tea dance at the Watch Hill Yacht Club on
the last summer weekend of 1942. His dress whites were impeccably
tailored and pressed and his eyes were the color of the hazy horizon
over Montauk. They waltzed—something by Victor Herbert, she
recalled—and the plum-colored sleeves of Rainey's afternoon gown
had fluttered in three-quarter time against the uncompromising
white of Commander Dudley's shoulders.

Now, the extraordinary warmth and fragrance of Indian summer
revived her whirlwind romance, her scant months as a wife—continuing to live with her widowed father in the large, shingled house
on the pond at Haversham, while John angled for weekend leave.
She had still felt like a bride, when the bridegroom vanished, aban-
doning her and the war effort and the United States Navy, for bluefish and Block Island and the spirit that moved him.

"The spirit that moved him"—even now, nearly four decades
later, Miss Rainey realized that she lacked the frailest notion what
such a spirit might have been. On their wedding night, in a large
cherry spool bed in the guest room at Haversham (her father had

considerately gone fishing with Judge Brimford immediately following the ceremony), John had wept in her arms, confessing his longing to be a warrior of the sea. He had petitioned to be sent to the South Pacific, attached to a cruiser or battleship. The Navy's continued refusal to make him a hero perplexed and unmanned him. Rainey had stroked his wet cheeks, reassuring him of his manliness, secretly hoping to conceive a son as the proof her husband needed.

By late spring, John Amos Dudley had his assurances: he received orders to join a heavy cruiser in the Aleutian Islands and Rainey was carrying his child. In June, three days before he was to ship out, he sailed in a rented skiff toward Block Island, alone, with fishing gear borrowed from Rainey's father. Weeks later, when the Watch Hill postcard had come, Dr. Roth had quietly paid the owner of the skiff and purchased new fishing tackle. Rainey, at three and a half months, had miscarried the child she had been so certain was a son. She understood that the man to whom she had promised herself was a coward. Beyond that, however, "the spirit that moved him" eluded her.

It was this, the mysteriousness of John Amos Dudley's spirit, that most tormented Rainey. The yearning to see her husband's face once more was not prompted by passion or bitterness. Those, like the humiliation, had passed. But she could not abide knowing her life had been shaped and confined by something whose nature she failed so totally to grasp. And she supposed she wanted her husband to look her in the eye, to renounce her outright, because she still cherished a hope that she might yet make a man of him.

For a time, government men had come to the house at Haversham, full of probing questions about the Lieutenant Commander who disappeared. Rainey and her father were both shamed by the accusations implicit in their questions and their flat, official eyes. But there was nothing to hide. When she received the picture postcard of the Watch Hill carousel (a New York postmark), Rainey had relinquished it to her government gladly. Her aging father, retired from medical practice, had been gentle, noncommittal, eager to avoid his daughter's gaze. He did not live to see the end of

the war, and Rainey felt her disgrace shortened his life. In her innocence, she had consorted with the enemy.

Now, as the sun beat down on the tin roof, Miss Rainey Roth
twisted stalks of marjoram into Advent wreaths, inhaled the heady
smells of dill and basil and oregano, and looked back on the chapter
of her life whose ending she would finally be able to write, thanks
to a numbered chance carelessly dropped on her garden path. She
fashioned nosegays of strawflowers to adorn the doorways of fussy
women with cheerful, orderly families. She filled them out with
sprigs of eucalyptus for scent. Rosemary for remembrance. And she
waited to hear from Franklin R. Alfino, Private Investigator.

The odd, misplaced hot spell passed and autumn returned. Now
the air had teeth in it. Miss Rainey removed her woolen cardigans
from the cedar chest in the attic and hung them outdoors to let the
wind lessen the pungent odor of southernwood. On cold mornings, she plugged in a small electric heater in her workroom. She
massaged her stiff fingers with warmed camphor oil at night.

It was a chilly overcast morning, and she was standing with her
back to the heater, pasting hand-lettered labels on bottles of pale
pink chive blossom vinegar, when Franklin Alfino returned. She
did not hear him approach until he opened the door, setting her
Japanese glass windchimes clashing.

"Good Heavens!" A handful of bright paper squares flew from
her hands and floated to the floor.

The detective squatted awkwardly and began to gather up the
scattered labels. "Scare you? Sorry."

"Startle a body out of her wits," Miss Rainey muttered.

Alfino straightened up and gave her a mildly reproving look.

"Don't mind me," she said.

"Get up on the wrong side of the bed?"

"It's getting up that matters." She tried to sound businesslike.
"Have you something to report . . . or do you just happen to be 'in
my neck of the woods' again?"

"Got anything around the house for lunch?"

"It's ten o'clock in the morning, Mr. Alfino."

The detective smiled good-naturedly. "I learned how to tell time at detective school, Miss Roth. Got any coffee?" He looked pointedly at an electric percolator on the corner of her workbench. It was plugged into an extension cord which reached, just barely, to an outlet halfway around the room.

"Herb tea. I do not approve of coffee."

"Don't know what you're missing. I'll settle for anything warm, though . . . even if it tastes like boiled socks."

Miss Rainey brewed tea in a tarnished copper kettle she took from the windowsill and placed it on the table along with two chipped earthenware mugs. Alfino cleared a space among the litter of vinegar bottles, labels, and glass cannisters of loose herbs. Without speaking, they sat side by side on the two rickety chairs which had once belonged to the austere dining room at Haversham. Miss Rainey took the mug without a handle and the chair with a loose hind leg.

"This isn't so bad," Alfino said.

"Lemon verbena, the herb of enchantment."

"You putting a spell on me?"

"I might try, if I thought for a moment it would get you down to business."

Alfino bowed deferentially. "All you gotta do is ask, good lady."

Miss Rainey's hands, trembling slightly, closed around her spotted brown mug. "I am asking," she said.

"I've found him."

"Where?"

"I don't know how to say this tactfully."

"Never mind that. Where is he?"

"In New Bedford. In a cemetery."

Miss Rainey Roth stared at Franklin Alfino. Her eyes, glistening with anger, were fiercely blue. "He's dead?"

"Almost fifteen years. I'm sorry . . ."

Her lips flattened out in a hard, straight line.

"Maybe it's just as well," Alfino said uncertainly.

Miss Rainey replied slowly, in a choked voice. "It simply is not . . . acceptable." She started to get up. Then, without warning, her mouth framing a small silent "o" of distress, she slumped to the floor in a dead faint.

She awoke on the horsehair sofa in her own front parlor. The air was musty, for the room was unused and unloved. Her father's fine furniture surrounded her, dusty and unforgiving. Franklin Alfino bent over her, covering her with his raincoat, a rumpled tan thing she had noticed when he first arrived: at last, something about him seemed to fall in with his occupation.

Miss Rainey came to like a person taking charge of a small emergency. "Don't fuss. I'm fine." When she sat up, too quickly, the color drained from her face. She dropped back against the sofa cushions. "I'm perfectly all right."

The detective wrapped the soiled sleeves of his coat around her shoulders. "Now, just take it easy for a few minutes."

"I never faint . . . must be coming down with something."

"A shock. Want some water?"

"What happened to him?"

"Your—."

"Husband," Miss Rainey said firmly.

"We'll talk about that later." Alfino looked uneasily around the cold, formal room. "Nice place you've got."

"We'll talk about it now, Mr. Alfino."

"You ought to—."

"Now," she repeated.

Alfino sighed. "Seems he drank himself to death. Put in a State institution in '65, died within a year. He was buried there. No living relatives, he told 'em."

Miss Rainey closed her eyes, nodding weakly.

"You sure you're all right?"

"He never even looked me in the eye." She turned her face to the rough, stern sofa-back, and the detective realized that she was weeping.

"It's finished," he said softly. "You're rid of him."

"No," she whispered. "I am not."

The following week, Miss Rainey sent a sizable check to Franklin R. Alfino, Private Investigator, for services rendered. She was free of debt, and nearly a thousand dollars were left from her lottery winnings. Her feet were on the ground, her business was unencumbered, her unfortunate past dead and buried. She tried to summon up satisfaction over the loose ends snipped from her life, and she kept about her work. In her herb garden, only the rue— that bitter shrub symbolizing repentance and said to restore second sight—remained green. She cut it back, pausing to bruise a handful of leaves and rub their oil on her forehead, for her head often ached. The Four Thieves . . . blind Adam . . . the Pharisees . . . it was a poor company she joined, anointing herself with rue.

The shop was doing a brisker business than in previous years. People seemed more interested in caring for themselves properly. Miss Rainey expanded her stock, devised more appealing labels and packaging, lectured at the town library and the Women's Club on the healing properties of common herbs. Exhausted at the end of each day, she took herself off to bed and courted sleep with hops tea and an inventory of her blessings. She was, after all, independent, content.

Something, however, had come over Miss Rainey Roth of Wyoming, Rhode Island. Mary Alice Potter, the town librarian, marked the change. So did Mr. Gencarella at the bank. Miss Rainey looked well enough, but her step seemed slightly less determined, her shoulders less straight. When she addressed the Friends of the Library, her ideas did not seem quite so "definite," Mary Alice said. The lines in her face were deeper, yet softer too, as if sorrow had won a victory over disapproval.

In short, Miss Rainey had been widowed.

The first Sunday of Advent was bitingly cold. A furious wind lashed the last leaves from the trees and brought small branches down with them. Wearing a severe black gabardine coat which had hung in the back of her closet for a dozen years, Miss Rainey went to the foot of her driveway, turned over her sign, and drove to New

Bedford, Massachusetts, the port from which the stern Captain Ahab had pursued his great white nemesis.

She had called Franklin Alfino the day before for directions to the hospital. At first, he had refused to give them to her.

"What do you want to do that for?" he said. "Let the past stay buried."

"This is *my* concern," Miss Rainey told him.

"Mine, too."

"Why should you make it your business?"

"Like I told you, good lady, some things still interest me."

In the end, however, Alfino had given the directions and even offered to accompany her. Miss Rainey had turned him down with unaccustomed gentleness. "I must do this myself. It's between me and—."

"Your husband," he said. "I understand." The detective sounded sad and old.

"Franklin?"

"I thought you didn't want to call me that."

"Our business is finished now," Miss Rainey said.

The State hospital was located to the west of the city, several miles off a straight, little-used highway. The cemetery, Alfino had told her, was to the left of the main gate, behind a grove of pines.

Miss Rainey was stopped at the gate. She rolled down the car window and informed the elderly guard that she merely intended to visit the cemetery. He told her where to park and waved her on without curiosity, pulling a plaid muffler over his jaw.

There were no other visitors in the graveyard, a small square tract of land made monotonous with rows of plain markers. Miss Rainey had no trouble finding the plot she wanted. It was identified by a gray granite slab the size of a dress box: J. A. Dudley, 1917–1966.

Wind tore through the trees. There was faint music from a nearby hospital building, but it could be heard only when the wind paused. The strains were brassy, but too sporadic for her to recognize. Miss Rainey stood beside the grave of her late husband, studying the two lines of letters and numbers meant to memorialize him, and trying to recall his face.

But even now, John Amos Dudley refused to look her in the eye. The face of the young Lieutenant Commander was darkly tarnished and dim, and the forty-nine-year-old drunkard buried here was unimaginable to her. Only a dazzling white sleeve and the color of the sky over Montauk came back to her. Miss Rainey waited. Behind the brutal wind, she thought she detected a waltz. But even as she listened, she knew she was making it up . . . as deftly as she had made up the contentment of her life.

When the breeze abated, the music made itself plain. A march— John Philip Sousa, if she wasn't mistaken. The false heartiness of parades and toy soldiers. Miss Rainey straightened her shoulders and gave a little shake of her head. Then she opened her handbag to remove a small pouch of unbleached muslin.

The dried herbs, mixed that morning, were comfortably rough and familiar to her fingers, something known and understood. She shook them from the sack, cupping them in the palm of her right hand. Then, when the wind picked up again, she tossed the handful of earth-toned bits and pieces into the swells of air. They flew from her hand and seemed to rise over her head before they dropped unevenly upon the final resting place of her estranged and long-gone husband:

> Rosemary for remembrance . . .
> Thyme for courage . . .
> And rue, the herb of grace.

Baby

Ivy Goodman studied at the University of Pennsylvania and Stanford University, where she was a fellow in the writing program. Stories from Heart Failure *have been included in the* O. Henry *and other anthologies. She is currently working on a novel.*

"*Ivy Goodman's stories are sharply original, sometimes brilliant, and often hilarious. Many take interesting, bold risks. Her style is spare and tautly controlled, her vision is both oblique and penetrating.*"
ALICE ADAMS, 1983

He shuttles from me, in Boston, to ex-wife and baby in Baltimore, to me, to baby. He vacations three weeks alone with baby. He wants to get to know baby. He wants custody of baby. And when he gets custody (last month he shattered a tea cup to prove how certain he is of getting custody), he wants me to help love baby. I kissed his hands, one finger bloodied, sliced by a jagged piece of china, and agreed to love baby. Already, more carefully than if they were my own, I love both the man and his baby.

Five months ago, I met the man at a party. Clearly, he wanted someone at that party. He is particular to a certain point, and then beyond that point he is not at all particular. For hours I watched him dance with a married woman who I knew would eventually refuse him. Eye to eye, hip to hip. Overheated, she took her vest off and stared at him as if that vest and the tight blue blouse beneath it mattered. Perhaps they did matter. But when she and her husband left, he came to me and talked about his baby.

"And how old is this baby?" I asked.

"Ten months."

"Do you have a photograph?"

"Not with me."

"Not in your wallet?"

"I don't have a wallet. But I have hundreds of pictures at home. Do you want to see them?"

"Yes."

"Should we go now?"

"Yes."

At least he had the integrity to wait until afterwards to bring out the baby. Naked, we sat in bed, turning over the baby in Maryland, the baby in Massachusetts, the drooling, farting, five-toothed baby, holding his toes in zoos and botanical gardens, lounging in trees, hammocks, the arms of his father, his mother. No, I was not spared the eleven duo shots of the girlish ex-wife and mother kissing the baby.

The beautiful mother of the baby. Will he go back to her? He doesn't go back. He goes on. Unknowingly, I, too, may be diminishing, a piece of the past that grows more evil with each new woman, each new recounting. The only unscathed one is that poor baby.

The baby. How does a woman who loves the father of the baby love the baby? By remembering that she is not the mother of the baby. When the father moves away, he will also take the baby. If I haven't already, I am doomed to lose both father and baby.

But why do I want them to begin with? When I could have an honest man and my own baby? Most days I am terrified by the thought of my own baby. About honest men: you must be honest in return, for who knows how long. But with the treacherous, you can be kind and honest while it lasts, knowing it won't last. In the end you suffer, of course. The surprise is how, and in which places.

Sometimes he held me all night. Sometimes when he heard me cry in sleep, he clawed my spine until I cried myself awake. When he planned a trip, I found the tickets on the bureau days before he told me he was leaving. ("By the way, I'll be flying to Maryland tomorrow." And after a pause, "Drive me to the airport at eight, would you?" Or, "Pack. You're coming with me.") For two weeks,

he telephoned every midnight, though now I haven't heard his
voice in sixteen days, and I tore open his last letter Saturday. It was
all about the baby. The baby is walking perfectly. The baby is making friends with other babies. In so many gestures and baby words,
the baby has stated his preference for road life with father, his dread
of that split-level crowded with mother, grandmother, grandfather,
and every baby toy available in greater Baltimore.

Yesterday, in stores, on the street, I laughed, waved, and clicked
my tongue at twelve babies, wheeled, cradled, backpacked, or carefully led by twelve women; yes, all twelve, women. He is probably
the only man on the Eastern Seaboard walking into a grocery at
10 A.M. without a wedding ring and with a baby. The woman he
leers at over piled grapefruit will want to laugh but won't, because
she's flattered, then will, because she's flattered. No wonder the
baby is making friends with other babies.

But I can't compete with strangers, pretending to be lured, as I
pretended to be, by his obvious glances, by his baby. He will stay
with one of them or another of them, or he won't stay. He will
come back, or he won't come back. Whatever his decisions, I knew
from the start they would have nothing to do with me.

All last night I drifted, nearing sleep but never finding it. I miss
him. According to plan, my ache spreads. I pit myself against myself. I'm losing.

I want another of our silent breakfasts, his head lowered to his
bowl, his spoon overturned near his coffee mug. I want to break his
mug. I want to do something to him.

He brooded. He thought he was entitled to brood. But his hor-
rors, described on cold nights, were no more horrible than mine;
he just thought they were. The stories he told and I listened to, I
would never presume to tell. And if I did, who would listen to me?

Because he only liked my hair down, when I pinned it up to wash
my face, I closed the bathroom door, but I closed the door for both
of us. What he didn't want to see, and more, I wanted never to
show him. And what he has seen I want now, impossibly, to take
from him, before he mocks it to amuse his next woman.

His woman. His women. He's stuffed a battered envelope with snapshots of us, already including one of me, full lengths, with legs crossed or, in a blur, crossing, heads turning, mouths speaking. He interrupted us and then, camera swinging from his shoulder, moved on. His ex-wife, mother of the baby, is actually his third ex-wife. From the glossy pile I try to guess the first two, but can't. Bodies, faces, wives, lovers, blend. We look tired; we are tired. Thinking practically, we want a good night's sleep and wonder if he'll leave soon. But we also think our shadowed faces have been brushed by moth wings. We feel more haunted than he. When he whispered what he thought was sad, we spared him what we knew was sadder. We let him pout, in a corner, alone. But even children keep their secrets. Right now, what is he thinking? All those silent times, what was he thinking?

In a friend's house, in a crowded room, I remember looking at him. He looked back. He shook his head. He could have been bedazzled. He could have meant we'll leave soon, but not yet. Or he could have wanted me to vanish.

Is he enigmatic, or is he just myopic? He's said himself that his eyes stare when he strains them. He should wear his glasses. I wonder, alone with the baby, does he wear his glasses? As a novelty, he was married the last time in thin gold-framed glasses.

Wed in March, parents in August, estranged in November, and now, divorced, he and his ex-wife hate each other. If I said, "I'll give you another baby," would he marry me?

I don't want a baby. No, I do want a baby. I covet babies. But which are instincts, and which are yearnings? Do I feel heartbreak or the rattle of dwindling ova? What do I want so, when I lie awake, wanting? And what if I did have his baby? He would leave me and try to take the baby.

In green motel rooms, does he rest his elbows on the rails of portable cribs and watch the sleeping baby? When he slept with me, I watched him. His ribs, wings, spread, closed in, spread, closed in. He strained. I wanted to make breath easier for him.

He was losing hair. He was losing weight. His skeleton was rising out of him. Each night, new bones surprised me. My fingers

stumbled. I want him again. I still want him. But my desire is di-
verted toward bedrolls, pillows, small animals seen from a distance,
and other women's babies. Or is my desire itself diversion?

I worry about what I'll do because I know what I've done. Also, I worry about that baby.

And at dusk, when the telephone rings and I answer it, I recognize his whimper, wavering behind his father's voice, his father, who, after weeks of silence, has called to ask if I know it's raining. "Yes, here it's been raining. Where are you, where it's raining?"

"We're both in a phone booth, about ten miles south at a Texaco."

"And you're coming back?"

"Yes. Soon."

Almost before I hear them or see them, I smell them, tobacco, baby powder, wet wool, cold; and after he puts the sleeping baby on the couch and touches me, just tobacco, wool, cold. "How's the baby?"

"A pain in the neck the last hundred miles, but fine now."

The baby, his face creased by his bent cap brim, stretches one fist, then brings it close, licks it.

"His cap."

"Would you take it off? I have to get another suitcase from the car."

When I bend down, the baby turns his head; his back curls. The cap slips, and I pull it free and put it on a chair. It is that simple. In the middle of the floor, where he'll be safer, I smooth a blanket for him. When I lift him, soft, willing, but weighted down by heavy shoes, he nestles. I untie the shoes. By the time the door slams, he is covered with his own yellow quilt and still sleeping. All the while, sleeping. His father says, "You've tucked him in, thanks. Too tired to talk. Tomorrow. And nothing's settled."

No, nothing's settled. In our bedroom now, flung across the bed, the other traveler also sleeps, his trousers damp, dragged black at the cuffs from the rain. I grab his sneakers by their heels and tug. When they hit the floor, he groans, rolls. His shirt wrinkles up above his rib cage.

"Too tired to talk. Tomorrow." If he hadn't been so tired, he might have laughed at his own joke. Why now, at the end, should we talk?

In the kitchen, I sit, the only one awake in this sleeping household. I don't want the man. I don't want the baby. But when the baby cries, I go to the baby.

Crows

Dianne Benedict teaches at the University of Southern Maine. She has
published in the Atlantic, MSS, fiction internationale, *and other magazines*
and is currently at work on a novel.

". . . uncommonly good stories by an uncommonly gifted writer . . . absolutely
singular in their effect on the reader, riveting, compounded of mystery and joy,
filled with luminous, often eerie connections. Benedict is the genuine article,
an artist who writes with individuality, clearness of expression, and sincerity."
RAYMOND CARVER, 1982

Evening was spreading over the long sweep of the land, darkening
the prickly-pear cactus into soft, hulking shapes that appeared to be
folding slowly towards the ground, like sheep for the night. A man
was traveling along the shoulder of the road. He was a tall, gaunt
man with a head that jutted forward, and he carried a shotgun
swinging easily in one hand. He moved lightly, almost but not
quite running. He wore an olive-green jacket and a felt hat, both
greased with sweat, and a pair of heavy wool pants that lacked a
number of inches in meeting up with his shoes.

Suddenly all the long, careless bones of this man drew together,
as if someone had tugged on a string at the center of him, and in
the space of a few seconds he had melted soundlessly into the ditch
at his side, raised his gun to the bead, and, without pause, pulled
the trigger. In the deepening, slow-breathing evening air, the sound
of this shot breaking barrier after barrier across the countryside
was like the end of the world.

The man darted forward a few paces and froze. Then the string
at his center fell slack, and, pushing his hat back on his head, he

rose to his full height, and spit sideways at a cedar post. He cracked his gun open and removed the spent shell.

A few yards ahead of him something rustled the weeds in the ditch. A large black fan spread open there, then another, and the thing bumped forward, scrabbling along the rocky ground, and then sank on its side.

The man cradled the gun in his arm, went forward and stood looking down at the thing in the weeds.

"Half-shot you a crow, have you, Myron?" he said. "Well, shit!"

The old clay-colored truck barrelled noisily through the growing darkness. Beneath the clatter of the stones in the truckbed, the tires hummed monotonously on the concrete road, and the tinny music from the radio drifted in snatches over the darkening range like reflections from a brightly colored Chinese lantern over a vast black lake.

Everything inside the cab was bathed by the green-white light from the dash. A small, plastic dancer in a real grass skirt was secured by a suction cup to the shelf behind the seat, and a pair of giant foam-rubber dice hung from the rearview mirror.

The old concrete road that the truck was moving on passed eventually in front of a nightspot called The Abandoned Hope. This was a place near the reservoir, with live music and a few cabins around it, and was very popular with the colored folk.

Next door to The Abandoned Hope was a small, run-down establishment for buying and selling used cars. It was owned by a man named Rich Stutts, a wiry, short-legged individual who dressed, winter and summer, in army fatigues with the sleeves ripped off the shirt. When the clay-colored truck was still about ten miles down the road, Stutts was standing in front of a fragment of mirror that he had propped up in his kitchen, combing his carrot-colored hair forward into a shelf over his eyes. Before long he and a new girl he had arranged to have for the evening and the two people in the truck would all join up together.

The young man in the truck, whose name was Jim Wesley White, drove with his arm resting on the open window. He steered with one thumb pressed against the bottom of the steering wheel. He

wore a dark maroon shirt with a white stripe in it and clean khaki
pants, and his straight brown hair, freshly wetted and parted in the
middle, still showed the marks of the comb. He was twenty-one
years old. He smelled of starching and ironing and Old Spice co-
logne, and he had a look of mystical innocence in his dark blue eyes.

Every few minutes he glanced at his companion. This was a
young woman with heavy, dark-brown hair held back by two tor-
toise-shell combs. She wore a flower-print dress with white cuffs
and collar, and she had a handkerchief with pansies on it tucked in
her belt. She sat with her hands in her lap, mile after mile, looking
out the open window.

After they had gone a long while without conversation, Jim
Wesley made a small adjustment to the rearview mirror. "Have you
ever been out to the lake?" he said.

"Yes," she said.

He looked carefully into the mirror from several angles. "Do you
know a man out there name of Stutts?" he said.

"Yes."

"That's where I work. I work at his place," he said.

"What do you do there?"

"Fix cars," he said.

"He has owned that place a long time," she said.

"Yes," he said. "He says he knows you."

She turned and looked at him for the first time since they had left
the city. "What did he say about me?" she asked.

"Oh, I don't know. I guess he said something about how you
played the organ in church. I said I knew that, naturally."

"I didn't belong to the church when I knew him," she said.

"Oh," he said. "Well, I guess he knew of it somehow."

Again, they drove in silence. Jim Wesley thought about the time,
a little more than a week ago, when he and Stutts were sitting on
the old split-up car seat in front of the shop eating freeze-dried
salted corn out of the little packages that were sold in the vendor.

"I knew her ten years ago when she was maybe sixteen years old,"
Stutts had said, and then he had had a great deal to tell about her,
most of which was impossible to believe.

"It's not the same one," Jim Wesley had said.

"It is. I know her. It's her." Stutts patted his pockets and brought out his cigarettes. "She was altogether different then," he said. "It was like some kind of voltage always coming out from her. Wasn't any way to understand her. She just started following me around. Just started coming out here to the lake all by herself in her Daddy's car. By God, I still puzzle over her."

"The way I heard it, she won't go out with anybody," Jim Wesley said.

Stutts laughed at him and flicked a kernel of corn at him that struck him on the forehead. "Maybe she would with a virgin," he said.

Jim Wesley reached over and emptied one of the bags of corn into Stutt's breast pocket and then laid his hand on the bulge. "Miss Eugenia," he said, "Would it make any difference if I told you I was a virgin?"

"Darling boy, it surely would," said Stutts. "I have to confess a weakness for virgin boys."

"Well, here I am," Jim Wesley said, and he grabbed Stutts by the head, and Stutts shoved him hard so that he fell off the seat onto the ground. He had wrapped his arms around Stutts' legs then, and Stutts had fought him off and kicked dirt on him and had gone, laughing, back into the shop.

Now, riding in the truck, he stole glances at her. She was quiet, strong-looking. Her arms were smooth and white, and the curve of her throat moved him, made him feel as if he were sinking, drowning even.

Before the talk with Stutts, he had never thought much of her. When she played the organ in church she had always seemed plain and somewhat awkward, sitting up on a level above the congregation. He had always thought of her, when he thought of her at all, as a sort of handmaiden of the Christ among the lilies that looked down on everyone from the stained-glass window over her head. But after Stutts had spoken with him about her, he had come up and had a conversation with her on the lawn in front of the church. She had said to him in her slow voice, as though it didn't even take

any thinking over, that yes she would go with him to the lake, come
Saturday night, or wherever he wanted to go.

Her father, a large man with pale, shaking hands, had been sitting on the porch swing when Jim Wesley drove up to the house.
The father was drinking wine from a plastic glass, and the bottle
was on the floor under the swing. The man's handshake was moist
and needful. His eyes begged for something. He had been a widower for years. Eugenia had stood at the edge of the porch steps,
looking out over the yard while Jim Wesley extricated himself.

Now, riding next to her in the truck, he thought about what
Stutts had told him about the way she had been. She had got religion, evidently. He pictured pulling the combs from her hair on
each side, watching it fall forward.

Her hands with their long, smooth fingers rested in her lap, the
palm of one turned upward. It was still with him, from when she
got into the car, the way her legs had swung in together, long and
strong under the thin, flowered cloth.

She would at least go walking with him by the lake, he thought.
Stutts would have the cabin ready like they had planned, but they
wouldn't necessarily have to use it. He didn't know if they would
use it. Sometimes, when he looked at her, he wanted to go into the
cabin with her like he had thought about; but at other times, especially when he looked over at her hands, at the one so relaxed with
the palm turned upward, he would feel a dull cold in his legs and
belly, and then it seemed to him that all that business related to the
cabin was impossible even to consider.

She couldn't say why she had come with him. Remembering
back, she thought perhaps she had come with him because the
smell of his after-shave lotion reminded her of being in school, and
she had momentarily slipped back to that time when, whatever a
boy asked you, you said yes.

Then she remembered distinctly that the moment he'd asked her
to come with him she'd had a sudden vision of the house she lived
in with her father, and how dark it was in a certain corner where the
stair turned, and up a little higher, on the second landing, a small

wire cage that had hung there as long as she could remember, with a few hulls still in the feed cup and the little wire door standing open.

When he had asked her out, she had been excited to picture sitting on the steps of the porch for the next few evenings thinking about going. Even though he was too young for her. She had felt a little pull, like the tension of a spring, under her breastbone.

She had been aware of him a long time at church. She had been very drawn to him for about a year now, maybe, and it had made her happy to have this feeling for him secretly without him knowing. She was struck by how perfectly proportioned everything was about him—the shape of his head, his brown hands that she could tell were not hard like a man's usually were, his eyes under the straight brows looking as though nothing could ever damage him, or even touch him, like stars glimpsed remotely through a tear in the clouds.

She wasn't able to look at him while they drove. She watched, in a long sweep of sky, the gold that the sun had left deepen into red. On the radio, a man was singing about how loving a woman was like being taken by the ocean farther and farther from shore.

"Look up ahead," Jim Wesley said. He was leaning forward peering through the windshield. The truck slowed.

"It's Myron Bless," he said.

"Who is that?" she said, but her voice was covered by the whine of the gears as they pulled off the road.

They drew up alongside a man in a felt hat and a jacket that was out at the elbows. The man squinted against the headlights and then stepped closer to the truck and bent down to look inside. He had a cracked-open gun slung over one arm, and with his other hand he held a crow by its thick black feet.

"Hey there, Myron," said Jim Wesley. "What are you doing out here?"

"Guess I'm after crow," the man said. He had a voice like a nail coming out of the wood slowly. "Or else they're after me."

Eugenia, watching the crow's head, saw a topaz eye appear, and then the man stepped back and smacked the head against a cedar post. After that he gave the crow a hard little shake as if he expected

something to fall out of it, and the beak and eye widened simulta-neously and there was a great swelling of feathers ending in a shudder.

"I wouldn't keep on with that business," Eugenia said, but then the man was coming towards them and looking inside again.

"I'm about ready to fold it up," he said. "You going to the lake, I'd appreciate the ride."

"Climb in," said Jim Wesley. He was already shifting gears. The man tossed the crow carelessly into the ditch behind him and went thumping up into the truck bed, and then they were once more on the road.

"Isn't much to look at, is he?" said Jim Wesley.

"Who is he?" she said.

"Myron Bless. Works for Stutts," he said.

She turned around and looked through the dusty back window at the felt hat that rubbed against the glass.

"What does he do?" she asked. She remembered the defiant topaz eye, the clenched black feet.

"Whatever he's told," he said.

Stutts took the girl by the wrist and pressed her hand up into the small of her back. He steered her through all the slow-moving black people on the dance floor. He found a little space for them to move around in, and he put his hands on her hips as she began to pick up the beat of the music. She was a new girl, a real dresser. She had on a tight-fitting silver dress with a halter top, and a cluster of rhine-stones on a black ribbon around her neck. She had arranged her red hair into a twist on top of her head, and under the blunt-cut bangs her eyelids glistened with green and silver dust.

When the musicians stopped for a break, Stutts took the girl over to the bar. After he had ordered the drinks, he put his hands on her back and massaged her neck a little, and she smiled and gave him a long look that said, yes, she was feeling that way, too. He offered her a cigarette and she took it and ran it slowly through her fingers while he lit the match.

The bartender brought the drinks and wiped the beads of water off the bar with his apron. "Jim Wesley White was looking for you a while back," he said.

Stutts swung around on the stool and looked out over the barroom, which was so dark and crowded it was hard to recognize anyone, but then he saw Jim Wesley and Eugenia sitting together at a table by the door.

The girl in the silver dress leaned close and said, "Who's looking for you?" and he squeezed her arm, high up where he could feel the warmth of her underarm, and then he left the bar and made his way across the room towards the other two.

When he leaned down between them and said, "I can get you a better table," Eugenia drew back as if there had been a bright light turned on her and looked up at him with her face tight as though against the glare of it.

Stutts said, "Miss Crawford and I have met before, or do I disremember," and she said, "No, that's right."

White smiled back and forth at the two of them and said, "What do you know about that."

Then the girl from the bar came up and asked to be introduced.

It was well into the evening when Stutts asked Eugenia to dance. He picked a slow number and pulled her to him as soon as they reached the floor. She moved lightly against him, not holding onto him noticeably, but not pulling away, either.

"Been a long time, isn't it?" he said, and she said, "Since what?"

"Since we were dancing together," he said.

She made no reply.

"Hell, since we got this close or anything," he said.

"It was nine years ago," she said.

"I always did remember you," he said. He drew back and looked down at her. She was looking away to the side.

"I knew you only about a month in the summer, I think maybe it was ten years ago," she said.

"But you never did forget me, neither."

"That's right," she said.

He smiled down at her. "You remember all that?" he asked her.

She looked up at him with that look like being under too bright

a light again, and said, "Do I remember all what?"

"You and me," he said.

"And the others?" she said.

He thought she meant maybe some other girls who must have been in the picture at the time, but she said, "I mean those others you liked to bring along," and then he remembered. He remembered a night when he had taken her out to the other side of the lake, and they had picked up two of his buddies on the way. He remembered getting her to lie with him in the back seat. The other men had sat up front, he recalled, drinking their beer slowly and acting like they weren't watching, only they were watching. He recalled how she had lain with him, not pitching in so as you would notice, but not pulling away either.

"I never did understand about that," he said.

She stopped dancing and stood back from him and looked up at him with an expression he couldn't put a name to.

"I mean that whole business there at the end," he said. "That's what we're talking about, isn't it?"

"It was a long time ago," she said.

"Well, sure," he said.

"But I still remember it," she said.

He stared at her. She had taken a handkerchief from her belt and was pressing it where the sweat glinted on her upper lip and under her eyes. A large man behind her bumped against her shoulder and she dropped the handkerchief, but she was walking away by then and she didn't stop to pick it up.

Eugenia walked with Jim Wesley on a path crossed with roots under some live oak trees on their way to the cabins. The cabins were duplexes, sided with brown asbestos shingles. They stood in a row, with carports between them. Beside each door grew a young cedar tree about the size of a ten-year-old child.

"We can probably sleep in the truck if you're worried about how it looks," Jim Wesley said.

"There's nobody looking at us," said Eugenia.

"Or I could maybe go leap off the pier," he said laughing, "and if I didn't drown I'd probably come up sober." He could barely walk. She had to keep her arm around him.

They reached the step of their cabin, and she took the key from him and opened the door.

"We're lucky to have a place," she said.

"Hell, yes, we have a place," he said. He held onto the doorsill and put his other arm around her shoulders. "Stutts would have given us *any* place. Hell, we could have had *his* place."

"He had this place ready all along," she said.

"Oh, I don't know if you can go so far as to say that," he said.

"You are too drunk to lie," she said. She put an arm around his waist and helped him through the door. He stood there looking around as though he'd never seen a bedroom before in his life.

The walls of the room were covered with a dull brown wallpaper that had strips of some kind of flowers in it. A merciless glare fell sharply on everything from a small ceiling fixture with brass arms and four glass tulips. There was a spindly iron bed covered with a quilt, and a dresser with a round mirror in a frame of heavy roses. Thrown down on the cracked linoleum, with its border of ivy vine, were a half-dozen rag rugs.

Eugenia led Jim Wesley to the bed. He fell upon it and immediately lay still and went to sleep. She sat beside him, looking for a long time at the dark window where she saw herself reflected. Then she slipped his shoes off his feet, placed them under the bed, and went into the bathroom.

While she was there she was sure she smelled the smoke from Stutts' cigarettes. He'd been in there, alright, she thought. He'd been in there, picturing how it would be. Well, he could never have in mind the way a thing really was. He could never have any part of it. He would always be thinking one thing, and the way it really was would be another. What did she care what he thought he had? She could let him have it, it was no part of her.

She was washing her face when she saw the two rubbers on a shelf over the sink. She stood with the water dripping from her face, thinking, of course, one for tonight, and one for in the morning. She picked one up and slipped it out of its little paper band and looked

closely at it. Then she put the paper band back on it and laid the
rubber on the shelf exactly where it had been. It was nothing to her.

She came out of the bathroom and walked barefoot over to the
door to switch off the light. She took off her dress and slip in the
moonlight and hung them in the closet, and then she took off her
brassiere and folded it and put it in the single drawer of the stand
beside the bed.

She started to undo Jim Wesley's pants, but he came alive suddenly, distressed and feverish-looking. "It was those damn mice got
under the clutch plate," he said. He pushed her roughly away and
got up and stepped out of his pants. Then he got back in bed,
under the covers. She watched the pinched look ease from around
his eyes, and then he was asleep again.

She got in beside him and looked for a long time at his face.
There were pale, milky shadows moving over him. The moon was
bright in the room, and, in the brightness outside, she could see
heavy rocking shadows cast down by the live oak trees.

She lifted back the quilt and then the sheet. He lay on his side
with his legs drawn up. His hands were pressed together between
his thighs. She opened his shirt and folded it back and laid her hand
on his chest. She put her mouth where his neck curved into his
shoulder and moved closer to him and pressed her breasts against
him. She slipped her hand down over his ribs and round over the
curve of his back and after that she took a long time feeling him
everywhere, slowly, because there was no reason not to in the quiet
room, no reason at all.

Sometime later, in the room on the other side of the wall, Myron
Bless eased himself down into a wicker chair. He had a package of
cigarettes in his pocket that he'd taken off of Stutts. When he took
the package out, he found that he was down to the last cigarette.
When he took that one out he flattened the package and made a
hard twist out of it and dropped it on the floor.

It was dark in the room. Every now and then the blind would
billow out at the window and then rest back with a little tapping

sound. Myron pinched the last inch of the cigarette between his forefinger and thumb, and each time he took a draw he held it up and watched the ember.

He was thinking about his first time and the boy it had been with. He hadn't thought on all that in a long time. He eased back into his memory gingerly, feeling all along if it was wise, and he knew, remembering, that that first one was the only one worth thinking back on. He had always known that. Long, boney, waterfront trash that boy had been, that first one, name of Kelly from a family of brothers that worked a trawler. Was no place to meet with him except under the wharf. They hadn't known the first thing about it, hadn't even known enough to bring something to put under them. It had only been just feeling each other, showing each other a little at a time, until the boy had told him one night that some other boy had showed him the way. Behind the unblinking ember, Myron laughed low in his throat. That's what the boy had called it, "the way," as if there was only that one. This is the way, the boy would say, and there in the dark wedge under the wharf, with chinks of light sliding over them as they moved, and now and then a heavy tread on the boards above them from some bloke come out to piss—there they would have what they wanted, and it was all there with that boy, by God, more than it had ever been again. He watched the tiny glowworms winding on the ember of the cigarette. You spend a lifetime looking, he thought, and all along it was only just that once, but you could never guess it. Not until it was all played out from here to hell and back, and it had let go of you, finally, and you didn't care no more. It was all only brackish water save for a time going too fast under a wharf, the deep sun-red of the arms starting at the shoulder and then the long white length of that boy, all hipbones and the hollows in the flanks, all that warm slippery business.

He felt for the ashtray on the stand beside the chair and ground out the cigarette.

Stutts would have that new girl with him, so there was no going home. Maybe he would walk by the lake until the first light, or maybe he would bed down in the boathouse. It was the sound of

the water under the wharf made that a good place. Stutts would
sleep late with the girl. Time to check in on them would be around
ten, maybe eleven. Be about then they'd be ready for breakfast.
Maybe today they would go on the shoot. It had been the crow he
had got by mistake had put him in mind of it, and he had brought
up the idea when Stutts had come home with the girl, and Stutts
had said, hell, why not, if he was back up on his feet by then.

Myron opened the door without touching the knob and eased
the screen-door open and stepped out onto the porch. He looked
down the long, shadow-banded path towards the lake. He felt the
moonlight on his face and shoulders, blue and bright and quiet. He
patted his pocket for the cigarettes, then remembered they were
gone. After a moment he stepped down onto the path.

Eugenia knew there was someone in the other room. There had
been no sound, but the smell of smoke had come again strongly,
and she knew with some slow-rising sense that there was someone
there, and then she heard a small sound on the path and knew that
he had gone.

She got up and took her watch out of the pocket of her dress and
looked at it, and then she went and stood in front of a picture hanging on the wall between the two rooms. It was a picture of three
cowboys around a fire, with a horse tied up in the background. One
man was playing the harmonica and the two others were smiling at
each other across the fire. One of the smiling men was bent forward
passing a plate with a fish on it across to the other one.

Eugenia went up and took the picture down and stood looking
at a hole in the wall. She put her hand in the hole and felt wood at
the back of it. Then she found the place on the picture where there
was a slit in the paper just wide enough to look through. She put
the picture down and went out onto the porch.

The door to the other room was ajar, and when she went in, the
smell of smoke was strong and also the feeling was very strong that
the person had just left.

She switched on the lights. On the floor, propped up against the
wall between the two rooms, was a picture of a Japanese woman

holding a small brown bird on the back of her hand. On the wall above the picture there was a length of wood that could be pushed aside. When Eugenia pushed it aside and looked through, she saw Jim Wesley asleep in the moonlight, uncovered except for one leg wrapped in the sheet.

She turned and looked about the room. The bed looked as though it was made up with only the spread, without any sheets or blankets underneath. There were cigarette butts in an ashtray beside the chair. She bent to pick up a twisted cigarette package that lay on the floor, knowing it was a package of Stutts' Lucky Strikes even before she spread it open.

"He was watching us," she said.

She moved in front of the long mirror over the dresser. Slowly she raised her arms with the wrists crossed and looked at herself that way. She was the color of plaster in the harsh light. Her dark nipples were stark on her white body and her shoulders were nothing but bone. Her eyes were like live coals far back in a cave.

She leaned over and pushed an ashtray across the glass top of the dresser slowly until it reached the edge and dropped off. There was a vase on the dresser also, half full of water but without any flowers in it, and she pushed that slowly over the edge, too.

Then she crossed the room and sat on the edge of the bed. She sat there looking down at her hands pressed together between her knees. After a while she lay back. She lay stretched out on the bed for a long time, with her eyes open, under the harsh overhead light. It was like being under the eye of the sun in the desert. Some time later, when the dawn came, she was still lying there in the same position, but her eyes were closed by then and she was asleep.

Later that day Jim Wesley sat beside Eugenia in the back of the truck taking a hard ride. Stutts was up front, driving, with the girl from the night before beside him, and also Myron Bless. They drove over rough terrain, swerving constantly to avoid the prickle-bush and low mesquite, heading out for a place Myron knew about that he said was virgin ground.

Jim Wesley would have had no wish to speak, even if he could

have been heard over the crack of stones on metal. He rode along with his eyes fixed on the guns. There were five guns—the three shotguns, and the two rifles for the women. Packed alongside of them was a wooden toolbox, a cooler full of drinks, and a small battery-operated gramophone that Stutts had wrapped up in a blanket.

It was a long ride. It seemed to Jim Wesley like it would go on forever. They had been driving across open country for an hour, and now it was well on towards evening, with the sun sinking low enough to be flattening out, and the beginning of a thin pollen-colored haze drifting up from the horizon.

After a while the truck lurched and slowed down as Stutts shifted gears; then they took a sudden turn and picked up speed again. Jim Wesley hauled himself up, bracing against the wind, and saw that they were approaching three great wide-spreading live oak trees, darkly silhouetted, behind which the sun was going down very deep-colored and swollen.

When they were about a quarter mile from these trees, they came to a table of stones that fell away to the trees and beyond them, and Stutts stopped the truck at the edge of this rubble and got out and came around to open the back end. Then Myron got out and came around, too, and they hauled out the toolbox and three of the guns and the blanket with the gramophone wrapped up in it, and headed for the trees.

Jim Wesley stood in the truck watching as they made their way over the stones. Behind him, Eugenia sat turned in on herself, with her arms around her knees. She was dressed in a long-tailed khaki shirt and a pair of army pants of Stutts'. There was no sound except a slow, melancholy country beat coming from a radio inside the truck.

After a few moments the door of the cab opened slowly and Stutts' girl climbed down, her skirt stretching taut over her thighs. She had on the same spike-heeled shoes and silver dress she'd worn the night before, and a small radio hardly bigger than a package of cigarettes hung from a strap on her wrist. Without closing the door of the truck, she began to make her way unsteadily over the stones, following the men.

"Time to decide," Jim Wesley said.

The music drifted back to them from the girl's radio.

"You going to come?" he said.

Eugenia didn't answer.

"Whatever happened last night, I'm sorry," he said, and, when still she wouldn't answer, he said loudly, "only I swear to God if it's anything like I think it is I only wish I could remember it!"

"What do you wish it was?" she said.

"I wish it was just what you think."

"Well," she said, "Then that's what it was."

He thought for a moment. "I don't know that for sure," he said.

She rolled up the cuffs of the army pants. "I'm tired of the whole business," she said. She crawled to the end of the truck and dropped to the ground. He followed her and dropped down beside her and took hold of her arm. Her face turned hard and she tore her arm away from him and started after the others.

He hauled out the cooler with the drinks in it and the two remaining guns and hurried to catch up with her. The day was growing unbearably thin for him, yet still he was caught up in an expectation that was without name or reason, and he rushed foolishly after her, stumbling over the stones, with the two guns clutched awkwardly against him, and the cooler getting tangled up with his legs.

When he was even with her, she stopped and put her hands in her pockets and turned halfway towards him. "You were asleep," she said.

"When?" he said.

She lifted the edge of a stone with her foot, turned it over carefully. "You don't even have any idea of it. About all that," she said.

"About all what?" he said, and she glanced at him, frowning, with her face tight against him and then she turned and walked away.

"Listen," he said.

"I'm tired of the whole business," she said.

"Now, wait a minute," he said, and he began to hurry after her

again, but then he stumbled over the cooler and had to set it down, hard, on the ground in front of him. "What the hell's the sense in keeping secrets?" he called, but she had gotten far away by then and had no interest in even turning around to look at him, and so he didn't care to call out to her any longer.

"Bitch," he said softly.

He left the cooler sitting where it was. He went on towards the group of people under the trees. Someone else was going to have to come back for the cooler. It wasn't going to be him. The sun, setting behind the trees, cast long shadows towards him. He stopped and looked back at the truck. The door on the passenger side was still open. The truck looked like it was waiting for him. It was his truck. He didn't like it the way Stutts had driven it over the rough terrain. He was always careful about his truck, treating it as if it had feelings, and it had lasted him a long time. Stutts could ruin a truck in a day. But it was no matter to him, he could always get another one, easy.

Jim Wesley turned and continued, entering the shadow of the trees. No one in the group looked at him. Eugenia was backed up against the trunk, with her shoe off, searching around inside of it for a stone. Myron had his knife out, scraping away at what looked like a three-inch section of bamboo. Stutts lay stretched out on the blanket.

The girl in the silver dress sat off to one side. She was turning the dial on her radio slowly from station to station, searching for something. Snatches of voices slipped out, now a woman, now a man, now a line from a song, broken off.

The first crow appeared out of nowhere. No one saw it come, but suddenly it was there, moving along one of the high-up branches. Myron pointed it out to the others. "Here they come," he said.

Then there was another one, and they all saw that one, and the girl in the silver dress got really excited to shoot at it, but Myron said, "Chrissake, hold onto her, Stutts!" Just then, Jim Wesley called out, "Throw me one of those callers!" and Myron threw him one of the callers he had carved out, and then Myron and Jim Wesley began sending out calls that sounded like crows in a terrible rage.

"By God, they're coming!" said Stutts, and he put a record on the little gramophone he'd brought out there. When the record had picked up speed, he set the needle on it and turned the volume up on a recording of about a thousand crows all calling at once. This sound lifted and filled the space, and Myron and Jim Wesley blew more loudly on the callers, getting really excited over the sound of all the crows on the record.

Then there came the first answer from far away in the dark curtain of dust that the wind had blown up off the countryside. It sounded like maybe a half-dozen crows answering from different locations. But then it was as if a tidal wave of crows burst through some smothering barrier with a sound that intensified swiftly until it drowned out the record, and crows began dropping down out of the darkening sky into the trees. In a few seconds, the upper branches were thick with crows, all of them calling, and hundreds more dropping and swooping, until the sky was completely blacked out, and then the men took up the guns and began to shoot.

The crows fell heavily, like stones, and lay on the ground flapping and scrabbling, but still they came as if there was no end of them, flying lower, more brazen, many of them right into the guns. There was no time to count or even take satisfaction in the dead. There was only the rustling mass descending, ever-replenishing, deafening them, and the men loading up and drawing a bead, and blasting off, and doing this over and over, and all the while there were the ones in great number who were moving over the branches, calling and flapping as if there was nothing any different from every other day of their lives.

Then, over the terrible noise of the crows and the guns there came another sound, which was the girl in the silver dress screaming and screaming. Jim Wesley, when finally he heard this, looked over his shoulder and saw the girl with her hands to her face yelling towards Eugenia who lay close-by on the ground with a dark stain

spreading beneath her. He gazed without comprehension at this
scene and lowered his gun, sensing in that moment that he was the
only one shooting. Myron held his gun with the barrel pointed
down, and was shaking and white in the face. Stutts had dropped
his gun and was waving his hands as if to make everything quiet,
and was approaching with careful steps the place where Eugenia lay
looking so strange.

The crows overhead went on calling, but the record had played
out, and it was quieter, now, after the guns. No one spoke and the
girl had stopped screaming.

Stutts went down beside the figure on the ground and bent close
over it, but at first didn't touch it.

"She had the gun on you, Stutts," Myron said.

"She had what?" said Jim Wesley.

"I didn't have no other choice, she had the gun on you," Myron
said, this time louder, and then he dropped his gun and sat down
on the ground with a low cry.

Half an hour later Jim Wesley sat in the back of the fast-moving
truck, along with the gear, which had been thrown in helter-skelter.
The guns were vibrating and traveling over the truck-bed, first this
way and then that. When one of them got too close to him, he
would reach for it and throw it over the side of the truck.

The record player still had the little record on it, and the arm
with its needle kept bouncing back and forth across it.

He held the body where they had placed it across his knees,
wrapped up in the blanket. Again and again (it seemed to him he'd
been doing this for days) he had to keep covering it up. Still, she
kept getting exposed.

"We'll be there in a minute," he said repeatedly.

He gazed steadily at a streak of red trapped between two black-
nesses along the horizon. Above that began the wide expanse of the
night, with already a few stars.

The Phototropic Woman

Annabel Thomas grew up in Columbus, Ohio; she earned her B.A. from Ohio State University and wrote for the Columbus Citizen-Journal. *She now lives in the small farm community of Ashley, Ohio, where she writes unceasingly.*

"Whether the tale is grim, terrifying, haunting, or heart-wrenching, her manner of telling is exactly right. This is what marks Annabel Thomas's fiction with the rare stamp of originality and distinguishes her work among contemporary short stories. Her ability to move from scene to scene in story after story, each characterized by its own special style, makes us wonder where all these voices are coming from. Surely not from a single writer? . . . Affecting no moral, told flatly and directly in wonderfully accurate dialogue, her stories stick in the memory like a sad tick. I think it inevitable that Annabel Thomas will soon be recognized widely for the skilled and talented writer she is."

DORIS GRUMBACH, 1981

The woman was rolled up in a woolen blanket. It covered her body and even her head so that her world was warm and soft as an un-born's. When the alarm went off, she got out of bed and poked up the stove.

She put water to heat and when it was steaming she stripped to the waist and washed in the basin. She pulled a sweater over her head and plaited up her hair. While she drank a mug of strong black tea, she read the survival book.

After she put the shack in order, the woman took a coil of rope and a box of candles and walked up the sun-speckled path through the locust thicket between the green mossed rocks big as sheep sheds. She had worn the path carrying and dragging the provisions the book recommended to the cave.

The cave smelt of damp sandstone and of dust and still air. She

dropped the rope beside the boxes of canned goods and was counting the candles when she heard a noise like hundreds of nine pins falling onto a wooden floor. When she turned round she saw dirt and rock pouring into the mouth of the cave. Before she could move toward it, the opening was completely closed and she stood coughing in blackness.

The woman felt her way to the boxes and found the coal oil lantern and the matches. When the wick caught, the light reflected from a hundred rock surfaces overhead and around the edges while the middle was murky with floating dust. It was like standing inside a gem.

She took a pickax and dug where the entrance had been. She kept digging until she was too tired to dig any more.

"There's no use to that," the woman said.

In fact she wondered if she should try to get out at all, at least right away. Had she seen a flash of light just before the dirt came down? The woman stood still a long time thinking what she should do.

She began by pacing off the room. It was twenty by fifteen feet. Then she felt the roof, tracing it back to where it closed down like a clamshell.

She took the pickax and pried gently where the roof joined the floor. As she widened a crack in the stone she felt air rush through. She worked slowly and hesitantly, half afraid of digging out into poisoned air.

When the hole was large enough, she took the lantern and crawled into the opening. Working forward on her belly, she wriggled down through mud thick as grease. Her hair became caked and her clothes clogged with it. It went up her sleeves and down into her shoes.

The tunnel began to spiral like a corkscrew and to taper so that she got stuck sometimes, then squirmed loose and so at last came out of the tunnel onto the floor of a large room.

Wherever she shined the light she saw pillars with rock hanging from them in folds like cloth. She couldn't see the top of the room.

She circled the walls. There was no way out except the way she'd come in.

Back in the upper room, she scooped out a trench with the pickax, laid large flat stones over the trench and closed the cracks with pebbles and mud. At the higher end she built a chimney from a small hollow tree limb. At the lower end she placed a handful of shredded bark and struck a match to it. She added twigs, then larger sticks from the supply of squaw wood she had gathered and stored in the cave. She kept the fire small. Every move she made came straight out of the survival book. She called up the pages in her mind's eye, then did what they said. When the fire burned steadily, she cooked soup.

Working and resting, then working again, the woman slowly enlarged the tunnel, hacking out hand holds and foot holds until she could pass up and down easily. At the far end of the lower room she found a trickle of water spreading thin and soundless over the face of the rock. She set a bucket to catch it where it dripped off a projection. By feeling her pulse, she calculated the minutes it took for the dripping water to fill the bucket. Each time she judged twenty-four hours had gone by she made a mark on the cave wall with a piece of sandstone. One day she totaled up the marks. She had been in the cave somewhat over twelve days.

As time passed, the woman gradually made herself a proper home in the upper room. She arranged the boxes for chairs and a table, cooked good meals on the fireplace she had built and after she had eaten, spread a blanket over the warm stones and slept.

She wondered what was going on outside. Was the world burnt to ashes? Were scarred people picking about through swelling corpses, twisted metal, broken glass? Or was everything as it had been and the sun shining calm and warm down through the leaves spotting the path. The thought of the sun gave her heart a twist as if a coal of fire had touched her in the breast.

Below the water trickle in the lower room, the woman discovered a small underground pool in a rock basin.

"The old fishing hole," she said, for in the pool were strange white fish.

Instead of swimming away from her, they froze in the water when she reached for them. She seined them out easily with her skirt. They were three or four inches long. On either side of their heads, she found bulges covered with skin where the eyes had been.

She slit the fish open, gutted them and pinned them with thorns to a smooth log which she propped close to the fire. The book had told how.

"Survival," the woman said to the fish. "Mine, not yours."

On one of her fishing trips, she noticed, in a small recess filled with boulders on the far side of the pool, what appeared to be a piece of cloth caught beneath the bottom stone. It was of a coarse weave like burlap. She couldn't pull it free. Every day she passed by it she felt of the cloth.

"What is it?" she said.

Finally she took along the pickax and pried the boulders loose, rolling them off, one by one, across the floor. She worked gingerly, afraid of starting a cave-in and burying herself. As each boulder fell away, more of the cloth showed until she could see a large bundle wedged into a depression. She bent forward and lifted away the final stone, then started back, giving a little shriek.

"God in heaven," she said. "It's an Indian!"

"He won't scalp you," she added a moment later, peering down. "He's been dead so long the meat's gone dry on his bones."

Although the long hair was much as it had been in life, the skin was blackish and hard and part of the skull was bare. The fiber blanket lay in patches over the rib cage. Beside the corpse was a small piece of gourd and a bundle of reeds tied together with grass.

"Came in out of a storm," the woman said, "and here he is still, poor bastard."

Leaning down to touch the Indian's blanket, the woman saw that the recess was a crawl way into yet another room.

She called the upper cave, "Home," and the second chamber, "the Indian Room." The third, the new one, became, "the Bat Room." The third room was fair sized though not so big nor so beautiful as the Indian Room. When the woman first heard the bats squeaking from a great distance overhead, she set the lantern on a rock and dug out handholds and footholds in the wall with a can lid. Following the ·method described in the survival book, she slapped the hand grips first and listened to hear if they sounded loose or cracked before going up carefully. She eased her foot into the vertical slits, twisting her ankle sideways, slipping in her toe, then straightening the ankle.

Now and then she paused in her climb to light a candle and have a look around. Once she saw a cave cricket, palest white and long-legged, creeping up the rock. Later she came upon the disintegrating body of a millipede with a white fungus encasing it like a shroud.

Pulling herself onto a ledge, she suddenly clapped her hands over her ears to shut out what sounded like the roaring of the biggest airplane motor in the world. Stretching her candle up at arm's length, she saw the bats, very high up, in a vast smoky cloud.

The ledge where she stood held a pool of bat droppings, a wide brown lake smelling of ammonia. As the candle light slid across it she saw it move. She bent over, shining the light full on it. It was seething with living creatures. Tens of thousands of beetles, flat worms, snails, millipedes, and mites were swimming on the surface or crawling on the bottom of the guano. All of them were colorless and all of them were blind.

Where the bats came in, she couldn't tell. She felt no air and saw no light. When the rock of the walls grew too hard to dig, she had to climb back down. She never came in sight of the ceiling.

Next she explored a number of small passageways opening off the Bat Room. Most dead-ended, choked with fallen rock. The rest opened onto horrifying drops. One descended and became an underground stream which she waded until the roof closed down to the water. Then she turned back.

The woman now believed that she had examined every room and passageway accessible to her and that there was no way out of the cave.

She settled into a routine of fishing, cooking, eating, and sleeping. Time flowed on, sluggish and slow. She hung in it, drowsily.

But she dreamed strange dreams. And all her dreams were about light. At first she couldn't remember them but woke with only the

imprint of brightness on her eyes like an aftertaste on the tongue.

Later, she recalled scenes in which she lay doubled inside a giant egg, walled away from the light. As she beat on the shell, stretching toward the light, she could feel the light outside straining toward her. At last, with a cracking like a mighty explosion, she straightened her arms and legs sending the shell into bits. As she thrust forth into hot brightness, she looked to see if it were the sun or the flash of an explosion that beat upon her but she never found out.

When the coal oil was gone and the woman began to use the candles more and more sparingly, the shape of day and night blurred and faded from her life. Her meals became irregular. She ate as often as she felt hungry. Sometimes she forgot to eat at all for long stretches. She let the bucket overflow or forgot to mark on the wall so often that at last she lost all track of how long she had been in the cave.

Once, as she opened a can by candlelight, she lifted the lid and looked at her reflection in the shiny tin circle.

She saw that her face and arms had grown pasty. Her clothes were colorless from dirt and wear. She had broken her glasses when she climbed the wall of the Bat Room so that she peered at herself through eyes slightly out of focus. The skin hung loose on her cheeks and drew taut across the sharp bridge of her nose. Her hair, trailing loose on her shoulders, was pale with dust.

The candle sputtered, brightened, then, burned to its end, died. She reached for another. The candles rattled against one another in the box. So few left? Her hands shook, counting them. How many more hours of light? Not many. Then the dark.

As the woman let the candles fall from her fingers, a strange restlessness came upon her. She moved to the cave mouth and felt of the mass of dirt and rock which covered it. She caught up the pickax and dug until she couldn't lift it for another stroke.

After that she often counted the candles and as often dug at the entrance. Blisters broke on her hands and bled. Sweat dripped off her chin. Her body burned. It was as if she felt the light through the tons of dirt over her head, pulling her toward it whether she wanted to go or not. She dug until her arm went numb. Then she threw herself on the floor and slept. When she woke, she dug again.

Sometimes she dropped the pickax and fell to tearing at the dirt and rocks with her fingers. Afterwards she cleaned her hands and wrapped them in strips she tore from her skirt.

At last she left off digging and circled the Indian Room and the Bat Room each in turn again and again, feeling of the walls, climbing where she could gouge out a hand and foothold, going as far up as she was able, then dropping back.

Next she reexamined each of the passageways at the end of the Bat Room. One passage ended in a shallow pit carved into the stone with walls round like a chimney and stretching up out of sight. Down this chimney, it seemed to the woman, there poured like steady rain a strange dark light.

She placed her back against one wall of the chimney and lifted both her feet onto the wall opposite. She pressed a hand against the rock on either side of her buttocks and so levered her body off the wall. She inched her way up, alternately pressing her feet against one wall and her back against the other. Soon the chimney narrowed so that she was forced to use her knees instead of her feet and after a time she began to slip.

She slid down, caught herself, and started up once more. Her back and knees were raw and bleeding. The portions of her sweater and skirt covering them had worn away. She slipped again, reached out her hands to catch herself, tried to hold onto the sides of the pit, could not, and fell heavily, shot down like a stone, and hit the cave floor with a yell loud enough to wake the dead Indian.

When she tried to stand, the woman's ankle wouldn't bear her weight. It took her a long time to drag herself back to the Home Chamber. Once there, she mixed a poultice of mud and spread it on the ankle from the middle of the calf to the instep. Gradually it hardened into a cast.

The woman lay wrapped in her blanket on the warm stones while, slowly, her bruises and scrapes began to heal. She used to talk to herself aloud a good part of the time. Now, she fell deeper

and deeper into silence until her thoughts lost the shape of words
and shot through her brain in strange flashes of feeling and impulse.

In her dreams she repeated the accident and repeated it, always
walking with the sensation of having been, in falling, drenched
with light. She slept, woke, ate, slept again. Her ankle ached less,
then not at all. When she judged enough time had passed, the
woman took a small stone and pounded the mud cast gently so that
it cracked and fell away. She walked up and down the home cave
until her ankle grew strong.

When she was able to return to the Indian Room and the Bat
Room, she again explored the walls and passages, ending at last
with the underground river. She waded the stream to the point
where the overhead rocks narrowed down to touch the water. The
river deepened as the roof came down so that she stood in water to
her armpits.

She filled her lungs and swam downstream under the rocks. Feeling with her fingers that the roof still touched the water and still
touched and still touched, she swam back.

She tried again. Then again. Before each try she breathed in and
out rapidly and so was able to stay under water longer. With each
attempt she went further until, when she felt the roof begin to rise,
she pushed on and broke from the water into a narrow tunnel with
air at the top and headroom enough to stand upright.

Back in the Home Chamber, the woman took the rope into her
lap. She ran a few feet of its cold damp length through her fingers.
The day she had carried it to the cave, it had been warm from the
sun. She tore a strip from the bottom of her blanket and tied it to
the rope. She added another strip and another until she had tied on
the whole of the blanket.

At the river, she knotted one end of the rope around her waist
and looped the other over a rock projection. Wading slowly downstream, she felt a slight push of current at the backs of her legs. Her
thigh touched a fish hanging still in the water.

Swimming to the spot where she had stood before, she walked

on in waist-high water. She could reach out her hands and touch both walls of the tunnel that held the river. The roof hung a few feet above her.

The woman moved on in blackness, trailing the rope. When she rubbed her eyes she saw pale flashes far back inside her head.

Several yards beyond the point where she'd turned back before, she began to feel the roof closing rapidly down again, grazing her head so that she must stoop to go forward. When her feet lost touch with the bottom she began to swim.

The water was numbing cold. Her clothes hung on her like the metal plates of a suit of armor. Only her head was above water and still the roof brushed her hair and she felt it closing, closing.

The woman took several quick, deep breaths, filled her lungs, and dove down through the water. Leveling off, she shot ahead rapidly, keeping a steady forward push with arms and legs, hands and feet. She continued on for the length of her body, then her body's length again. And again. As she swam she waited for the tug at her waist that would tell her she had reached the rope's end, the point of no return. When it came, she slipped the knot and swam out of the rope, leaving it to curl in the water behind her.

Her lungs began to ache in earnest. The blood, pounding behind her eyes, filled her head with glances of bright color. Stubbornly she kept up her steady breast stroke, her frog kick, until the expanding and contracting of her muscles became the structure of her consciousness.

She tried to remember her life outside the cave but she could not. She tried to recall the details of her days in the Home Chamber, the Indian and the Bat Rooms but they were washed from her brain leaving only the sensation of inward scalding light creating, destroying her in its struggle to be born.

JAMES FETLER

The Indians Don't Need
Me Anymore

James Fetler has been published in the Atlantic, Paris Review, Commentary,
Transatlantic Review, *and elsewhere. He has received a National Endowment
for the Arts fellowship in creative writing and was awarded the Gold Medal
for Fiction by the Commonwealth Club of California. He teaches English
at Foothill College near San Francisco.*

*"His work is mature and exquisitely crafted. The cycle of pieces on the solitude
of old age is near perfection, as compassionate, precise, and moving as any
contemporary fiction dealing with aging in America."*
FRANCINE DU PLESSIX GRAY, 1980

I

I suppose that was it: the last of my Alcatraz runs. I won't be hauling any more clothing and food to the entrenched Indians. It's a
series of very long tacks from the Palo Alto yacht harbor to the
Rock—a whole day's trip when the winds aren't good—and I finally had to admit as I was tying the *Wanderer* up the last time that
I'm not really helping the American Indian Movement all that
much with the few boxes of blankets and canned goods I've been
able to buy or collect around here. Legal aid would be better, along
with some solid political support. Ritchie wants a big generator.
There's the psychology to think about, too. They've got enough blankets and Spam. And now that Nancy has finally remarried, and it's
clear that my contract will not be renewed at Peninsula State,
I'm ready to clean out my cottage, get rid of the hookah and the
scented drip candles, and try again some other place.

186

The

Indians

Don't

Need Me

Anymore

I used to think all those shuttles in the sloop were a sign of my altruism at work. Social concern. But the truth is I found a great solace in watching the winds and the tides when I first started sailing last summer. Handling a tiller was good therapy, it kept my body and mind occupied and took me away from the traps I had set for myself. And having a meaningful destination made my hours on the water more rich—it was more than just sliding around. When I looked at the hull of the boat the other day I could see it's absorbed a real beating from the northwesterly winds. I'll have to unload it even though it's a bad time to sell. I can't afford it any more.

I'm going to start packing. Roll up that Harpo Marx poster tacked over my desk. That grin has been getting on my nerves. And there's something else telling me it's time to stop licking the wounds. Once again I can feel the machinery about to start grinding in me. Sparrow noticed it, too: he said I look as if I'm about to lock myself into a different position. Since the children have finally accepted their new Field & Stream dad, who will give them the discipline and care they both need and deserve, I might as well get on my feet. I've used up the bay.

2

As I was sailing away from the Indians today I had to finally admit that the life I've been trying to hammer together has left me empty and raw. I hadn't expected that. *Fulfillment* and *actualization* seemed easy enough to wrap up and take home when I had Abraham Maslow on the lectern before me, reinforced by my neatly typed notes and the formulas clearly outlined on the board. Even the pointer I swung back and forth felt authentic.

As the *Wanderer* was sailing under the Bay Bridge I found myself staring straight up at the massive steel girders, and that brought back the feel of the rigid geometry that would press against me at Peninsula State—in the classrooms, in the faculty lounge, even down by the tennis courts—and that little flash took me back to the Friday last May when I lost my cool while doing Tolstoy. Everything seemed to be pushing against me that Friday. Even the side-

walks on campus were slamming up needlessly hard against my
arches. Off and on, over a period of several months, I'd been trying
for one final clarification between Nancy and me, despite this new
IBM man in her life who happened to hit it off beautifully with the
kids, and for a short while we seemed to have worked up an actual
glow between us, with the widower temporarily on the sidelines,
but already I could sense the glow dying, since nothing was happening, we couldn't really change the deep core of whatever we
were. *No good, no good,* I kept thinking, remembering the glow that
was starting to spread out to Laura and Alex, *already they're lighten-
ing up, not nearly so tense, no longer crying at night, but it isn't going to
work, and this glow in the children is a terrible thing to see.* I had just
had them over for the weekend: the zoo, Marine World, rattling
cable cars out to Fisherman's Wharf, just the three of us having a
ball, no apprehensive Mom snapping *Alex needs his nap!*, no griping
about garbage sacks or the dog's bone on the couch—and then
wham! as I was walking across campus and thinking back to that
marvelous weekend, I found myself aching for leaves to rake, weeds
to yank out of the ground, dirty dishes to wash, someone else flushing the toilet, the sounds of can openers, the slamming of doors. I
was also hung over. The night before, loaded on sherry, I had driven
down Hopkins Street with the headlights off. Craig's 4-wheel drive
Toyota was parked in my former driveway, and all the curtains were
drawn in the house. I kept reminding myself as I drove back to the
cottage not to let this sort of thing happen again.

3

It was a hot Friday. I was sweating so hard in my bush jacket and
turtleneck jersey that I finally wadded a couple of paper towels
under my armpits, but the towels got soggy and slid down the
sleeves. Sparrow and my other colleagues were ambling from class
to class in their usual short-sleeved drip-dry shirts like NASA engi-
neers, but I stuck to the turtleneck and boots I'd decided would

188

The

Indians

Don't

Need Me

Anymore

best represent the real me, plus the other bold touches designed to impress and seduce undergrads—the torn jeans and the shades. That was part of the contract, I figured, getting the Camaro crowd turned on to Yeats and Flaubert using all the theatricals at your command, including the proper cosmetics. You had to relate.

By the time my 2 P.M. class had dragged around that Friday I could feel the bad ache in my shoulders and neck. Every time I thought back to the split in my life, and the way it was bruising the kids, I would start to concoct weekend jaunts in my mind—Mendocino, Carmel, the whole family packed into the Hillman convertible along with a fictitious sheep dog I would throw in to finish the scene (Jip wasn't quite right for the part) like a Standard Oil billboard. But I could never imagine us alone, just Nancy and me. Not comfortably. Too much distance had crystallized between us, and it wouldn't thaw out. I couldn't imagine myself totally alone with her, the two of us seated at a restaurant table, a couple of menus and an ashtray between us, and this was peculiar because I know I felt jealousy and remorse, especially after Craig started coming around. It grated against me, and yet it was clear I would have to accept the brute fact that those crystals were permanently there. So would she. Shortly before moving into the cottage, I had told her, *You won't accept this until later, but the truth is you'll get nothing good out of me until after we've split. You're still young—you deserve a fresh start.*

As I walked into class I could spot a real bummer in the making. Their eyes told me, the tilt of their frames. I pushed them through ten, fifteen minutes of the Tolstoy, clutching my chest, acting out Ivan Ilyich's torment and death, everything but the actual screaming, but when I finally finished my performance they responded with a silence so solid and compressed you could haul it away in a furniture van.

I leaned against the desk: artificial pearls cast out to genuine swine. "So what's he saying—*Ivan Ilyich's life had been most simple and most ordinary, and therefore most terrible*—what does that mean?"

Their eyeballs were barely twitching. I waited. Nothing. I could

see Sparrow standing outside, as though checking me out. George
McManus was meditating on his thumb. A girl yawned.

I threw my stuff into the briefcase. *Zap*: there was the Toyota again, parked directly behind Nancy's green Maverick. "You're really disgusting," I said quietly and walked out, leaving them sitting there with their plywood expressions. I went to my car. *They haven't learned how to decipher the plain printed page!* I was feeling so bad I left tracks. I could hear Sparrow yelling to me. I ignored him. I had heard it all before.

The faculty lot seemed to be buckling with heat. I left the Menlo Park campus by way of El Camino Real and winced all the way into Palo Alto, the sun rubbing my eyes like a file. As soon as I approached my own turf I felt better. The tree-lined avenues felt cool, almost damp, and the elegantly decaying old houses dating back to the '80s and '90s, with their towers and panes of stained glass, the verandas and warped picket fences, were comforting: a world decomposing, waiting for the bulldozers, a dark falling-apart, a rich calm. Rows of diseased palm trees. Cast-iron sprinklers revolving on the lawns. I drove up to my cottage holding my breath. I listened: no motorcycles, no rock and roll. I relaxed.

4

The little place I'd been renting the last couple of years sat directly in back of a once-magnificent estate dating back to the founding of Stanford University. Since the end of the Korean War the big house had been gerrymandered into several small units, but the owners, an elderly couple in Burlingame, were merely sitting on the property, waiting and watching the land values climb, and so they had let the old mansion with its thick, crazy hedges and fruit trees disintegrate, one window and board at a time. When I moved into the cottage the week Nancy filed for divorce, the last of the tenants, a bachelor accountant who kept plants in his room, was in the process of moving out. *It's impossible*, he confided to me as he hauled

190

The

Indians

Don't

Need Me

Anymore

out his flowerpots, *the plumbing doesn't work. Take a look at the roof.* The roof was full of bare patches where the shingles had come off.

So for several months the Victorian relic stood empty and dark. It was balm for my soul. I had my secluded retreat less than ten blocks away from my previous home, and Laura was able to drop by after school to visit with me whenever she felt like it. *This is your cottage, you know*, I assured her. *Most kids have only one home, you've got two, how about that. Huh?* She came around fairly often, especially at first, because she thought it was all kind of neat, but sometimes the whole situation confused her, and she'd squint at the light-blue light bulbs with the Tiffany shades, and the candles, and the hookah that set me back sixty-five bucks, and the posters of Harpo and W. C. Fields, and ask, *Dad, how come you're living like a teenager?*

But I had the lush, untended gardens all to myself, with the pigeons working their wings like propellers in the palms, and the lime trees and bougainvillea, the secluded green circles of clover and moss where I'd stretch out after work and accept the sun into my pores, Ravel drifting out of my windows like smoke. I was suffering over Nancy, of course, and over the other women who were plowing themselves through my life, creating the usual gouges and cuts. They came and they went, but invariably they came on too strong, leaving their toothbrushes, badgering me over the phone late at night, and I wasn't ready for any of that, not with my old world still heavy on my mind. I fixed the young ladies nice beef stroganoffs and bought a good water bed, but they didn't know when to quit. And the aching slid forward and back in my chest.

5

Then the free spirits moved in.

I was fixing my chicken and rice one tranquil afternoon, Casadesus filling the cottage with *Le tombeau de Couperin*, when a couple of young men in bib overalls loped into the kitchen. Could they borrow my john? They had taken out a lease on the big house and

found all the toilets clogged. They used my bathroom, phoned the plumber, and went out to their VW bus. Ten minutes later they were back at my door.

Got any boards around here?

Boards?

Boards. Planks. That front lawn is awfully damp.

I went out with them. They had backed their bus, which was loaded with mattresses and food, up to the front door, and the wheels had sunk in on either side of the cement walk. I looked at the furrows gouged out by the spinning rear wheels.

I haven't got any planks.

The taller of the two pulled a rubber band from his wrist and grabbed the back of his mane and twisted it. He slipped the rubber band on. *Might as well unload. Want to give us a hand?*

I spent the next couple of hours hauling in pots and pans, sacks of flour and rice, boxes of canned goods, and of course the mattresses.

You've sure got a lot of mattresses.

Yeah.

That night I slept my best sleep in weeks, no moaning, no dreams, and I awoke the next morning with my arms aching but my head very bright. I hadn't had a single slug of sherry before hitting the sack, and it felt novel and good to wake up with a clean skull and all the headpieces fitting into place. When I glanced out the window I saw, in addition to the VW bus, a converted milk truck and an Easy Rider bike. I went outside. The milk truck had Oregon plates and was coated with dust.

When I came home from the campus that night a strange Studebaker pickup, outfitted with a wooden camper complete with a stovepipe and a kerosene lantern hanging from the doorknob, was occupying my stall in the carport, and now there were two motorcycles on the lawn. The rear wheel was off on one of the choppers, and a pockmarked kid wearing a floppy leather hat with a turkey feather was working on the chain. I parked my Hillman in the street and walked over. He glanced at me.

192

The

Indians

Don't

Need Me

Anymore

You happen to have a torque wrench?

No.

He resumed his tinkering.

Do you know who belongs to that truck?

What truck?

That Studebaker in the carport.

He shook his head. *Nope.*

6

Troubled in spirit, I went into the cottage, and while I was trying to grade a few papers before supper—*The Celebration of the Dionysian Principle in Hesse*—I could hear yet another set of pistons roar up to the front of the house, and then voices, this time the laughter of skinny girls, *Oh wow, out of sight!* and then an electric guitar started blatching out chord after chord from one of the rear dormer windows of the big house—no progression, no melody, just a blatching of random chords. I got up and closed all my windows.

Well. I thought about it. They were, after all, leasing the place and its grounds for hard cash, and were therefore entitled to run their commune any way they saw fit. And besides, they were healthy and young and conditioned to live in a world full of amplification and pounding exhausts.

The week before, I had just finished doing *Gatsby* at school, and it struck me just then that there were some connections between that Fitzgerald milieu—all those parties and motor excursions and teas—and the blatching of the electric guitar. I flashed myself back to my twenties and late teens, to the boarding house in New Haven where the volleyball boys raised the same banal hell every day and got predictably smashed on a few cans of beer every alternate night, and then to my basement cubicle on Chicago's North Side, where there wasn't fresh air and my only companion was an elderly muscatel·freak who had lost control over his bladder, and then to the long, lonely rides on the El to my classes in Jackson Park, the solitary meals and the stark cafeterias with tiled floors and walls and all

the menial jobs, one after the other, as I worked my way through
the first years of graduate school, before Nancy showed up. And then I realized I was biting my lip over the free spirits in their kibbutz because I had never had anything like the contact they'd worked out for themselves, creating a network of interests in some ways not really so different from Scott Fitzgerald's golf games and midwinter proms. Faces and places and names. At their age—at the age of nineteen or twenty I'd be walking along Lake Michigan completely alone, my brain turning inward as usual, absorbed in its own processes, my loneliness following my tracks like a dog, just the surf of the lake on one side and the whine of the Outer Drive traffic on the other. The Beatles hadn't been invented. Acapulco gold didn't exist. Small wonder I found such a refuge in Nancy the moment she came on the scene in my Age of Johnson class, and that I dug into her like a clamp for eleven long years. And this explained, possibly, why I found the spontaneous gregariousness in the big house, along with the noises it brought, so unsettling. The free spirits made me think of the volleyball boys in New Haven, and the tiled cafeterias, and the muscatel freak.

7

But at any rate, the big house was silent that Friday. No blatches, no bikes. Two mongrels were lying on their sides in the middle of the alley, paws stretched out stiff, like freeway fatalities. I circled around them and parked and went into my place. I had ceased troubling my head over the portable kiln someone had tilted on its side in the bed of primroses and then apparently abandoned, or the overstuffed chair with the cigarette burns sitting under the pomegranate tree, or the empty wine jugs on the porch, the deer skulls propped up on the fence. They were simply a part of my life, like the smog hanging over the Santa Clara valley, the decanter of sherry on my desk. My folders and notes were jammed into the briefcase like wallpaper samples I was being paid to hustle. They had little connection with the slippery feel of the children as they

194

The

Indians

Don't

Need Me

Anymore

sat face to face in the tub, my hands soaping their necks, or with the strained mouth of their mother those feverish early months when I wasn't quite sure where I'd be sleeping that night, and her whispers as we sat side by side on the steps of the back porch, the kids watching cartoons on TV, *What do you need that you can't get from me?* and her sudden stiffening as my fingers touched her elbow.

I stared out the door of the cottage. The unexpected silence had caught me off guard. My mind started picking through past memories the way a pick probes for fragments of food. I sat down at my desk. Harpo was grinning at me. My journal was lying on top of a stack of term papers, like a press. I opened it at random—any entry would do. This one went back a few years, to the period when everything was presumably still intact:

> *April 12, 1966. Again the chloroform on the tongue, nothing working between us, the rooms of the house like compartments for storing up silence. We poke at our dinner and strain to concoct dialogue, but the forks make more noise. Strangers at least have perfunctory exchange, a few ceremonial nods. Sparrow says I look terrible again. All evening I found myself hassling Laura about her Mary Poppins record, TURN IT DOWN! TURN IT DOWN! and finally I gave her a crack across the rear that set her spinning. I'd like to understand my machinery better, figure out what exactly is freezing me up and then making me boil. Poor design. Everybody gets caught. Mean irritations and lust.*

8

I heard a motorcycle drive up to the big house, then the VW bus. A bird started beating its wings inside me. I had papers to grade, work to do. Now the camper, horn honking. I slammed shut my journal and stuck it up on the shelf.

In the past, when the pressures built up, I could always drop over at Nancy's, have a cup of Sanka and play with the children and Jip

for a while. Mow the lawn. Following the divorce we became toler-
able friends, almost close, since we finally had something in common, and there were nights when I tortured myself over her. When
I wasn't entertaining some woman, I kept pictures of Nancy on my
desk. And then suddenly, before I was ready for him, her IBM ad-
mirer showed up and declared Nan off limits to me. Suddenly it
was no longer possible to cruise over to Hopkins Street and ring
the doorbell whenever I felt the need for that bell. I guess I had
figured on keeping the whole business on ice over there, tucked
away for emergency use. She finally had everything that I wanted
for her, and it hurt.

I fixed myself a pan of tuna and noodles. *Forge on!* I kept telling
myself. After dinner I started grading the papers, the decanter at
my side. When I finished the sherry around ten I got into the car
and drove to the Green Goose. I stayed there for a couple of hours.

Then I remember it's raining, but lightly, and I'm driving down
Hopkins Street with my lights off, and there's that Toyota again in
the driveway, and the windows are dark. I drive on, down Middle-
field Avenue, and I turn up some side street and notice I can't get
the wipers to work, although I keep twisting the knob back and
forth, and then I feel a peculiar bump which I can't account for, and
suddenly I'm chugging in second gear not on the street but up the
manicured lawn of the Wesleyan Methodist Church, unable to
stop, my foot sliding off the clutch pedal, and then I notice the
windshield's got cracks in a number of places, and I get the car back
on the street and somehow manage to navigate it home.

The next morning, when I finally struggled to get out of bed and
go out to the carport, and when I saw how the front end had been
flattened by some incredible flattening machine, I simply turned
around and crawled back to bed. I didn't know what I'd hit. I didn't
want to find out. The questions didn't come until several days later.
I should've known better, of course, and reported it at once. Sparrow says the delay cost me my job. Yesterday he said, *Go join the
Indians up there on the Rock.*

It isn't clear what exactly is happening on Alcatraz. Sparrow claims they are going to dig in permanently. *Time* says in its cover story: GOODBYE TO TONTO. It's obvious that the kind of relief they've been getting will have to give way to something more substantial. Ritchie is right. He poured me a cup of coffee from his thermos today and said, "Send us a couple of good electricians. And a big generator."

He was looking at me strangely—he seemed almost embarrassed. A Coast Guard cutter was idling a few hundred yards away. It hurt me a little to hear Ritchie talk like that, after all the heavy seas I had plowed the *Wanderer* through, and he must have noticed, because he said, "Look, you've done a great job. Everybody has done a great job." Then he leaned forward. "Mind if I say something?"

"What?" The coffee was sloshing out of the cup.

"Aren't you pushing yourself a bit hard?"

I stared at him.

He gave me the same kind of look I would sometimes lay on my students. "The first time I saw you ram that little boat into the dock I said, *Jesus, now here is one wild character!* You remember?"

I laughed. Then I saw his expression. "What is it, Ritch?"

The boom was beginning to swing. Ritchie grabbed it. "Don't get me wrong, I'm not trying—." He shifted his weight. "You don't look very healthy."

"I feel fine."

"Look, it isn't my business, but you really look bad and it's bothering me. The others have noticed it, too. We don't want anyone jeopardizing their health. You look worse every time you come out. How much weight have you lost, anyway? That's an awfully long trip you've been making in the boat—it'd be a lot simpler to haul the stuff up to the city in your car. Drop it off at the Center. I mean you know we appreciate every sack of potatoes we get, but—you really look bad. You look like you've lost—."

"Okay, Ritchie." I handed him the cup. "You're probably right."

"It's senseless to burn yourself out. We're not hurting that bad."

"Okay, Ritch."

He kept holding the boom so it wouldn't swing out. "It's time we got moving on something more solid." He backed away. "Like a big generator. There's the psychology to think about, too."

"All right, Ritch."

As I pushed the sloop off he saluted me by shaking his fist. The sails luffed and snapped, suddenly filled with wind. I shook my fist back, but I could see that the Indians don't need me anymore.

Places We Lost

*Mary Hedin lives, writes, and teaches in Marin County, California. Her
stories have been published in the* Best American *and* O. Henry *collections.
She has won the McGinnis Award for Fiction and the
Great Lakes Colleges Association Award.*

*"Mary Hedin writes generous, beautifully conceived, consistently trustworthy
short stories. A few sharp images, a few lines of dialogue, and her characters
spring to life—people worth watching, listening to, caring about. These are
stories as stories ought to be, finely crafted, concerned, moving."*
JOHN GARDNER, 1979

That house was more than ordinarily loved. My father had built
and sold houses all over the south side of Minneapolis. Almost
every year, we had moved into and out of one of them. Move in, fix
it up, sell it. That was the pattern. But that house was built just for
us. It was a high-gabled, English country-style house, and when we
moved in, mother announced that that was it. She had had her fill
of moving, and she had things just the way she wanted them there,
from the clever limed-oak phone niche in the hall to the breakfast
nook with its trestle table and built-in benches.

Four years later, we were in the middle of the Depression. My
father no longer built houses. He worked at intervals for a sash-and-
door shop. Mostly he was home. In those days, shabby-looking
men knocked on our door and asked for food, and abandoned cats
howled in the alleys at night.

In spite of that, we children did not understand. Buddy was still
a baby, and Jenny and I were fed. We were clothed. We heard the
words—Depression, breadlines, WPA, Mecklenburg scrip. They
had a grand and mysterious sound, and we did not comprehend

them. When father announced, one day, that the sash-and-door shop had closed, it meant less to us than the quick change in weather that was moving March from winter to spring.

Then, on a Friday night in May, an evening warmer than the calendar allowed, Jenny and I grew keenly aware of the change and loss threatening us all. That it came then, on the same night that Jenny came to something else, launching the risk and deceit which harmed us all, was not, perhaps, entirely coincidental.

Usually, Jenny and I were among the first to be called home from the evening games. That night, no one called us. We marveled, at first, at our unexpected freedom. We played Kick the Can furiously as the evening turned dusky, crowding the last minutes with the greatest amount of pleasure. Even after most of the children had gone home and we were much too tired, we played on. At last, there were just three of us—Jenny and I and Carrie Bergman, whose parents had gone to church and didn't know she was out.

We huddled by the telephone pole that had been goal and watched the final excessive blooming of stars in the altogether darkened skies. Still no one called. Jenny looked at me, caught between wanting to be called and wanting to stay there in the dew-sharpened, strange night air. The trees were high black shadows against the lighted sky. Beneath them, fireflies scudded over an unseen earth. Down the avenue, the houses in formal rows were large and remote from us. At last, our sense of freedom grew so immense that we were strange in it, unsure of it, and wanted to escape before it swept us toward things we only sensed and did not wish to know.

"Let's go," Jenny whispered. "Let's go," Carrie agreed.

We turned and ran our separate ways. I clutched Jenny's hand and pulled her as fast as I could down the alley, across the grass, up the concrete walk to our back door. The house was still there. The kitchen windows facing the alley were dark, but the double windows of the dining room gave out an old light.

I stopped when we reached the steps. "Jenny, did you hear mother calling us?" I whispered.

"No, she didn't," Jenny warbled. "She never called us."

"Jenny, we're going to get spanked." I was gloomily sure of it.

Jenny stood still, considering. The crickets' warnings riddled the dark. Finally, she tugged like a fish at the hand in which I still held hers. "Come on," she said carelessly. "Let's go in."

"We'll get spanked." I repeated.

Jenny tossed her head. The fair hair moved like wind in the scant light. "Well, I don't care. I'm going in. Come on, Berit. Let's go." She started up the steps; but on the second one, she stopped. Her hand left mine. Her head leaned toward the night. "Shh," she whispered. "Listen."

I stopped, I waited. I heard nothing. "What? What do you hear?"

"Shh," Jenny whispered again.

Then I heard it, the faint, fine tissue of sound, a thin belling of woe, moving without source into and out of the night.

The sound came again, and we both knew it for what it was. Tenderness quavered out of Jenny's throat in a whispered, half-sung cry. "A kitten. It's a kitten." She went blindly from me towards whatever dark place she thought the sound came from, crooning, "Here, kitty, kitty. Here, kitty." I could hear, in the quick, breathless callings, that extravagance of love which was Jenny's gift and liability and which poured from her toward any small furred thing she ever saw.

Plaintive, haunting mews were coming in answer to her calls. Then both murmurs and mewing ceased, and Jenny stood beside me, holding something against her chest. "Look at him, Berit. Oh, look at him, how tiny he is."

I could not see the kitten in the darkness but she couldn't keep him, anyway. She knew that. She was always bringing home hungry cats, and father never let her keep one. "Put him down, Jenny. Come on. We have to go in."

"He's so tiny, Berit. Look. He's lost, Berit, poor little thing."

I heard the small, rich thrum, the purring. I started up the steps saying, "Put him down, Jenny," and she came after me and didn't put the kitten down. I stopped outside the door, the knob cold and damp in my hand.

"I'm going to ask." Jenny said. The dark prevented seeing; but I knew from the sound of her slow, soft words that in her wide eyes there was that look of determination I was never able to defeat. I

wiped my palm against my skirt and pulled open the door.

The weathers of my father's nature blew violently from sublimity and joy to outrage and despair. His knobby, sharp-boned face was seamed and creased by his moods, as lands are marked by their climates' demands. To hear my father angry did not astonish. To hear him shouting at mother gave room for apprehension. But she, who usually would not speak to him unless he was calm, was answering his anger with anger equal to his own, her voice raised to a near shout. In bewilderment, we both stopped on the dark side of the dining-room door.

"Don't be so unreasonable, Emma!" he shouted. "It has to be done."

"No. I will not let you."

"We have to live. It's that simple. What do you think we'll eat? Leaves off the trees, perhaps?"

"Not the house," mother cried in a loud sharp voice. "We don't have to sell the house. We're eating. We're not starving. Not the house!" She sat at the table, the light of the dining-room fixture falling on her coppery hair, her face now lowered into her covering hands.

My father paced around her, circling the round oak table, stopping to lean over her bowed body, and shouting into her ears. "Not starving! Not starving, she says!" With each word, he stabbed the air in front of her with a thrust-out forefinger. "Women! Masters of logic! We'll live in a nice house. We'll walk around with empty bellies, and then, when it's too late, we'll lose the house, anyway. We'll see the day the bank forecloses, that's how it will be!"

From the dark kitchen we watched, trying to find meaning in the storm of words. Why would we sell the house? How could you lose a house? Where would we be if we were not there in that house?

My mother dropped her hands from a pale face in which her eyes were two places of darkness. Then she stood up and put that white face close to my father's knotted one and shouted. "No. No. No."

His mouth snapped like a trap. His lids slitted down against his eyes' fury. His brows were one black streak across the blazing forehead. Overhead, the light fixture still trembled with the shouts, which had frozen now into total silence. Under the flickering, fragmented light, they stood dumbly unyielding, unforgiving, sudden hate flung up between them that grew into a wall of silence, from which neither could move and which neither could destroy.

In that cold, walled silence, the breaths I drew shook past a thick tongue and a closed throat. Against my arm, Jenny's arm trembled with dismay, and we stood locked, two small girls caught on the outer edge of their anger.

Then, in Jenny's arms, the kitten stirred; lifted a small, sleepy head; mewed faintly.

Both faces turned toward the door, turned from anger to remembrance and surprise.

"What are you girls doing here?" My father's bellow was a lesser anger. "Why aren't you in bed?" Then his black brows rode up, up on his corrugated forehead. His eyes pulled wide open. "What's that?" he shouted. "Get that cat out of here!"

In spite of all, Jenny's desire gave sufficient courage. "I thought we could keep—," she ventured, on a high, frail note.

"Get that cat out of here!" He plunged around the table toward us.

We stumbled back toward the safe dark behind us.

But mother had already wheeled from her place, and she came to us with her arms spread, like a winged, red-haired angel. She swept both of us away in the white arc of her arms, away from my black-browed, bellowing father, crying over her turned, sharply defying shoulder, "Stop shouting at the children." His huge fist crashed upon the shining table as she herded us through the kitchen to the back door, where Jenny lowered her arms and gave up the tiny kitten to the larger, cold night.

Upstairs in our bed, we lay cradled in each other's comfortless arms. Jenny's tears dampened the pillow beneath my cheek. Her questions—"Berit, where will the kitten go? How will we lose the house, Berit? Berit, do you think the kitten will die?"—went with us unanswered, threatening, even as we moved hopeless, helpless, into the distance of sleep.

I awakened to total quiet. The light of a late-rising moon had

taken our room. Black shadows of quivering leaves flickered in
changing patterns against the white wall. Even before I reached out,
I knew that the place beside me was empty. Jenny was gone. I listened. I felt the empty space. I raised up on one elbow, looked
about the room. "Jenny?" I whispered.

No answer. Had she gone for a drink? To the bathroom? I listened for the sound of running water, for the flush. I heard no
sound. I shook the sheet from my legs. I got up. Gooseflesh fled
along my arms, between my shoulders. I tiptoed around the bed.
My shadow grew long and strange upon the white wall and moved
before me as I left the room. I went along the hall, down the stairs,
stopped at the bottom. From my parents' room, the usual deep
drawn breaths issued in forgetful counterpoint.

"Jenny?" The whisper met with consuming silence. I dared once
more. "Jenny?"

There was a tick of noise in the kitchen. A door? Opening? Closing? Then I heard the tiny, singing wire of sound. The kitten.
I slipped over the smooth, moon-sheathed linoleum floor to the
back door.

The moonlight lay like water upon the concrete steps. Its light
made a clearness deprived of detail, sharper than reality. Jenny
crouched on the step, her long hair fallen past her face so that its
ends swept the glittering steps. Her arms were lifted from her sides,
and the curve of her hands was shaped to the saucer's circle. The
tiny kitten, spraddle-legged and quivering, looked frail and blue in
the moon's light, fumbling at the offered milk.

She had not heard me. I looked down on her and the kitten, set
there like a carving in the wash of light. I gave up a giggle. "Jenny,"
I scolded, "what are you doing?"

She turned her face to me, looked at me, not surprised, but with
absolute assurance, as though getting up in a deserted, half-finished
night to feed a stray kitten she could not keep was an entirely reasonable and expected action. "He's hungry." Her lips fluttered between smiles and woe. As she turned back to the kitten, the silvered
sheath of her hair fell again over the curve of her cheek, hiding the

look on her face as her whispers of love and comfort fell upon the kitten's peaked, attentive ears. The fear and unhappiness from which we had taken our sleep were gone. Watching her there, sturdy and strange in the moon-whitened gown that covered even her human feet, I took from her the tiny blue kitten, the lapping tides of stirring moon-watered air, forgetfulness and wonder for myself.

But in the day that followed, and in the long, tense days following it, there was little such relief. A great silence stood between my mother and my father, and it was not peace. Whatever occasional dialogue went between them began abruptly, ended impotently.

Each day, father walked the long way to the Loop. Late in the afternoon, he pulled open the back door, shrugged his coat from weary, humped shoulders, and dropped it to the bench in the breakfast nook. Like someone very old, cautious of his aches, he lowered himself down beside it. Mother set a dishpan full of water on the green linoleum floor in front of him. He tugged at stiff shoes, sticky socks. He dropped his hot, abused feet into the water, moved his toes, groaned. He leaned his elbows on the table, his head on his hands, and growled out tales of jobs gone, homes lost, businesses closed. "America, America," he muttered. "Land of broken promise." On the radio, Father Coughlin's speeches, dreary stock quotations, glum news reports fed his despair.

And mother turned only silence against his words. Hearing his grim, unpatriotic speeches, she suffered, perhaps, the pain and embarrassment burning in me. When he was away, she attacked her chores as though she were fighting a battle involving dust mops and laundry tubs and vacuum cleaners. She didn't walk; she ran, as if victory depended on vigilance, and I knew the battle she waged somehow involved her differences with my father. Buddy was cutting his molars, and when she sang comforting, foolish rhymes to him, rocking him toward rest he could not find, her own face held weariness and pain.

But that she hid from father. She turned toward him a cool, impersonal mask, and he showed her a constant, impersonal and frowning bitterness. They remained if not enemies, antagonists, keeping mind and flesh and soul to resistance.

Jenny paid no attention to their warfares. The kitten had claimed her, and there was room in her thoughts only for it, how to care for it, how to keep it for her own. The Saturday morning after that moonlit night, she found a cardboard box in the basement. She sneaked rags out of mother's ragbag. She tucked the box with its nest of rags in a green hollow of the wild honeysuckle crowding the corner of the empty lot next door. She smuggled milk out to it.

From then on, each morning when we started down the alley to school, I had to wait on the damp concrete, shivers riding up and down my legs, while she crept through the dew-wet branches to see the kitten and leave it bits of her lunch.

When we got home in the afternoon, she poured herself a glass of milk and went out on the back steps to drink it. In a few minutes, she brought the emptied glass back to the sink, and then she was gone. I knew she was going to the kitten's hiding place with a jar of milk held against her stomach. And the kitten seemed to know. At least, it made that bush its home and did not betray Jenny by following her home, as kittens usually do.

At first, the necessary deception cost Jenny something. There were fever and shyness in her darkened eyes; a deepened color burned her cheeks, and it seemed that the demands of conscience gave off the same signs of danger as disease. Or perhaps the burning of cheek and eye was, even in the beginning, not the mark of guilt, but only a sign of the heart's whole mission. At any rate, she was changed, and I thought someone ought to notice other than me. No one did.

The passions my parents themselves were enduring took them from their ordinary perceptions. Jenny went her dedicated, deceitful way. I warned her, and scolded her, and worried, and Jenny ignored all that.

On the last Sunday in May, I went down the stairs into the kitchen full of morning sun. I felt at once, in spite of that wealth of brilliant light, that the air was drained and empty. My mother stood by the stove as though she leaned on the spoon moving slowly through the pan of oatmeal. In the heaviness of lids lying over her inward-looking eyes, in the droop of her head, there was defeat.

My father leaned over the Sunday paper, spread out upon the trestle table. He looked up; brows lifted; his teeth gleamed in a showy smile. "Well, there's a fine sleepyhead!" His laugh was loud and not free.

I knew the fine show was for mother, and she was getting no comfort or amusement from it. I could not laugh and only blushed. Father picked up the funnies he never allowed us to see until after we were home from church. He gave them to me, and I held them and looked at the gaudy, foolish colors and didn't feel like reading them.

"When is he coming?" my mother said, her eyes not lifting from the spoon.

I looked up from the funnies and out the window at the quiet yellow morning and saw Jenny wandering down the alley in her red sweater, her head bent toward the kitten in her arms.

"This afternoon," father answered, and he looked out the window and saw Jenny, too. "Whose cat is that?" he shouted, his anger easier and truer than his joy had been.

I jumped, hesitated, and found deception easy enough to practice. "I think it's Carrie Wallstrom's," I murmured, and, suffering, went and took Buddy, where he leaned from mother's hip, drooling on his fresh shirt. "Stop that Buddy," I fussed, and wiped away the bubbles he blew from his wet, laughing mouth.

My father studied the paper again. "Stop acting as though it's my fault!" he suddenly shouted.

My mother's hand dropped the spoon and fell to her side. She stood with her head lowered to her chest and turned away from us. My father stood up, looked at her, and stomped out of the kitchen, down the basement stairs, banging the doors behind him. . . .

It was noon, and we were eating lunch in the breakfast nook when the doorbell rang.

"That will be Johnson," father announced. His brown eyes shone at mother.

She did not look up to see it, but the spoonful of custard she was lifting toward Buddy's wide-opened mouth stopped in mid-air. Buddy's mouth stretched a wide and wider O. Suddenly it blared

out a great, wounded bellow. Mother jumped. She popped the
spoon into Buddy's mouth. The howl split off. Father went from
the kitchen, and mother began to shovel the filled spoon at Buddy's
mouth faster than he could swallow.

"Hurry, girls," she said. Her red head dipped toward the dining-room door. "Shush, girls."

The voice joining my father's was a high-pitched man's voice, with a singsong motion to it that hid its sense.

But father's bugle-noted words came clear. "The floors," he said. "The floors are of first-grade oak. And the hardware. Throughout the house, the finest. Look at that fireplace. Wisconsin stone. Had the best mason in the business lay that fireplace. See how those edges join? Beautiful. The dining room," he said. "Fourteen by sixteen."

They came into the kitchen, my father walking with arms folded across his chest, the rolled sleeves of his shirt showing the muscle lying smooth and heavy beneath the browned skin, his jaw out, his mouth stern and glad. Beside him was a taller man, thin in the body and loose-looking under the pin-striped cloth of his suit. His long legs lifted and dropped in a slow, light step, like the legs of a water spider. His oiled cap of gray hair lay flat and smooth over a crown that was as oval as an egg.

"Mr. Johnson, my wife." My father's smile was for Johnson, his frown for mother.

"How do you do," my mother answered, and her tone was light and armored. She moved from table to sink like a dancer, with dirty dishes in her hands.

Mr. Johnson looked down from his high place. His face slipped into and out of a quick, promising, unreliable smile. His small, light eyes ran from corner to corner, taking in the whole room.

"Inlaid linoleum," my father said, looking coldly at my mother's straight back.

"Ah, yes." Mr. Johnson paused. "The stove should go with, of course," he said. "It fits so nicely there."

There was a jerk in the arc of my mother's arm as she lifted plates from the table. "We'll keep the stove," she said.

Johnson looked at my father. His smile, tolerant and fluid, slid over his face.

A band of red flared across my father's high-boned cheeks and took his ears. "There are plenty of cupboards," he said. "Look at this large storage closet."

"That comfy breakfast nook should catch someone's fancy." Johnson's chant was comforting.

They went to tour the bedrooms.

Afterward, my father came back to the kitchen. He sat down on one of the benches by the trestle table in the nook and looked out the white-curtained window at the leaves of the one great oak tree, holding the sun sharply on their scalloped edges. He looked at the leaves as though he needed to study the intricacies of their twined and shadowed shapes. He said nothing at all.

My mother went to the table. She put her hands on the table's edge. Now she looked down on father as though she were a teacher and he a recalcitrant student. "Well, what did he say?"

My father looked not at her, but only into the dense clusters of leaves. "Forty-five hundred. He says forty-five hundred."

My mother's hands dropped from the table's edge, went to her sides, came up again, and sat on her hipbones in the shape of fists. Her lips pouted with contempt. Her chin lifted. She stared down at father. The light in her eyes snapped out at him. Her hair and cheeks looked on fire. She stood there growing straighter and taller and blazing more vividly with each short moment until she burst into rocketing words.

"Forty-five hundred? Forty-five hundred dollars? Why, that's ridiculous! It cost that much to build. That doesn't even allow for labor! What about that? Isn't your labor worth anything? If that Mr. Johnson thinks we're going to sell this house at a price like that, he's mistaken, that's what he is! Why, I'll sit here till doomsday before I let you give away this house for forty-five hundred dollars!"

But her indignation didn't touch father. Neither the day's heat nor the last of her words affected him. He sat on the bench, looking out at leaves, as though some cold winter had frozen him to the spot, and when the flare of mother's words faded, it seemed that

gray, dreary smoke drifted down over us all, darkening my mother's
face so that what had been marvelously brilliant became paled and
drained before our eyes. But father didn't see that, either.

"Axel, you can't sell for forty-five hundred," my mother whispered at last.

"Mortgage, twenty-seven hundred." (He was counting only to himself.) "Rent, probably twenty-five a month. That's three hundred. Food, a hundred a month. Fifteen hundred. One year. It'll do for one year. Perhaps stretch it some. By then, maybe—."

And then he turned from the window and looked at mother; but she bent from his haunted, calculating look, down to Buddy squeezing her knees. She lifted him up and went away with him, murmuring. "Don't cry, Buddy. There, now. Don't cry."

Johnson came and went at irregular intervals. He brought one or two prospective buyers, who went through the house in a desultory way and did not return. My father still walked to town each day and returned with hurt feet and a bad temper. Jenny was in the empty lot almost all of the time. She named the kitten Tiger, although he had a gray coat with a white bib. Mother was quiet and remote. The frown between her fair brows seemed permanent.

Then it was late June, and we were out of school. The blue days were long and unseasonably hot. Mornings we played in the shade of the oak in the back yard, and afternoons we retired to the damp coolness of the basement and played there. Mother answered an ad in the paper and began to do piecework for a knitting mill. She got twenty-five cents for each finished sleeve. It took her six hours to knit one sleeve. Father forecast total disaster. "Democracy," he intoned. "A beautiful intention. Failed!"

We went to Powderhorn Park on the Fourth of July. We sat on high hills ringing the small pond and watched the fireworks spray across the close, dark sky. At the end, a box of fireworks blew up, and the show ended precipitously in a wild spatter of sound and brilliant, confused flares, rockets, Roman candles and fire fountains. "Fourth of July," Father shouted. "Last rites."

In the middle of July, the middle of the day, we were in the basement, canning peaches. Jenny and I had slipped the wet, limp skins from the fruit. Mother had halved them, stoned them, slid the yellow rounds into the green Mason jars that stood in rows on the newspaper-covered table. On the small, two-burner gas stove, sugar syrup simmered over a blue flame. The cool air was heavy with sweetness. Mother lifted the pot of syrup from the stove.

The doorbell rang.

"Shoot. Who can that be?" She set the pot back on the stove, lifted the corner of her wet, stained apron, and wiped the fine beads from her forehead. "Berit, run up and see."

I ran up the stairs, through the shade-drawn rooms to the front door. As I reached the door, the flat, dull buzz repeated. I pushed down the latch; pulled at the heavy door with both hands, and almost fell forward into the blast of white light.

"Well, hello, little girl, is your mother home?"

I recognized that high voice. I peered into the sun and up. Behind Mr. Johnson I saw another form, a large bulk of darkness, someone strange, a woman. A buyer. Important.

I banged the door shut and ran back through the dim rooms and down the stairs, shouting, "Mother, it's Mr. Johnson. And someone else."

Upstairs, the doorbell buzzed. Mother dropped her hot pad and towel, ran ahead of me up the stairs, through the house to the front door. "Excuse me," she said, when I pulled the door open again. "Please come in."

Mr. Johnson looked at my mother as though he towed behind him a cargo of untold value. His face was several shades brighter than usual, his grin wider and looser. "This is Mrs. Faulk." He flapped his hand like a flag.

She had a forward-thrusting, presumptuous bosom, a chin tucked forbiddingly back toward a stiff neck. Her black eyes looked all around coldly, possessively, taking everything in and giving nothing out. She swayed into the living room behind the shelf of her bosom like a captain looking over a ship's bridge. "The shades," she commanded.

Mr. Johnson rushed to a window and jerked at the hoop on the string of the shade.

"I'll do that, Mr. Johnson." My mother's voice was new, and I turned and saw that she had learned in one swift lesson the art of condescension. She went from window to window, her back and mouth stiff. The hot sunlight broke into the room's summer shade.

"Wisconsin stone." Mr. Johnson gestured grandly toward the fireplace.

Mrs. Faulk exhaled audibly through her thin nose. She pushed at the carpet with the perforated toe of her black oxford.

Mr. Johnson stooped and flung the carpet back. "Good—excellent condition, the floors," he cried. "Fine housekeeper, fine, fine."

Red spots marred my mother's cheeks. Her lips closed in upon themselves. "I will leave you, Mr. Johnson. Excuse me." She turned away with her chin high, signaling indifference. She shooed us children down the stairs ahead of her into the basement. She lifted the syrup from the burner and poured it into the jars filled with mounded peaches. White steam rose around her. She blew a long breath up toward her hair, lifted an arm, wiped her forehead.

"Is she going to buy the house, Momma?" Jenny looked toward the stairs, as if she expected to find those cold black eyes staring down at her.

Mother didn't answer.

We were to move to a duplex on Cedar Avenue. It was a high, narrow, scabby-looking building. Its brown paint was flaking.

Black screens on the windows and front porch gave it a sinister aspect. The patch of ground that was its front yard was burned dry, and the bushes flanking the steps were woody and tangled. Traffic was steady down Cedar Avenue. At regular intervals, streetcars roared through its steady hum.

"It's temporary," father repeated, as we toured the empty, high-ceilinged rooms.

My mother eyed inadequate closets; high, narrow windows.

"I can put shelves over the stove," father said, as we trailed through a small kitchen. "The children can sleep three in one room for a while," he asserted, standing in the center of a lightless bedroom. "After all," he shouted at my silent mother in the small, square living room, where dark woodwork looked soft and disintegrating under too many coats of varnish and stain, "what do you expect for twenty dollars a month?"

"Who's complaining?" my mother said, and walked out the door and out to the car at the curb.

But whatever anxiety and pain touched the rest of us still did not touch Jenny. She went about with her face looking like a flower with sun on it. As long as she had the kitten to be sometimes cuddled, sometimes played with and murmured to, nothing else affected her.

But I knew, if Jenny did not, that her strange impregnability was doomed. Time, which she ignored, was still inexorable. Days dawned and turned and passed into swift, forgotten nights. When six or seven more had gone, Jenny would have to abandon her kitten to his makeshift home in the empty lot, and her present happiness would shatter into loss.

On the last day of July, early in the morning, father's friend Lars arrived at the house with an old truck. Draperies were down, folded into huge cardboard cartons and covered with sheets. The rugs were rolled into cylinders. The house echoed when we spoke.

Father was furious with energy. He shouted at all of us. "Get that box out of there. Berit, open that door. Let's get that chest next, Lars. Emma, bring the hammer. Berit, get Buddy out of the way."

Everyone but Jenny hauled and shoved and carried and ran. She was not around.

It was past noon when they went off with the first load. Lars was driving. My mother sat beside him, smudged and disheveled, holding Buddy on her knees. My father stood on the crowded platform of the truck, leaning his elbows on the cab's roof. I was left behind to watch the house.

As soon as the truck rumbled out of sight, I ran to the empty lot to find Jenny. The high, covering weeds were dry. They scraped at my legs as I ran. At the far corner of the lot, the tumble of honey-

suckle shimmered where sun touched it. The tiny yellow blossoms
gave off light as though of sun themselves, and as I came near the lit
place, the air was suffused with fragrance.

"Jenny?" I whispered, as though the place would be marred by
ordinary sound. She did not answer. "Jenny?" I moved a branch,
and in the deeper light, I saw her there, lying face down on the
patch of ground smoothed with use. Her long hair was tumbled
over her neck and face. The gray kitten jumped about her, hissing
softly and clawing at the strands of her hair. The light was golden
upon them, and in its dapple, they seemed private and privileged.

"Jenny!" I said harshly, although why I scolded her I was not sure.
She flung back her hair and looked at me.

"Jenny, come on home," I commanded, though when I came, I
had no plans for ordering her away. The sight of that much happiness somehow made it seem necessary to save her from it.

Jenny sat up and took the kitten into her arms. It lay in the folds
of her smooth arms, a soft gray bundle collapsed into comfort. The
kitten's wide eyes narrowed down, and a lush rumble of purring
filled the shady den. Jenny looked at me, her own eyes grown
heavy-lidded with secrecy and willfulness. She shook her head. "I'm
not coming. I'm going to stay here."

"Jenny, come on. They're coming back. You can't stay here
forever."

Jenny looked only at her kitten. She stroked it, and her face began to assume a look of dreams and separation. Then she stopped,
shook the hair from her face, sighed. "I'm hungry, Berit."

I could do nothing but go back across the burned grasses to the
disordered kitchen and make peanut-butter sandwiches and take
them to her with a glass of milk.

I watched while she ate the sandwiches and drank the milk. She
stopped drinking before the milk was gone. She held the kitten and
tilted the glass, so that he could lap up what was left. I sat and
rested and did not say all the things I had already said too often.
Now more than ever, she would not listen to what I said, and if I
felt sorrowful and full of foreboding, perhaps by now I also envied

her for being able to give so wholly what I, possibly, could never give—a desire and love so entire that it could not conceive disaster, although what it risked challenged all realities.

Perhaps I guessed, too, that for one like Jenny, so much more possessed by what she found within herself than I, that it was not a matter of choice. Even if she admitted that she would lose her kitten and her believed-in unreality within a few short hours, that knowledge would not diminish or alter her commitment, and she would have to accept and endure the suffering which was the price of her gift.

Then I heard the truck's faulty motor clattering up the avenue, I left Jenny in the honeysuckle and ran back to the half-emptied house before father and the gloomy-faced Lars climbed out of the truck.

I ran with them from room to room, as they heaved and hauled the rest of the afternoon.

It was after five, and the hot day was dulling down toward a ruddy evening when father wearily brushed his hands on his haunches, looked around the emptied rooms, said, "Well, I guess that's it. Let's go."

He closed and locked windows and doors, strode out to the truck, and was halfway up on the seat behind the steering wheel when I grabbed his sleeve.

"Jenny. We have to get Jenny."

Surprise sent his eyebrows high up his sweaty forehead. "Jenny? Where is she?"

I pointed to the empty-looking lot. "Over there."

"Well, go get her." He pulled his leg up and settled down behind the wheel. I shook my head. "Hurry up," he shouted, and I ran again over the weeds, knowing what would happen.

After he called the third time, I trudged back to the truck. "She won't come."

"What do you mean, she won't come? Where is that girl?" father demanded.

I pointed to the corner of the lot. "Over there. In the honeysuckle bush."

He jumped out of the cab and went down the walk and across

the vacant lot, shouting, "Jenny, Jenny," in a huge voice, his long legs pumping furiously. I ran after him and saw him rummage through the tangle of branches and stand tall and momentarily arrested when he uncovered her there.

Color and weariness and anger deepened in his face as he looked. He took it all in at once—the nest in the box, the tin for food, the look of custom within the den, Jenny kneeling there on her cleared ground, her kitten against her breast, her eyes at last barren with fear. There was that moment of silence, each one looking, disbelieving, upon the other.

Then father burst into rage. "What in God's name are you doing here?"

With that shout, Jenny changed, stiffened, turned adamant with desire. In eye and mouth and uptilted chin, her will was pitted against his own. "Go away," she shouted. "Go away!"

A snarl like anguish rolled from father's throat. With flaming face and burned eyes, he bent and grabbed the animal from Jenny's arms. He held it by the neck in one hand. The kitten's body arced and twisted. It spit and clawed. Its pointed teeth yearned in the arched red mouth. The claws whipped at father's arm.

Jenny flew at father. She beat on his chest with hard fists, kicked wildly at his legs. Leaves and light shook over the three of them in a whistling, spattering storm.

The fury on father's face became a look I had never seen. That snarling sound repeated in his throat. He wrapped a large, wrenching hand around the kitten's wild, twisting form and turned it fiercely away from the hand that held the kitten's head.

The tiny crack broke through the spitting and the hissing and Jenny's crying, and, in immense silence, the kitten fell from its single, violent shudder and lay broken, looking only like a dirty rag, upon the ground.

With one long cry, Jenny fell upon it there. Father reached down and grabbed her and flung her over his shoulder. He plunged through the fragrant, blossoming branches and ran toward the truck.

We were not what we had been. What was known was gone. What was new was strange. The darker light and limited space of the place in which we lived robbed even the furniture of familiarity. But if the place in which we lived was bleak, it was less than the bleakness each of us found within ourselves. For Jenny and I could not forget. We would never forget; we knew that. And we could not understand at all.

Those summer days, Jenny sat on the chipped concrete steps in front of the duplex and looked at the paper-littered, track-scarred street and did not see what she looked at. Not even the abrupt, pain-ing roar of the streetcars changed the flat disinterest on her face.

If father saw her there, her small round chin held on one up-turned palm, unwilling or unable to play, his frown pulled blackly across his face. "Let her sit," he'd say roughly. "She'll get over it."

But in his eyes there was a distance that had not been there before.

On a leaf-strewn day in October, Jenny and I walked home from our new school. Early evening already blended shadow to dusk. A skinny, half-wild cat darted out at us from the shelter of a low tree. Jenny screamed when she saw it and ran, terrorized and sobbing, the long block home.

When I went into the kitchen she stood in mother's arms, crying and shaking, her dropped books scattered across the floor. Mother looked at me for the explanation Jenny could not give, and father turned the same mystified and worried look from where he was, half up from his chair at the table.

"A cat. She saw a cat."

The look then that went from father to mother, and from her to him, was so stunned and so cold, so knowing and so burdened that I stood in the center of it, a prisoner in its harsh winter.

Then my father turned away. He laid his arms and head upon the table. His shoulders heaved and humped; but I would not have known those shaking sounds were sobs had he not suddenly pushed away from the chair and fled from the house out into the fallen dark. When he rushed by, I saw the tears runneling his face.

And so we could forgive. We lived through those years to years
more comfortable. We knew again times of happiness and of love.
Looking back, I know that if mother had needed that house less, or
if Jenny had been a less willful child, or father a less passionate man,
or the times easier, there would have been less hurt. But where we
live and where we love, we must, it seems, bear a plenitude of pain.

Terror

Lon Otto's second collection of short stories, Cover Me, *was published by Coffee House Press in 1988. He spent 1989–90 in Central America, writing a novel,* Temper, *and beginning work on a new novel,* The Flower Trade. *He lives in St. Paul, Minnesota, with his wife and their two children.*

"Lon Otto has range and he has intelligence, a great deal of intelligence. But what distinguishes his stories for me is the clear sense of authority in his work. I get a sense of eloquent, even beautiful, shoptalk in his stories, not verisimilitude, or not just verisimilitude, but something the next step up—actual presence perhaps. What we used to call 'vivid,' but vivid from the inside—illuminated vivid. His work has rhythm and pacing. It has, from story to story, surprise, the shifted gears of differentiated concerns. One would not think that the man who wrote 'Submarine Warfare on the Upper Mississippi' could possibly be the same fellow who wrote 'A Regular Old Time Miser' or that either of these writers could also claim 'Welfare Island.' Yet there it is. A Nest of Hooks *reads like a sort of museum, a beautifully curated warehouse of strange and wonderful things."*
STANLEY ELKIN, 1978

The White Arab Gelding plunged and jerked against the longe line at his nose; martingale and side-reins snapped his head back as he reared or tucked low, trying to buck. Again she snapped the long, light whip that never touched him, and again he bucked, backed away, pulling her across the soft earth and sawdust footing of the indoor ring. She snapped the whip hard, hauled back on the longe line. "Trot!" she said, "trot, dammit!" He jumped back once more; reared. Then, suddenly obedient, he began trotting in the circle described by the twenty-foot rope. She moved in a little circle of her own in the center, following him, keeping herself focused on his driving hindquarters, the long whip trailing back from her other hand. "Canter!" she said, and after a moment's hesitation he shifted into the rolling gait that she wanted. "Good," she murmured, following him in her little controlling circle in the middle. "Good." When he slipped back into a trot she had only to raise the whip and speak to him once before he resumed cantering, circling mechanically in the cold, damp ring, his hooves ringing now and then on small stones, sometimes clashing together with a louder, hollow sound.

As the woman and horse moved in their small and large circles, the man leaned against the wooden railing, watching them, his back turned to the row of tie stalls that faced the ring. The stalls were almost all occupied, the horses having been brought in to be fed. They ate steadily, their tails to him. He stamped his feet on the cold concrete, buried his hands deeper in his coat.

When they were done here, then he could go home and take a hot bath and eat supper. When her horse was shod and she had finished her riding lesson and groomed her horse, fed him a last apple or carrot, then he could go out to his car and drive them through the late winter darkness on rutted, frozen roads and narrow county roads and the highway and the interstate back into the lighted city where he would forget the rank, steaming smell of the stable. He would drop her off at her apartment, she would not ask him up, though she might, perhaps, and he would drive through residential streets to his home, park in his garage and step finally into his warm kitchen, leaving his shoes in the entranceway.

A door in the wall across the ring slid open and a man in a T-shirt and heavy leather apron crossed the ring toward him. It was Dave, the farrier, who was to reset her horse's shoes before her evening lesson. "That's the way," the farrier shouted, climbing up on the railing beside him. "Run her legs off, burn up some of that orneriness." The woman hadn't had a chance to exercise the horse in several days, and it was stiff and jumpy from confinement in the ten-by-ten box stall. The farrier perched himself on the rail beside the man, who was grateful for the company, and followed the movement of the horse closely. "She's forging pretty bad, all right," the farrier observed after a moment. The man looked at him, and the farrier explained, "Her hooves are hitting together. Forging. We'll have to change the angle of her hooves a little, slow up them rear feet. Now, if she was running barefoot, Mother Nature would take care of it." The farrier's shaggy hair curled at his neck, dark with sweat in the cold stable.

In a few minutes the woman finished longeing the horse and led him back to the enclosed double line of stalls behind the far wall of the ring. She snapped slack chains to his halter from each side of the walkway and fed him an apple from the palm of her hand, saying comforting, encouraging words to him. "Oh, I love you so much!" she said to the horse, her arm hugging his neck. "You know I do," she said, "you know I do."

"She'll be all right," the farrier said, patting the horse's side and neck. "We'll get along fine, won't we," he said, scratching at the base of his forelock, wrapping his hand a moment around one startled ear, drawing the head down, then releasing it. "You have to let them know who's boss," he said. "That's the name of the game."

As the farrier straightened out the clinched-over nails in the first front hoof and pried off the shoe, the woman watched closely, squatting on her booted heels beside him. The man leaned back against the rough boards behind her, then squatted beside her, then rose and wandered around the other side of the horse. He examined the neatly arranged tools in the farrier's work box—pincers, small pry-bars, crooked-bladed hoof knife, sledgehammer, nails, brass caliper of some sort—and envied, as he always did, professionals working with tools, people who knew what they were doing. The woman, squatting beside the farrier, had the air of a colleague rather than a client.

The man stood, walked off toward the far end of the stable. In the closed area of the stalls the air was thick with the smell of manure and urine. He looked at his watch; it was after six. Her car was in the shop, so he had picked her up after work to bring her out for her lesson, which wouldn't begin until seven. He hadn't had anything to eat, and he hadn't had a chance to change his clothes. But when she had called the office to ask him to take her to the stable, it was the first time they had spoken in more than a week. He had decided that he didn't care, and then she had called.

He peered into a lightless stall, decided it was empty, then noticed a dark-brown horse standing motionless in back. If it had not been merely a convenience for her. If she had not merely needed a ride to the stable and thought of him, as one who knew the way by heart. If she. If she and he. But that was over; this sudden friendliness between them where there had been tension in good and bad times proved it was over. Which was why he had said, sure, yes, I'll pick you up after work. What was why? What did she want? He turned back, brushing something, straw or something, from his coat sleeve.

There had not been much progress. The farrier talked constantly and worked with an agonizing slowness. He clipped a ragged crescent from the front edge of a hoof and tossed it to the old, fat labrador that had been watching. As the dog grabbed the scrap and chewed at it, growling ecstatically, the farrier leaned against the horse and explained why dogs like hoof paring so much, and told them about a collie he had had when he was a kid, who was scared to death of horses but would come cowering and cringing around when someone was shoeing. The farrier was wiry and boyish, good-looking. As he told his stories he grinned frequently, baring his widely spaced front teeth. The man remembered something he had been told at a party the summer before, a cookout in the pasture of another stable. The woman had told him that most of the horse owners in this country are women, and farriers were said to get a lot of incidental sex. The man thought of Gerard Manley Hopkins' "Felix Randal."

There had been a farrier at that cookout, not Dave, a different one, a big, beefy man, silent and sullen, arrogant. The man had never met this farrier, had never met any farrier before. The man was a stranger to most of the horse people at the cookout, and had only known the woman for a few weeks. He sat on the tailgate of a pickup truck and watched the huge fire, drinking beer with the silent farrier. After a while the farrier loosened up a little and began picking up some of the younger women and pretended to be about to throw them into the fire. The women squealed and protested, and one tall, angry, rawboned woman, sitting on the ground before the fire, said, "When a woman says *no*, it doesn't *necessarily* mean, 'Overpower me!'" She was very sarcastic. Nobody except the man seemed to hear her, and she repeated the statement several times. The man sat on the tailgate, opening another beer, and wondered if he should tell the farrier to cut it out, but that would have been another male fantasy, and might well have ended in humiliation.

He wasn't sure what the woman would have wanted. On the way to the party, the woman had told him she didn't want to go to New York with him. After the cookout, walking arm in arm with him across the hilly pasture, she asked him what he thought of Ed. "The farrier?" he said. "I liked him at first. He seemed what a farrier should be. Afterwards, he was just another asshole bully."

"You were expecting Felix Randal," she laughed. It was the truth. "Kay wants to sleep with him," the woman said. Kay was her best friend among the horse people. The man snorted in disbelief, and the woman said, "Well, he *is* awfully attractive." He couldn't figure her out. And later, when he had returned from New York and she talked about living together, he felt a sudden panic which must have shown on his face, for she had laughed out loud. Later, he changed his mind, but thought that she had changed, too, and so he said nothing, and they just slid along in a relationship that kept him constantly confused and uneasy, even when most happy.

Having finished talking about his dog, Dave hunkered down again beside the hoof he was working on, cleaned the frog with a blunt hook, checked the angle with the yellow brass gauge. He told them the angle in meaningless degrees. "Now, some farriers," he said, "would give her special built-up shoes to stop that forging." He held the hoof cocked on the heavy leather apron covering his thighs. "But me," he said, "I try to let Mother Nature take care of it. Just give her a little better angle," he said, working on the hoof with a big rasp, "then let Mother Nature do her thing." The farrier then told them about the old Indian in Montana who had taught him everything he knew about horses. He told them what he had learned in farrier school, and he told them what he learned from books. "Following Mother Nature," he said, "that's the name of

the game."

When the farrier finally came to the fitting of the first shoe, it was nearly time for her lesson, though her instructor had not yet arrived. The farrier filled his mouth with the sharp shoeing nails; as he was about to tap home the first nail, he told them, through the nails, how important the first two nails were, and then he spat out all the nails and showed them how the nail was curved on one side, straight on the other side from point to head, so it would curve out through the hoof wall, rather than digging back into the quick. "You have to listen to Mother Nature," the farrier said. "She says she don't want nails in the quick. That's the name of the game. Kick your head in otherwise."

By the time the farrier had finished the two front hooves, it was a half hour past the time of the woman's lesson. Her instructor strode in then, a tall, thin woman with glasses, and insisted they begin at once. And so the woman saddled and bridled her horse and led him into the ring half-shod, while the farrier began work on another horse. "You take your time," the farrier shouted to her, as she disappeared through the passageway into the ring. "I'll finish her up when you're done. I aim to please, that's the name of the game."

The man watched the farrier begin the ear-scratching routine with the new horse and was going to stay there, but then he followed the woman into the open arena and crossed over to the other side. From behind the railing he watched her circle the ring under the glittering glassed eye and furious orders of the instructor. When the woman's hands were not straight enough, or her heels not low enough, or her back not erect enough, the instructor would shout at her savagely, as if personally insulted by each invisible error. And yet the woman's body seemed to him to move in perfect harmony with the horse: formal, controlled. Her jaw was set with concentration, and her lips were tight and pale. Her eyes looked straight ahead without emotion. From behind the far wall came the muffled sounds of the farrier's hammer pounding a shoe into shape.

The man's feet were growing painfully cold. He stamped on the concrete and thought about horses' hooves and iron shoes. The woman was taking the horse across low jumps now. The man was hungry and cold, but watched her for a while more, his throat tightening each time she approached the hurdle. Finally he gave in to his discomfort and retreated into the club room that was built into a corner of the stable. In the room there was a picture window that looked out into the arena; he stood before it, watching the woman and horse, silent through the glass, the instructor's harsh voice indistinct.

After a few minutes the man went to buy a soda from the machine that stood in one corner. The room was shabby and comfortable, warm, furnished with old stuffed chairs, a sofa, hideous lamps on blond end tables, and a television that was always on. The prettiest of several girls who worked at the stables was sitting on the sofa, watching television. The man picked up a horse magazine from the stack on one of the end tables, sat down with it, and watched the girl, who was really very pretty, watching the show. Like everyone there she wore boots, Levis, flannel shirt, and down vest. She looked good, lounging on the old couch, watching television without expression.

Another time when he had been out to the stable, this girl had come into the club room with a pail of dark water and a bottle of Lysol, her arm black to the elbow, stinking. "Been cleaning out my gelding," she had announced, and she and the woman had laughed, discussing what worked best for that unpleasant job. Another time he had watched the woman do it to her own horse, dipping her fingers in petroleum jelly, then reaching far up into the penis sheath of the edgy horse, dragging out a muddy, tar-like crud on her finger tips. As she reached in, the horse had raised one hoof slightly, and he had had to look away.

As the man finished his soda, a boy of eighteen or nineteen, the son of the stable owners, came in and sat down beside the girl and gave her a little hug. He watched the show for a minute, then began to unwrap the supper he had brought in a paper bag. He took out a banana, nudged her, and began drawing the skin back slowly.

"Is this the way you like them?" he asked. She turned, looked at it a

moment, then turned back to the television. "I've seen better," she
said, and the boy laughed. She ignored him after that, and after
he finished the banana and a sandwich, the boy rested his arm on
the sofa back behind her, not touching her, and became engrossed
in the show.

The riding ring was empty. The man left the club room, meeting
the instructor coming in, who was talking to herself. He crossed
the arena and found the farrier working on the woman's horse
again, the woman beside him, speaking soft words of praise into
the horse's soft-furred ear. The farrier was tired by now and talked
even more, worked even more slowly, than before. He was telling
the woman about the types of horse to watch out for: horses that
have domed foreheads, that show a lot of white around the eyes,
that are yellow in color.

The man leaned against a wall near them, numb now from waiting so long. The farrier was telling about a wild mustang he'd
bought in Montana and brought back the year before. "That little
horse looked so fierce," he said, squatting beside the patient horse,
"the vet wouldn't go into the stall with him to give him his shots.
I spent most half of fall building a stockade for breaking that son of
a bitch. Nine foot high stockade. Finally I got some of my buddies
over to help, and got the animal out into the stockade. I was scared
to death, but then I just jumped on him bareback, like that Indian
in Montana taught me. Expected to get thrown a mile. Well, damned
if that bastard didn't act as calm as pie, went around that stockade
like he was born in it, never bucked once. Hell, in a week the kids
were riding him!" The farrier chuckled at his story, then turned to
his work again. The woman, who was feeling relaxed and cheerful
after the lesson, asked the farrier questions about everything he was
doing. The man wondered if she thought the farrier was attractive.

He watched them for a while, then walked down the line of
stalls. A huge, roman-nosed, gray stallion, a prize-winning jumper,
was champing on a frayed, wet piece of wood he had torn from his
stall. Curious, eyeing the man warily, the horse extended his mas-

sive head toward him over the gate of his stall as he passed. The man stopped, and the horse jerked back a little, nickering, letting the scrap of torn wood fall to the concrete floor of the passageway.

Feeling a sudden surge of compassion for the high-strung, powerful animal, a vague pity that nearly drew tears to his eyes, the man leaned over, and with two fingers he gingerly lifted the dark mass of pulped, sopping fibers, swung it once, and tossed it back into the stall. And the great gray horse startled, started back in his stall from whatever it was that was arcing suddenly towards him, reared, wild-eyed and screaming, pawing the ground and pounding his enormous, battering hooves against the boards of his stall in terror.

Sunday Morning

Pat Carr was born in Grass Creek, Wyoming, and has lived in Cali, Colombia, and various places throughout the South and Southwest. Her first collection of stories, The Women in the Mirror, *was followed by others, the latest of which is* Sonachi. *She teaches creative writing at Western Kentucky University in Bowling Green.*

"Pat Carr's stories have solid, traditional virtues—excellent prose, skillful dramatic structure—and they are especially impressive for the variety and depth of their subjects. A clear moral vision prevails throughout and the most delicate and exquisite psychological situations are rendered with subtlety and good effect. She is the kind of writer who, with remarkable consistency, produces stories that are at once finely controlled and significantly moving."
LEONARD MICHAELS, 1977

"Just take it easy. It doesn't hurt that much."

His voice was suave, calm, practiced.

The pain welled out, radiating, cutting her in half so sharply, so abruptly that her breath stopped. There was nothing but the white pain filling her, consuming her. Then it started receding, drawing back into itself somewhere inside that was not a part of her, and she remembered that she wasn't supposed to hold her breath, that she was supposed to pant like a dog instead.

"Now see."

He put his hand heavily on the white swathed mound and she felt it and knew it was a part of her he was touching, something that had belonged to her but somehow didn't anymore.

She moved her ankles against the straps, the metal against her heels, but she couldn't see them over the mound.

It started again.

She knew she could stand it, she was prepared for it, and she remembered to open her mouth and take in the short choppy bits of air. But it was worse than she'd thought as it swelled, carrying her with it behind her closed eyelids and passed what she could stand.

"Just relax," the nurse said from somewhere outside the pain. "They're coming along nicely now, doctor."

It went down again, lowering her with it onto a glass shelf. But she'd tensed against it and she was stiff.

"Breathe, breathe. That's the girl."

She should concentrate on relaxing the next time it came, telling herself it couldn't win, but a woman was screaming through a wall in the next cubicle, and she couldn't close out the sound enough to think herself calm.

"Listen to the one Dr. Davis got," the nurse said.

As it started, a hand pressed down on the mound and it fought against the hand, sharpening itself, breaking her in two. She wanted to push the hand away, but both of hers were strapped down and she could only move her head from side to side.

Breathe, breathe, pant like a dog next time.

She didn't know if it was actually worse or if she was merely giving in to it a little more each time, letting it swallow her, melt away a little more of her, feed on her from inside, grow each time.

When it recoiled, she wouldn't be blind and could focus, hear their voices.

She didn't know how long it had been coming, receding, its swells of brilliant pain sweeping her up, out, faster, the lowerings shorter, almost without a chance to pause. She lost contact with time and her arms and legs knotted into clenched muscles.

Then "I see the head coming," he said.

But somehow that didn't mean anything in the grip of the terrible grinding pain. She tried to rise above it, to breathe, but she couldn't find the rim of it and her lungs wouldn't work around it.

"Push now."

Again and again, faster, one swell coming before the last had quite gone down. Moans were close around her and she felt the clamminess of her forehead like blood.

"Push!"

She had to defecate but the pain clamped around her and it was as if her insides were crashing through the partition of her bowels.

"There!"

A great rushing, bursting, shattered the glass shelf.

"There," one of them said again.

It receded again and a hand touched her. It had gone down enough for her to open her eyelids.

He was holding up a baby. A slick blue yellow body, long and lifeless, a narrow and hairless animal.

Then he slapped his hand against it and the body quivered, took a breath that washed through it in a pink flood and changed the yellow. It let the breath out again in a fierce cry.

He gave it to the nurse who began busily wiping it at another table as the pain started again.

She gasped and was betrayed. It hadn't ended. She moaned.

"That's the afterbirth coming now," he said complacently and put his hand on the white mound again.

She looked at it startled even over the pain. It hadn't gone down, hadn't changed at all and yet the baby was already out. But then she could see it ripple, looser than it had been, sway as the pain came and went, lessening, lessening.

"Do you feel that?"

He was sitting at the foot of the table below the mound and she couldn't see him.

She waited to see if there was anything to feel. "No."

"I'm sewing you up now, but I didn't think you'd feel anything. Usually the pressure of the head has deadened everything."

He went on talking and she could see the long rough strand pull up in a hemming motion as he sewed.

Her muscles ached with excruciating stiffness and the waves of pain were still coming, going. But it had weakened, it was over and she knew it.

The woman next door was still moaning.

They had taken the baby away and she realized she hadn't asked what it was. That didn't seem to matter somehow.

Without interest she let them do whatever they were doing. She lay racked, waiting.

Finally they released her ankles and wrists, but the cramps didn't go away immediately as she'd thought they would. The nurse brought another stiff new sheet and recovered, rearranged her. They put a needle in her arm and hooked it to colorless tubes that ran to a colorless liquid in a bottle above her head.

"There we are."

In a bright glare of lights two white suited men wheeled her out into the hallway.

Whitney was there and pressed her hand with his until her bones hurt. He was smiling, patting her hand all the way down the hall to the room.

The baby was already there in a white bassinet laced with a blue ribbon over the top and she wondered if that meant it was a boy.

They wheeled her next to it, rolled her and the colorless tubes onto the hospital bed there beside the bassinet, covered her with the stiff sheet and a white cotton spread.

"Is this ours?" He was peering down into the curve of the bassinet.

It wasn't, it was hers, but she looked over, not to have to say it, looking toward but not really seeing the baby, and nodded.

C. E. POVERMAN

A Short Apocryphal Tale of the Sea My Father Would Deny Anyway

C. E. Poverman has published three novels since The Black Velvet Girl—
Susan, Solomon's Daughter, *and most recently* My Father in Dreams. *He
has finished a new collection of stories and is working on a novel. He works and
lives in Tucson with his wife and two children.*

*"Poverman takes us to new places, new cities of the imagination. He is adept,
surprising, sometimes harsh and frequently very funny—a real discovery."*
DONALD BARTHELME, 1976

My father's always been a tyrant at sea. This year it got so bad, my
mother absconded even before we left the Florida coast. She is
waving goodbye from the dock, Ruby is leaning against the mizzen-
mast behind my father, and I am midships striking my father's
owner pennant—a scalpel crossed with a long-stemmed martini
glass.

Now Ruby is telling about the rickshaw boys who couldn't stop,
skidded on the ice, and went through the whorehouse; my father is
laughing so hard he is spilling his martini on his fly. Ruby is the
only person who makes my father laugh like this.

Each year Ruby and my father laugh all the way across the Gulf
Stream, through the Bahamas, back across the Gulf Stream and up
to spring training.

231

There, of course, at spring training, my father comes in every day on special passes from Ruby, my father who had never cared for baseball before Ruby sailed with him, and he watches Ruby stretch his six foot eight inch frame under the late winter southern sun, watches him go into his wind up, raise his thirty-eight inch arm kick up his leg and release the wonderful hard white baseball from his fingertips. My father sits up in the stands wearing brown and white saddle shoes and a boater, drinking soft drinks and eating hot dogs and keeping his tan. He watches Ruby throw terrific fastballs, sliders, and get his fast and slow breaking curve working. My father, who never cared for baseball, can actually see Ruby getting his stuff day by day. Ruby frequently looks up at my father in the stands and then throws a beautiful untouchable curve. After my father sees to it Ruby gets his stuff, he flies home to take up his practice of mending shattered and broken bones, twisted spines, etc. For the first time in his life, he reads the standings, at least of Ruby's team and probably the other teams, because to know where Ruby's team is he has to know where the other teams are.

My mother stayed on the dock. Just Ruby, my father, and me. We sailed from cay to cay, spearfishing and laughing. With my mother gone, I found out things I'd never suspected about my father. One was that he made terrible scrambled eggs. Much too dry.

Here is the blowfish I speared the other day, spines still extended, semi-inflated, lashed to the mainstay. I took him for a grouper in about twenty feet of water and went speeding in for the kill. He disappeared under a coral head with my spear sticking through him. When I tugged he came slowly swimming toward me trailing clouds of blood, his body inflated the size of a basketball, his spines extended. I let go of the spear gun and swam backward into Ruby, I started, I turned to see Ruby, his lips puffed up around the mouthpiece of his snorkel, his hair streaming his body an ashen underwater pallor; in the one-way mirror of the sea shining in his mask, I could see his eyes bulging; he was trying to keep from laughing underwater . . .

On the surface, gasping, snorkel spat out, mask pushed back,
Ruby treaded water, laughed, sucked huge gasps of air, laughed,
sank, treaded water harder, laughed, sank, laughed . . .

Ruby varnished the blowfish, presented it to me in a sunset ceremony, then lashed it to the mainstay at head height—his head
height.

We had a good time sailing from cay to cay.

We ate the tails of crayfish and grouper when I could tell the
difference.

Ruby and I sleep aft of the forepeak, Ruby sleeping in the star-
board bunk and myself in the port bunk. The bunks come together
against the forepeak. In fact, Ruby's legs are so long they curl
around the bottom of his bunk into the bottom of my bunk. We
sleep with our heads full astern on opposite sides of the V, our feet
the meeting, our heads the points of the V.

I was in the process of untangling my feet from Ruby's one
morning when I noticed there was blood on the sheets. I sat up
suddenly and hit my head on the deck. Years of cautious sitting up
forgotten, I sank back onto the pillow holding my head and weeping tears of rage at my father's boat. I sat up slowly. I untangled my
sheets, parting them gingerly like the tissue on birthday neckties,
I pulled one foot toward me, then the other, but my feet were
whole and uncut, white as wild daisies. Ruby's . . . were still oozing
blood in several places. He slept soundly, his Roman nose plowed
into the pillow.

He couldn't put any weight on them. There was no point in even
trying. I brought him breakfast in bed. As he ate, he told my father
and me he'd been winning last night in the gambling clubs across
the cay. Roulette. Blackjack. Craps. Etc. There, he'd met a lithe-
some young creature, taken his winnings, and gone on to a native
bar far from the beaten path. About the time Ruby's new lady ex-
cused herself for a run to the ladies' room, a man appeared at the
door, had anyone seen his wife, the bar got quiet, Ruby figured out

who the man's wife was, the man in the doorway was giving a dem-
onstration with his fishing knife, if I catch the man who is with my
wife tonight, I am going to do this, and he swiped at the air, and
this, swipe, and this, stab, and this, lunge, and this, ha!, Ruby into
the men's room as she comes out of the lady's room, 2 plus 2, Ruby
pushed out the bathroom window, pulled himself through . . . out
to the road and running in the dark his sandals still under the bar
stool and running down the road as a car's headlights went on and
the headlights coming down the road growing bigger behind Ruby
almost on top of him sprinting spring training early this year on
these crushed coral roads the car right behind him he veered and
dove into the brush which grew tight up against the road the car
swung to shine its headlights after him into the brush and all four
doors opened. Men disembarking. Ruby crawled on all fours out of
the headlights, up, and sprinting through brush across coral, the
men veering, lost, hard to see them in the dark, like Korea again,
black on black, sudden noise behind Ruby, one of them on the
right track collided with Ruby's . . . right fist. And Ruby got away.
Much later, he doubled back to the road, met the girl and took her
to a beach.

That made my father smile under his mustache as though he'd
just performed the first successful pelvis transplant.

But the feet.

Ruby sat on a bunk in the main cabin where—using the overhead handrails—he'd managed to limp the four or five steps from
the bow. Hands locked behind his knees, he slowly raised one foot,
then the other. My father kneeled on the floor, put on his trifocal
surgical glasses, and gently took each of Ruby's feet in hands—
torn, blackened, embedded with grains of coral, bloody—my father shook his head and got a strange look on his face—perhaps
sad, perhaps wistful—and told me to bring a large basin of warm
salty water.

The ash of my father's Schimmelpinnck falling into the water as
he placed Ruby's foot in the basin . . . ash floating, a grey smudge,

gone . . . My father applied antiseptic ointments to Ruby's feet,
lightly wrapped them in gauze, gave Ruby some antibiotics, and told him to stay off his feet. He took the Schimmelpinnck out of his mouth. And don't worry.

A blow came in. We left the dock and anchored to ride it out. With his feet propped up on a cushion and his lap covered with yards and yards of beautiful white dacron, Ruby mended sails while we wound and unwound above our anchor.

On about the second day, I dropped my father's Zippo lighter overboard. Between blasts of wind, when the water surface would clear, I could see the lighter down there on the bottom. My father asked once if anyone had seen his lighter and I shrugged. He gave me an odd look. I kept watching the Zippo on the bottom. It was the size of half a dime. I was afraid some currents might cover it with sand and I'd lose sight of it.

Late the second day, I dove. Underwater, the lighter grew to the size of a waffle iron as I approached. I dove closer and closer and then my ears began to ring, my sinuses ached, and I choked back a gag as my lungs got hot. My dive lost momentum I stretched out my hand for the lighter, I was nowhere near, I tipped my head up and beat it for the surface driving my fins the hull of the boat hanging above like a face without features, I burst to the surface spitting out the snorkel mouthpiece and gasping for air.

My father was in the cockpit. All I could see was his head, his profile, really; he was staring up toward the bow, somewhere beyond the bow, his head in profile, his bent nose, his grey hair blown up in wisps like mare's tails, his mustache and his Schimmelpinnck stuck beneath his mustache the ash at the tip hanging on in the wind . . .

. . . closer I startled up a ray buried in the sand he winged slowly away trailing sand I grasped for the lighter in my hand a cloud of sand rose I rolled on my side and looked over at the anchor buried in the sand magnified about the size of a Cadillac the anchor line thick as a tree going slack and taut with the tugging of the hull, the line rising going up disappearing through the surface of the water cut off hanging like an Indian swami's rope through the water the grey sky silvery I went back up.

When I hauled myself on deck, my father took the Schimmelpinnck from between his lips, taking a swim?, I held up the dripping lighter between my fingers, but didn't grin, when did that go over he said in such a way I felt as though he had added it to a wearisome list in his head, he put the Schimmelpinnck back in his mouth.

Below, I took the Zippo out of its case, unscrewed the spring for the flint, washed the whole thing in fresh water and lighter fluid and put the spring and the cottony insides and the case behind the stove to dry out.

During the days, the boat would swing and shudder in the wind and thousands of miles of clouds would blow over our masts. I'd watch the people passing on the road along the shore, the men walking or with bicycles, the women moving on their errands. On the fishing dock, the men would come in at odd times and stand up side to side against a long board to gut their catches. Knives flashing, they'd slit the fish and throw their guts into the water. I tried to figure out which one was the husband and which one caught the fist. At night, sudden black shadows would drift in and out of the circles cast by the dock and street lights into the water as the sharks would feast on the fish guts.

Every morning and evening my father would take Ruby's feet in his hands and examine them for signs of infection and progress. He would smear them with ointment and give Ruby his antibiotics for the day.

About the fourth or fifth morning of the blow, I woke to find

Ruby's bunk empty. He was standing and moving about the cabin
pretty easily. He brought me a cup of coffee in my bunk.

After breakfast, I went topside with the lighter closed in my
hand. My father was watching the clouds breaking up. He turned
to me. I opened my palm. Then I handed him a cigar out of his
sportshirt and ground him up a flame. The flame covered my hand
in the breeze while my father puffed and got his Schimmelpinnck
going. As I handed my father the lighter, he looked steadily at me
behind the clouds of smoke in what I thought was an odd look.
The lighter dropped heavily into his pants pocket and clanked his
change. He nodded, puffed his cigar, and turned his eyes back up to
watch the weather. The sky was blue overhead.

Ruby came topside and got into a conference with my father. We
needed diesel and water. Ruby watched the fishing dock several
moments. He moved back and forth in the cockpit. My father and
Ruby looked at each other. We needed diesel and water.

We had both the diesel and water hoses going wide open in our
tanks with Ruby watching the fishing dock out of the corner of
his eye when there was some movement. The fishermen—six or
eight—had stopped working and were standing in a group.

The town dock was about four or five hundred yards from the
yacht dock. The fishermen moved faster the closer they got, but no
one was running. When they grouped at the end of the yacht dock,
my father neatly squeezed off the diesel and quickly handed the
hose back up to the dockmaster.

I saw Ruby pick up a winch handle.

That was good enough for me. I picked up a winch handle and
stood ready to slip the dockline.

They stood over us, their brown feet making several rows. Maybe
twelve or fifteen men. They stared silently at Ruby who from the

high bow and with his great height rose and fell with the motion of the boat at their eye level on the dock. A number of them had their hands behind their backs and were shifting nervously about.

One of the men, you Ruby Whittaker?

Ruby didn't answer.

I say, maan, you Ruby Whittaker pitch Red Sox?

The man took a baseball glove from behind his back and made writing motions.

I got Ruby a magic marker from below.

Ruby signed the glove: Good Fishin', Ruby Whittaker, Red Sox.

They peeled off their shirts and Ruby spread them fluttering on the deck and signed them.

Baseballs. Softballs.

Radio on full blast, Ruby!, I listen faar at sea, maan, pitch good, maan, last year pitch good against Yankees, I listen in ma boat at sea . . .

Ruby signed the radio.

You gone have good pitching dis year, maan?

Several of the men were looking curiously at the varnished blow-fish lashed to the stay. Maybe these people think varnished blowfish is a delicacy?

. . . the bills of caps, the sweatbands of caps, the brims of straw hats, the palms of hands, the diesel pump, the back of a ten-year-old boy, everyone happy even though the magic marker didn't show up against his sun blackened skin . . .

My father watched proudly from the helm.

Ruby looked at me once and shrugged.

Once out at sea, I struck my father's owner pennant from the spreader—the scalpel crossed with the martini glass. I raised the bloodied sheet to the masthead where we flew it all the way across the shoal of the Grand Bahama Bank, off the bank and out into the deep blue of the Gulf Stream and on to where the Gulf Stream meets the dull blue-green water in a line off the Florida coast. There, I struck the sheet.

My father couldn't make it to spring training that year, he had to go home and fix things up with my mother. He wasn't such a tyrant on shore.

As spring training progressed into the exhibition games and Ruby still hadn't gotten his stuff really working, my father got more and more depressed. He'd stand at the window with the sports page in his hand and stare at the robins in the front yard. He'd sometimes shake his head and look the way he had when he took Ruby's feet in hands.

The grass got greener. The elms leafed and became thick. Exhibition games progressed into the regular season schedule. I knew he was blaming himself for not being there at spring training, but I thought he was being foolish for such a wise man. There's only so much a man can do—even for the national pastime.

Tickets

Barry Targan's most recent collection of stories is Falling Free. *He teaches at the State University of New York, the University Center at Binghamton. When he is not teaching or writing, he tries to sail as much as possible and to garden.*

"In Harry Belten and the Mendelssohn Violin Concerto, we find in wondrous plenty the full range of short story voices and possibilities. There is a bright originality casting long shadows of grand tradition. Barry Targan is a gifted artist who tells his stories with great energy and with graceful care. This is a rich and various gathering, an admirable addition to the small body of genuinely distinguished fiction made in and for our time.

The winning book has in my judgment the best claim for its consistent excellence and maximum variety of character, setting, action, and implication within a unity of personal experience and concerns. Targan is not overtly experimental, but he is strong, solid, graceful, and often very subtle."

GEORGE P. GARRETT, 1975

Morris Jacobi sat at his kitchen table with his forearms resting on the damp plastic tablecloth. His wife Helen had just wiped it with a sponge for the third time in the half hour of his warmed-over supper. Had Morris noticed, he would have expected the scene to which his wife's insistent cleaning was always prelude. But he was weary and did not notice. The time was seven-thirty.

Morris held an empty dessert cup in one hand and with the spoon in his other hand scored channels in the remaining traces of chocolate pudding. From time to time he would put the empty spoon, upside down, into his mouth and leave it there for maybe a minute. In such an interval Helen turned away from the sink to him.

240　　"You want another?" He forgot about the spoon in his mouth

and started to answer her. He stopped trying to speak and removed it.

"What?"

"You want another pudding? You've been scraping the cup now
for so long I don't even have to wash it. You still hungry?" The
thought that he could still be hungry, or might be hungry, caused
her to frown. She left the sink and came to the table.

"Some coffee, maybe," he said.

"Coffee keeps you up. Even the Sanka keeps you up," she reminded him. "With you I think maybe it's mental. So many things
are mental today. You know what I mean?"

"Tea, then," he said.

After Helen had boiled the water and poured him the cup of tea
and cut a wedge of lemon, she sat down opposite him and began to
turn slowly the pages of a *Woman's Day* that lay in front of her.
Morris, with his tea as with his chocolate pudding, seemed to rumi-
nate. He sipped slowly and only at long intervals. The tea became
cool. Morris was silent. After fifteen minutes, the tea almost gone,
Helen looked up from her magazine and told her husband that Mr.
Feldman from the synagogue had stopped by that morning and
wanted to know whether the Jacobi family wanted the fifty or the
one hundred dollar seat tickets. Morris looked at his wife without
pain, and with certainty said, "None of them. Not the ones for fifty
or a hundred." Then, "What seats? What tickets?"

Helen told him they were seat tickets for the high holidays.

"Yeah," Morris said, "well, we don't need seats for a hundred
dollars or even fifty. We can sit on the benches downstairs like always and for nothing. God's God," he added.

"Out here," Helen explained, "they don't have a downstairs. You
can't even get inside without having tickets." "So we don't go,"
Morris answered. "What? It's the first time we ever missed?"

"It's different out here, Morris," Helen said, finally allowing her
voice to rise. She closed the *Woman's Day*. "Out here I got to see
these women almost every day. You go to the city and who knows
you? But me, every day, every single day except I should be sick or

something I got to see them. So how can I explain not having tickets for the holidays?"

"Explain to them you are up to your ears in debt. Explain to them you just bought one half of a shoe-store and one whole house in Green Acres, where the tax assessment is fifty bucks a thousand." Morris got up. "Tell them you can't afford it. Tell them the truth." He had finished. He walked into the living room, but even before he could turn on the TV Helen was at his ear demanding, now stridently, "What? Are you crazy?"

It was a question to which Morris had addressed himself with frequency in the past six months.

Riding in the dirty train that brought him slowly out of the city to his home he would ask himself if, in fact, he were not crazy. Especially on Thursday and Friday nights, when he would not get home until after ten or eleven o'clock (the store stayed open for a special shopping night and for stock taking), would he question the sanity of his motives and gains. His observations were direct and his conclusions, like an unbalanced ledger, fierce.

For twenty years come April he had sold shoes for Slotkin and Novick—Sampler Shoes, Inc. Slotkin was now dead for over a year and Novick, too old himself (though hale) to handle the business alone, convinced, easily and sensibly, the Widow Slotkin to sell her half of the business to Morris. It was for all three parties a solution, or, to Morris at that time, so it had appeared. Now he wondered.

Before he became a partner he had earned less money, so spent less, lived less spaciously but in greater communion with his wife and daughter and son, and had come to move well and fondly in a neighborhood whose identity in the city had not been lost. All these conditions of his middle-age life had been changed. In place of his substantial savings stood debts which he often felt would be liquidated only with part of (God forbid!) his life insurance. For the frenetic, suffocating joys of his children growing up stood now the boundlessness of the late trains and his weariness. And—stone upon stone—for twenty years of faces and colors and shapes stood the cold, treeless silence of Green Acres and the dogs which charged at him out of, it seemed, all the driveways on the long block at whose end he lived. Morris alone in Green Acres owned no car.

Jolting through the night Morris would look at himself in the train window and try to catch his reflected eyes. He could not escape his own arithmetic. He had traded in one whole existence for another, disagreeable one. Tricked by the convenience of Slotkin's death and Novick's need, Morris had reached out and taken. In an easy, pleasant, lawyer-ish afternoon he had attained the long goal of many men. It was not until some little time after that he realized such a goal had never been his. He felt, as in a bad tasting business deal, that he had been taken advantage of by life. For what? For this had he gone down on his knees to the world for twenty years? Was this what twenty years of sweaty feet added up to? "Shmuck," he hissed at his companion cringing in the window.

"Never again will I ever leave this house, Morris Jacobi. I shouldn't be able to go to *shule* on Yom Kippur. And the children? Think of the children. All their new friends inside and them standing out front, alone." Helen groaned and sank down on the sofa.

"What are you talking about," Morris countered. "That's all them kids go to the synagogue for anyway, to stand outside and *kibbitz*. You think any of them know or care what's going on inside. Ha! Don't make me laugh. A couple of days off from school, that's all it means. The Yom Kippur Social Club. Ha! Don't make me laugh." But Helen was at him.

"You should talk. You're such a good Jewish man? Look who's making who laugh. Besides, they should be able to go if they want to." Again she sank back in the sofa. Two small fists inside of him beat quickly and sharply at Morris's heart. "Gas," he thought, but he was wrong. He turned on the TV and a dark truce fell upon the house until morning.

Morning, breakfast particularly, had become the best part of Morris's day. It was the one family meal throughout the week, not counting Sundays. Both he and the children had to take buses, he to the train station and they to the regional school four miles away. After breakfast Morris, Harry, fifteen, and Barbara, thirteen, would walk the long block together to the bus stop, the children ani-

matedly challenging the day, Morris listening, occasionally questioning, and always being asked to assent to something. Joy of his
joys. Five minutes. At the bus stop they cut him cold to join their
respective knots of new, quickly-made friends. His bus came first,
and without a wave, he mounted to be torn even further away.
"Aaaah," his breath would escape from him.

That morning at breakfast Helen continued her offensive. As
soon as she had placed the grapefruit, unscalloped, in front of them
she began. "When are the holidays, children?"

Harry answered, "Late, this year. Rosh Hashonah starts sun-
down the eighteenth. Yom Kippur the twenty-seventh."

"No school. No school for three days this year," Barbara added.

"This year you'll go to school . . . all three days, too," Helen
threw at them and turned quickly away to the stove for the coffee.

"What?" the children screamed together.

"You heard me," Helen screamed back at and over them. "Ask
your father." Morris gagged on his toast.

"Why are you torturing the children," he asked of her, quietly.
Shame flickered in her eyes, but what was begun was begun. Morris
said, "Always the children have never gone to school on the high
holidays. This year is no different." Harry and Barbara hoorayed.

"Sha!" Helen silenced them. "O but this year *is* different. Before
always, *always*, they had a synagogue to go to. This year, no. So,
no synagogue, so no sense not going to school. The three days
shouldn't be a total loss. That's that."

"What do you mean we don't have a synagogue?" Harry asked
his father. "What about Beth Israel? We just joined it."

"Get your coats," Morris said. "Hurry. We'll miss our buses."

Surprisingly and, to Morris, gratifyingly, for four and a half
minutes of their walk to the buses the children said nothing. Only
when the three were almost upon the bus stop did Harry ask,

"What's going on Dad? Are we going to *shule* for the holidays or
not?" What could Morris say?

"Harry, I don't know." His bus had arrived. Morris sprang eagerly
toward it, but before he could bring himself to enter he turned and
called out after the boy moving toward his school friends, "Harry,

Harry. I don't think so." And then he was in the bus convincing himself that biting off the tongue already poised between his teeth would solve nothing.

Business was unusually—unreasonably—good that morning. Even so, though it absorbed much of Morris, it did not absorb all of him. Nor did the hurried business conference in which he and Novick, but especially he, decided to reorder double on the imitation Capezios which had sold so incredibly fast (one hundred pair in a week) absorb all of him. It took a solid hour of shouting on the telephone to bludgeon out of Krinsky the jobber a promise that was worth something, a promise that he would deliver the shoes by tomorrow, and a lunch-hour rush that lasted two lunch hours to totally absorb Morris. At two-thirty he settled down to a sandwich and coffee in the box-crowded, leathery-smelling backroom. Out in front it was absolutely quiet, for once a good sound, for once, even, satisfying. Morris bit into the sandwich with appetite.

Halfway through Morris's lunch Novick came back to him, worried. "Morris," he worried out loud, "two-hundred-fifty Capezios is a lot of Capezios. You think maybe we should maybe order half?"

Morris smiled, finished the last eighth of his sandwich, and said, "Abe, we got a good price on them because of the size of the order, right? Right! And who was it twenty years ago said to the young salesman, 'You got to have the stock. It's the stock makes sales'? So, what do you think? I ordered two-hundred-fifty pairs of *black* Capezios? Abe, Abe, we got every kind of Capezio made and back-ups." Morris was feeling good, positively. He waxed on. "And Abe, look at the price. For what we bought them even if we sell only half we almost break even." Morris settled back pleased, but the look on Abe Novick's face did not change.

"Morris," he began, "it ain't none of all you said, which is true, but something else altogether. These crazy demands, like for the Capezios. They don't last long. All my life in this business I've seen the same thing. All of a sudden like, they want something. One, maybe two weeks, and you couldn't give it away. And especially with the Capezios. We don't sell them now, before it gets cold and rainy, we ain't *going* to sell them this year." Novick frowned deeper. "That's a lot of money locked up in stock," he added after a moment. His visage was black.

Morris was perturbed. Not that it was uncharacteristic of Novick to worry and to disturb others with his worries; Morris was used to that. But he was not used to Novick worrying so deeply, so insistently, especially when he, Morris, could not see the cause of it. After all, even though what Novick said was true, it was still all hypothetical. What, under the sun, *couldn't* happen? Finally, why hadn't Novick thought of all this when he consented to the order in the first place? Why was he coming now to lay this thing at his feet?

"So?" Morris asked, a touch sharply. "If the fad lasts one week or two weeks what's the difference? At the rate we're selling we'll get rid of enough. Some stock you always got to end up with."

"No, no," said Novick shaking his head in gentle, preparatory commiseration. "You don't understand."

"Frankly, I don't," Morris broke in. He got up, ready—wanting—to return to the store, to the selling of the damned Capezios. "Frankly, Abe, I just don't know what you're talking about." He turned and started out.

"The holidays," the old man called after him. Morris spun around.

"What? WHAT?" Morris shouted at him, visions of conspiracy racing through him. Novick, frightened at the sudden turn, drew his left shoulder up an inch and inclined his head down an inch in gesture of defense.

"The holidays," he whined. "We got to close for the holidays. Three days this year."

"*Oi gotteneu*," Morris groaned, turning white. He sank back into the leathery smell of the storeroom onto a shipping carton and groaned again.

Novick was to him in a moment, solicitous, hovering, fretful. Morris, in turn, felt impelled to calm the agitated older man. And both were returned, outwardly at least, to stableness, to the decorum of businessmen, as two customers entered the store.

"I'll get them," Morris said, rising from the carton. Waiting on people was what he was best at. It calmed him to do something he could. To Novick he said, "Call Krinsky and halve the order." But Novick's eyes pleaded. "O.K.," Morris relented, "cut it two-thirds." Novick smiled for the first time that afternoon and went for the phone.

As Morris entered the front he felt a little restored. Part of his pre-lunch ease he had forced to return. "So, look," he reflected to himself, "the world is still turning. Who said it should all be smooth?" But in three seconds even this glaze of calm was shattered. The two superbly dressed men waiting for him were no customers. They were Feldman and Katz from Beth Israel. They had come to sell him tickets.

After introducing themselves Mr. Feldman said, "A nice business you got here Mr. Jacobi." Mr. Katz nodded. Both of them cast about appreciatively.

Morris said, "A nice business I'll *have* when, I should live long enough, it's paid for. And then only half. My partner Novick is over there." He pointed to the cash-out counter behind which Novick was talking into the phone. Feldman and Katz didn't bother to look. They took his word? They didn't care. "What do you want?" Morris asked.

"Could we talk to you? A minute? In the back maybe?" Katz spoke and gestured to the storeroom with his eyes. Morris turned and led them there. They entered and all sat down on the cartons. Feldman began.

"Your wife called me this morning and asked me to talk to you about the tickets."

"Did she tell you why?" Morris asked. "Did she tell you I said we wouldn't buy any tickets? Did she tell you that?" Feldman flushed slightly. Morris knew that Helen didn't tell him anything. She didn't have to. Feldmans always knew such things. Feldmans also knew how to twist your arm. But not this time. Morris braced himself.

"No," Feldman said, "your wife didn't say anything. She just asked I talk to you about the tickets. You say you don't want any. You don't have to tell me anything, but I ask, as a Jew, as belonging to the same congregation, why?"

"I can't afford it, and besides, I just paid two hundred dollars not so long ago just to join Beth Israel. Why should I pay extra for the holidays?"

Feldman smiled. It was the answer, the reaction, he wanted and expected. He attacked swiftly and with a merciless reasonableness. "Mr. Jacobi, Beth Israel couldn't exist on membership dues alone. The additional assessment for seats at the high holidays is really part of the congregation's financial responsibility." Morris waited for more, but there was no more. Who needed more?

"Why, why is the financial responsibility so high in Green Acres?" Morris asked. "Why does God cost so much?" Feldman, Katz, and even Morris himself were surprised and embarrassed at the question. What, after all, had God to do with all this? Katz tittered.

"Why does *everything* cost so much in Green Acres?" Katz and Feldman laughed appropriately, but Morris thought it was a good question. And then Novick entered, distraught, miserable, his sparse white hair flattened down on his soaking pink head.

"Go," he muttered, fluttering toward the telephone with his hand. "Go, Krinsky." Morris dashed out of the storeroom.

During the first ten minutes he argued on the phone with Krinsky about reducing the order, two customers came into the store. Novick did not reappear and Morris could not chance letting Krinsky go. His whole argument turned on convincing Krinsky that it was not too late to cancel, that it was not out of Krinsky's capable hands nor, even, out of the large province of his heart. The customers, annoyed, left. Feldman and Katz came forward, themselves caught by their desires to pull Morris into the holiday congregation and by their own, other temporal demands. A third customer entered the store, but Krinsky's capitulation was nowhere in sight. Where was Novick? "Abe," Morris shouted toward the storeroom, but there was no Novick nor an answer. Krinsky became obstinate, Morris frenzied (was Novick dead?). "Nazi," he shouted into the telephone. "Do you want our blood?" Krinsky hung up. Morris groaned. He had gone too far. The third cusomer left. Novick reappeared.

"I was on the toilet," he explained, apologetically. Morris spun
on Feldman and Katz.

"You want to look at a nice pair of shoes, maybe?" He was shaking. His eyes were antic. Feldman and Katz looked at each other quickly and then away. They started toward the door.

"What's the matter?" Morris demanded. "I got the only shoe store from Green Acres, from Beth Israel even. Why don't you buy your shoes from me?" He looked at their shoes and saw his answer. Leather like that even Morris' jobbers didn't see. The door eased itself pneumatically shut after them. Morris ran for the back room. He came out with his hat on, his coat partly. He ran for the door.

"Where are you going?" Novick screeched after him, clawing the air.

"Out," Morris shouted, and, even louder, "for a walk." But the phone rang to arrest him. Maybe it was Krinsky? It was Helen.

"Morris, Morris, speak to Barbara, speak to our baby. What did you tell Harry this morning? Tell the baby it isn't so. Tell her she can go to *shule*." Her voice rang with the great histrionic Jewish sense of tragedy.

"It is so," Morris blasted back at her. "She can't go." He hung up and walked out into the busy flush of people and was swirled away.

Morris walked a good distance but not aimlessly. He walked back to the neighborhood in which he had lived for the twenty years before the arrival of his swift sloop of fortune, of partnership and Green Acres. In this place he had become a husband and a father. Among these people of these streets he was neither more nor less than what he was. He was Morris Jacobi, seller of shoes, married to Helen, getting matronly fat, father of Barbara and Harry who had a good head for numbers, should maybe someday be an accountant. That was Morris Jacobi, but who was this stranger walking up the five steps of the synagogue entrance?

"Who are you," the *shamus* asked. Morris groaned. He could not say. "What do you want?" he asked, now suspiciously. Fremick, the old *shamus*, was dead, had died just four months ago—Morris had heard. Fremick would have known him. But this new *shamus*? This alien? Morris caught himself. Who was new here, who was the alien?

"Again I ask you, Mister," the *shamus* broke in on him. "What do you want here?" He was insistent.

"I want to see the rabbi," Morris blurted out. He had not come to the synagogue to say that, or to say anything, but having said it, now it seemed right.

"The rabbi's not here. Come back for evening services." The *shamus* folded his arms. Then Morris asked the *shamus* if he could bring his family to the synagogue for the high holidays. The *shamus*'s lips tightened across his teeth, his nostrils sprang hissing into the air, and the cleft between his eyes became a crevice.

"Only," he struck out at him, "if you're a Jew."

Morris fled.

Riding homeward that evening Morris, soul-sore and troubled, had his solution. He and his family would worship at Rodeph Sholom just as in all the years past. Indeed, the solution became more than a solution, it became a pleasure, a warm indulgence. Not even the occasional thought of two-hundred-fifty pairs of Capezios marching through the night toward his store could much disturb him. He settled back into his seat and, at partial peace, watched out of the window the autumn-touched September day conclude.

Morris entered his home to be attacked by his wife's strident accusations and by his children's cold, demanding eyes. They, the children, had been brought up to respect always their father but, alas for this moment anyway, Morris thought, to believe always their mother. Nevertheless, he thought, he had a good hand. For a minute or two more he would play it close to the vest. Why not? For what he had paid let him enjoy himself a little. Finally he held up his hands, over his head, like Moses.

"Enough," he said, and they were silent. "We'll go to *shule*."

"Yaaah," they shouted, laughing. The children hopped.

"To Rodeph Sholom," he added.

"O no," they screamed. Barbara began to cry, Helen to pull her hair. Morris, stunned, considered himself. "Some card player," he

thought. Putz, shmuck, schlemeil, dope, nut, jerk. To that cadence
he moved into his gleaming kitchen to serve himself supper. But *Barry*
who could eat? *Targan*

In the darkened living room Morris sat before the unfocused TV.
He saw nothing. Somewhere behind and above him his alienated
family moved. A slammed door, a call, a sewing machine—all insistently, reproachfully excluding him. Inside of him the little fists
beat him black and blue. "Mercy," he pleaded, but nothing happened. At nine-thirty the doorbell rang. It was Uncle Charlie,
Helen's uncle, Uncle Charlie who had been very good to the
Jacobis, had, even, been the co-signer of the great loan which had
bought for Morris all he now had. Uncle Charlie was a rich and
successful man and a leader of the congregation.

"Hel-*lo* Morris. What are you doing, contemplating your navel
here in the darkness? Ho Ho." Some kidder, Uncle Charlie.

"Hello Charlie," Morris said, "Come on in." But Charlie was in.
"Let me help you with your coat." But the coat was already off. "I'll
call Helen." But Helen, who had heard the doorbell, was already
there. Morris tried to wonder why Charlie had come to his house
at nine-thirty that night, but he knew.

"Uncle Charlie," Helen said with affection, and went to embrace him.

"*Mädchen,*" he answered. They hugged. "How about a nice
hot tea?"

"Of course," she said. She took him by the hand and led him into
the kitchen. Morris followed, snapping off the TV as he passed it.

They sat around in the small talk of families and friends while
Helen made the tea. The tea made and half drunk, Charlie began.

"What's this Helen says you're not going to synagogue for the
holidays?"

"We are going," Morris answered.

"O?" Charlie smiled, glancing at Helen questioningly.

"To Rodeph Sholom," Morris added.

"O!" Charlie frowned. "Why to Rodeph Sholom and not Beth
Israel? You belong to Beth Israel." The phone rang before Morris
could answer. It was Krinsky.

"Jacobi," he said, "I can cancel half but not two-thirds, certainly not two-thirds at the price I'm giving you . . . or anywhere near the price I'm giving you. A half but not two-thirds." There was a silence before Morris answered.

"Fine," he said. "A half will be fine." Another silence. "Krinsky. What I said this afternoon. I'm sorry."

"Forget it," Krinsky said. And then he said, "Right then I could have cancelled half." And then, low, "I should have. It wasn't right. Who can sell Capezios Rosh Hashonah, Yom Kippur?" He added his goodnight, Morris his, and they hung up. Morris came back to the table.

"So," Charlie said, "I repeat. You belong to Beth Israel. How come you're not going there for the holidays?"

"Beth Israel wants to sell me tickets. At Rodeph Sholom it's free." Suddenly dizzied with fear at what was about to race out of him into words, he struggled to embrace the hard rock of experience of this life his years had won him, to cling to the mountain's striated face and walk its slim but certain path. But he tripped and, though at once sickeningly spun about by the vagaries of his belief, said, "Like it should be." Out of the dimmest gene and corpuscle sprang five millennia of suffering to assail him. Morris was scared, but the little fists of pain were gone.

"What do you mean 'Free?'" Charlie snapped at him, his blood rising, his ears red. "In this world nothing's 'free.' Was your store 'free?' Was your house 'free?' When you joined the synagogue why didn't you talk about 'free' then? Here!" Charlie reached into his breast pocket and withdrew a check. He flipped it onto the table. "A hundred dollars. Two tickets."

"No," Morris said. Helen caught her breath.

"No? NO?" Charlie couldn't believe it. Neither, quite, could Morris, who could? "So if 'no' explain, please, why not."

"It's a matter of . . . principle," Morris said, the word almost sticking in him.

"*Principle*," exploded Charlie in thunder. "What's a man your age, married, two kids yet got to do with principle?" Morris, himself, wondered. "And let me tell you, Mister *principle*, something else. It ain't *principle* what built Beth Israel *or* Rodeph Sholom. It's this." He hit his fist down upon the check. "And lots more of it." But there, Morris knew, Charlie was wrong.

Charlie rose, picked up the check, and walked over to Helen. "Here," he said, "you keep this until your *meshugana* husband wises up. I got to go." He and Helen walked out of the room. Morris, after a moment, followed.

At the door, ready to leave, Charlie paused and, calmly and softly, said to Morris, "You should think some about your wife and kids before you do this thing." He paused. "And about me, too. What would it look like for me, my own family don't show up? Good night," he said and left. But in two seconds there was pounding on the door. Morris opened it. Charlie stood before him, livid. "For shame," he shouted. "For shame you should do this to me and your family." He clenched a fist and raised it above his head, shaking. "When you needed help for the business did I come? Now what is it so big a thing we ask of you? On your knees, you should go down on your knees praying from us forgiveness. For shame you should do such a thing."

"For shame I do it," Morris shouted back and slammed the door in his face. He jumped back from the door, and from his wife demanded candles.

"What?" asked Helen.

"Candles," he demanded, louder, angry. "*Shabbas* candles."

"What?" she asked again, frozen. But Morris was gone, into the kitchen, into her precise, determined cupboards rooting about in frenzy. She followed him. He emerged from the scattered cupboards holding in his hands two *Jahrzeit* candles, memorials for the dead.

"These were all I could find," he shouted, as if to make it clear to her. He smashed the two drinking glasses of wax against the enameled drain board of the sink, chunks and splinters of glass pattering and tinkling everywhere, specks and smears of blood springing out upon his hands. It was not to death that he would offer.

"O God," Helen screamed. The children, dumb, appeared in the doorway. Morris jammed the mounds of candles down on the table, searched for and found a match and struck it. He lit the candles.

"*Oi, oi, oi, oi,*" Helen moaned. The children came to her. Morris extended his arms, his palms flat out in front of him high over the burning candles, and then brought his hands back to his face, his bloodied fingers covering his eyes. He repeated the gesture.

"Morris, Morris. What are you doing?" Helen called to him.

"Praying," he said, and did. "*Boruch Ato Adonoy Eloheynu Melech Ho-olom Borey Pree Hagofen.*"

"Morris," Helen screamed, chilled. "That's the blessing for wine."

"It's the only prayer I know," he said. And lifting his wounded fingers again and again to his eyes, prayed on into the night.

The End of the World

Natalie Petesch has published nine works of fiction; several have won national awards. Her novels include Seasons Such As These, the odyssey of katinou kalokovich, Duncan's Colony, *and* Flowering Mimosa. *She is the author of the short fiction collections* After the First Death There Is No Other, Wild with All Regret, Soul Clap Its Hands and Sing, *and, most recently,* Justina of Andalusia and Other Stories.

"These are stories written for the most part in a deceptively straightforward and purified manner which permits the images and incidents, the ideas and sentiments, the style and shapes to have, like a shout in a silence, their full effect. There is a sense throughout of the author's restraint, which sometimes gives the impression of conventionality, for these stories are, at bottom, very traditional, yet it is just this 'holding back' which ends in convincing the reader of the confidence the author has in skill and material. . . . Although these stories, then, have a familiar center, they prove once more what care and execution, discipline and certainty, can accomplish."

WILLIAM H. GASS, 1974

Kaethe Kluge—Kate to her friends—was blonde, chunky and loved a good laugh. She believed the end of the world was coming, not in any religious sense, but simply, casually, with no diabolical intent but just the way under-the-arms is the first place a dress rips. It was the sweat that did it, there was nothing one could do about it. Some of Kate's friends were joining communes, they foresaw the end of the nuclear family. Others were laughing or nodding themselves to death on grass or smack; but Kate stayed away from all that, preferring to go out neither grinning nor sleeping but in her right mind. When the time came she was going to stand on a mountain top (she imagined herself somewhere in Nevada), and watch the fire storms from L.A. shake the trees out of their roots.

In the meantime one had to survive, and one stayed clear of jobs that could be called commitments. Kate could have told her friends a dozen ways to survive besides selling their books. But the best way of all, the blood bank, she simply kept to herself, knowing that it took more stomach than most, and scorning any one-upsmanship with her friends.

The first time, she herself had keeled over. The sight of the cold-looking instruments and of her own blood welling into the plastic tube was what did it. But she had got used to it. All her friends knew of it was that twice a month Kate disappeared for the week-end, turned up with fifteen dollars which she promptly spent at the students' co-op for a bag of brown rice, a sack of pinto beans, three pounds of powdered milk and a can of soy bean oil. As to fresh vegetables, that kind of thing, it was rumored that Kate was often seen sauntering down Milford Avenue with an open shopping bag—out on maneuvers, they said.

But the fact was that Kate rarely found it necessary to use her shopping bag for edibles; she reserved it instead for such inarguable necessities as toothpaste, scotch tape and notepaper: she claimed she was keeping a journal for the time capsules, something she predicted would become a popular fad toward the end.

All this required no preparation and no regimen, she could let things slide. But when she met Jésus Quatre-vingts (was it his real name? her friends asked; but Kate only shrugged: if it was *his* name, it was real), she understood at once that he was a threat to her freedom. Waiting for the end of the world was a safe enough thing, she had discovered, but falling in love quite another. For the first time in her life she was seized by a desire to buy land, plant seeds, overcome popular prejudice by being a perfect example of something.

Quatre-vingts was very tall and lean, his pupils seemed ringed with iridescent shades of blue to light purple like the throat of a pigeon. And he had those corkscrew earlocks that, as a child, had made her weep when she had realized that they were nailing Him down to the cross. In the picture the sweat had run from His curls,

just like Quatre-vingts' when she had met him at the blood bank.

She had had no supper that evening and was feeling woozy anyway. She was thinking, when she got the money she'd go out and
blow a third of it on a steak at Masschio's. To-hell-with-it-you-only-
live-once, you know, that sort of thing. Not far from her were a
couple of winos, grumbling that it was taking so long today. One
of them had come fifty miles, from over the state line and claimed
he was dead tired: though he didn't stop talking for a minute. He
was explaining the ropes to the younger guy alongside him, who
didn't want to have a thing to do with it, but listened anyway, the
TV set being out of order. The old guy sold his blood like apples:
he was a professional; he said they didn't keep track of you if you
travelled from one town to another; you could go in every week to
a different one and they wouldn't notice. Only he wasn't feeling up
to it any more. The wine built up your blood but it didn't do much
else good. He went on to show a sore elbow that hadn't healed.
Also some black-and-blue spots on his legs. "Bad sign," he said.
"You're not usin' up the sugar fast's you're takin' it in." The other
wino nodded indifferently. It was clear that he was fresher, newer at
the trade and he was bored by stories of failure; he had his own row
to hoe, all he needed was a gallon of Gallo, he said, and he'd be
ready for the job in the morning. "Job? What job?" asked the older
man. The younger seemed to reflect a moment, caressing his veins
tenderly. "Clean-up man. A couple of churches over to the Hill district." "You gonna clean churches for the *colored*?" The older man's
ruddy face turned beet-red with disgust.

It was at this point Quatre-vingts had come in. He was bare-
footed and that was all Kate could see, as she was lying down, waiting her turn. The attendant had directed him to a table beside hers.
She had noticed how slowly he swung his body back onto the table,
briefly balancing his weight on the palms of his hands, then with a
great sigh he leaned his head back on the table as though he had
come there to rest. He turned to look at Kate. His eyes were so
deep in his head they seemed sculptured in a vein of stone, with the
rings of the pupils shading chromatically outward from the dark

pool at the center. As Kate lay there staring, she felt herself falling into his vision as soundlessly as a swimmer who knows his own power and the depth of the plunge. They lay there silently a few moments, then seized by her own comic demon, Kate had cried out with mock terror: "I'm innocent, innocent! Let me go, and I'll tell all. . . ." Quatre-vingts had grinned and muttered under his breath in movie tones, pseudo-heroic: "Just stick with me, do exactly as I say, and we'll both get out of here alive—I promise you that." During the interval before the attendants return they plotted strategies of "escape." . . . Quatre-vingts had begun to laugh, his joy and recognition resounding through the blood bank.

When he laughed, Kate noticed that he had several teeth missing. It had made her heart ache as though she herself had lost something precious, not having been there when he lost them. She would have said something to comfort him, perhaps: it was clear to her that at this rate, he'd never have money for new ones. Perhaps it was that she was already lightheaded and supperless, but the dark wounds in the laughing mouth had hit her like a bomb, her mood of merriment had suddenly vanished and, instead, a tear rolled down her cheek.

Quatre-vingts had risen from the table. Her eyes fell to the omega sign he wore around his throat; she could see the bones at his neck, thin as knives; and she continued to cry.

"Say, kid, why're you crying? Hey, don't do that. You'll be out of here in a minute. . . . It won't hurt. You won't feel a thing, I mean it."

She knew it was only hysteria and hypoglycemia (or whatever the damned word was) but she couldn't stop. "For a lousy fifteen bucks," she whimpered. "For a goddam lousy fifteen bucks," she sobbed, "they'd crucify Jesus himself."

"Say, kid, how'd you know my name?" he laughed.

And that's how they fell in love. On their way out of the place, the two winos stared at them, they were already holding hands. "Where those two think they're goin'?" demanded the younger sourly. "They're gettin' married," announced the older as if he'd known them all his life. "Oh yeah? And what the fuck they gonna live on?" "Blood," chortled the old wino. "They gonna live on blood."

When Kate had told her mother about Quatre-vingts, Mrs. Kluge had sighed and reminded Kate that she had already been through one marriage to a sweet-looking angel who hadn't made enough money to support his habit.

"But, Mother," Kate argued good-naturedly. "It was you taught me not to be money-minded—told me all about the Rich Man, the one who was going to get his fat stomach stuck in the eye of the needle."

"But that doesn't mean you have to go and marry every bleeding heart you see, does it?" said Mrs. Kluge.

"Well, all I can say is," Kate continued, "that you have only your-self to blame. All those pictures of Him you used to keep tacked all over the goddamned wall. So now naturally when I see anybody looks like him, I just fall all over myself to be in love first thing."

Mrs. Kluge had accepted the injustice blandly. "Well, when you get pregnant, be sure and tell 'em it was the Holy Ghost. . . ."

"Mother . . . people don't get pregnant anymore," Kate said.

Her mother raised an eyebrow. "They don't? . . ."

Kate hadn't answered: because regardless of mother-warnings Quatre-vingts was who Kate wanted, even if the end of the world were to be tomorrow. And on that subject, he and she were of one mind. They believed that People had had it, that Population and the Unthinkable were going to get them before too long. So they made love as though they were on a Sunday school picnic that was scheduled to last till the last megaton bomb. And theirs could have continued to be the savored joy of those who shut themselves off from the plague to tell each other stories, except that (of course, Quatre-vingts said) Kate became mysteriously pregnant. At first they couldn't dig it, and cursed the statistical warranty of the pill-makers who, they said, were probably also turning over a few shares in maternity hospitals. Then they laughed and said what the hell, why not? Having a kid wouldn't halt the apocalypse, but one slightly breathing child wouldn't pollute the air very much either.

But vitamins, iron pills, calcium tablets—these had never been among Kate's inarguable necessities. Such items strained the image of colossal indifference she had used to make as she strolled through the open-shelf drug stores: she was getting too big, in her sixth month, to look indifferent to anything. So Quatre-vingts decided they would swing it somehow with two blood bank visits a month (his), plus one night a week washing glasses at the local bar. And he brought home the entire ten bucks too; the owner of the bar didn't even bother to take out social security, health insurance, that kind of crap intended for when the world was young.

The baby was to be called Consuelo—their Consolation: what else had they found that distracted them so utterly from Armageddon? They found themselves considering unheard-of sacrifices for this generation they believed they'd never live to see. Quatre-vingts even started talking about going to school—they paid people to let themselves be taught how to teach other people, he explained. But Kate was not ready for such commitments. Besides, all her teachers had been a drag, she said: products working to produce products for the Establishment. So Quatre-vingts said, "O.K. Let's wait and see." Meanwhile he enrolled in a course in Hindi at the Free University. "Who knows? Maybe we'll go to India, learn how to be non-violent." Kate smiled and echoed dreamily: "Who knows?"

The seventh month, the eighth, and finally the ninth. Money was more and more tight, they wouldn't take Kate at the blood bank. She couldn't have swiped a hair pin without the Keystone cops coming after her, she was that big. Then towards the end of the last month she noticed for the first time a tremor in Quatre-vingts' hand as he poured their coffee; and he began falling asleep in his chair, his hand dropping silently to the floor. Kate suspected he was taking side trips, away from the inner city, to blood banks where they didn't know him. How many trips she couldn't know, but he brought things home regularly—safety pins, teething rings, calcium tablets. She began to be afraid for the first time in her life, but said nothing. It was too close to the last week of her time.

At last they thought her time had come, but it turned out to be false labor; then the doctor required x-rays, measurement of the pelvis and all that. The bastard just wants to scare me, Kate decided.

Make it look like twins, quints, Caesarean sections and concomi-
tant appendectomies. Make himself look like a big Herr Doktor.
But finally the doctor simply directed Kate to take some pills and to
sit with her feet propped up: what the hell, what Chinese peasant
sat around with her feet propped up to have a baby? She ignored
the doctor and her ankles swelled up like cotton candy.

Twelve days later the doctor was proved right. "O.K., O.K.," she
was ready to admit she was wrong; it had been a bad scene, but
now it was over and they had their Consuelo. Kate had been in the
hospital over a week and they were going to release her as soon as
they'd run a series of tests on Consuelo. The tests turned out O.K.
Consuelo was a great kid, and that was lucky, at least. They had
their future, their consolation.

But suddenly the future broke in two, leaving only Consuelo.
Kate, who had been awaiting the end of the world for so long, was
shocked but unastonished: it was a way for the world to end.

During the second week of her hospitalization—she'd been very
sick, one bad scene after another, with fever and mastitis and freaky
nurses—Quatre-vingts had been found slumped up against a fire
hydrant along Second Avenue, not far from the blood bank—
sound asleep. A friend who had picked him up knew instantly that
he was not drunk, just wasn't getting enough oxygen in his brain to
stay awake. "Christ," the friend had said, offended and grieved, "if
you needed money that bad, why didn't you ask me?" "I need
money that bad," Quatre-vingts had replied, "and now I'm askin'."
The friend, however, didn't have any bread himself: what he had
was a lead on a job. Not a nine to five, but something cool that
would keep them together, Consuelo, Kate and Quatre-vingts.
A job that paid real bread and they could put money in banks instead of blood, "ha ha," the friend had joked encouragingly. And he
got Quatre-vingts a job at the check-out counter of the Shop 'n
Save. Most of the night it was quiet, the friend said, you read or
dozed by the counter. In the early morning the breakfast shoppers
would hurry in, half-asleep, for a loaf of bread, a carton of milk,
that sort of thing. On this particular morning, along with the silence, had appeared an armed robber—or rather two or perhaps

three: nobody ever figured it out, nobody was ever really arrested, though a suspect was picked up in the desert in California and beaten up by the fuzz just for show. The killers had ordered Quatre-vingts into the food locker, filled his head full of holes and left him to freeze. He was found by the morning sweep-out man who was the first to open the cooler. Quatre-vingts lay in a pool of half-frozen blood.

He was shot up so badly they wouldn't even open the coffin. At least that's what they told her. The company had paid for the funeral. Plastic flower wreaths ringed the coffin, which seemed to Kate not much bigger than a shoe box: though Quatre-vingts was tall, very tall. At another time the cheap wreaths feigning melancholy affluence would have fired her with rage. But Kate was thinking hard and without amusement that the guy in the shoe box, whoever he was, certainly was not Quatre-vingts. The whole thing was a put-on. What it was: Quatre-vingts had wanted to go to India, that's all; and he and his friends had planned this hoax between them. The rest of the world might believe it, but not she, not she. Somewhere in India Quatre-vingts was meditating; so it was clear that the thing to do was to follow him there.

So as soon as the funeral was over, Kate returned to their room, packed a small duffel bag and strapped Consuelo across her bosom, hammock-fashion. She stopped off at the local Family Service long enough to pick up a check they had promised her "to help make her way in the world again," then she flew one-way to Amsterdam. From there she wrote her mother that she was going to walk to India, begging all the way. And she did.

The Woman from Jujuy

H. E. Francis' latest collection of stories is A Disturbance of Gulls. *A Fulbright scholar (Oxford) and three-time Fulbright lecturer (Argentina), he translates Argentine literature. His work has appeared in the* O. Henry, Best American, *and* Pushcart Prize *volumes. In 1989 he received an honorary doctorate from the University of Alabama. He lives in Madrid, Spain.*

"H. E. Francis is a truly gifted writer who manages, in each of his stories, to concentrate with splendor and pathos on a single theme: the oneness of all things, the terrifying completion of the individual who contains within himself the entirety of life. The character who dies violently but in a moment of illumination in a town dump which is actually a kind of paradise of his own creation, the character who discovers in his wife the lives of dead soldiers whom he loved in the war, the character who realizes that the insanity of the woman he loves is precious and really his own—in each instance some multiple interior existence affirms the power and beauty of life and the terrible distances between us. But the important thing is that Francis has found new ways to generate from ordinary language a writing voice at once familiar and yet surprising as well and, in its richness, worthy of his amazing human vision and limitless compassion. His work is shockingly profound."

JOHN HAWKES, 1973

Throughout the province she was famed for her infamy. She was shameless and everyone shunned her. She moved among them like an object of fate, indifferent. Her eyes seemed a perpetual black night in that dark face. Her thick mass of hair was blacker than crow, never washed or combed. It hung in matted clusters. In the wind they leaped up like a riled nest of snakes about her placid face. She had no possessions but the black dress, the torn black shawl, ashen with dust and dirt, which she draped loosely over her back and arms, black cotton stockings, the dark blue *alpargatas* torn and breaking on her feet, and always over one arm the enormous patched burlap which served as a mattress on hot days, as a blanket on cold nights when she stretched out at full length to sleep on the pavement.

You might see her at the most crowded noon on the main street, San Martín, ambling among the hundreds dodging around her in and out of stores, or standing in the midst of traffic pouring out of the Mercado Central on Las Heras, or strolling along the wall of the *zanjón* that cuts across the city, staring into the canal water. She sat wherever it occurred to her, with her hand out. She was not like the other beggars. They mouthed and trembled, wore easily moulded pain on their faces, and stealthily counted their gain. They had friends and families, a place to go, and made profits. But she held out her hand as if expecting nothing but accident or grace: to eat, no more. When anything came her way, she simply pocketed it. Her eyes—aimed at the end of the street, far above the passers' heads, or through them—were always clear and peaceful, her face easeful, often with the faint shadow of a smile. You might see her sitting against Gath y Chaves, on the sidewalk near the Cine Radar, by Casa Heredia, in the *parquecito* by the Teatro Gabriela Mistral, eating—as if even the pedestrians did not exist—from an opened tin of tuna or potted meat, her gaze too filled to include them.

What was she doing in Mendoza?

"All the beggars end up in Mendoza," people said, "because it is rich and there is much sun and no rain, they can sleep anywhere."

She was thirty but she looked ageless now.

She was from the far north, a *jujeña* from the province of Jujuy. She was from a house of children, thirteen, fourteen—she was not sure—nor did she know her father. She lived in an isolated hut by the river, crowded in with those who were left, and did whatever they told her—pounded meal, picked herbs, set traps for now and then a *liebre*, but mostly went for twigs and fuel and stole whatever food she could to help the family keep alive. And when the time came, she worked in the field with her mother and her mother's man and the children old enough.

That's where Lucas first saw her.

She did not see him. He saw her. She was fifteen. She was so pushed with tasks by her mother and her mother's man and the children that she had not yet lifted her eyes to men, though she knew the fumblings of children, laughs and jokes and gropings in the night, playthings of little animals. And she did not think. There were things that happened. What did not happen she did not know.

But Lucas happened. "Your name?" he said, working in the row beside her. She looked up at him. He was tall and made her feel small. She had never felt small before. His face was sweating, and his shirt all wet, and the hair where the shirt was open. Even his white teeth were so wet they seemed to be sweating, and his tongue in his open mouth. "Lucía," she said, and he threw back his head and she saw how red his lips were, and thick, when he laughed, and how his chest swelled, and she felt strange so she looked down, and when she looked back up, she felt stranger because he was looking at her but not laughing now, so she crouched down, bending her head to the earth, dizzy with the smell of it and the plants, not daring to look up until he said, "I see you tomorrow, Lucía," laughing that laugh she did not yet understand, and watched him down the furrow, tall and thin-hipped and straight, his buttocks firm under the loose trousers. Then her eyes gripped the furrow; she wanted to laugh, to cry—she did not know. She was glad when the others called "Lucía!" because it was getting dark.

He worked fast. He far outstripped her. He was furrows away by the end of the first hour of the morning, and she did not look again. But twice in the morning he called "Hola, Lucía!" and flagged her. She nodded, but did not flag—she could not make her hand move—but she felt red, her whole body felt red and she wanted to cry. She went down on her knees, tearing roots up hard all day. The baskets filled. In the afternoon he said, "Leave your baskets. I'll help you when the time comes." Her eyes widened. She always carried her own baskets; she did not even think if they were heavy. She did not speak now. And when he came, at dark, and the children were calling "Lucía!" he said to them, "Go. She'll be along," and carried her baskets to the end of the furrows. She walked up and down behind him.

With the last one he said, "Come, Lucía," and took her hand. She could hardly keep up, he was so tall. He stopped by the willow and turned to her and took her shoulders and dropped his hands over her breasts and arms and waist and drew her up off her feet and suddenly she could not breathe, she felt his sweat hot and burning, it made her burn, and so fast his hand came down over her breasts and tore down her dress she knew she was going to die. His hard beard burned over her face and neck and breasts until she wanted to scream with it and when he opened her legs she did cry out but with such a groan of pain and pleasure together that her hands could not hold him close enough, could not, and he said, "Sí," and she felt how hot the ground was, for the first time the smell of earth came into her, he was gripping the whole earth, she was the whole earth, she came up to meet him, and suddenly for the first time the sky tore her eyes open, it came in, she had never seen it, blue—and red with the sun burning far.

He left her there. She did not move for a long time. She did not want to move. She watched the blue die and the red die, and the dark grow and slowly turn to moony night with a glow of silver. She listened to the soft flow of river, the thinnest rush of wind, the plants, the earth in soft breakings, and herself—the brush of her skin, her breath moving, the quiet river in her, and the sky. The others were calling "Lucía!" again. She rose. She was covered with dust, twisted, her dress torn and stained; she clutched the stains, holding him in them—and smiled. It had happened. It seemed the first thing that happened, and the last. It was not a dream. It was more real than dreams. She did not want to dream any more.

In the morning he was gone. The work was over. He was a migrant worker—he went from province to province: there were *palmitos* by the jungle, peanuts, avocados, sugar cane south in Tucumán, artichokes, grapes in the *viñas* of Mendoza, wheat in the *trigales* and alfalfa on the pampas—it did not matter.

She followed him. When they were all asleep, she stole her

mother's black shawl and slipped away—taking the highway south
to Salta, where others moved as the days grew hotter. She never
spoke to anyone, simply followed the movements of small groups
going south, not even thinking it was a miracle when—perhaps because she was young or quiet or apparently confident or stoic—
people gave her bits of bread, cheese, salami, some *fideos*. Sometimes she stood on the edge of a field and, seeing her, someone
offered her work, rare and unexpected since mostly entire families
were contracted for the harvest; or invited her to share; and more
and more frequently—she came to know the look—there were
men's sly offers of a night's rest which gave her a taut stomach and
she went on, not comfortable until the clean moon whitened the
barren flats and the far mountains, without a soul on the horizon.
When occasional cars passed, a truck or one of the buses, she tried
to duck, make a rock or a bush, until it had disappeared. This way,
she worked from place to place. She was alive now, she would
not die. He was somewhere ahead—she did not even know his
name yet.

It was not long—ten or twelve weeks—before she saw him for
the first time. From Salta she had gone the logical way: to Tucumán
and the canebrakes. She grew used to the road. Her life was dust
and heat. In one of the *barrios* of Tucumán, when she felt near lifeless with hunger, dried out from thirst, she happened on an open
doorway, an old house with a rich tiled patio overlapped with vine
leaves, filled with palms and geranium and garden, and an old
woman eyed her. "*Hambre*, eh?" The face was stone but the voice
soft. She dropped her eyes. "Come. . . ." The woman stretched her
hand, but she would not let her touch her. She would let no one
touch her.

She stayed over two months, doing all the chores, not abused but
with a motion which allowed her perhaps two hours in the afternoon when the old woman, Doña Melinda, took the siesta. It was
then she made the rounds of the *cañas*, first one, then the other,
never duplicating. With a kind of instinct, she moved systematically
over the zone. And then one day, standing at the edge of a *cañaveral*,

motionless, she turned slowly—with a habit she had developed of letting her eyes trace from one side of a field to the other, encompassing it all bit by bit—and she saw the familiar form straighten up. She would have recognized it anywhere, the same long black hair falling off the right side, the wide shoulders, the narrow hips, that loose blue shirt opened nearly to the waist and the loose gray trousers strapped about with a wide brown belt, and the black *alpargatas*. She sat down and watched him. She felt a fierce flow come up as if from the earth and pulse through her.

He did not see her sitting distantly at the edge of the brake that day or the next, but on the third day he looked several times as if curious and before the afternoon was over he had even ventured down the brake to stand and from a good distance look at her. At first she was not sure he knew her, but after a while she was convinced that he had satisfied himself because he turned away, then stopped, looked back, and laughed loud, shaking his head, then went back to work. That day she did not return to Doña Melinda's but sat there, and every day throughout the season, until the fields were clean. He did not again come to her and look and laugh, though she knew each morning he had seen her arrive and take her place.

Nobody knew why the strange girl was there. They saw her, they said what they would no doubt, but she listened to no one.

When the harvest was over, he was gone again. She expected it now. There came a quiet rhythm of drift in her. She knew that he was ahead somewhere, with the sureness of inevitability. If she moved thus far day after day, even if she missed him in one place, fortune was such that tomorrow she would cross him at another. There was no doubt to it. It was the same to her as the movement of the sun and the moon and the stars. She also knew she had to follow their motion. It was inside her as it was in them, and it impelled her as they were impelled, and she wanted that—because always at the end of that motion he would be.

After so many months, she knew he too expected her, though he seemed never to have mentioned her to anyone else, even when they commented on the stranger like a dark bird at the edge of the field

or orchard or even, when he went into the canning factories, outside the plant. She saw, when he arrived—if she was early—that he
checked, assuring himself that she was there. Perhaps he thought
it was uncanny at first—how she found him; how miraculously
within a fairly brief period after his arrival on a new job, as if by
sorcery, she materialized. Then it was evident that he could gauge
the period between the beginning of a new job and her appearance
and that he had accepted but ignored her.

She made no overtures to speak to him or anyone who knew
him. There was no gesture of harassment, no reminder that they
had ever met—except the ritual of her apparition. She came like an
embodied spirit. Only once in the first three years did he speak to
her—and then as if he did not actually know her. He must have
drunk too much wine because he railed as her mother's man used
to—crying out in a fury that broke his words, a mixture of swear-
ing and anger and no sense and some anguish: " . . . bitch, go back
to your other world . . . black bird, eats out the heart and sucks
blood . . . never again, no . . . with my own bare hands kill, yes,
next time kill . . . vulture, never to let alone nobody, not even
when I close my eyes, that black thing there, in the dark night,
yes, witch. . . ." She understood nothing except that he really did
know her, it had to be. As certain as the pulse of blood through her,
she knew too that one day he would speak—not such words as
these, but other words—or what was that first afternoon for? She
was alive. She did not know that before. Something would come.
She did not know what, but she would wait. She believed the moment was always there just ahead, so she did not need to speak. It
would come.

In time her face and arms and hands had changed color; they had
become darker, browned deep so her eyes were quick with light in
her head, her arms and hands stronger from work in the fields, in
this house or that pension, from washing and scrubbing, sometimes lugging buckets in a factory, sometimes other menial tasks;
but her face, oily and dark, did not dry out. Something in the life
began to accustom her body to so little food that in the periods
when she had more than enough merely to subsist, she even gained

weight, her face round. Later her body widened a bit as if the hips balanced better for walking, her legs planted farther apart by habit.

Bits and snatches of cloth, clothes, burlap—thrown into refuse—she saved, replacing so the change was almost unnoticeable the things she came away with, weaving dirty threads, cord, string into the shawl, hoarding the burlap so that whenever she worked for anyone she could sleep nearby. But less and less frequently as time went on was she given work, because she did not keep herself up, her body knew no water, her hair was matted and dusted, and so conditioned was she to her own odors, never anyone else's, that she recognized no need. In Jujuy they had never washed—only once or twice she had gone into the river, but so long ago she must have been four or five. So she became an unchanged image, recurring as persistently as a sign in one province after another. When people passed her, there was an almost imperceptible recognition, as of a malignant sign fortunately grown no larger, and a shift of eye which negated her presence therefore. Occasionally, in the cities, now and again someone dropped pesos into her hand. She never said like the beggars "*Que Dios le bendiga*," for she knew in some way food would always come; she did not even look into her hand. When she passed the market she bought what the change would buy and sat wherever she was to eat a small portion of it. She wrapped the rest in the burlap.

They lived forever in the warm seasons, he moving with the sun and growth, she behind . . . Buenos Aires, Rosario, Córdoba, Mendoza, San Juan, San Luis, Tucumán, La Rioja, Jujuy, El Charco. . . . She knew all the *barrios*, the streets, the *centros* as if by some primordial memory, though she saw nothing, she talked of nothing— she had no one to talk to, perhaps no voice left, for she never muttered even to herself and for her few purchases she pointed. It was only her eyes that spoke. They looked far.

After the first months—and for all the years she traveled—the men, perhaps because she was so unkempt and dirty, no longer tried to take her. Nor did people try to get rid of her overtly. There were many beggars since Perón's betrayal of the República. What could you do?

He did not stop. He did not marry, though there were many women. She did not care. She knew he had recognized her, he expected her. He would have sent her away otherwise, though she knew that too was impossible. When the sign came, she would know it.

She waited fifteen years.

It came in March during the *Fiesta de la Vendimia*, the annual grape harvest—the greatest event in all the province of Mendoza—when wine runs in blood-red spurts from the public fountains, free, and the ritual of the grapes is offered: blood pressed from the grapes, from deep in the earth, the pulse, and into the mouth; and the ancient dances and song fill the air and the blood. Sometimes she saw him dance the *gato* and the *cueca* and laugh and sing so alive, and a remote stirring from the field of Jujuy came into her and she felt she was very close.

Often those years in Mendoza she went for rest to the old ruins of a church on Fray Luis Beltrán Street. Green grass grew in the shade, and vestiges of marigold and *enamorados del sol*; it was cool against the stones, and night made a roof over the fallen church. Nobody bothered her there. The neighborhood too was accustomed to the emptiness of the ruins. He knew she stayed there—she had found the place not far from the pension he usually stayed in, near the plaza, farther down the street. That building was old and crumbling now; they would condemn it soon surely; but to her it was the same as always, as he was: though he was weathered and his eyes tired, and thin, but still not forty, and young, to her he was the unchanged youth in the field of Jujuy.

That afternoon the bishop blessed the vines on the Plaza Independencia with an enormous crowd around. The week of joy and holiness had begun. At night she walked the several kilometers to the Greek amphitheater, *el teatro griego*, to see the panorama of dances and song under lights that went into the mountains as far as God. After, she went down into the city. There was dancing on the plazas and she went where, always, he would be—and watched for a long time. She had a seething inside her from so much joy around her. Once she crossed his gaze—he looked long at her—and for an instant she felt this must be the moment, but his look was filled with anger and hatred, not the first time, and she told herself that did not matter, she was used to it, it was to be expected, where there was such hatred there was feeling. She knew his feeling—she remembered. Almost she spoke. But when she saw his look, she turned away and went back to Luis Beltrán to curl up against the great overshadowing column where she liked to lie on such warm nights on her burlap.

The three boys were there—she knew them on sight; they must hang about as always, but she ignored them. She did not fear them because once she had overheard one tell the others, "She must smell like that to keep us away and stay pure." She pretended not to hear. It made no sense to her. She knew only her own body now. She stretched out to sleep. But in a minute they were standing over her. She had not expected that. She bolted up, sitting, curious, startled. But before she could speak she was booted in the neck and side, hauled up by her arms and struck in the face and stomach and breasts—and then remembered nothing more. They must have dropped her in the corner, thrown her burlap over her, because when she woke she was covered, she could scarcely move, she felt broken, she wanted to scream; but she could not, dared not, move, the slightest breath tore like fire through her. She thought she was blind, but there was sun through the burlap, though she could not raise her hand. She felt paralyzed. She did not know how long she lay there, she never knew, but she felt a burning over her, more in her side than anywhere else; and when finally after long effort she moved, she felt her hand tear with a terrible pain from her side, she felt herself in her hand as if she were holding her body in it. For the first time she smelled herself, a stench she could not bear, worse than rotting fish. She wanted to speak but she could not, her mouth was taut, and even the sounds in her throat ached. When she remembered the first kick, her throat felt as wide as her head. She fainted and in spells came to, but she could not remove the burlap, she could scarcely get her breath.

Then it was she had the dream—for a moment even fell into it as if she *wanted* to dream: someone tore away the burlap, the sun

poured down over him so quick and full and bright that her eyes
pained, needled. She wanted to cry the name she had heard shouted
in the fields, that thousands of times ran over her silent tongue,
Lucas! But no sound came and she felt dry even to dying. She was
not dreaming; surely she was dying. But his voice broke. "Lucía!"
he cried. She felt the voice in his hands; his hands were on her,
burning, breaking her body till she wanted to cry out, scream, but
in joy too. Her name! He remembered, he spoke her name. She
wanted to scream *Lucas* before the vision disappeared. And then in
an instant when he released his hands and stared at her unbelieving,
with a glitter like tears in his eyes, all the pain came back, her body
racked with so many pains, she knew it was real. She opened her
mouth to speak to him, but it would not open. *Lucas!* She wanted
him to know she knew him. Still she looked—she would not close
her eyes—but suddenly he vanished. She must have fainted because
when she saw again, he was still there only talking to her now fast,
fast, words she could not even understand. ". . . years, and me, for
me. . . ." He was tearing at her clothes. She felt now his hand over
her side, and she moaned. He heard it, he *did*, and he touched her
and she knew she would die now. The blood in her burned. She
never knew such joy though the pain was too terrible, more terrible
when he himself shouted with a look of pain and terror and thrust
his face down against her, against her side, where she could see now
the terrible mass; and he clutched her, sucking at her, licking like
Rubio's little dog in Jujuy, licking; and she screamed *No, Lucas, it's
all right, I can die now*, feeling the whole pulse of the earth come
into her so that she could not stand the burning pain and joy; and
his head sucking at her deep putrid wounds touched her hand and
his hair fell between her fingers. . . .

He carried her to the *zanjón*, which was empty of water except
for a narrow meander in the center, and washed her wounds, put
water in her mouth, and laid her on the burlap, under a footbridge.

In the night he brought her food. "Listen," he said, "it's dark.
I'm taking you now into my pension, but you must not cry out, no
matter how much I hurt you." She could not fathom the despair of
that man. She wanted to tell him nothing mattered, she had had

her sign, but she could not speak, only to make a sound even she did not recognize from her own body. Maybe she would die. But she did not want to leave him alone. Maybe now, after all the years, he did not want to be alone. Maybe she had been in him all those years. She nodded.

He carried her stealthily into the pension, across the patio to his door. Everyone was sleeping. She knew he would have a hard time keeping the secret. On the bed she went to sleep or fainted at once. She never knew how long she slept, but when she woke it was to the shouts of a woman, the *patrona*, screaming, "No filth in here! Look at the rot! I'll have bugs! You filthy *puta*, getting beat up and kicked out of any man's bed. Left you here and didn't come back, eh? Get out! Out, you filthy bitch! Joaquín!" They pushed and kicked and thrust her out, despite her shrieks of pain, and dumped her by the gutter, the dry *acequia*. Painfully she sat up. She held onto a tree root, leaned her head, gasping, against the tree. Where was he? She crawled to the plaza across the street and stretched out on a bench. In the morning she tried to walk. She sat on the plaza with her hand out.

Where was he?

After, in the five days that followed, every day she went back and sat before his pension, farther off now because of the fury of the *patrona*. She watched the same *pensionistas* go in and out, but never Lucas. She would wait, if need be, until he returned. And then on the fifth day she went closer. Perhaps from long experience, sitting as he did in a front window, one of the old men knew who she was. He crossed the street and strolled about the plaza as always—it was as if each time he went round he was coming closer, like the sun and the moon and the stars and something in her own blood. She waited. "You . . . " He seemed not to know how to say, or what. She dropped her eyes, her head. "Lucas . . . ," he said. Instantly she raised her head. The sound of his name from someone else's lips maddened her. "He died—yesterday," the man said, "in the *villa miseria*, near the park. The boy, there—" he indicated the pension, "told me. At Alonso's house, in the *villa miseria*." She could not fathom it: they were words, a nightmare. And then she moaned,

she could not stop moaning. When a crowd gathered at some distance, she pulled herself up. . . .

Lucas!

She went to the *villa miseria*. A wind came up, a sea of dust rose
over the park, the *viento sonda* was coming, the *villa miseria* was
thick with rolls of dust, it poured down between the mud huts.
Children kept playing everywhere; outside, in some doorways,
women were cooking; rags fluttered over all the window holes. She
stopped a little girl. "*Hija* . . . ," she said. Her own voice struck her
with fright, a phantom's. She did not recognize the sound. Her
throat resounded, hollow. "*Hija* . . . " The words pained her: "*La
casa de Alonso?*" "*Allá*," the girl fingered. She turned. The blown
tierra burned her eyes, her lungs ached. "Lucas?" she said in the
doorway. An old woman came close: "*Muerto*," she said. "Where?
Where's Lucas?" she cried. "Dead—there, in the Hospital Emilio
Civit. Poison." "Poison?" she said. "What from?" "Who knows?
Poison. I told you," the woman said, dropping the curtain. *Poison?*
From *her?* "Lucas!" she cried, as if she had regained full power of
her voice. It thrust up like a stone scraping harsh and terrible. She
shouted in fury, raged, as if her arms themselves flagging the shawl
bellowed against the sand and air and mountains and the invisible
sky beyond.

"Lucas! I killed you, *I*, Lucas!" The children gathered, men and
women came from their *chozas*, they stood in the smiting sand listening, watching her beat her breasts and wail.

"Ay, Lucas, I waited for the sign all the years, I knew the sign,
but I did not know—Ayyyyyyyyyy!" She screamed, she fell, her fingers dug the earth, her face pressed into the dirt. But even when
she fell and they thought she could not get up, she rose to her
knees, she turned to them, she shouted, "You see what a man is! He
saved my life—*mine*. For me, who hounded him, he died. And
who else would suck the wounds of a beggar, I ask you! Such a
man! Ayyyyy, Lucas, you saved my life, yes—" But her rage rose,
her rancor knew no limit. "But you left me here, you left me *here*,
you, you—I curse you, Lucas, I curse you. Ayyyyyyyyyy." And now
she stretched full, her arms rose, the black shawl blew. And she

cried out, "Lucas, I swear, I swear before God and these wit-
nesses—all my life I will do penance. You *hear* me, Lucas? All the
life left to me I will follow you still—" But the wind blew her
words, the sand smote, the people went back in, the children
laughed at her and threw clods. Dust filled her mouth.

She went down through the park to the city. For a while every
night she went back to Luis Beltrán to sit before the pension. He
did not come.

Around the ruins of the old church they put a high iron grating
to protect them or to keep vagrants and children from danger—
who knows? So she took to the streets again, stopping whenever
she was tired—sometimes on San Martín in front of Casa Muñoz
with her arms stretched out on the flagstones, stiller than a nun,
staring up at the sky she first really saw fifteen years before, indifferent to the people passing, sometimes during siesta on the shady
side of La Rioja Street, or Salta, or San Juan—it made no difference—crossing her arms over her breast, letting the deep blue sky
come down into her quiet eyes.

The Burning

Jack Cady has published six novels, including Singleton *and* McDowell's
Ghost. *He has lived in the Pacific Northwest for the past twenty-five years
and currently teaches writing at Pacific Lutheran University in
Tacoma, Washington.*

"Jack Cady's The Burning *has stories that are quite honestly unforgettable —
one might almost wish to 'forget' them, because of their power to haunt and
disturb, if it weren't for the obvious compassion that underlies their art. The
stories are direct, uncluttered, unpretentious. Which is not to say that they
aren't ambitious—they are very ambitious indeed. It takes no special critical
power to recognize in Cady an exceptional writer, who is not just promising
but has already achieved some remarkable feats. The Burning will introduce
an important new writer and will do honor to the Iowa School of Letters
Award for Short Fiction."*

JOYCE CAROL OATES, 1972

Sunlight gleamed as Singleton and I walked down the hill to the
charred wreckage of what had been a truck. Gates was dead, and
the breeze lifted sooty material that mixed with the valley smells of
weeds, flowers, and diesel stink. Manny was in jail. Nothing more
could be done for Gates, but now Manny was sitting in his own
fire, burning because he was kind, because he was gentle.

Traffic was moving as usual on the long slopes; only an occasional
car slowed, its occupants looking over the scene of last night's fire.
The truck drivers would know all about the trouble, and they did
not want to see. Besides, there was a hill to climb on either side of
the valley. They could not afford to lose speed. I knew that by now
the word of the burning had spread at least a hundred miles. As far
as Lexington, drivers would be leaning against counters listening,

with wildness spreading in them. Singleton and I had not slept through the long night. We revisited the scene because we felt it was the final thing we could do for both men.

Close up the sunlight played on bright runs of metal where someone had pulled the cab apart hoping to recover enough of Gates's remains for burial. An oil fire, when the oil is pouring on a man, doesn't leave much. Only the frame and other heavy structural members of the truck remained.

"If he had only been knocked out or killed before the fire got to him . . ." We were both thinking the words. Either might have said them.

"His company's sending an investigator," Singleton told me. "But since we're here, let's go over it. They'll be sure to ask."

"Are you going to pull?"

"No." He shook his head and ran his hand across his face. "No. Next week maybe or the week after. I'm not steady. I called for three drivers. That's one for your rig too."

"Thanks. I've got vacation coming. I'm taking it."

The road surface along the wreck was blackened, and the asphalt waved and sagged. It was a bad spot. The state should have put up signs. Forty-seven feet of power and payload; now it seemed little there in the ditch, its unimportance turning my stomach. I wanted to retch. I felt lonely and useless.

We walked to the far hill to look at the tire marks. Narrow little lines which swung wide across the other lane and then back in, suddenly breaking and spinning up the roadway. Heavy black lines were laid beside them where the driver of the car being passed had ridden his brakes and then gone on up the hill. Coming down were the marks Gates made, and they showed that he had done what a trucker is supposed to do. He had avoided at all costs. The marks ran off the road.

I never knew him. Manny, tall, sandy-haired, and laughing, was my good friend, but I did not know Gates. I did not know until later that Singleton knew him.

We had picked Gates up twenty miles back on the narrow two-lane that ran through the Kentucky hills. We rode behind him

figuring to pass when he got a chance to let us around. It was
early, around 3 A.M., but there was still heavy vacation-season traffic. Manny was out front behind Gates. My rig was second behind him, and Singleton was behind me. Our three freights were grossing less than fifty thousand so we could go.

Gates's tanker must have scaled at around sixty thousand. Even with that weight you can usually go, but his gas-powered tractor was too light.

It slowed us to be laying back, but there was no reason to dog it. He was making the best time he could. He topped the hill by June's Stop and ran fast after he crested on the long slope down. He had Manny by maybe two hundred yards because Manny had signaled into June's.

When he signaled I checked my mirrors. Singleton kept pulling so I kept pulling. When he saw us coming on, Manny canceled the signal and went over the top behind Gates. It allowed enough of a lag for Gates to get out front, and it kept Manny from being killed.

We took the hill fast. You have to climb out the other side. I was a quarter mile back, running at forty-five and gaining speed, when I saw the headlights of the little car swing into the lane ahead of Gates's tanker. The driver had incorrectly estimated the truck's speed or the car's passing power.

It was quick and not bad at first. The tanker went into the ditch. The car cut back in, broke traction, and spun directly up the roadway. It came to a stop next to Manny's rig, almost brushing against his drive axle and not even bending sheet metal, a fluke. The car it had passed went onto the shoulder and recovered. The driver took it on up the hill to get away from the wreck and involvement.

Manny was closer. He had perhaps a second more to anticipate the wreck. He had stopped quicker than I believed possible. It was about a minute before the fire started. I was running with my extinguisher when I saw it, and knew I would be too late.

"I wish he'd exploded," Singleton said. He kicked up dust along the roadway. He was too old for this, and he was beat-out and shaken. The calmness of resignation was trying to take him, and I hoped it would. I wondered to myself if those clear eyes that had looked down a million and a half miles of road had ever looked at anything like this.

"Exploded? Yes, either that or got out."

"He was hurt. I think he was hurt bad." He looked at me almost helplessly. "No sense wishing; let's go back up."

After the wreck Singleton had backed his rig over the narrow two-lane, following the gradual bend of the road in the dark. He had taken the two girls from the small car into his cab.

I had stayed a little longer until Gates's burning got really bad. Then I brought the little car in, feeling the way I feel in any car: naked, unprotected, and nearly blind. I was shaking from weakness. The road was blocked above. There was no oncoming beyond the pot flares. The cop with the flashlight had arrived ten or fifteen minutes after the wreck. Behind me the fire rose against the summer blackness and blanketed the valley with the acrid smell of number-two diesel. Because of the distance, Manny's rig seemed almost in the middle of the fire and silhouetted against the burning, though I knew he had stopped nearly fifty yards up the roadway. My own rig was pulled in behind him; its markers stood pale beside the bigger glow. As I was about to go past the cop, he waved me over.

"Where you taking it?"

"Just to the top," I told him. "The girls were pretty shaken up. Don't worry, they won't go anywhere."

"Think they need an ambulance?" He paused, uncertain. "Christ," he said. "Will that other cruiser ever get here?"

"What about Manny?" I asked.

"In there." He nodded to where Manny sat in the cruiser. The lights were out inside. He could not be seen. "I'll take a statement at the top. You'll see him at the top."

I wanted to call to Manny, but there was nothing I could do. I took the car on to June's Stop. Rigs were starting to pile in, even stacking up along the roadway. Cars were parked around and between them, blacked out and gleaming small and dull in the lights from the truck markers. Most of the guys had cut their engines. It would be a long wait.

Singleton's truck was down by the restaurant. Inside around the

counter, which formed a kind of box, drivers were sitting and talking. A few were standing around. They were excited and walked
back and forth. I wanted coffee, needed it, but I could not go in. At
least not then. A driver came up behind me.

"You Wakefield?" he asked. He meant did I drive for Wakefield.
My name is Arnold.

I told him yes.

"Your buddy took the girls to Number Twelve. He said to come."

"As if we didn't have enough trouble . . . "

"He's got the door open." The guy grinned. He was short with a
light build and was in too good a mood. I disliked him right away.

"Listen," he said. "They say there's going to be a shakedown."

"Who says?"

"Who knows? That's just the word. If you left anything back
there, you'd better get it out. Check it with June." He meant guns
and pills. A lot of companies require them in spite of the law. A lot
of guys carry them on their own, the guns I mean. Pills are Ben-
zedrine, Bennies, or a stronger kind called footballs. Only drivers
who don't know any better use them to stay awake or get high on.

"I've got it right here," I told him, and patted my side pocket.
"I'll hang onto it myself."

"Your funeral," he said, grinning. He gave me a sick feeling. He
was a guy with nose trouble, one who spreads his manure up and
down the road, a show-off to impress waitresses. "Thanks," I said,
and turned to go to the motel room.

"Hey," he yelled, "what do you think will happen to him?"

"You figure it out." I went over to the motel, found Twelve, and
went inside.

The room had twin beds. Singleton was sitting on one, facing
the two girls on the other. One was kind of curled up. The other
was leaning forward still crying. Vassar, I thought. No, nothing like
that on 25 South; University of Kentucky likely, but the same sorry
type. I edged down beside Singleton. "Why do you bother?" I asked
him. "To hell with them." The girl bawling looked up hard for a
moment and started bawling worse.

"I had room," she bawled.

We were all under a strain. The diesel smell was bad, but the other smell that I would never forget had been worse. Even away from the fire I seemed still to smell it.

"You thought you had room!" I yelled at her.

"No, really. I was all right. I had room." She was convinced, almost righteous. At some other time she might have been pretty. Both were twenty or twenty-one. The curled-up one was sort of mousy-looking. The one who was bawling was tall with long hair. I thought of her as a thing.

"No—really," I yelled at her; "you had no room, but keep lying to yourself. Pretty soon that'll make everything OK."

"Leave it, Arn," Singleton told me. "You're not doing any good."

He went to the sink to wet a towel, bringing it to the girl. "Wipe your face," he told her. Then he turned to me. "Did you bring their car?"

"I brought it—just a minute. You can have them in just a minute." I was still blind angry. "Old, young, men, women, we've seen too many of their kind. I just want to say it once." I looked directly at her. "How much have you driven?"

For a moment it didn't take; then she understood.

"Five years."

"Not years. Miles."

"Why—I guess—I don't know. Five years."

"Five thousand a year? Ten thousand? That would be plenty; you haven't driven that much. Five years times ten is fifty thousand. That's six to eight months' work for those guys down there. *You had no room!*" I bit it out at her. She just looked confused, and I felt weak. "I'm ready to leave it now," I told Singleton. "I should have known. Remember, we've got a friend down there."

"I've got two."

He looked different than ever before. He sat slouched on the bed and leaned forward a little. His hands were in his lap, and the lines and creases in his face were shadowed in the half-light from the floor lamp.

"Who was he?" I asked.

He looked at me. I realized with a shock that he had been fighting back tears, but his eyes were gray and clear as always. The silver hair that had been crossed with dark streaks as long as I had known him now seemed a dull gray. The hands in his lap were steady. He reached into a pocket.

"Get coffee." He looked at the girls. "Get two apiece for everybody."

"Who was it, Singleton?"

"Get the coffee. We'll talk later." He looked at the girl who was curled up. "She's not good."

"Shock?"

"Real light. If it was going to get worse, I think it would have. Maybe you'd better bring June." He got up again and tried to straighten the curled-up girl. He asked her to turn on her back. She looked OK. She tried to fight him. "Help him," I told the one who had been bawling.

The restaurant was better than a hundred yards off. A hillbilly voice was deviling a truck song. June was in the kitchen, I told her I needed help, and she came right away. Business is one thing, people are another. She has always been that way. She brought a Silex with her, and we walked back across the lot. In the distance there was the sound of two sirens crossing against each other.

"The other police car."

"That and a fire truck," she told me.

June is a fine woman, once very pretty but now careless of her appearance and too heavy. It is always sad and a little strange to see a nice-looking woman allow herself to slide. There must be reasons, but not the kind that bear thinking about. She had a good hand with people, a good way. She ran a straight business. When we came to the room, she asked us to leave and started mothering the girls. We went outside with the coffee and sat on the step.

"I'm sorry," I told him. "I shouldn't have blown up, but for a minute I could have killed them. I hate every fool like them."

"It's their road too."

"I know."

"Everybody makes mistakes. You—me—nobody has perfect judgment."

"But not like that."

"No. No, we're not like that, but she won't ever be again either. She has to live with that."

I understood a little more about him. He was good in his judgment. It was suddenly not a matter for us to forgive. There was the law. It had nothing to do with us.

"Manny never held those brakes against you," he told me.

Once I had checked his truck for him, and he had a failure. I wanted to say that it was different.

We sat listening to the muffled sounds from the room behind us. Soon, off at the downhill corner of the lot, headlights appeared coming from the wreck. The state car cruised across the lot. It stopped at the end of the motel row. Singleton stood up and motioned to him. The car moved toward us, rolling in gently. The cop got out. Manny was sitting in the back seat. He was slumped over and quiet. When the cop slammed the door, he did not look up.

He was an older cop, too old to be riding a cruiser. In the darkness and excitement there had been no way to tell much about him. He was tired and walked to us unofficially. We made room for him on the step. He sat between us, letdown, his hands shaking with either fatigue or nervousness.

"Charles," he said to Singleton, "who was he?"

"You'd better have some coffee," Singleton told him. He reached over and put his hand on the cop's shoulder. I poured coffee from the Silex, and he drank it fast.

"Gates," said Singleton. "Island Oil. When Haber went broke, I pulled tanks for two years." He stopped as if reflecting. "He was pretty good. I broke him in."

The cop pointed to the car. "Him?"

"Manley, Johnny Manley."

"You're taking him in," I said. "What's the charge?"

"I don't know," the cop told me. "I wouldn't even know what

would stick. His rig's half out in one lane. If you're going to say I
need a charge, then I'll take him in for obstructing the road."

"I didn't mean that. I'm not trying to push you. I just wanted to
see how you felt."

"Then ask straight out. I don't know what I think myself till I get
the whole story."

Singleton walked to the car. He leaned through the window to
call softly to Manny. Manny did not move, and Singleton leaned
against the car for a little while as the cop and I sat and watched.
A couple of drivers came by, curious but respectfully silent, and the
cop ran them off. June came out with a chair and sat beside the
steps. The two girls came out and stood quietly. I looked at them.
They were both young, pretty, and in the present circumstances
useless and destructively ignorant. I could no longer hate them.

"Is that him?" one of them whispered.

"Yes." I felt like whispering myself. It seemed wrong to be talking about him when he was no more than ten yards off, but I
doubted that he was listening to anyone. He was looking down, his
long body slumped forward and his hair astray. His face, which was
never very good-looking, was drawn tight around his fixed eyes,
and his hands were not visible. Perhaps he held them in his lap.

"They can't prove nothing," the cop said. "I bet he gets off." He
stood up. "Let's get it over with; we've wasted time."

Singleton came back then. "Tell me," the cop said to him.

"He won't be driving again. I don't know what the law will do,
but I know what Manny can't do. He won't take another one out.
You can take her statement on the accident"—he pointed at one of
the girls—"and his"—he pointed at me. "I was just over the crest—
couldn't see it very well. What I can tell you about is afterward,
but"—he turned to the girls—"I want to tell you something first
because maybe you ought to know. I've known that man yonder
seven, eight years. He's a quiet guy. Doesn't say much; really not
hard to get to know. He likes people, has patience with them.
Sometimes you think he'd be more sociable if he just knew how to
start." He hesitated as if searching for words.

"I don't know exactly how to tell it. Instead of talking, he does nice things. Always has extra equipment to spare if the scales are open and the ICC's checking, or maybe puts a bag of apples in your cab before you leave out. Kid stuff—yes, that's it, kid stuff a lot of the time. Sometimes guys don't understand and joke him.

"When he finally got married, it was to a girl who started the whole thing, not him. She was wild. Silly, you know, not especially bad but not the best either. She worked at a stop in Tennessee and quit work after she married instead of going back like she planned. The guy has something. He did good for that girl. I don't know what's going to happen to them now, and it's none of our business I guess, but I just thought you ought to know."

He turned back to the cop. "I came over the crest and saw Manny's and Arnie's stoplights and saw Arnie's trailer jump and pitch sideways till he corrected and got it stopped. I pulled in behind them, and they were both already out and running. Before I got there, I saw the fire. He could tell you more about how it started." He looked at me. I was thinking about it. I nodded for him to go on because it was very real to me, still happening. I wondered if maybe I could get out of having to describe it. I knew there would have to be a corroborative statement, so as Singleton told it I thought along with him.

He did a good job of the telling. He had gotten there only a minute or so after Manny and I were on the scene. Manny jumped from his cab, dodged around the car with the girls in it, and ran to the wreck. I took only enough time to grab my extinguisher. When I got there, Manny was on top of the wreck trying to pull Gates out and holding the door up at the same time.

The tanker had gone in hitting the ditch fast but stretching out the way you want to try to hit a ditch. It had made no motion to jack-knife. The ditch had been too deep, and instead it had lain over on its side. All along there—for that matter, all through those hills—the roadside is usually an outcropping of limestone, slate, and coal. In the cuts and even in the valleys there is rock. Until the truck was pulled off, there would be no way to know. It was likely that the tank and maybe his saddle tank had been opened up on an outcrop of rock. There was a little flicker of fire forward of the cab.

Gasoline, I had thought, but it did not grow quick like gasoline.
The diesel from his tank was running down the ditch and muffled it
some at first.

I went for it with the extinguisher, but it was growing and the
extinguisher was a popgun. Manny started yelling to come help him,
and I whirled and climbed up over the jutting wheel. Singleton was
suddenly there, grabbing me, boosting me up. I took the cab door
and held it up, and Gates started to yell.

Manny had him under the shoulders pulling hard, had him about
halfway out, but he was hung up. I believe Gates's leg was pinched
or held by the wheel. Otherwise Manny would not have gotten him
out that far. Manny knew though. He knelt down beside him
staring into the wrecked cab.

The fire was getting big behind me, building with a roar. It was
flowing down the ditch but gaining backward over the surface rapidly. I gave Manny a little shove and closed the door over Gates's
head so we could both reach him through the window. He was a
small chunky man—hard to grasp. We got him under the arms and
pulled hard, and he screamed again. The heat was close now. I was
terrified, confused. We could not pull harder. There was no way to
get him out.

Then I was suddenly alone. Manny jumped down, stumbling
against Singleton, who tried to climb up and was driven back, his
face lined and desperate in the fire glow. Manny disappeared running into the darkness. Where I was above the cab, the air was getting unbearably hot. The fire had not yet worked in under the
wreck. I tugged hopelessly until I could no longer bear the heat and
jumped down and rolled away. Singleton helped me up and pulled
me back just as screams changed from hurt to fear; high weeping,
desperate and unbelieving cries as the heat but not the fire got
to him.

I was held in horrified disbelief of what was happening. Outside
the cab and in front of it were heavy oil flames. Gates, his head and
neck and one hand outside the window, was leaning back away
from them, screaming another kind of cry because the fire that had

been getting close had arrived. The muscles of his neck and face were cast bronze in the fire glow, and his mouth was a wide black circle issuing cries. His eyes were closed tight, and his straining hand tried to pull himself away.

Then there was a noise, and he fell back and disappeared into the fire, quietly sinking to cremation with no further sound, and we turned to look behind us. Manny was standing helplessly, his pistol dropping from his shaking hand to the ground, and then he too was falling to the ground, covering his eyes with his hands and rolling on his side away from us.

"If I'd known, I wouldn't have stopped him," Singleton told the cop. "Of all the men I know, he's the only one who could have done that much."

He hesitated, running his hand through his graying hair. "I didn't help, you understand—didn't help." He looked pleading. "Nothing I could do, no use—Arn didn't help. Only Manny."

The girls and June were sobbing. The sky to the eastward was coming alive with light. The cop who was too old to be riding a cruiser looked blanched and even older in the beginning dawn. I felt as I had once felt at sea after battling an all-night storm. Only Singleton seemed capable of further speech, his almost ancient features passive but alive.

He looked at the patrol car where Manny still slumped. "They can't prove he killed a man. There's nothing to prove it with. They can't even prove the bullet didn't miss, and in a way that's the worst thing that can happen. You see, I know him. You think maybe he'll change after a while—maybe it will dull down and let him live normal. It won't. I sat with him before you came and did what I could, and it was nothing. Do they electrocute in this state or use gas? If they were kind, the way he is kind, they'd do one or the other."

American Gothic

Philip O'Connor's works include two story collections, Old Morals, Small Continents, Darker Times *and* A Season for Unnatural Causes; *a novella,* Ohio Woman; *and two novels,* Stealing Home *and* Defending Civilization. *A third novel,* Finding Brendan, *is scheduled for publication in 1991. His stories have appeared in prize anthologies, including the* Best American Short Stories. *He is Distinguished Research Professor at Bowling Green State University, where he helped initiate the M.F.A. program in creative writing.*

"O'Connor has the true Irish gift of telling a tale for all it's worth, but he also has the sophistication of narrative technique and the plain fidelity to his American experience to keep his stories from being only charming. They are taut and painful too; that is to say, they ring true."

GEORGE P. ELLIOTT, 1971

The events of that summer drift back slowly, darkly, like scenes from the dim gray movies we watched from the top of the highest balcony at the old Fox Theater on Market Street. We broke in through a side entrance late at night, crept past sleepy-eyed ushers clad like Marines in full dress, fled along the walls of the brightly lit stairways and landings, climbing upward, toward the darkness. Once, I recall, we arrived in time for the stage show, Duke Ellington and his band, playing again their hits of the late forties, but mostly we got there in time only for the feature film, or part of it. We took our seats and gazed down, hushed and myopic, as the theater darkened into a great bluish cavern, the smoky air flooded with music and the scenes of the film began to sweep relentlessly past us.

George was a little round foreigner, Greek or maybe Italian, and he had very bad eyes. We stole bottles of wine when he was in the lavatory in the back. Even if he heard us in the store, it took time for him to come up front, and then he couldn't see who it was until he got very close. We always got away.

It was Ditch's idea to steal. He was bigger, older and tougher than most of us. There were always boys like him around, in the neighborhoods or at high school or even working in libraries, where you might not expect them. You did what they said.

For some reason Ditch liked me. When I first arrived at the library, Ditch took the easy shelf (a wall of books at the west end of the reading room) away from Charlie and gave it to me. Charlie complained, saying he had been a page for two years and had earned the easy shelf. "Tough shit," said Ditch, who had been there longer than anyone and was head page. I thought he'd go on and give Charlie a reason—I was too new, too stupid for anything but the easy wall—but he didn't. Charlie shut up and took a hard section of shelves on the south wall: Fiction, R to Z.

On Saturday night, when it wasn't busy, all the pages met in the stacking room just behind the reading room desk. It was the best place to drink the wine. Miss Sweet worked the reading room desk on Saturday nights. She was a tall woman with a long bony face and sleepy eyes. She was very old, near retirement. She did not seem to notice us making noise.

Usually only the old men who in the daytime sat in the park across the street were in the reading room late at night. A lot of them if it was a cold night. The page who was on duty had to look under tables at closing time (11:00) because sometimes the old men lay down and slept there. At ten-forty-five Miss Sweet came into the stacking room and said, "Jackie, don't you think it's time to ask the gentlemen to leave?"

I always was careful to be polite to Miss Sweet because she was so old. "Yes, Miss Sweet," I said, "I'll do it right away."

"Thank you, Jackie," she said, and then she looked at us sitting slovenly on the tables beside the books piled for shelving on Monday morning. "Good night, boys," she said.

"Good night, Miss Sweet," most of us said, but someone, at
Ditch's prodding, always added something like, "you old witch."

"Tsk, tsk, tsk," she said if she heard, which she usually didn't.
"Whoever made that remark should be ashamed of himself."

"Are you ashamed of yourself, Charlie?" Ditch said.

"I am."

"Then apologize."

Charlie said, "I'm sorry, Miss Sweet."

"I'm surprised at you, Charles."

"I won't do it again, Miss Sweet."

When she closed the door, we laughed. Charlie, or whoever happened to make the remark, did not worry. He knew that Miss Sweet would never report him.

Once Ditch signaled me to say something funny to Miss Sweet, but I couldn't do it. When she left the room, he looked about and said, "One thing I hate is a guy with no sense of humor." But he didn't let them know he meant me. Later, when we went to the park in Civic Center after stealing the wine, he didn't speak to me, however, and I knew I'd failed him.

The others helped me get rid of the old men. There were always a few who lay across a pair of chairs or got under a table, and slept. When we finished with the ones who were seated, we wiggled the chairs of the sleepers, and kicked at the few who remained under the tables. I kicked them lightly on their butts, as most of the other pages did, but Ditch kicked hard. The old men groaned when Ditch kicked them and once one old man got sick and threw up.

We went to George's after work. George had long hours. From six in the morning to midnight. It was harder to steal wine late at night. He was always behind the counter then. Ditch sent one boy in by himself to buy a candy bar and start a conversation. Then another boy drifted in and stood behind the first boy so that George's vision was blocked by the first boy. The second boy backed up to the wine shelf across from the cash register and plucked off one or two bottles. He then nudged the first boy, who said good night to George and turned toward the door, giving the second boy time to go out ahead of him with the concealed wine. If George called to the second boy, "What you want?" he said, "I was just waiting for him (the first boy)." We had more wine.

I couldn't do the stealing. When I told that to Ditch I thought he'd jump all over me; he didn't. He said only that I had to do something and I'd better be willing to cover for someone else who could. I told him I didn't mind covering.

"You'd probably drop the bottle and break it anyway."

The others laughed.

"Guys that live with their mothers have no guts. You got to get tough, Jackie. My old man and I have a fist fight about every other day. How would you like that?"

I wouldn't, I told him.

I'd seen his father, who once came to the reading room, claiming Ditch had stolen some money from his drawer at home. The father drove a semi-truck for a paper company. He was about five-six but weighed (according to Ditch) two hundred pounds. It looked more like three hundred the night he came to raise hell with Ditch. He wore a tight black t-shirt his muscles were just about to rip to shreds. He told Ditch to give him back the money. Ditch said he didn't have it. The father put him up against the back wall of the stacking room and searched him. While the father slapped at his pockets and looked into his wallet, Ditch turned around and grinned and winked at the rest of us, who watched. When the father left the stacking room, Ditch called him a dumb runt. He said his old man picked on him because he was afraid someday Ditch was going to lay him out for good. "And I am," he said fiercely. "He'll think his truck ran over him."

If there was a good movie at the Fox on Market Street, we went to the side and pried open an exit door. If there was something interesting at Civic Auditorium, like the annual boat show, we snuck through the delivery entrance at the back and saw it. Sometimes we went to one of the pool halls on Market Street and put our money together for a couple of games. One of us kept the bottle rolled up in his jacket. When anyone got thirsty, he took the jacket and went to the men's room.

Early in the morning (1:00) we all got on a streetcar, one that went through Twin Peaks tunnel. It was usually empty. When the car entered the tunnel, we started through it unscrewing light bulbs, or maybe we stood in back pulling the conductor's bell. The conductor complained, but Ditch or one of the older boys pushed him against the back window and cursed at him and said he was going to throw him off the car if he didn't shut up. He shut up. I enjoyed unscrewing the bulbs and didn't mind pulling the rope on the bell, except when the conductor started to complain. When I pulled pranks Ditch stood back and laughed, delighted. Much of my pleasure came from making him laugh. When the motorman sensed the lights going off, he sped up. The car went so fast it zigzagged from side to side. One of the older boys climbed out on the raised cowcatcher in back and went the rest of the way in the open air, screaming like Tarzan. If there were other riders, we cursed at them and did crazy things like offer them wine. The streetcar had to slow down for a turn at the end of the tunnel. That's when we jumped off. There was a workman's ladder before the car reached the end of the approachway, where there might be police cars.

We were usually out of wine by then. For a while we stood under a telephone pole and listened to someone tell dirty stories. Finally we split up and walked home in little groups, singing and throwing rocks at street lights.

Then the library hired a new page. The biggest difference we noticed between him and us was not his color—we all knew a few black kids at school—but that he carried a knife, a long, thin pocket knife. When I say the biggest difference we noticed I mean the biggest difference Ditch noticed because if Ditch didn't notice something you noticed you figured it wasn't worth noticing, and you stopped noticing it.

We were in the stacking room getting louder and louder one Saturday night when Abner pulled out the knife. Abner had hardly spoken the first couple of days he worked there. He sorted his books and put them on the reading room shelves and went to whomever was working at the desk and asked was there anything else he could do, and if there wasn't he went to a corner of the stacking room and read a magazine that looked like *Life* but had blacks on the cover.

We were drinking when Ditch looked up and saw the knife. Abner was working on his fingernails.

"What you got that for?" he asked.

Abner wasn't drinking with us. He looked up with his big frog eyes. "What?" he said.

"The knife," Ditch snapped. "Why do you need a big pocket knife to fix your nails?"

Abner looked at the knife and then at Ditch. He didn't answer. Aside from Ditch he was the strongest looking boy in the room.

"Hey," said Ditch, getting off his chair. "You hear what I said?"

"I heard," said Abner, who was looking at the magazine again.

"Well?"

Abner looked up slowly, right at Ditch. "I don't know."

"Gimme that," said Ditch.

Abner held the knife in his right hand. It was still open. The tip of the blade was pointed toward Ditch's middle.

"You hear?" said Ditch.

Abner didn't move.

Just then Miss Sweet opened the door and said, "Jackie, don't you think it's time to ask the gentlemen to leave?"

"Yes, Miss Sweet. I'll do it in . . . a few minutes."

"Hurry now," she said, standing at the door. "It's getting late." She wasn't looking at Abner's knife. She probably wouldn't have seen it if she had been.

I couldn't move, too interested to see what would happen between Ditch and Abner when the door closed. No one made fun of her that night. We were all waiting.

But Abner raised his head. Slowly he closed the magazine and then the knife. He stood up and slid the knife into his pocket. He did not look at Ditch as he walked past him to the door.

He had cooled things off, but you would have had to be stupid blind not to know that sooner or later Ditch would go at Abner or

Abner at Ditch. Sometimes one or two of us went home early, but that night everyone tagged along.

In the vacant lot beside George's store, Ditch said, "Abner's first night with us. I think Abner ought to steal the wine." No one had asked Abner to come along, but he had. "How about it, Abner?" he said. It was dark there in the lot. Looking, you could not see Ditch's sneer, but you could hear it in his voice.

Abner's big eyes, intense and curious, were shining in the light of a distant street lamp. "Explain the stealing," he grunted. He sounded a little scared now.

Someone told him how it was done, and then Ditch said to Abner, "Okay, you buy the candy bar, and I'll get the wine."

But someone said, "He can't go. George won't let Negroes in his store."

"That's right," said Ditch. He looked at Abner. "You're lucky you're a Nig." He came down hard on the "Nig."

He waited for Abner to jump at the word. But he didn't.

Ditch stole the bottle while Charlie covered.

When we got to the pool hall, Abner said good night.

"Where you goin'?" Ditch said.

"I don't know how to play, man."

"You're gonna learn, man," Ditch said. He arrogantly broke between a couple of us, grabbed Abner's shirt and pulled him up the pool hall stairs. Abner didn't resist at all. I was surprised, certain by now that Ditch was afraid of nothing. He reminded me of an oversized Jimmy Cagney the way he swaggered; in fact, he sort of looked like Jimmy Cagney in the face. "C'mon, Nig," he said, heading for a corner table. The rest of us followed.

Ditch took a table only for himself and Abner. For nearly two hours he tried to show Abner how to play. Every few minutes he called him stupid and grabbed the stick away from him and bent down to show him what he was doing wrong.

Finally we all stood and watched, waiting for Abner to blow up, sure he would. But he didn't.

When it was over, Ditch slapped him on the back and said, "What you think of this game?"

Abner, despite the abuse Ditch had given him, shrugged and said, "Ain't bad."

There were looks of disappointment all around. A terrific fight hadn't come off. I was relieved, sure one of them would have ended up in the hospital. Knowing Ditch, however, I didn't think he was finished with Abner yet. Neither did the others, I guess. Everyone tagged along when we started up Market toward the tunnel entrance. Every once in a while Ditch would duck into an unlighted store doorway and the rest of us would follow. There we'd drink some wine. Abner drank too, slowly at first, making horrible faces. But then he stopped making faces and drank faster.

For a while Ditch seemed pretty friendly to him, but then he started saying things about Abner's toughness. "He's not a bad pool player now, but how does he go in a fight? That's what I'd like to know." When he spoke, he addressed everyone but Abner.

Abner knew how to handle it. He played deaf.

But then Ditch got onto the knife again. "Why does he carry that thing anyway? Can't he fight like the rest of us? I've heard about these Pachukes and Niggers."

Finally, fearing the worst, frightened, I said, "Why don't you lay off, Ditch? Abner isn't bothering anyone."

"The hell he ain't. That knife of his bothers me."

"What's wrong with a knife?" someone said.

"I didn't say anything was," said Ditch. "I just want to know."

Someone added, "My old man says the streets are getting so full of punks everyone is going to have to carry a gun or a knife pretty soon."

"Your old man is chicken shit," said Ditch, giving the boy a sidelong look. He turned back to Abner. "How about it Abner? How come you carry a knife?"

We were nearing a doorway. Abner stopped and looked up, fixing his eyes, now nearly closed from the wine, on a dark building across the street. "Man," he said thoughtfully, in a kind of lighthearted squeal, "I don't know. I just don't know."

Abner's tone seemed to anger Ditch. "The hell you don't," he said, facing Abner, his clenched fists on his hips.

Now Abner looked patiently up at a trolley wire.

"How long you been carrying it?"

Abner looked at him coldly, "Don't know."

"Where you from?" someone said.

"Alabama," he said.

"You didn't carry a knife there?" Ditch said.

"No."

"No wonder Niggers come to San Francisco," said Ditch to everyone but Abner. "It's the only place they're allowed to carry knives. Niggers and queers and foreigners and old people. All the outcasts come to San Francisco."

Abner's eyes were back on the trolley wire. Finally he let out a noisy sigh. He shook his head. "I carry it because I carry it. I guess that's about all I can say."

"Well, that ain't a reason," Ditch growled. "How 'bout you givin' it to me to carry?"

"Uh uh," said Abner, putting his hand on his pocket. "Can't do that."

"Otherwise I just might have to take it."

Abner backed out of the doorway we had entered. "You just come on then if you have to, I ain't giving it up by myself."

Ditch could not seem to decide whether or not to move after Abner. He crouched down, glared at him, and then straightened. He stuck out his forefinger and said, "God damn you, Nig. You're gonna gimme that before the night's over."

"'Fraid I can't, Ditch," Abner said politely.

"Streetcar'll be here in a minute," someone said. "Let's have a drink." We hurried to the tunnel streetcar stop and drank.

The conductor, also black, watched us suspiciously as we got on. The streetcar was nearly empty. We went peacefully to the center of the car and sat down.

Ditch explained our operations to Abner. As he listened, he seemed uneasy. Now and then he looked back at the conductor. "What do you do this for?" he said.

"To pass the time," said Ditch. "But tonight we're gonna just sit here and watch you. You're gonna do all the work. You got yourself a real daddy back there. You give him some real fun. And if you don't, we're gonna take away that knife, and I'm gonna personally beat shit out of you." He was sitting very close to Abner. Several of his closest followers were leaning over them.

I had been trembling since the conversation in the doorway. I knew whose side I'd be on if a fight started. Not Ditch's. That made me even more nervous. I said from across the aisle, "Ditch, why don't you leave him alone?"

"Shut up," Ditch said. "You're still a baby. When you turn into a man, you give me advice."

Abner was clearly frightened. He sat very still, staring straight ahead. Then he rose slowly and walked back to the conductor. The conductor kept his eyes warily on him. Because of the loud noise of the streetcar echoing through the tunnel, you could not hear what Abner was saying.

"Quit starin'," Ditch said.

We turned around and faced the front, waiting to hear bells ringing or glass breaking. Nothing happened for a long time, and then there was a yell. We looked back but could see neither Abner nor the conductor. Ditch was the first to leap out of his seat and race back.

We found them on the floor. The old conductor's mouth was bleeding. Abner was sitting on top of him, about to bring his big fist down once more. Ditch grabbed his fist. Then he held his free hand to keep the rest of us away. He seemed to want to be sure of something before he really stopped Abner. Every time Abner broke free and struck, we all, even Ditch, flinched. Finally Ditch pulled Abner off the conductor. The beaten old man lay there and looked fiercely up at Abner. He muttered one word: "Traitor!" Abner was grunting like a chained and angry dog, fighting to get back at him. The streetcar began to slow down. Ditch pulled Abner away, and we moved quickly to the open step.

There was some wine left. We killed it in silence in an unfinished house on a hill several blocks from the tunnel entrance. Sitting around a dusty future bedroom, we could see through the window

the tops of many houses. All the roofs were coated in blue moonlight. The new neighborhood was like those most of us lived in.
The house, the bedroom itself, was identical to many of ours.

Abner was alone in a corner, still panting heavily. He had said
nothing from the time we left the streetcar.

"Hey, Ab," someone called, "how did it start?"

Abner stopped panting. He hesitated, then said, "He made me
an insult."

"Huh?" said Ditch.

Facing Ditch, speaking in a low voice that made me think it had
to be either that or shouting, he told us he had gone to the back of
the streetcar, not intending to play with the bell, not intending to
do anything, just to stand there with the conductor, then get off
at the end of the tunnel and leave us. He looked across at Ditch,
hesitated, then said, "If you would have come back there, man, I
wouldn't have let you do anything. Know that?"

Ditch said, "Bullshit," and started to stir as if he were going to
get up and go across the room. He didn't, too interested, as all of us
were, in what Abner was going to say next.

"First thing is he calls me a minstrel boy. He says, 'You got your
face painted up, just for the show, didn't you, boy?' I asks him what
he means by that. He says my face was painted. Underneath it I was
white just like those others, meaning yours. He says go ahead and
steal my money 'cause that's what those white boys do. I start to tell
him I'm not going to do anything but he don't listen and says I'm a
little field slave and lots of things and I tell him shut up but he don't
and then he calls me a traitor to my own race and that's when I hit
him." Abner stood up now, had walked over to the window and
was looking out. "You can't make me one. He can't. Nobody can.
What'd he have to say that for?"

"It don't matter," said Ditch.

"I ain't a traitor. He shouldn't of said that."

"That's right. That's right," said Ditch, wanting to get on to
something else.

Abner turned abruptly. "I hate you, man." He was looking squarely at Ditch. He shook his head and turned back to the window. He reached into his pocket and slowly removed his knife.

Ditch, on the floor, started squirming back, fussing with his jacket as he moved.

I thought this was going to be the fight we'd all hung around for. But Abner, with a flip of his hand, tossed the knife out the window. He turned back, again to Ditch. "I ain't afraid of you," he said. "I hate you but I ain't afraid."

"Hey!" Charlie, against the wall was pointing. "What's that?"

I turned.

Something was glistening in front of Ditch. In the dim light I could see him moving it back, to the side, toward his jacket pocket.

"It's a . . . it's a gun," said Charlie, who was closest to Ditch.

The gun was back in Ditch's pocket. He had taken it out when Abner had shown the knife, but now it was back, secure in his pocket.

I was stunned the moment Charlie had said "gun." Ditch was liable to do nearly anything, but a gun . . . That seemed to turn all else inside out. I juggled with the recognition, not knowing what to do with it.

Charlie seemed to speak for all of us: "You never told us about that, Ditch."

"Whyn't you mind your own god damn business?"

"But . . ."

"What the hell you think I did with the dough I stole from my old man, buy candy bars?"

"Jesus," Charlie said. "Jesus Christ!"

Abner hadn't moved.

"Whyn't you sit down?" Ditch said to him, making it a command, not a request.

"Don't want to."

"You better," Charlie said. He turned to Ditch, then back to Abner, finding in the passage of his eyes a new knowledge that had to be communicated. He had known Ditch longer than any of us and seemed certain when he said, "He'll use it."

"I ain't sitting down," Abner said.

"Sit!"

"Jesus," Charlie whispered.

Ditch's hand glided back, as if responding to the pull of an invisible rope.

Someone made a whimpering noise.

"Please don't take it out again, Ditch," I said.

He didn't seem to hear. Or maybe the attention he was getting urged him to go through with it. He removed the pistol, very small, held it in front of his stomach, pointed at Abner's stomach, raised his left hand to the weapon, and made the hammer click back.

Charlie had come a certain distance and could seem to go no farther: "Jesus."

Abner had backed all the way up against the window, eyes wide, a pair of brightly burning lights fixed on the pistol.

"Sit down," Ditch said.

He didn't move.

I stood shakily.

"Sit down." This time it was for me.

"Ditch," I said weakly.

"Sit down."

But something drew me forward. While I sensed the danger, I was not acting to challenge it; I was just moving, the way Ditch's hand had moved toward the gun, as if that was the thing I, my rope, was causing me to do next. I saw something moving on the other side of the room. One of the others. Also moving toward Abner. Charlie. He was coming in slow mechanical steps, approaching from the other side.

"Everybody sit down!"

In a moment Charlie was next to me, in front of Abner, facing Ditch.

"What the hell you two doin'?"

"Put . . . put it back in your pocket," Charlie said.

"Yeah, Ditch," someone said from behind him.

"Why should I put it back?" Ditch said in a new uncertain voice. "If he had a knife, why can't I have this?"

"You got to put it back, that's all," Charlie said, trying to sound calm.

"Got to, huh?"

"You just got to," Charlie said. "You just got to, Ditch."

My legs quivered. They seemed about to give way. I could feel Charlie's arm next to mine. I wasn't facing Ditch defiantly, I was just standing there, before him, in front of Abner, beside Charlie, waiting for something that had started finally to stop, as if it was bound to stop, the way a downpour of rain that interrupts a game on the street has to stop.

"You . . . you might shoot *me* . . . or *Jackie*." Charlie had been searching and now he'd found what he wanted. "That's why, Ditch."

In a moment there was a click, hammer forward, and the gun went down to his side. "That's a good enough reason," he said, seeming relieved. "Yeah."

When the gun was back in Ditch's pocket, Abner stepped forward, opening a space between Charlie and me. He took a few steps toward Ditch, then turned and moved to the door. Quickly he was gone. The room went silent. Then someone got up in back and went out, following Abner. Then someone else. Before I realized what was happening, Charlie left me and went out. The door was open now. Abner had closed it behind him, but the second person to leave had left it open, and it was still open and, one by one, everyone was leaving. Finally there were only Ditch and me.

"Pricks." Ditch was still seated. He mumbled the words into the floor: "Nigger lovin' pricks."

I stood there, not knowing what to say to him, then—it seemed the only choice I had—I left the room too.

"You're one of them too, you baby!" he yelled after me. "The only reason I didn't shoot you is 'cause you're such a god damn baby!" He kept shouting but I couldn't make out what else he said.

The others were walking ahead of me, in a line, all walking separately, twenty, thirty, forty yards apart, about six altogether. I felt strong walking behind them. I thought Ditch might be coming along behind me; that frightened me, but I didn't look back; I kept

myself from looking back. I wanted to keep feeling strong. Way up
in front was Abner. When he approached the corner where you
turned toward the streetcar stop, a street light from behind shone
on him in a way that momentarily made him seem white; someone
else. But by the time he reached the corner the harsh light went off
him and he was himself again. One by one they went around the
corner. I was the last one around.

At the car stop we talked about what happened. Someone said
Charlie and I had more guts then the whole god damn U.S. Army.
Charlie denied it. He said it would have taken more guts for him to
pick up someone else's bloodied body which is what he would have
had to do if Ditch had pulled the trigger on Abner. I hadn't thought
of that, but it made sense. Anything might have made sense. I still
didn't know why I'd done what I'd done. Finally someone asked
Abner, who had thanked Charlie and me about twenty-five times
already, if he was going to stick it out at the library.

"Why not?" he said.

It took a while for his answer to sink in but then there were nods
all around. Of course. Why not? Why not for any of us.

Ditch never did arrive at the car stop. Funny, but no one looked
toward the corner to see if he'd come around. No one seemed to
care. I guess if he had come around and tried something, with or
without gun, none of us would have backed off, unless maybe he'd
gone crazy and come around shooting.

On Monday Charlie arrived at work a little late. He told us he'd
run into Ditch in a soda fountain on Mission Street. Ditch, he said,
was quitting the library. "He told me his old man was getting him a
job on the trucks, riding as back-up driver for the old man himself."

I thought someone would laugh at the reason as phony. No one
did. Maybe it *was* the true reason. Ditch had recently turned eighteen, was old enough to get a chauffeur's license. I pictured him in
the truck cab beside his father, fingering the pistol in his pocket.
Firecrackers, I thought, if they ever got into an argument.

Charlie also said Ditch had had a message for Abner. Charlie delivered it straight-faced. "He said he'd meet you any time or any

place. No weapons. Just bare fists. You just name it." Charlie kept his laughter inside until he finished. Then he broke up, slapping his hand hard on the top of a stack of books. Abner was grinning, just shaking his head and grinning.

Later someone cut a picture of a cooked chicken out of *Family Circle* magazine and stuck it on the wall above where Ditch used to sit. In red crayon across the chicken was Ditch's name. For days there were a lot of jokes and insults about Ditch.

One day, when we were all laughing, Abner stopped and looked at the chair at the end of the stacking room. It was the only chair in the room, the one from which Ditch had tossed his orders, the one from which he'd challenged Abner. Abner kept looking at the chair, finally turning away with a fearful gaze. "That white-ass son-of-a-bitch nearly killed me," he said as if he just now became aware of the fact. His remark was good for more laughs, but also for a subsequent silence in which we all, I think, started to weigh what had nearly happened.

There weren't many jokes after that. Now and then I'd get puffed up and think it had been like a no-bull western movie, and I'd size myself up with the latest cowboy actor who'd hooked me with wondrous moves. But most of the time, often when I was alone in the stacking room, I'd look at Ditch's chair or some other object that reminded me of him and feel a low chill, testicles turning to ice cubes, remembering. At such times I'd get out, maybe go stack some books or head for the reference room and get a drink of water.

It occurred to me once that Ditch might have been right in what he'd said about me being a baby, even that night in the house, especially that night. I remembered the way infants crawled out on ledges or into the paths of cars if you let them. Maybe I'd done something like that. I hoped, was pretty sure in fact, that it had been more than that. I never did know for certain and finally just stopped worrying about it.

The Beach Umbrella

Cyrus Colter, a lawyer, born in 1910 in Noblesville, Indiana, began to write in his mid fifties. He has published stories and novels comprising, to date, seven books. He is an emeritus professor at Northwestern University, where he held the Chester D. Tripp Chair in the Humanities.

"Cyrus Colter is what a writer is and always has been—a man with stories to tell, a milieu to reveal, and people he cares about. The reader becomes absorbed, learns, and finally cares in the same way."
VANCE BOURJAILY, 1970

"When I came upon his tales, amidst all the others in the contest, I suddenly found myself having a lovely time. He was telling me all sorts of magical things about life I'd never known before. I was so grateful."
KURT VONNEGUT, JR., 1970

The Thirty-first Street beach lay dazzling under a sky so blue that Lake Michigan ran to the horizon like a sheet of sapphire silk, studded with little barbed white sequins for sails; and the heavy surface of the water lapped gently at the boulder "sea wall" which had been cut into, graded, and sanded to make the beach. Saturday afternoons were always frenzied: three black lifeguards, giants in sunglasses, preened in their towers and chaperoned the bathers— adults, teen-agers, and children—who were going through every physical gyration of which the human body is capable. Some dove, swam, some hollered, rode inner tubes, or merely stood waistdeep and pummeled the water; others—on the beach—sprinted, did handsprings and somersaults, sucked Eskimo pies, or just buried their children in the sand. Then there were the lollers—extended in their languor under a garish variety of beach umbrellas.

Elijah lolled too—on his stomach in the white sand, his chin cupped in his palm; but under no umbrella. He had none. By habit, though, he stared in awe at those who did, and sometimes meddled in their conversation: "It's gonna be gettin' *hot* pretty soon—if it ain't careful," he said to a Bantu-looking fellow and his girl sitting nearby with an older woman. The temperature was then in the nineties. The fellow managed a negligent smile. "Yeah," he said, and persisted in listening to the women. Buoyant still, Elijah watched them. But soon his gaze wavered, and then moved on to other lollers of interest. Finally he got up, stretched, brushed sand from his swimming trunks, and scanned the beach for a new spot. He started walking.

He was not tall. And he appeared to walk on his toes—his walnut-colored legs were bowed and skinny and made him hobble like a jerky little spider. Next he plopped down near two men and two girls—they were hilarious about something—sitting beneath a big purple-and-white umbrella. The girls, chocolate brown and shapely, emitted squeals of laughter at the wisecracks of the men. Elijah was enchanted. All summer long the rambunctious gaiety of the beach had fastened on him a curious charm, a hex, that brought him gawking and twiddling to the lake each Saturday. The rest of the week, save Sunday, he worked. But Myrtle, his wife, detested the sport and stayed away. Randall, the boy, had been only twice and then without little Susan, who during the summer was her mother's own midget reflection. But Elijah came regularly, especially whenever Myrtle was being evil, which he felt now was almost always. She was getting worse, too—if that was possible. The woman was money-*crazy*.

"You gotta sharp-lookin' umbrella there!" he cut in on the two laughing couples. They studied him—the abruptly silent way. Then the big-shouldered fellow smiled and lifted his eyes to their spangled roof. "Yeah? . . . Thanks," he said. Elijah carried on: "I see a lot of 'em out here this summer—much more'n last year." The fellow meditated on this, but was noncommittal. The others went on gabbing, mostly with their hands. Elijah, squinting in the hot sun, watched them. He didn't see how they could be married; they cut

the fool too much, acted like they'd itched to get together for weeks
and just now made it. He pondered going back in the water, but
he'd already had an hour of that. His eyes traveled the sweltering
beach. Funny about his folks; they were every shape and color a
God-made human could be. Here was a real sample of variety—
pink white to jetty black. Could you any longer call that a *race* of
people? It was a complicated complication—for some real educated
guy to figure out. Then another thought slowly bore in on him: the
beach umbrellas blooming across the sand attracted people—slews
of friends, buddies; and gals, too. Wherever the loudest-racket tore
the air, a big red, or green, or yellowish umbrella—bordered with
white fringe maybe—flowered in the middle of it all and gave
shade to the happy good-timers.

Take, for instance, that tropical-looking pea-green umbrella over
there, with the Bikini-ed brown chicks under it, and the portable
radio jumping. A real beach party! He got up, stole over, and eased
down in the sand at the fringe of the jubilation—two big thermos
jugs sat in the shade and everybody had a paper cup in hand as the
explosions of buffoonery carried out to the water. Chief provoker
of mirth was a bulging-eyed old gal in a white bathing suit who,
encumbered by big flabby overripe thighs, cavorted and pranced in
the sand. When, perspiring from the heat, she finally fagged out,
she flopped down almost on top of him. So far, he had gone un-
noticed. But now, as he craned in at closer range, she brought him
up: "Whatta *you* want, Pops?" She grinned, but with a touch of
hostility.

Pops! Where'd she get that stuff? He was only forty-one, not a
day older than that boozy bag. But he smiled. "Nothin'," he said
brightly, "but you sure got one goin' here." He turned and viewed
the noise-makers.

"An' you wanta get in on it!" she wrangled.

"Oh, I was just lookin'—."

"—You was just lookin'. Yeah, you was just lookin' at them
young chicks there!" She roared a laugh and pointed at the sexy-
looking girls under the umbrella.

Elijah grinned weakly.

"Beat it!" she catcalled, and turned back to the party.

He sat like a rock—the hell with her. But soon he relented, and wandered down to the water's edge—remote now from all inhospitality—to sit in the sand and hug his raised knees. Far out, the sailboats were pinned to the horizon and, despite all the close-in fuss, the wide miles of lake lay impassive under a blazing calm; far south and east down the long-curving lake shore, miles in the distance, the smoky haze of the Whiting plant of the Youngstown Sheet and Tube Company hung ominously in an otherwise bright sky. And so it was that he turned back and viewed the beach again—and suddenly caught his craving. Weren't they something— the umbrellas! The flashy colors of them! Yes . . . yes, he too must have one. The thought came slow and final, and scared him. For there stood Myrtle in his mind. She nagged him now night and day, and it was always money that got her started; there was never enough—for Susan's shoes, Randy's overcoat, for new kitchen linoleum, Venetian blinds, for a better car than the old Chevy. "I just don't understand you!" she had said only night before last. "Have you got any plans at all for your family? You got a family, you know. If you could only bear to pull yourself away from that deaf old tightwad out at that warehouse, and go get yourself a *real* job . . . But no! Not *you!*"

She was talking about old man Schroeder, who owned the warehouse where he worked. Yes, the pay could be better, but it still wasn't as bad as she made out. Myrtle could be such a fool sometimes. He had been with the old man nine years now; had started out as a freight handler, but worked up to doing inventories and a little paper work. True, the business had been going down recently, for the old man's sight and hearing were failing and his key people had left. Now he depended on *him*, Elijah—who of late wore a necktie on the job, and made his inventory rounds with a ball-point pen and clipboard. The old man was friendlier, too—almost "hat in hand" to him. He liked everything about the job now—except the pay. And that was only because of Myrtle. She just wanted so much; even talked of moving out of their rented apartment and buying out in the Chatham area. But one thing had to be said for her: she never griped about anything for herself; only for the family, the kids. Every payday he endorsed his check and handed it over to her, and got back in return only gasoline and cigarette money. And this could get pretty tiresome. About six weeks ago he'd gotten a thirty-dollar-a-month raise out of the old man, but that had only made her madder than ever. He'd thought about looking for another job all right; but where would he go to get another white-collar job? There weren't many of them for him. *She* wouldn't care if he went back to the steel mills, back to pouring that white-hot ore out at Youngstown Sheet and Tube. It would be okay with *her*—so long as his paycheck was fat. But that kind of work was no good, undignified; coming home on the bus you were always so tired you went to sleep in your seat, with your lunch pail in your lap.

Just then two wet boys, chasing each other across the sand, raced by him into the water. The cold spray on his skin made him jump, jolting him out of his thoughts. He turned and slowly scanned the beach again. The umbrellas were brighter, gayer, bolder than ever—each a hiving center of playful people. He stood up finally, took a long last look, and then started back to the spot where he had parked the Chevy.

The following Monday evening was hot and humid as Elijah sat at home in their plain living room and pretended to read the newspaper; the windows were up, but not the slightest breeze came through the screens to stir Myrtle's fluffy curtains. At the moment she and nine-year-old Susan were in the kitchen finishing the dinner dishes. For twenty minutes now he had sat waiting for the furtive chance to speak to Randall. Randall, at twelve, was a serious, industrious boy, and did deliveries and odd jobs for the neighborhood grocer. Soon he came through—intent, absorbed—on his way back to the grocery store for another hour's work.

"Gotta go back, eh, Randy?" Elijah said.

"Yes, sir." He was tall for his age, and wore glasses. He paused with his hand on the doorknob.

Elijah hesitated. Better wait, he thought—wait till he comes back. But Myrtle might be around then. Better ask him now. But Randall had opened the door. "See you later, Dad," he said— and left.

Elijah, shaken, again raised the newspaper and tried to read. He should have called him back, he knew, but he had lost his nerve— because he couldn't tell how Randy would take it. Fifteen dollars was nothing though, really—Randy probably had fifty or sixty stashed away somewhere in his room. Then he thought of Myrtle, and waves of fright went over him—to be even thinking about a beach umbrella was bad enough; and to buy one, especially now, would be to her some kind of crime; but to borrow even a part of the money for it from Randy . . . well, Myrtle would go out of her mind. He had never lied to his family before. This would be the first time. And he had thought about it all day long. During the morning, at the warehouse, he had gotten out the two big mail-order catalogues, to look at the beach umbrellas; but the ones shown were all so small and dinky-looking he was contemptuous. So at noon he drove the Chevy out to a sporting-goods store on West Sixty-third Street. There he found a gorgeous assortment of yard and beach umbrellas. And there he found his prize. A beauty, a big beauty, with wide red and white stripes, and a white fringe. But oh the price! Twenty-three dollars! And he with nine.

"What's the matter with you?" Myrtle had walked in the room. She was thin, and medium brown-skinned with a saddle of freckles across her nose, and looked harried in her sleeveless housedress with her hair unkempt.

Startled, he lowered the newspaper. "Nothing," he said.

"How can you read looking *over* the paper?"

"Was I?"

Not bothering to answer, she sank in a chair. "Susie," she called back into the kitchen, "bring my cigarettes in here, will you, baby?"

Soon Susan, chubby and solemn, with the mist of perspiration on her forehead, came in with the cigarettes. "Only three left, Mama," she said, peering into the pack.

"Okay," Myrtle sighed, taking the cigarettes. Susan started out.

"Now, scour the sink good, honey—and then go take your bath. You'll feel cooler."

Before looking at him again, Myrtle lit a cigarette. "School starts in three weeks," she said, with a forlorn shake of her head. "Do you realize that?"

"Yeah? . . . Jesus, time flies." He could not look at her.

"Susie needs dresses, and a couple of pairs of *good* shoes—and she'll need a coat before it gets cold."

"Yeah, I know." He patted the arm of the chair.

"Randy—bless his heart—has already made enough to get most of *his* things. That boy's something; he's all business—I've never seen anything like it." She took a drag on her cigarette. "And old man Schroeder giving you a thirty-dollar raise! What was you thinkin' about? What'd you *say* to him?"

He did not answer at first. Finally he said, "Thirty dollars are thirty dollars, Myrtle. *You* know business is slow."

"*I'll* say it is! And there won't be any business before long—and then where'll you be? I tell you over and over again, you better start looking for something *now*! I been preachin' it to you for a year."

He said nothing.

"Ford and International Harvester are hiring every man they can lay their hands on! And the mills out in Gary and Whiting are going full blast—you see the red sky every night. The men make *good* money."

"They earn every nickel of it, too," he said in gloom.

"But they *get* it! Bring it home! It spends! Does that mean anything to you? Do you know what some of them make? Well, ask Hawthorne—or ask Sonny Milton. Sonny's wife says his checks some weeks run as high as a hundred sixty, hundred eighty, dollars. One week! Take-home pay!"

"Yeah? . . . And Sonny told me he wished he had a job like mine."

Myrtle threw back her head with a bitter gasp. "Oh-h-h, God! Did you tell him what you made? Did you tell him that?"

Suddenly Susan came back into the muggy living room. She went straight to her mother and stood as if expecting an award.

Myrtle absently patted her on the side of the head. "Now, go and run your bath water, honey," she said.

Elijah smiled at Susan. "Susie," he said, "d'you know your tummy is stickin' way out—you didn't eat too much, did you?" He laughed.

Susan turned and observed him; then looked at her mother. "No," she finally said.

"Go on, now, baby," Myrtle said. Susan left the room.

Myrtle resumed. "Well, there's no use going through all this again. It's plain as the nose on your face. You got a family—a good family, *I* think. The only question is, do you wanta get off your hind end and do somethin' for it. It's just that simple."

Elijah looked at her. "You can talk real crazy sometimes, Myrtle."

"I think it's that old man!" she cried, her freckles contorted. "He's got you answering the phone, and taking inventory—wearing a necktie and all that. You wearing a necktie and your son mopping in a grocery store, so he can buy his own clothes." She snatched up her cigarettes, and walked out of the room.

His eyes did not follow her, but remained off in space. Finally he got up and went back into the kitchen. Over the stove the plaster was thinly cracked, and, in spots, the linoleum had worn through the pattern; but everything was immaculate. He opened the refrigerator, poured a glass of cold water, and sat down at the kitchen table. He felt strange and weak, and sat for a long time sipping the water.

Then after a while he heard Randall's key in the front door, sending tremors of dread through him. When Randall came into the kitchen, he seemed to him as tall as himself; his glasses were steamy from the humidity outside, and his hands were dirty.

"Hi, Dad," he said gravely without looking at him, and opened the refrigerator door.

Elijah chuckled. "Your mother'll get after you about going in there without washing your hands."

But Randall took out the water pitcher and closed the door.

Elijah watched him. Now was the time to ask him. His heart was hammering. Go on—now! But instead he heard his husky voice saying, "What'd they have you doing over at the grocery tonight?"

Randall was drinking the glass of water. When he finished he

said, "Refilling shelves."

"Pretty hot job tonight, eh?"

"It wasn't so bad." Randall was matter-of-fact as he set the empty glass over the sink, and paused before leaving.

"Well . . . you're doing fine, son. Fine. Your mother sure is proud of you . . ." Purpose had lodged in his throat.

The praise embarrassed Randall. "Okay, Dad," he said, and edged from the kitchen.

Elijah slumped back in his chair, near prostration. He tried to clear his mind of every particle of thought, but the images became only more jumbled, oppressive to the point of panic.

Then before long Myrtle came into the kitchen—ignoring him. But she seemed not so hostile now as coldly impassive, exhibiting a bravado he had not seen before. He got up and went back into the living room and turned on the television. As the TV-screen lawmen galloped before him, he sat oblivious, admitting the failure of his will. If only he could have gotten Randall to himself long enough— but everything had been so sudden, abrupt; he couldn't just ask him out of the clear blue. Besides, around him, Randall always seemed so busy, too busy to talk. He couldn't understand that; he had never mistreated the boy, never whipped him in his life; had shaken him a time or two, but that was long ago, when he was little.

He sat and watched the finish of the half-hour TV show. Myrtle was in the bedroom now. He slouched in his chair, lacking the re-solve to get up and turn off the television.

Suddenly he was on his feet.

Leaving the television on, he went back to Randall's room in the rear. The door was open and Randall was asleep, lying on his back on the bed, perspiring, still dressed except for his shoes and glasses. He stood over the bed and looked at him. He was a good boy; his own son. But how strange—he thought for the first time—there was no resemblance between them. None whatsoever. Randy had a few of his mother's freckles on his thin brown face, but he could see none of himself in the boy. Then his musings were scattered by the return of his fear. He dreaded waking him. And he might be cross.

If he didn't hurry, though, Myrtle or Susie might come strolling out any minute. His bones seemed rubbery from the strain. Finally he bent down and touched Randall's shoulder. The boy did not move a muscle, except to open his eyes. Elijah smiled at him. And he slowly sat up.

"Sorry, Randy—to wake you up like this."

"What's the matter?" Randall rubbed his eyes.

Elijah bent down again, but did not whisper. "Say, can you let me have fifteen bucks—till I get my check? . . . I need to get some things—and I'm a little short this time." He could hardly bring the words up.

Randall gave him a slow, queer look.

"I'll get my check a week from Friday," Elijah said, " . . . and I'll give it back to you then—sure."

Now instinctively Randall glanced toward the door, and Elijah knew Myrtle had crossed his thoughts. "You don't have to mention anything to your mother," he said with casual suddenness.

Randall got up slowly off the bed, and, in his socks, walked to the little table where he did his homework. He pulled the drawer out, fished far in the back a moment, and brought out a white business envelope secured by a rubber band. Holding the envelope close to his stomach, he took out first a ten-dollar bill, and then a five, and sighing, handed them over.

"Thanks, old man," Elijah quivered, folding the money. "You'll get this back the day I get my check. . . . That's for sure.

"Okay," Randall finally said.

Elijah started out. Then he could see Myrtle on payday—her hand extended for his check. He hesitated, and looked at Randall, as if to speak. But he slipped the money in his trousers pocket and hurried from the room.

The following Saturday at the beach did not begin bright and sunny. By noon it was hot, but the sky was overcast and angry, the air heavy. There was no certainty whatever of a crowd, raucous or otherwise, and this was Elijah's chief concern as, shortly before twelve o'clock, he drove up in the Chevy and parked in the bumpy, graveled stretch of high ground that looked down eastward over the lake and was used for a parking lot. He climbed out of the car, glancing at the lake and clouds, and prayed in his heart it would not rain—the water was murky and restless, and only a handful of bathers had showed. But it was early yet. He stood beside the car and watched a bulbous, brown-skinned woman, in bathing suit and enormous straw hat, lugging a lunch basket down toward the beach, followed by her brood of children. And a fellow in swimming trunks, apparently the father, took a towel and sandals from his new Buick and called petulantly to his family to "just wait a minute, please." In another car, two women sat waiting, as yet fully clothed and undecided about going swimming. While down at the water's edge there was the usual cluster of dripping boys who, brash and boisterous, swarmed to the beach every day in fair weather or foul.

Elijah took off his shirt, peeled his trousers from over his swimming trunks, and started collecting the paraphernalia from the back seat of the car: a frayed pink rug filched from the house, a towel, sunglasses, cigarettes, a thermos jug filled with cold lemonade he had made himself, and a dozen paper cups. All this he stacked on the front fender. Then he went around to the rear and opened the trunk. Ah, there it lay—encased in a long, slim package trussed with heavy twine, and barely fitting athwart the spare tire. He felt prickles of excitement as he took the knife from the tool bag, cut the twine, and pulled the wrapping paper away. Red and white stripes sprang at him. It was even more gorgeous than when it had first seduced him in the store. The white fringe gave it style; the wide red fillets were cardinal and stark, and the white stripes glared. Now he opened it over his head, for the full thrill of its colors, and looked around to see if anyone else agreed. Finally after a while he gathered up all his equipment and headed down for the beach, his short, nubby legs seeming more bowed than ever under the weight of their cargo.

When he reached the sand, a choice of location became a pressing matter. That was why he had come early. From past observation it was clear that the center of gaiety shifted from day to day; last Saturday it might have been nearer the water, this Saturday, well back; or up, or down, the beach a ways. He must pick the site with care, for he could not move about the way he did when he had no umbrella; it was too noticeable. He finally took a spot as near the center of the beach as he could estimate, and dropped his gear in the sand. He knelt down and spread the pink rug, then moved the thermos jug over onto it, and folded the towel and placed it with the paper cups, sunglasses, and cigarettes down beside the jug. Now he went to find a heavy stone or brick to drive down the spike for the hollow umbrella stem to fit over. So it was not until the umbrella was finally up that he again had time for anxiety about the weather. His whole morning's effort had been an act of faith, for, as yet, there was no sun, although now and then a few azure breaks appeared in the thinning cloud mass. But before very long this brighter texture of the sky began to grow and spread by slow degrees, and his hopes quickened. Finally he sat down under the umbrella, lit a cigarette, and waited.

It was not long before two small boys came by—on their way to the water. He grinned, and called to them, "Hey, fellas, been in yet?"—their bathing suits were dry.

They stopped, and observed him. Then one of them smiled, and shook his head.

Elijah laughed. "Well, whatta you waitin' for? Go on in there and get them suits wet!" Both boys gave him silent smiles. And they lingered. He thought this a good omen—it had been different the Saturday before.

Once or twice the sun burst through the weakening clouds. He forgot the boys now in watching the skies, and soon they moved on. His anxiety was not detectable from his lazy posture under the umbrella, with his dwarfish, gnarled legs extended and his bare heels on the little rug. But then soon the clouds began to fade in earnest, seeming not to move away laterally, but slowly to recede into a lucent haze, until at last the sun came through hot and bright. He squinted at the sky and felt delivered. They would come, the folks would come!—were coming now; the beach would soon be swarming. Two other umbrellas were up already, and the diving board thronged with wet, acrobatic boys. The lifeguards were in

their towers now, and still another launched his yellow rowboat. And up on the Outer Drive, the cars, one by one, were turning into the parking lot. The sun was bringing them out all right; soon he'd be in the middle of a field day. He felt a low-key, welling excitement, for the water was blue, and far out the sails were starched and white.

Soon he saw the two little boys coming back. They were soaked. Their mother—a thin, brown girl in a yellow bathing suit—was with them now, and the boys were pointing to his umbrella. She seemed dignified for her youth, as she gave him a shy glance and then smiled at the boys.

"Ah, ha!" he cried to the boys. "You've been in *now* all right!" And then laughing to her, "I was kiddin' them awhile ago about their dry bathing suits."

She smiled at the boys again. "They like for me to be with them when they go in," she said.

"I got some lemonade here," he said abruptly, slapping the thermos jug. "Why don't you have some?" His voice was anxious.

She hesitated.

He jumped up. "Come on, sit down." He smiled at her and stepped aside.

Still she hesitated. But her eager boys pressed close behind her. Finally she smiled and sat down under the umbrella.

"You fellas can sit down under there too—in the shade," he said to the boys, and pointed under the umbrella. The boys flopped down quickly in the shady sand. He started at once serving them cold lemonade in the paper cups.

"Whew! I thought it was goin' to rain there for a while," he said, making conversation after passing out the lemonade. He had squatted on the sand and lit another cigarette. "Then there wouldn't a been much goin' on. But it turned out fine after all—there'll be a mob here before long."

She sipped the lemonade, but said little. He felt she had sat down only because of the boys, for she merely smiled and gave short answers to his questions. He learned the boys' names, Melvin and James; their ages, seven and nine; and that they were still frightened by the water. But he wanted to ask *her* name, and inquire about her husband. But he could not capture the courage.

Now the sun was hot and the sand was hot. And an orange-and-white umbrella was going up right beside them—two fellows and a girl. When the fellow who had been kneeling to drive the umbrella spike in the sand stood up, he was string-bean tall, and black, with his glistening hair freshly processed. The girl was a lighter brown, and wore a lilac bathing suit, and, although her legs were thin, she was pleasant enough to look at. The second fellow was medium, really, in height, but short beside his tall, black friend. He was yellow-skinned, and fast getting bald, although still in his early thirties. Both men sported little shoestring mustaches.

Elijah watched them in silence as long as he could. "You picked the right spot all right!" he laughed at last, putting on his sunglasses.

"How come, man?" The tall, black fellow grinned, showing his mouthful of gold teeth.

"You see *every*body here!" happily rejoined Elijah. "They all come here!"

"Man, I been coming here for years," the fellow reproved, and sat down in his khaki swimming trunks to take off his shoes. Then he stood up. "But right now, in the water I goes." He looked down at the girl. "How 'bout you, Lois, baby?"

"No, Caesar," she smiled, "not yet; I'm gonna sit here awhile and relax."

"Okay, then—you just sit right there and relax. And Little Joe"—he turned and grinned to his shorter friend—"you sit there an' relax right along with her. You all can talk with this gentleman here"—he nodded at Elijah—"an' his nice wife." Then, pleased with himself, he trotted off toward the water.

The young mother looked at Elijah, as if he should have hastened to correct him. But somehow he had not wanted to. Yet too, Caesar's remark seemed to amuse her, for she soon smiled. Elijah felt the pain of relief—he did not want her to go; he glanced at her with a furtive laugh, and then they both laughed. The boys had finished their lemonade now, and were digging in the sand. Lois and Little Joe were busy talking.

Elijah was not quite sure what he should say to the mother. He did not understand her, was afraid of boring her, was desperate to keep her interested. As she sat looking out over the lake, he watched her. She was not pretty; and she was too thin. But he thought she had poise; he liked the way she treated her boys—tender, but casual; how different from Myrtle's frantic herding.

Soon she turned to the boys. "Want to go back in the water?" she laughed.

The boys looked at each other, and then at her. "Okay," James said finally, in resignation.

"Here, have some more lemonade," Elijah cut in.

The boys, rescued for the moment, quickly extended their cups. He poured them more lemonade, as she looked on smiling.

Now he turned to Lois and Little Joe sitting under their orange-and-white umbrella. "How 'bout some good ole cold lemonade?" he asked with a mushy smile. "I got plenty of cups." He felt he must get something going.

Lois smiled back, "No, thanks," she said, fluttering her long eyelashes, "not right now."

He looked anxiously at Little Joe.

"*I'll* take a cup!" said Little Joe, and turned and laughed to Lois: "Hand me that bag there, will you?" He pointed to her beach bag in the sand. She passed it to him, and he reached in and pulled out a pint of gin. "We'll have some *real* lemonade," he vowed, with a daredevilish grin.

Lois squealed with pretended embarrassment, "Oh, *Joe!*"

Elijah's eyes were big now; he was thinking of the police. But he handed Little Joe a cup and poured the lemonade, to which Joe added gin. Then Joe, grinning, thrust the bottle at Elijah. "How 'bout yourself, chief?" he said.

Elijah, shaking his head, leaned forward and whispered, "You ain't supposed to drink on the beach, y'know."

"*This* ain't a drink, man—it's a taste!" said Little Joe, laughing and waving the bottle around toward the young mother. "How 'bout a little taste for your wife here?" he said to Elijah.

The mother laughed and threw up both her hands. "No, not for me!"

Little Joe gave her a rakish grin. "What'sa matter? You *'fraid* of that guy?" He jerked his thumb toward Elijah. "You 'fraid of gettin' a whippin', eh?"

"No, not exactly," she laughed.

Elijah was so elated with her his relief burst up in hysterical laughter. His laugh became strident and hoarse and he could not stop. The boys gaped at him, and then at their mother. When finally he recovered, Little Joe asked him, "Whut's so funny 'bout *that*?" Then Little Joe grinned at the mother. "You beat *him* up sometimes, eh?"

This started Elijah's hysterics all over again. The mother looked concerned now, and embarrassed; her laugh was nervous and shadowed. Little Joe glanced at Lois, laughed, and shrugged his shoulders. When Elijah finally got control of himself again he looked spent and demoralized.

Lois now tried to divert attention by starting a conversation with the boys. But the mother showed signs of restlessness and seemed ready to go. At this moment Caesar returned. Glistening beads of water ran off his long, black body; and his hair was unprocessed now. He surveyed the group and then flashed a wide, gold-toothed grin. "One big, happy family, like I said." Then he spied the paper cup in Little Joe's hand. "Whut you got there, man?"

Little Joe looked down into his cup with a playful smirk. "Lemonade, lover boy, lemonade."

"Don't hand me that jive, Joey. You ain't never had any straight lemonade in your life."

This again brought uproarious laughter from Elijah. "I got the straight lemonade *here*!" He beat the thermos jug with his hand. "Come on—have some!" He reached for a paper cup.

"Why, sure," said poised Caesar. He held out the cup and received the lemonade. "Now, gimme that gin," he said to Little Joe.

Joe handed over the gin, and Caesar poured three fingers into the
lemonade and sat down in the sand with his legs crossed under him. Soon he turned to the two boys, as their mother watched him with amusement. "Say, ain't you boys goin' in any more? Why don't you tell your daddy there to take you in?" He nodded toward Elijah.

Little Melvin frowned at him. "My daddy's workin'," he said.

Caesar's eyebrows shot up. "Ooooh, la, la!" he crooned. "Hey, now!" And he turned and looked at the mother and then at Elijah, and gave a clownish little snigger.

Lois tittered before feigning exasperation at him. "There you go again," she said, "talkin' when you shoulda been listening."

Elijah laughed with the rest. But he felt deflated. Then he glanced at the mother, who was laughing too. He could detect in her no sign of dismay. Why then had she gone along with the gag in the first place, he thought—if now she didn't hate to see it punctured?

"*Hold the phone!*" softly exclaimed Little Joe. "Whut is *this*?" He was staring over his shoulder. Three women, young, brown, and worldly-looking, wandered toward them, carrying an assortment of beach paraphernalia and looking for a likely spot. They wore very scant bathing suits, and were followed, but slowly, by an older woman with big, unsightly thighs. Elijah recognized her at once. She was the old gal who, the Saturday before, had chased him away from her beach party. She wore the same white bathing suit, and one of her girls carried the pea-green umbrella.

Caesar forgot his whereabouts ogling the girls. The older woman, observing this, paused to survey the situation. "How 'bout along in here?" she finally said to one of the girls. The girl carrying the thermos jug set it in the sand so close to Caesar it nearly touched him. He was rapturous. The girl with the umbrella had no chance to put it up, for Caesar and Little Joe instantly encumbered her with help. Another girl turned on their radio, and grinning, feverish Little Joe started snapping his fingers to the music's beat.

Within a half hour, a boisterous party was in progress. The little radio, perched on a hump of sand, blared out hot jazz, as the older woman—whose name turned out to be Hattie—passed around some cold, rum-spiked punch; and before long she went into her dancing-prancing act—to the riotous delight of all, especially Elijah. Hattie did not remember him from the Saturday past, and he was glad, for everything was so different today! As different as milk and ink. He knew no one realized it, but this was *his* party really—the wildest, craziest, funniest, and best he had ever seen or heard of. Nobody had been near the water—except Caesar, and the mother and boys much earlier. It appeared Lois was Caesar's girl-friend, and she was hence more capable of reserve in face of the come-on antics of Opal, Billie, and Quanita—Hattie's girls. But Little Joe, to Caesar's tortured envy, was both free and aggressive. Even the young mother, who now volunteered her name to be Mrs. Green, got frolicsome, and twice jabbed Little Joe in the ribs.

Finally Caesar proposed they all go in the water. This met with instant, tipsy acclaim; and Little Joe, his yellow face contorted from laughing, jumped up, grabbed Billie's hand, and made off with her across the sand. But Hattie would not budge. Full of rum, and stubborn, she sat sprawled with her flaccid thighs spread in an obscene V, and her eyes half shut. Now she yelled at her departing girls: "You all watch out, now! Dont'cha go in too far. . . . Just wade! None o' you can swim a lick!"

Elijah now was beyond happiness. He felt a floating, manic glee. He sprang up and jerked Mrs. Green splashing into the water, fol-lowed by her somewhat less ecstatic boys. Caesar had to paddle about with Lois and leave Little Joe unassisted to caper with Billie, Opal, and Quanita. Billie was the prettiest of the three, and, despite Hattie's contrary statement, she could swim; and Little Joe, after taking her out in deeper water, waved back to Caesar in triumph. The sun was brazen now, and the beach and lake thronged with a variegated humanity. Elijah, a strong, but awkward, country-style swimmer, gave Mrs. Green a lesson in floating on her back, and, though she too could swim, he often felt obligated to place both his arms under her young body and buoy her up.

And sometimes he would purposely let her sink to her chin, whereupon she would feign a happy fright and utter faint simian screeches. Opal and Quanita sat in the shallows and kicked up their

heels at Caesar, who, fully occupied with Lois, was a grinning water-threshing study in frustration.

Thus the party went—on and on—till nearly four o'clock. Elijah had not known the world afforded such joy; his homely face was a wet festoon of beams and smiles. He went from girl to girl, insisting that she learn to float on his outstretched arms. Once begrudgingly Caesar admonished him, "Man, you gonna *drown* one o' them pretty chicks in a minute." And Little Joe bestowed his highest accolade by calling him "lover boy," as Elijah nearly strangled from laughter.

At last, they looked up to see old Hattie as she reeled down to the water's edge, coming to fetch her girls. Both Caesar and Little Joe ran out of the water to meet her, seized her by the wrists, and, despite her struggles and curses, dragged her in. "Turn me loose! You big galoots!" she yelled and gasped as the water hit her. She was in knee-deep before she wriggled and fought herself free and lurched out of the water. Her breath reeked of rum. Little Joe ran and caught her again, but she lunged backwards, and free, with such force she sat down in the wet sand with a thud. She roared a laugh now, and spread her arms for help, as her girls came sprinting and splashing out of the water and tugged her to her feet. Her eyes narrowed to vengeful, grinning slits as she turned on Caesar and Little Joe: "*I* know whut you two're up to!" She flashed a glance around toward her girls. "I been watchin' both o' you studs! Yeah, yeah, but your eyes may shine, an' your teeth may grit . . ." She went limp in a sneering, raucous laugh. Everybody laughed now—except Lois and Mrs. Green.

They had all come out of the water now, and soon the whole group returned to their three beach umbrellas. Hattie's girls immediately prepared to break camp. They took down their pea-green umbrella, folded some wet towels, and donned their beach sandals, as Hattie still bantered Caesar and Little Joe.

"Well, you sure had *yourself* a ball today," she said to Little Joe, who was sitting in the sand.

"Comin' back next Saturday?" asked grinning Little Joe.

"I jus' might at that," surmised Hattie. "We wuz here last Saturday."

"Good! Good!" Elijah broke in. "Let's *all* come back—next Saturday!" He searched every face.

"*I'll* be here," chimed Little Joe, grinning to Caesar. Captive Caesar glanced at Lois, and said nothing.

Lois and Mrs. Green were silent. Hattie, insulted, looked at them and started swelling up. "Never mind," she said pointedly to Elijah, "you jus' come on anyhow. You'll run into a slew o' folks lookin' for a good time. You don't need no *certain* people." But a little later, she and her girls all said friendly goodbyes and walked off across the sand.

The party now took a sudden downturn. All Elijah's efforts at resuscitation seemed unavailing. The westering sun was dipping toward the distant buildings of the city, and many of the bathers were leaving. Caesar and Little Joe had become bored; and Mrs. Green's boys, whining to go, kept a reproachful eye on their mother.

"Here, you boys, take some more lemonade," Elijah said quickly, reaching for the thermos jug. "Only got a little left—better get while gettin's good!" He laughed. The boys shook their heads.

On Lois he tried cajolery. Smiling, and pointing to her wet, but trim bathing suit, he asked, "What color would you say that is?"

"Lilac," said Lois, now standing.

"It sure is pretty! Prettiest on the beach!" he whispered.

Lois gave him a weak smile. Then she reached down for her beach bag, and looked at Caesar.

Caesar stood up, "Let's cut," he turned and said to Little Joe, and began taking down their orange-and-white umbrella.

Elijah was desolate. "Whatta you goin' for? It's gettin' cooler! Now's the time to *enjoy* the beach!"

"I've got to go home," Lois said.

Mrs. Green got up now; her boys had started off already. "Just a minute, Melvin," she called, frowning. Then, smiling, she turned and thanked Elijah.

He whirled around to them all. "Are we comin' back next Saturday? Come on—let's all come back! Wasn't it great! It was *great*!

Don't you think? Whatta you say?" He looked now at Lois and
Mrs. Green.

"We'll see," Lois said, smiling. "Maybe."

"Can *you* come?" He turned to Mrs. Green.

"I'm not sure," she said. "I'll try."

"Fine! Oh, that's fine!" He turned on Caesar and Little Joe. "I'll
be lookin' for you guys, hear?"

"Okay, chief," grinned Little Joe. "An' put somethin' in that
lemonade, will ya?"

Everybody laughed . . . and soon they were gone.

Elijah slowly crawled back under his umbrella, although the sun's
heat was almost spent. He looked about him. There was only one
umbrella on the spot now, his own; where before there had been
three. Cigarette butts and paper cups lay strewn where Hattie's
girls had sat, and the sandy imprint of Caesar's enormous street
shoes marked his site. Mrs. Green had dropped a bobby pin. He
too was caught up now by a sudden urge to go. It was hard to bear
much longer—the lonesomeness. And most of the people were
leaving anyway. He stirred and fidgeted in the sand, and finally
started an inventory of his belongings. . . . Then his thoughts flew
home, and he reconsidered. Funny—he hadn't thought of home all
afternoon. Where had the time gone anyhow? . . . It seemed he'd
just pulled up in the Chevy and unloaded his gear; now it was time
to go home again. Then the image of solemn Randy suddenly
formed in his mind, sending waves of guilt through him. He forgot
where he was as the duties of his existence leapt on his back—
where would he ever get Randy's fifteen dollars? He felt squarely
confronted by a great blank void. It was an awful thing he had
done—all for a day at the beach . . . with some sporting girls. He
thought of his family and felt tiny—and him itching to come back
next Saturday! Maybe Myrtle was right about him after all. Lord, if
she knew what he had done. . . .

He sat there for a long time. Most of the people were gone now.
The lake was quiet save for a few boys still in the water. And the sun,
red like blood, had settled on the dark silhouettes of the house-

tops across the city. He sat beneath the umbrella just as he had at one o'clock . . . and the thought smote him. He was jolted. Then dubious. But there it was—quivering, vital, swelling inside his skull like an unwanted fetus. So this was it! He mutinied inside. So he must sell it . . . his *umbrella*. Sell it for anything—only as long as it was enough to pay back Randy. For fifteen dollars even, if necessary. He was dogged; he couldn't do it; that wasn't the answer anyway. But the thought clawed and clung to him, rebuking and coaxing him by turns, until it finally became conviction. He must do it; it was the right thing to do; the only thing to do. Maybe then the awful weight would lift, the dull commotion in his stomach cease. He got up and started collecting his belongings; placed the thermos jug, sunglasses, towel, cigarettes, and little rug together in a neat pile, to be carried to the Chevy later. Then he turned to face his umbrella. Its red and white stripes stood defiant against the wide, churned-up sand. He stood for a moment mooning at it. Then he carefully let it down and, carrying it in his right hand, went off across the sand.

The sun now had gone down behind the vast city in a shower of crimson-golden glints, and on the beach only a few stragglers remained. For his first prospects, he approached two teen-age boys, but suddenly realizing they had no money, he turned away and went over to an old woman, squat and black, in street clothes—a spectator—who stood gazing eastward out across the lake. She held in her hand a little black book, with red-edged pages, which looked like the New Testament. He smiled at her. "Wanna buy a nice new beach umbrella?" He held out the collapsed umbrella toward her.

She gave him a beatific smile, but shook her head. "No, son," she said, "that ain't what *I* want." And she turned to gaze out on the lake again.

For a moment he still held the umbrella out, with a question mark on his face. "Okay, then," he finally said, and went on.

Next he hurried to the water's edge, where he saw a man and two women preparing to leave. "Wanna buy a nice new beach umbrella?" His voice sounded high-pitched, as he opened the umbrella over his head. "It's brand-new. I'll sell it for fifteen dollars—it cost a lot more'n that."

The man was hostile, and glared. Finally he said, "Whatta you take me for—a fool?"

Elijah looked bewildered, and made no answer. He observed the man for a moment. Finally he let the umbrella down. As he moved away, he heard the man say to the women, "It's hot—he stole it somewhere."

Close by, another man sat alone in the sand. Elijah started toward him. The man wore trousers, but was stripped to the waist, and bent over intent on some task in his lap. When Elijah reached him, he looked up from half a hatful of cigarette butts he was breaking open for the tobacco he collected in a little paper bag. He grinned at Elijah, who meant now to pass on.

"No, I ain't interested either, buddy," the man insisted as Elijah passed him. "Not me. I jus' got *outa* jail las' week—an' ain't goin' back for no umbrella." He laughed, as Elijah kept on.

Now he saw three women, still in their bathing suits, sitting together near the diving board. They were the only people he had not yet tried—except the one lifeguard left. As he approached them, he saw that all three wore glasses and were sedate. Some schoolteachers maybe, he thought, or office workers. They were talking—until they saw him coming; then they stopped. One of them was plump, but a smooth dark brown, and sat with a towel around her shoulders. Elijah addressed them through her: "Wanna buy a nice beach umbrella?" And again he opened the umbrella over his head.

"Gee! It's beautiful," the plump woman said to the others. "But where'd you get?" she suddenly asked Elijah, polite mistrust entering her voice.

"I bought it—just this week."

The three women looked at each other. "Why do you want to sell it so soon, then?" a second woman said.

Elijah grinned. "I need the money."

"Well!" The plump woman was exasperated. "*No*, we don't want it." And they turned from him. He stood for a while, watching them; finally he let the umbrella down and moved on.

Only the lifeguard was left. He was a huge youngster, not over twenty, and brawny and black, as he bent over cleaning out his beached rowboat. Elijah approached him so suddenly he looked up startled.

"Would you be interested in this umbrella?" Elijah said, and proffered the umbrella. "It's brand-new—I just bought it Tuesday. I'll sell it cheap." There was urgency in his voice.

The lifeguard gave him a queer stare; and then peered off toward the Outer Drive, as if looking for help. "You're lucky as hell," he finally said. "The cops just now cruised by—up on the Drive. I'd have turned you in so quick it'd made your head swim. Now you get the hell outa here." He was menacing.

Elijah was angry. "Whatta you mean? I *bought* this umbrella—it's mine."

The lifeguard took a step toward him. "I said you better get the hell outa here! An' I mean it! You thievin' bastard, you!"

Elijah, frightened now, gave ground. He turned and walked away a few steps; and then slowed up, as if an adequate answer had hit him. He stood for a moment. But finally he walked on, the umbrella drooping in his hand.

He walked up the gravelly slope now toward the Chevy, forgetting his little pile of belongings left in the sand. When he reached the car, and opened the trunk, he remembered; and went back down and gathered them up. He returned, threw them in the trunk and, without dressing, went around and climbed under the steering wheel. He was scared, shaken; and before starting the motor sat looking out on the lake. It was seven o'clock; the sky was waning pale, the beach forsaken, leaving a sense of perfect stillness and approaching night; the only sound was a gentle lapping of the water against the sand—one moderate *hallo-o-o-o* would have carried across to Michigan. He looked down at the beach. Where were they all now—the funny, proud, laughing people? Eating their dinners, he supposed, in a variety of homes. And all the beautiful umbrellas—where were they? Without their colors the beach was so deserted. Ah, the beach . . . after pouring hot ore all week out at

the Youngstown Sheet and Tube, he would probably be too fagged
out for the beach. But maybe he wouldn't—who knew? It was
great while it lasted . . . great. And his umbrella . . . he didn't know
what he'd do with that . . . he might never need it again. He'd keep
it, though—and see. Ha! . . . hadn't he sweat to get it! . . . and
they thought he had stolen it . . . stolen it . . . ah . . . and maybe
they were right. He sat for a few moments longer. Finally he started
the motor, and took the old Chevy out onto the Drive in the pink-
hued twilight. But down on the beach the sun was still shining.

Iowa Short Fiction Award and
John Simmons Short Fiction Award Winners

1990
A Hole in the Language,
Marly Swick
Judge: Jayne Anne Phillips

1989
Lent: The Slow Fast,
Starkey Flythe, Jr.
Judge: Gail Godwin

1989
Line of Fall,
Miles Wilson
Judge: Gail Godwin

1988
The Long White,
Sharon Dilworth
Judge: Robert Stone

1988
The Venus Tree,
Michael Pritchett
Judge: Robert Stone

1987
Fruit of the Month,
Abby Frucht
Judge: Alison Lurie

1987
Star Game,
Lucia Nevai
Judge: Alison Lurie

1986
Eminent Domain,
Dan O'Brien
Judge: Iowa Writers'
Workshop

1986
Resurrectionists,
Russell Working
Judge: Tobias Wolff

1985
Dancing in the Movies,
Robert Boswell
Judge: Tim O'Brien

1984
Old Wives' Tales,
Susan M. Dodd
Judge: Frederick Busch

1983
Heart Failure,
Ivy Goodman
Judge: Alice Adams

1982
Shiny Objects,
Dianne Benedict
Judge: Raymond Carver

1981
The Phototropic Woman,
Annabel Thomas
Judge: Doris Grumbach

1980
Impossible Appetites,
James Fetler
Judge: Francine du Plessix
Gray

1979
Fly Away Home,
Mary Hedin
Judge: John Gardner

1978
A Nest of Hooks,
Lon Otto
Judge: Stanley Elkin

1977
The Women in the Mirror,
Pat Carr
Judge: Leonard Michaels

1976
The Black Velvet Girl,
C. E. Poverman
Judge: Donald Barthelme

1975
*Harry Belten and the
Mendelssohn Violin Concerto*,
Barry Targan
Judge: George P. Garrett

1974
*After the First Death
There Is No Other*,
Natalie L. M. Petesch
Judge: William H. Gass

1973
The Itinerary of Beggars,
H. E. Francis
Judge: John Hawkes

1972
The Burning and Other Stories,
Jack Cady
Judge: Joyce Carol Oates

1971
*Old Morals, Small Continents,
Darker Times*,
Philip F. O'Connor
Judge: George P. Elliott

1970
The Beach Umbrella,
Cyrus Colter
Judges: Vance Bourjaily
and Kurt Vonnegut, Jr.